HANDS DOWN

MARIANA ZAPATA

MARIANA ZAPATA

Hands Down © 2020 Mariana Zapata

Book Cover Design by RBA Designs

Editing by Hot Tree Editing and My Brother's Editor

*To my greatest friend
and teacher.
The absolute love of my life.
Dorian,
this book and my whole life
is dedicated to your memory.*

CHAPTER ONE

"The word is out! The Oklahoma Thunderbirds have signed quarter-back Damarcus Williams to a two-year deal worth $25 million. This move comes weeks after the organization announced that Zac Travis would enter free agency following five seasons in Oklahoma City. Michael B, is it over for Travis as a starting quarterback in the NFO?"

The good-looking man in a dark gray suit on the television visibly bristled before leaning forward into the camera. *"Have you* seen *him play these past two seasons? I don't know why the Thunderbirds waited so long to take him off the roster! I mean, are you* kidding *me? This deep in his career, he's only managed to lead a team into the playoffs twice! What—"*

"Blanca, what are you doing?"

Shit balls.

Instantly tearing my gaze away from the closed captioning flashing across the bottom of the television screen I'd had my eye on from about fifteen feet away, I only just barely managed to think about what I'd been in the process of doing before the image of a familiar-looking man in a gray, white, and orange football uniform had caught my attention.

Like it—*he*—always had.

"Changing the channel," I answered the man on the other side of the counter from where I was standing. I lifted the remote in my palm as proof.

Did he just call me Blanca again?

I knew without a doubt that my new boss was trying to bust me not working. He was always creeping around, popping up out of nowhere when you least expected him. Fortunately, I had probably only been watching the television for about a minute. Just long enough to recognize the man the commentators on The Sports Network were talking about and catch the beginning of their discussion.

My boss—one of my three new bosses, if I was going to be technical—stared at me blankly from where he stood across the counter, either thinking I was full of shit or trying to figure out how to turn what I'd been doing around on me so he could have an excuse to bitch.

Because that was what he did—really well, unfortunately.

So well that most of my coworkers had quit over the last month since the gym had been officially taken over by its newest owners. Asshole 1, Asshole 2, and The Decent Guy Who Was Unfortunately Never Around Who Might Also Be An Asshole If He Ever Spent More Than Five Minutes At Maio House. That was how we referred to them—at least those of us who were left.

Okay, maybe it was just me and Deepa who did, but I highly doubted it.

"One of the members asked me if I could change it," I kept going, lying out of my freaking ass at that point, but it wasn't like he knew that. I wasn't going to feel bad about it either, especially not when he was *still* butchering my name this long into knowing each other. I'd corrected him at least ten times and spelled it out for him twice, maybe more. B-i-a-n-c-a M-a-r-i-a B-r-a-n-n-e-n. Bianca because my sister had named me, Maria for my mom's abuela—her grandma—and Brannen because... it was my dad's last name.

"And it's Bianca. With an I. Not an L," I corrected the man who was now in charge of signing my paychecks, tapping in vain at the name tag on the left side of my chest with a smile that was 200 percent forced. On that note, I needed to get him out of here and back into his office before he really did find something to complain about.

Then again, as I'd learned, he could find something wrong with... well, everything. "Did you need something?"

Besides a life and a personality change. Maybe multiple enemas too, to get whatever was lodged up his ass out of there.

My boss stared at me for a second longer as he leaned against the counter I had been hired almost three years ago to work behind. The front desk for a gym was a place I had enjoyed working at up until exactly a month ago.

I didn't need to look at the front of the counter to know that the words MAIO HOUSE were painted across the front of it. The world-famous gym hadn't changed names when it had been officially sold a few weeks ago. The three investors —one of whom was Gunner, the man who couldn't remember my name to save his life—had bought the brand and the legacy behind a gym. Maio House had been in the DeMaio family for seventy-something years and had bred dozens of world-class athletes, starting with boxers when it opened, and now mixed martial arts athletes.

The atmosphere had been great before. The members were mostly all nice, and I had liked my coworkers. The DeMaios had been the best owners and managers, as well.

Then one day, out of the blue, Mr. DeMaio told us he was selling.

It had been the beginning of the end. By the time that first Friday had rolled around after the sale had been official, one of the other front desk employees, two people who manned the juice bar, and the assistant manager had quit. Within the following week, two more front desk employees, the custodian, and the gym's manager of two years had quit too.

Mostly because of this lovely human being.

He sucked.

I purposely made my smile go even bigger while I waited for the crappiest boss I'd ever had to tell me if he actually needed something.

Because we both damn well knew he didn't. He was just being a micromanaging butt-munch who loved harassing his employees, and today was my lucky day. Yay.

"No," Gunner the retired United Fighting League fighter replied with that annoyingly blank glare that had me wondering if he'd tried using it in the cage back in his prime. I'd looked him up the first day he had bitched me out for drinking a smoothie behind the front desk. *"I don't know how they ran things here before,"* the nightmare had tried to tell me two days after he'd started working here, *"but no food is allowed behind the counter, even if it's a smoothie from the juice bar. And no discounts either. You pay the price that's on the board just like every-body else."*

First off, I hadn't even gotten a discount when my coworker had made my smoothie. I'd bought it for the full price. The only time I ever got discounts had been if one of the managers or owners had offered it up in the moment. Secondly, it hadn't been like I'd been drinking it in front of customers. I'd sipped at it between people coming and going, while crouched behind the counter because I'd had to skip my lunch. And why did I have to skip my lunch? Because my coworker had quit the day before after Gunner had griped at her for asking to come in late so she could take her son to the doctor.

"I don't pay you to stand around watching TV, remember that," the man said in that tone that had me fighting not to roll my eyes.

Remember that.

Douchebag.

Feeling my fingers instantly curling into fists on their own, it took everything in me to keep my face neutral and my eyes normal width before I managed to say to my boss as sweetly as humanly possible, smiling sarcastically, "I know. Don't worry."

What he needed to worry about was getting a foot up his ass.

How the hell I'd gone from really enjoying working here, enjoying my coworkers and most of the members, to sitting in my car, waiting until the absolute last minute to clock in and having my keys in my hand a minute before my shift was set to end was beyond me. Mostly. I had even started checking the schedule to see what days Gunner was supposed to come in so that I could mentally brace myself.

Gunner's annoying ass rapped his knuckles on the counter one last time before he pushed off. I watched him walk around the desk and to the door that led to the pathway connecting the gym part of the building that I worked in with the other building next door that held what we called the MMA section since the majority of the people who trained over there were fighters.

I needed to get out of here.

And one day—one day soon—I would.

First, I just needed Deepa to find another job so that I wouldn't feel bad leaving her to fend for herself with this asshole. I'd been bringing it up at least once a day, but she still hadn't committed to quitting no matter how much she hated putting up with Gunner too. Hopefully sooner than later, she really would go through with it because I wasn't positive how much longer I was going to last here even now that I was only working part-time.

I needed to talk to her about it again ASAP. Maybe tomorrow morning when she was supposed to come over to my apartment to help me. We could look through job listings during our break. Yeah, that was a good plan.

Now, what was I thinking about before I'd gotten distracted?

A recipe. I'd been trying to work out a new recipe in my head. That was what I'd been thinking about when TSN— The Sports Network—had flashed that familiar man across the screen and I'd instantly gone for the remote to change the channel. It took me a second to get back to where I'd last been on the recipe train. Bananas and chocolate were about as far as I'd gotten before I'd been weak and got sucked into what the commentators were saying, even though I knew better. It wasn't like they ever said anything nice.

But anyway.

All the time I spent standing around thinking had been my favorite thing about this job before. It was time I could use working out recipe ideas in my head, weighing their pros and cons while I got paid. I liked getting out of the house and had made friends here. It had been a win-win.

And then Gunner happened.

My phone vibrated against my butt cheek, and I looked around to make sure Asshole 1 hadn't come back in and wasn't hiding around the corner, waiting.

He wasn't. At least I was pretty sure he wasn't.

Pulling it out, I took a peek at the screen, half-expecting a message from my sister since I hadn't heard from her all day.

I wasn't disappointed.

CONNIE LOVES PECKER: Do I need to help you find a date to Lola's quince?

Wasn't that... months away? And did you even *need* a date to a fifteen-year-old's birthday party? Sure, that part of the family was spending something like twenty thousand dollars on my second cousin's party; my sister had called to tell me how dumb they were for throwing money around like that when we all knew they couldn't really afford it. For Connie's fifteenth birthday, our parents had bought her an ancient car that didn't run; she still griped about it. For my fifteenth birthday, Mamá Lupe, my abuelita, my grandma, had given me money to go to a theme park in San Antonio, and my cousin Boogie had taken me for the day. I'd wanted to go to Disney, but there hadn't been money back then. My parents had said they would take me someday, but I was twenty-seven now and still waiting on them to hold up that promise.

But I was finally going to Disney World this year, and I was excited. It was my gift to myself for surviving Kenny and his bullshit. I was going to celebrate my future with mouse ears on.

I glanced up to make sure Gunner's creepy ass still hadn't magically appeared and sent my sister a response real quick.

Me: I need a date?

I had just barely slipped my phone back into my pocket when it vibrated with another incoming text. A second one came through before I even managed to pull it back out. But they weren't from my sister.

They were both from Boogie.

BOOGIE IS MY FAVORITE: Call me as soon as you get a chance

BOOGIE IS MY FAVORITE: Please B

I could count on zero fingers the number of times my cousin—my favorite cousin who was basically my brother and definitely one of my best friends, tied with my sister—had ever *asked* me to call him. He was allergic to phone calls. And he rarely ever texted me on the weekend either, especially now that he had a girlfriend again.

Gunner could suck it if he caught me; my cousin needed me.

I hit the phone icon on the message and put it to my ear. Boogie answered on the second ring, freaking me out even more. I could also count on one hand the number of times he'd answered any call from anyone on the first ring. I would know. I'd been with him a thousand times when he'd looked to see who was calling and then spent twenty seconds debating whether or not to answer.

"Bianca," Boogie whispered before I even got a chance to say hi or ask what was wrong. "Paw-Paw Travis is in the hospital."

"Oh" was what came out of my mouth first, mostly because my brain was still hung up on needing a date, the recipe I had been trying to figure out, how I needed to get out of here, and how much of a shithead Gunner was. But I caught on fast. I went straight for the name he'd said. *Paw-Paw Travis?* What were the chances...? "Oh shit. Is he okay?"

I looked around again. The coast was still clear, thankfully. Beside me, the new girl working the juice bar glanced at me before looking away again just as quickly. Nobody wanted to get busted. I couldn't blame her.

"I don't know," my older cousin rattled off quickly, bringing me back to the call as he sounded freaking distracted and like he was muffling his voice. "The ambulance took him a couple hours ago, and they're telling us he's in the back having tests done."

"I'm so sorry, Boogie. What can I do?" I asked, thinking that, if Paw-Paw had been kind of like a grandfather figure for me, he had been almost like a dad to my cousin—a second dad, but a dad nonetheless. As far as I knew, Boogie still went over to his house once a week to check on him, and that had been the case since he'd moved back to the Austin area a while back.

"I need you to do me a solid," he replied.

I watched the front door as a couple of regular members came in and headed straight for the front desk. I smiled at both of them, holding the phone up to my ear with my shoulder, and scanned their passes. "Whatever you need." There wasn't a single thing I wouldn't do for him, or for any of my loved ones, and I had a lot of them.

Paw-Paw included.

I'd never forget the kindnesses he'd paid me when I was younger. I hadn't seen him in a while, but the last time I had, he'd given me a big hug and asked me a thousand questions about how I'd been doing since the last time we'd seen each other—a year before that. When I was little, he'd pull quarters out from behind my ears. For one of my birthdays, he'd given me a pendant of a flamingo that had belonged to his late wife. I still had it in my jewelry box.

Guilt nibbled at my stomach as I sent a silent prayer up that he was fine. If he was, I'd do better. I could visit a little more, maybe each time I went to see Boogie. I could call to at least check up on him. I could send him some gifts. Boogie had complained to me not that long ago about how Paw-Paw was still trying to do too much for his age.

"—tell him."

"Have a good workout," I whispered to the members as I pulled the phone away from my mouth. "I'm sorry, Boog. What did you say? I'm still at work for another twenty."

My cousin repeated himself. "Zac's not answering his phone. I've tried calling him and so has his mom, but he isn't picking up. Can you go by his place and tell him?"

The hell did he just say?

He wanted me to go tell *Zac* his grandfather was in the hospital?

Zac Travis, who had been the starting quarterback of the National Football Organization's Oklahoma Thunderbirds?

The one the TV anchors had literally just been talking about? The man whose life I'd saved when we were kids?

Seriously, what the hell were the chances?

"Please, B. I wouldn't ask if I didn't have to."

Of course I knew that. Boogie rarely asked for anything. So, of course, *of freaking course,* when he did it would be something like this.

"But he's not picking up, and I've been blowing him up for the last hour. His mom's been trying to call him too and nada," my cousin rattled on, stress and worry hanging on his every syllable.

He'd used the same voice back when Mamá Lupe had been sick. But this was different.

My cousin wanted me to go tell his *best friend* that his grandfather was in the hospital because said best friend wasn't answering his phone.

It was that simple, and it made a whole lot of sense.

In a way, it was nothing.

My cousin wanted me to go tell his best friend, who I had known almost my entire life, who had loved me and treated me like a little sister once upon a time, that there was something going on with his grandpa because he wasn't answering his phone. Because he needed to know. Of course he did. Of course he should.

There was no reason for me to say no. No *real* reason for me to even hesitate. So we hadn't seen or spoken to each other in almost ten years; it wasn't like that had happened because we'd gotten into a fight or because I'd done something dumb to make things weird.

Nope. There was no *real* reason.

Just me being a coward.

And him... well, it didn't matter anymore.

"Bianca?"

"I'm here," I replied, looking at myself in the reflection of the long mirror that took up the majority of the wall directly in front of the front desk and juice bar where I stood all day. Even with my hair down, I could see the bags under my eyes from all the way over here. I'd stayed up too late watching this Turkish romance online last night, and it had been totally worth it. It wasn't like the gym members hadn't seen me at work on three or four hours of sleep on a regular basis.

But....

Why did he have to ask for this of all things? Then again, it was a Christmas miracle that it had taken this long for me to get put into this position in the first place: having to go see Zac. It wasn't like I'd thought I'd *never* see him again. Just not any time soon. Maybe the next decade. From the moment I'd heard that he was living in Houston, I'd kind of prepared for the fact that my time was coming to an end, and it had been pretty much a miracle of its own that my cousin had been working out of the country for the last couple weeks so he hadn't gotten a chance to come down to visit.

But now Boogie was asking.

I had made my choices, and so had he. There were no hard feelings.

Now, here we were.

All I had to do was relay the news to him. That was it. No big deal.

I held back a sigh and gave my cousin the only real answer I could. "Yeah, of course I'll do it."

I'd love to see him—Zac—under better circumstances. It wasn't like I hadn't tried over the last ten years. It had just never... worked out.

All right, maybe I could have tried a lot harder but hadn't. Okay, maybe I hadn't *actually* tried, period. Because deep inside of me, the wuss still ran strong in a few situations, but extra, extra especially when it related to Zac Travis. Time had healed a lot of wounds but not all of them. Not the fine, little ones with hairline fractures that really hit home.

But my cousin's best friend needed to know his grandpa was in the hospital. And if he wasn't answering his phone, and I lived in the same city where he was training during his off-season? It was probably fate.

An image of what the commentators on The Sports Network had been just talking about flashed through my head.

Oh well.

I would do anything for the people I loved, and I loved Paw-Paw Travis. And I had loved Zac. Despite everything, I still did, in a way, and more than likely, I always would.

But even if I didn't, I couldn't say no to Boogie.

"I get off work soon. Where do you think he is?" I managed to ask, ignoring that lump of dread and nerves in my belly at the idea of seeing him again after so long, especially today of all days. But maybe he'd already known it was happening. That the Thunderbirds were signing a new quarterback.

Yeah, that could be it.

And really, this could be worse. Going to see him, I meant. At least Zac had never known I'd been in love with him.

Thank God.

He'd just forgotten all about me.

CHAPTER TWO

I should have just gone home and eaten dinner in front of the TV.

I popped the last grape from the fruit cup I'd bought at the gas station into my mouth and stared at the massive house through my window.

This was the house that Zac was living in, according to the address that Boogie had texted me right after we'd gotten off the phone. I double-checked the numbers to make sure I had them right, and yep, I did. I mean, the code for the gate to get into the neighborhood had been correct as well... unfortunately.

Where else would I expect a millionaire to live? I was 99 percent sure he didn't actually own the house since he wasn't going to be staying in Houston long term, but that didn't change the fact his rent had to be out of his ass for a place like this. I'd seen pictures of Zac's home back in Oklahoma. Boogie had sent me a picture of himself draped across marble floors between a grand staircase made up of all iron and rich wood, head propped on his fist, with Zac lying on the floor beside him in the same position. It had made me smile.

Back when I had really known Zac, when he'd been my friend, he'd been rolling around in a car with no air conditioning and a bumper with so many dents he called them freckles. And now? Well, the last time Boogie had sent me a picture of them together, they'd been in some BMW that probably cost more than the house I'd grown up in.

But he'd worked hard for everything he had and more. The big house, nice car—or maybe *cars*—and positive attention. And according to my current view, he had plenty of people surrounding him too.

Of course he did.

He'd been busy all those times I'd texted him and hadn't gotten a response, I knew. That knowledge needed to comfort me the way it had a decade ago when we'd... lost touch. *Lost touch.* That's what I was going to call it.

From the look of it, the house he was in now was just as big and more than likely just as luxurious as the one he'd been living in back in Oklahoma—two stories, wide, and with a circular driveway. I was only a little bit surprised to see that it was packed with cars. So was the street in front of it.

Three people happened to be walking up the path in front to what was one of the biggest homes I'd ever seen, and they were nicely dressed. I pulled my car over two giant houses down and hoped like hell no one would call to get it towed.

And why the hell did he have to be having a party today?

I locked my car and sprinted across the street in my black tennis shoes, eyeing each mansion for a second.

I palmed my cell and looked down at the screen, triple-checking the address that Boogie had texted me, just in case.

Yep, it was still correct.

I opened my text messaging app before I forgot and shot my sister a new message. She still hadn't replied to me about needing a date to the quinceañera.

Me: I'm going into a house I've never been in before. If I don't text you back in an hour, call the cops. The address is 555 Rose Hill Lane.

I stopped, thought about it, and sent her another message.

Me: Don't invite anyone I don't like to my funeral.

Then I sent her another one.

Me: And don't forget to drop my laptop in a swamp if something happens.

I thought about it for another second.

Me: And don't forget you're the only one I want to clean out my nightstand. Wear gloves and don't judge me.

I slipped my phone back into my purse as I stopped in front of what had to be at least an eight-thousand-square-foot home and eyed the combination of brick and stone walls, telling myself that I had to do this. Boogie had asked.

And the sooner I did this, the sooner I could go home.

Through the oversized glass and iron door, I could spy a whole lot of people inside, but I still knocked. And of course, no one heard, or at least they pretended not to hear or look over.

I rang the doorbell, watching the people hanging out inside some more, and still nothing. Why there were so many people over was beyond me. It wasn't his birthday. He'd already been in Houston almost two weeks by this point. Maybe it was a party just for the hell of it. To celebrate entering a new chapter of his life without the Thunderbirds? If it were me, I'd probably be balled up on my couch eating marshmallows and crying. What did I know though?

I waited a little longer, hoping someone would happen to look over... but still, no one did. A couple of the guys I could see inside were huge, and my gut said they had to be football players too. Like Zac. That's why he was here in Houston now, because he was going to be training with some special people or something before the preseason started. From the bits and pieces I'd collected from my cousin's comments, he'd gone on a long vacation before coming here.

I wondered what he was going to do now that he wasn't with the Thunderbirds anymore.

Bouncing on the balls of my feet for a second, I eyed my Maio House polo shirt and decided not to give a shit. I knocked once more, and when still no one looked at me standing there awkwardly, I went for the freaking doorknob. I had to do this.

I turned it.

It opened.

All right.

I went in, closing it behind me and eyeing all the nicely dressed people inside. None of them had tuxedos or suits on, but they sure as hell weren't in collared work shirts. I suddenly wished I'd at least put a little more lipstick on before getting out of my car.

Whatever.

The house opened into a pretty but basic formal dining room on one side and an office on the other. The office just had a desk, a chair, and a printer in it. There was nothing hanging on the walls as I continued further into the home, eyeing what had to be who the hell knows how many people spilling through the next part of the open floor plan house with its vaulted ceilings.

Everyone was talking, and there was a movie playing on a big television that was mounted above the fireplace in the living room. I spied a couple more guys who had to be some kind of athletes from their muscle composition and postures, and one of them met my eyes and smiled at me. But he wasn't the football player I was looking for... even though I wouldn't mind looking at him under different circumstances.

Clutching my purse a little tighter, I slowly made my way through the living area, looking for that light-colored head of hair in a sea of freaking giants.

I tried to look at every face but couldn't find the one I needed. The one I used to know.

Even more nerves set up shop in my stomach with every minute that dragged by. I was going to find Zac, do what I had to do, and it was going to be fine. And yeah, I had bad news to give him but at least it wasn't worse news. He'd be polite. Maybe we'd smile at each other, and I would mostly mean mine.

I didn't hold anything against him.

I'd see the man I'd known, give him his message, and then go back to my life. Maybe I'd see him again in another decade, and maybe I wouldn't. It'd be easier to accept and think about this time around, at least.

I headed toward a sliding door near a breakfast nook that led outside, noticing that it kept being opened and closed as partygoers came in and out. I wasn't going to wonder if Zac was in a bedroom or not unless I absolutely had to. As I was going around two people who happened to be coming back inside at the same time I was going out, the sound of laughter had me turning. Spotting him.

I almost did a double take.

On a lounger, flanked between two women, was a man I had seen on television about an hour ago when the commentators had been discussing his career. From a starting quarterback for a baby franchise to... well, who the hell knew what now. My cousin's best friend. My old friend.

I visually sucked up the man I hadn't seen in person in forever as I made my way over, scooting through and around groups of people who weren't paying me any attention. There had always been... something about Zac. Something there wasn't exactly a word for that was part his good looks, but mostly something inside of him that drew a person in—that drew *people* in. Something almost magnetic, and I could tell it was still alive and well even from a distance.

That was one of the things that made him an ideal quarterback.

That and his huge heart.

At least I'd thought that in the past.

Zac's signature cowboy hat hid what I knew was dark blond hair shot through with strands of auburn and a little brown. One of the last few times I'd seen him live on TV, it had been pretty long. I caught a slice of a bright white smile —a smile I knew constantly lingered on his face—as he talked to one of the women sitting beside him. His long legs were stretched out in front of him, covered in jeans like always. Even when we'd been kids, I couldn't remember him ever being in shorts unless he'd been at the pool in long, baggy swim trunks that Boogie had always been trying to yank down.

I smiled at a couple of people who caught my eye as I picked my way through the crowd hanging around the patio, and luckily no one grabbed me and asked if I was lost or was in the wrong place.

Nerves made my stomach feel a little weird, but I ignored them. This was Zac. I had known him—known *of* him—for more than half my life. He had sent me Christmas presents for a while. I loved him, and he had loved me for a long time. He was best friends with the man who had been better than a brother to me.

So what if Zac was some big-shot famous football player?

So what if he had been on the cover of magazines?

Or been the face of a football franchise?

So what if one of the last times I'd seen him in person, his girlfriend at the time had crushed my precious, fragile self-esteem into tiny little pieces with her fake-ass smile and harsh words? I wasn't seventeen anymore. I didn't weigh my self-value against other people's opinions.

And really, more than any other question, so what if he hadn't responded to any of my calls or texts for years? I was over that, and I had been for a long time. I didn't resent him for being busy.

I rubbed my sweaty fingers against each other and pressed my lips together as I kept on going.

The pretty blonde sitting on his right was the first one to look up at me, and luckily, she smiled. The brunette on his left didn't. She didn't really make any kind of facial expression, but there was something in her eyes that I didn't need to be a mind reader to know was more like *what are you looking at, bitch?* Pssh. Like that was intimidating. You didn't know scary until you read what people thought about you on the internet.

It wasn't until my feet stopped in front of the three of them that the cowboy hat tipped up and a pair of light blue eyes, such a pure soft blue that they could have almost been called baby blue, landed on me, making their way to my face and staying there.

He watched me, still smiling that smile I'd seen a million times that was all mischief and good humor. At least he wasn't devastated by what had happened with his former team, right? That was good. Then again, I'd seen him smile when I'd known he was devastated. That was just what he did.

It took me a second, but I smiled back at him, just a little thing, wiggling four fingers at him that I was pretty sure he didn't notice because his gaze didn't move anywhere below my neck.

And the first thing I said to a man who had carried me around on his shoulders, who had given me rides around my abuela's neighborhood on the handlebars of his bike, was "Hi, Zac."

And no, no, that wasn't freaking bittersweetness creeping up my throat.

He blinked again, and he kept on smiling as he drawled in a voice that had gotten deeper over the years, "How's it goin'?" Casual and friendly like always. Just like fucking Zac.

I went up to the balls of my feet, keeping my gaze right on a face that, in person, I could see how much it had matured. The softness that had been there before, that had been all boyish and cute, had mostly disappeared, leaving a leaner structure with high cheekbones and a sharp jaw. Fine little lines bracketed down and along his mouth. He was thirty-four now, after all.

And he was even more handsome than he'd been as a teenager or as a twenty-something, especially when he was smiling the way he was right then. Crooked. Still easygoing and friendly. Big Texas personified.

He was welcome.

"Hey," I told him carefully, still watching his striking, tan face. "It's me."

Me. Twenty-seven, not seventeen. My hair was long and down. When I'd been younger, it had always been up because I hadn't known what to do with my curls other than straighten it. I wore makeup now too. Plucked my eyebrows. Lost some weight. But I was still me.

His smile widened a little more, but I could tell, I could just tell....

"Bianca," I said, going up to the balls of my feet again.

Zac blinked and still....

I looked from one of his eyes to the other, taking in the color that was still so rich, and realized... he didn't recognize me. He didn't... remember? Or, if he did, then he didn't give a shit.

There was no hug. No *"Bianca! Holy shit! It's been so long! I'm so happy to see you! What are you doing here?"*

He just kept right on looking at me, blankly but politely. And....

My heart sank. I didn't mean for it to. I hadn't thought it could or would. I didn't want it to, but it sank. To my stomach at least. Probably all the way to my toes though. Because he'd been one of the most important people in my life for fourteen years, and he didn't—

It didn't matter.

I was here for a reason, and regardless of whether he remembered me or not, that didn't change anything. He didn't remember me, but I remembered him.

I had never forgotten Zac. Unlike him.

My toes curled inside my sneakers, and I forced the smile onto my face through sheer will, burying the disappointment deep as I went for it.... Then burying it even deeper. In and out. Let's do this. "Can I talk to you in private?"

One of his cheeks hitched up a little higher before the man who had been to my birthday parties until he'd left for college at eighteen said, "Aww, sugar, we can talk right here, can't we?"

He was still saying sugar. Of course he was.

My toes curled a little more in my sneakers as I clung to that "sugar" and reminded myself again that I wasn't being annoying or an inconvenience right then. I was here for a reason. An important one.

"I think it'd be better if we talked in private," I tried to explain as part of my brain tried to accept that he either didn't remember me or didn't care if he did. I tried to tell

myself that it didn't matter what the case was. But I was
going to go with option A because option B hurt just a little
too much, even though it shouldn't have. "Zac, it's me. Bianca
Brannen." I tried again, just in case. "Your mom's been trying
to call you...." I trailed off, hoping he'd get it. Hoping he
wouldn't force me to accept that he knew who I was and just
didn't care, even if my brain was aware he hadn't felt that way
in a while.

He got something though, because his next blink was
slow. His gaze sharpened suddenly. His forehead furrowed.

He was gorgeous.

He sat up straight and stared at me with those light blue
eyes. For so long, I'd thought they were the kindest eyes in
the world, and that was saying something because I knew a
lot of good people. But none of them had Zac's eyes, and I
had no reason to believe he wasn't that same person still,
regardless of him dropping me like a bad habit. Boogie
wouldn't still be friends with him if he'd changed too much, I
knew that. Mamá Lupe used to call him mi cielo for a reason.
My sky. Because she saw the same things in him—that innate
goodness. She had loved him as much as she'd loved her
biological grandkids.

So I told myself two things.

One: I wouldn't be sad if he didn't remember me.

Two: I wouldn't be sad if he didn't want me around. I had
popped out of nowhere, and I was asking for his time when
he was busy. It wasn't like he was being mean or rude.

And you couldn't fake those eyes.

I swallowed and went up to the balls of my feet again like
it would really make me taller. The words felt thick in my
throat. *I am here for a reason.* "I'm not trying to bother you.
Boogie asked me to come. He's been calling you too and—"

This beautiful man who had been featured naked on the
cover of a magazine a couple years back got to his booted feet

in about half a second. His mouth suddenly dropped open as those blue, blue eyes moved all over my face fast, fast, fast, and I could barely hear him as he gasped, literally gasped, "Wait. *Bianca?*"

Oh.

CHAPTER THREE

I couldn't actually remember meeting Zac. I couldn't remember meeting Mamá Lupe or Boogie for the first time either. My most blurry, distorted memories all included them though, like they had been around forever. Like life before them hadn't been memorable enough.

In my head and in my heart, they had always been around. From the beginning. Like my arms and my eyes, they were just... there.

I *knew* that I'd met them when I was three, when my parents moved to Liberty Hill with fifteen-year-old Connie and me, their oopsie, their surprise baby late in life. Somewhere along the way, for all I knew the same day we'd gotten to Mamá Lupe's house, Boogie and Zac had been there, along with a couple aunts and uncles I'd never met that had lived down the street too.

It had been a whole new world, I guess, going from living with only my parents and Connie to being surrounded by all these strangers who were family. According to Mamá Lupe, I'd fallen right into it. They claimed I hadn't been shy, but I knew now how nice almost everyone on my mom's side of the family was, so it must have been easy to get used to my new environment because of them.

It became home. The house. The people.

My parents didn't stay there for long either. By the time I was four, they were gone—like they would be on and off for the rest of my life—off saving the world, and they'd left Connie and me behind with Mamá Lupe and the rest of the family.

What I *did* remember was the bossy, dark-haired boy who used to tell our other cousins to shut up when they'd call me "la güera"—the white girl, even though I was only half, stupid asses—and the almost-blond, skinny boy who was always over at my abuela's house. Both of them were always nice to me. I kind of remembered them sitting in her living room, helping me build shit with big blocks, but that's about as far back as I could go when I thought of them being present and there.

What I didn't remember was the day that I supposedly pushed Zac out of the way of a copperhead in the yard and apparently saved his life. Everyone else just told me about it. What I knew for sure was that the blond, skinny boy *was* always, *always* nice to me after that.

Both of them were—my Boogie and Zac.

And with time, I could pluck out a whole lot more memories with them after that. How they taught me to ride a bike. How they'd let me ride on their bikes with them, at least until we got caught and Mamá Lupe hollered from the front porch to put me down before they killed me, even though I wasn't scared.

If they didn't invite me and I asked, they always let me tag along. I remembered that—never feeling excluded, always being welcomed by them.

Those two, along with Connie and my grandma, made me feel loved and wanted.

Despite the gap in our ages, we grew up together. Me and

them. They got older and older and hung around less, but they never forgot about me. Not then. Not even the one who had gone from a pale blond and skinny to a dirty blond and still skinny.

They got licenses, and I got to go for rides. When there was a football game when they were in high school, I was the little kid who got to hang out with her cool older cousin. I was the girl who got waved at by the guy that every student and parent in the stands cheered for.

And when they left for college, I cried. But they still came back to visit, and I got to see them some weekends and every holiday.

And then I turned sixteen and fell in love with the blond-haired man-boy who was still skinny, but not as skinny, and treated me like a little sister.

And... life was never the same after that.

It took me a second, but I answered Zac, even as my throat ached and my stomach churned a little. "Yup. It's me. Bianca." I lifted my fingers again and gave them another wiggle that was pretty half-assed.

Eyelashes, that were somewhere between blond and brown, fell over those baby blue eyes. "No," he pretty much whispered in what sounded like disbelief. Maybe even shock.

I nodded back at him, serious as a heart attack.

Those eyes moved over my face again right before he lifted one of those big, big hands—I tried not to think about how I'd thought he had the biggest hands and feet I'd ever seen back when I'd been younger—and he gently set the tip of his index finger right beside the corner of my mouth. Literally maybe two millimeters away. Right over the beauty mark there that I had hated when I'd been younger. I'd tried covering it up with my aunts' and Connie's makeup at least a dozen times.

Zac's finger stayed right there as his gaze flicked back to mine and my old friend asked, still basically whispering in a stunned drawl, "*Peewee?*"

Oh.

He really hadn't known it was me?

Warmth filled my chest—relief, it was relief, just a little bit of it; I could admit it—as I gave him another little smile, a hesitant one if I was going to be honest with myself. "Yep" was all I gave him, mostly because it was all I could. Okay, all I *would.*

Zachary James Travis's—professional quarterback and my old friend—mouth fell right open, showing me all those white, perfect teeth before the hand he had beside my lip fell away, and the next thing I knew, he was shaking his head and stating loudly, definitely freaking surprised, "You're shittin' me."

I shook my head in return.

Apparently that response was all he needed, because before I could do or say anything else, Zac took a step forward and, in the blink of a freaking eye, that six-foot-three body was there. Right in my face.

Right in my face and then lifting me up into a hug that had my toes leaving the ground in the time it took me to blink as he said, loud and in what really did seem like he was overwhelmed, "I can't believe it," as he hugged me so tightly to him, to that big, hard frame, so close.

A few years ago, that would have instantly eased most of the tension in my body.

He *did* remember me.

He was happy to see me.

And I wasn't going to cry because he hadn't *totally*

forgotten me. Or that he wasn't all blasé about seeing me after so long either. I wasn't.

But I didn't totally relax. Because it had been almost a decade, and because even though I understood that he was busy and had hundreds of people who wanted something from him, it didn't erase the hurt from before. It didn't wipe out the memories of staring at my phone and wondering what I had done wrong to make him not want to be my friend after so long.

I wasn't scraps. I had a life too. A life I had worked my ass off for. I had people who cared and loved me for a reason, because I'd earned it. I thought I was a decent person, most of the time.

And regardless of all that, ignoring the fine fracture of pain I still felt, I still loved him. Not for a second had I ever not wanted the best for him. There hadn't been a moment in my life that I hadn't rooted for him despite him outgrowing me and then leaving me in the past.

He was happy to see me right then, and I'd take it.

I lifted my arms and wrapped them around his neck and hugged that long body back, tightly for all of a second, like I had missed the hell out of him. Because I had. Just for a moment, I pressed my forehead against a spot along his warm, smooth neck.

There was no harm in that. I used to hug the shit out of him all the time.

I wasn't going to think about why we hadn't seen each other in so long. I wasn't going to be sad that it might be another ten years before we saw each other again after this. At least I wouldn't be sad for one more minute.

After this hug and after what I needed to do, life could go back to normal.

"I can't believe it's you, Peewee," Zac Travis pretty much whispered with that still surprised voice, the Texas accent he'd inherited from spending so much time with his Paw-Paw, thick and sweet. He held me so tight and high, I could barely touch the ground. And I'd be a goddamn liar if I said I didn't notice how hard and muscular his chest felt pressed up against me.

One of those long arms loosened, and what had to be his palm cupped the back of my head in a gesture that surprised me even more as his rich and familiar laughter filled the ear closest to his mouth. "I cannot fuckin' believe it."

I couldn't help but smile a little against his cheek, still right there in those final moments I was giving myself to soak up his attention after so long, right against the chest I'd seen bare countless times before he'd had any hair on it, and let myself savor his unexpected joy.

When he lowered me enough so I could touch the ground again flat-footed, I looked at him, still smiling. Feeling happy and surprised too.

Relieved.

The handsome man I'd been in love with when I'd been younger and dumber grinned down at me with an amazed expression that lit up his features in a way that I would have bet my life against a month ago. Zac's gaze flicked down to everything below my neck for a split second before it was back on my face, probably taking in my Maio House polo, my plain blue jeans that were rolled up at the ankles because they were too long, and my plain black tennis shoes with white soles that made standing for eight hours a day bearable. And that beaming white smile went even wider before those strong arms went wide at his sides, his expression flushed and pleased and earnest and totally freaking Zac before the NFO. "I can't believe it's you. When the hell did you grow up, huh?"

Of course he couldn't believe it was me. He hadn't seen me in so long or even looked me up.

Andddd there went at least half my joy.

That was reality for you, a kick to the freaking vagina when you needed it and even more when you didn't need it.

He kept right on smiling brightly as those light blue eyes strayed all over my face while my spine went tight and my shoulders dropped at his comment. "Peewee, you're an adult," my once-upon-a-time friend added, oblivious to what he'd reminded me of.

But I was over that shit. So I nodded at him again and said, a little bit weakly, "Most of the time."

"What are you doin' here?" Zac asked in that same excited voice, still oblivious. His face was all angles now, and up close, his eyes were just as kind as always. His finger came up to tap my beauty mark again as he shook his head one more time. "I cannot believe you're here, livin' and breathin' in front of me."

I remembered why I was there.

I started to reach for the blond-dusted skin wrapped around the hard muscles of his forearm before stopping. What the hell was I doing? I lowered my hand back down to my side and forced myself to meet those light blue eyes so I could do this. "Can we talk in private?"

The big smile still on his face hurt my heart, especially when he glanced down at the hand I'd pulled back, and part of it slowly melted off. But he nodded after a second, his expression turning somewhere between confused and hesitant, picking up on my mood, I could only guess. "Wherever you want, darlin'," he agreed easily.

In other circumstances, in another lifetime, his next words would have made my day. They would have lifted me up and made my whole month. I had loved him—*loved him*—but for what were probably a hundred different reasons, we hadn't seen each other in almost a third of my life. "When'd this happen? *Do you live here?*" he asked like he'd instantly forgotten I wanted to talk to him in private. "I feel like I'm imaginin' this."

I am here for a reason. Right. He needed to know; the sooner the better. I had to stay on track. He didn't really... care. Not really. "Do you know where your phone is?" I asked him instead.

That got his smile to falter just like *that*. "No. I let somebody borrow it. I thought they gave it back...."

He was onto me. Maybe he'd finally put together what I'd said about his mom and Boog calling, about being sent here, about wanting to talk to him in private.

"Want to go inside?"

He started to nod before he stopped, every single line in his body dropping. His eyes moved from one of mine to the other as he asked, very, very carefully, the warmth in his expression disappearing by the millisecond. "Is it—" His Adam's apple bobbed. Those long, sand-colored eyelashes fluttered, and the pain, the worry, the terror was there as that voice that had been bright and welcoming four minutes ago pronounced three words. "Is it Paw-Paw?"

I didn't want to tell him out here in front of his friends, and I didn't need to look around his body to know that there had to be a handful of eyes set on us. On him. I could feel it. He had to know it too.

"He's at the hospital, and they're running tests. That's all I know. Your mom and Boogie have been trying to call you but...." *You haven't answered.* Because he'd lent someone his phone while he was having a party. But it wasn't like he couldn't put that together on his own.

The man who I'd assumed had spent the majority of his life laughing and smiling went stone-faced and pale in about half a second.

I needed to keep going.

"Boogie gave me your address and asked me to come look

for you. I got here as soon as I could," I explained, eyeing the arm that had been hanging loosely at his side and thinking about taking hold of his hand just like I had done to him countless times when I'd been little. Except now those fingers that I would have meshed through mine were million-dollar fingers while mine were in the thousand-dollar club. But I didn't take his hand. We weren't there anymore. I focused on that lean, subtly striking face with its laugh lines that were hiding and pink lips and those warm blue eyes. "Want to use my phone and call them in the meantime?"

Those eyes flicked down to me, and his Adam's apple bobbed again as he nodded and lifted a hand to rub right between pectoral muscles buff enough for that touch to make them form a valley. There hadn't been any muscles there back in the day, that was for sure. His head turned to the right, and he called out, "CJ! Can you call my phone? I gotta find it."

"You got it, Big Texas," whoever he'd been talking to responded in a deep, deep voice.

Big Texas. I doubted he still thought of me whenever someone called him that. I had a feeling it had been a long, long time since he had.

I shoved my phone toward him. The faster he did this, the faster I could leave. "If he'll call it, I'll help look for it while you get in touch with your mom."

Those blue eyes moved toward me but were totally and completely distracted, like I was there but wasn't. I couldn't say I blamed him either, not after how the day was going.

My thought was confirmed when he looked down at my phone with sightless eyes. The beaming, happy man from a minute ago was totally gone, and I figured he needed a moment. Or ten. But he really did need to call his mom or my cousin.

And I needed to help him find his phone so I could go home.

I turned around to figure out who he'd asked for help and found a man pretty much directly behind me with platinum, bleached blond dreadlocks tied up into a ponytail holding a cell phone to his ear and swinging his gaze around at the same time. He wasn't very tall—not like I was one to talk—but he was really fit. After casting one last glance at Zac as he stared down at my cell like he didn't remember how to use it, I faced the other man again and got his attention. Two dark brown eyes flicked down to me.

"Hi. If you'll call it, I'll look for it."

The pretty buff man eyed me with a nod, his gaze sliding to my polo shirt for a second before he said, "I'll keep calling until you find it."

"Deal."

It took a long time walking through the house and the crowd of strangers to finally find a ringing iPhone with a big crack across the screen in a half bathroom by the front door. I snorted.

This man who used to have an eight-figure contract had a phone with a cracked screen. It wasn't so different from the Zac I'd known who would use duct tape on tears in his jacket, had cardboard taped to his car window for two months after an ex-girlfriend broke it, and had always ordered from the dollar menu because it was cheaper than buying a meal at the drive-through.

He really hadn't changed that much over the years. It was nice. If life and people and fans and critics hadn't done it, I had a feeling nothing and no one ever would. And that was even nicer.

He'd been happy to see me, there was no hiding that.

I hit answer as **CJ Daniels—White Oaks** flashed across the screen. "Got it. Thanks." I got a grunt in return and hung up.

Zac's phone vibrated, and the screen illuminated. It was second nature for me to look at it.

NEW TEXT MESSAGES

AMY BLONDEWAITRESS OKC: [picture message]

And below that, there were older notifications.

KEISHA BLDIVORCELAWYER OKC: [picture message]

STACY BROWNBANKER OKC: Just heard about...

VANESSA: [two new messages]

AIDEN: Call me.

TREVOR: WHAT THE FUCK ARE YOU DOING. CALL ME BACK

Amy. Blonde Waitress. OKC.

Keisha. Blonde? Divorce attorney. OKC.

Stacy. Brunette banker. OKC.

And a Vanessa.

At least he had his way of remembering the... people he met.

For one tiny, stupid, unnecessary second, I wondered if he had any Biancas in his phone. But just as quickly as that question entered my head, I kicked it to the side, as far away as possible.

It was none of my business.

I made my way back through the house but couldn't find him in the yard where he'd been. When his friend, the guy with the dreadlocks met my gaze, I lifted Zac's busted-up phone to reconfirm I'd found it and gave him a thumbs-up with my opposite hand, earning me a jerky nod. Now where the hell was he?

"I think he went to his room," the blonde who had been sitting beside him called out from the same spot she'd been in, getting my attention. She pointed up.

She knew where his room was. That wasn't any of my business either.

"He was still on the phone," she went on, with her nice voice matching her pretty face. "Is he okay?"

I lifted a shoulder. I didn't know her. I wasn't going to spread Zac's business around, especially not to someone who may or may not have a description after her name on his phone. I couldn't imagine knowing or meeting so many people that I had to describe them to keep track of them. At the most, a few people had last names under my contacts.

Anyway.

"Thanks for telling me." I offered up a little smile that was genuine because she was being nice. I liked nice people.

But now I needed to figure out where he was, get my phone back, and bounce.

"How do you know Zac?"

I glanced down at the unfamiliar voice and found the other half of the Zac sandwich bread, the brunette who had given me a funky look, still giving me a funky one after asking her question.

I gave her the only answer I would or could, especially around someone who didn't give me nice-person vibes. "We're family." She could do with that whatever she wanted.

Her face said she didn't believe me even a little bit, but I didn't give a shit. I turned around and headed back inside after smiling goodbye at the other woman. Finding a staircase tucked by the living room, I headed up, taking in all the plain white walls that matched all the white downstairs too. I couldn't hear anything over the voices downstairs as I made my way down the hall, peeking into every open room.

Each one was different. The first one was mostly empty except for a modern queen-sized bed and dresser. In the second room was an exact replica with another queen-sized bed and brand-new, never-been-lived-in everything. The carpet was pristine too.

The third room I came across though had a king-sized bed that took up the majority of it, and there was a medium-sized flat screen mounted to the wall. The closet door was open inside, I could see a hint of clothing hanging. On the bed was a T-shirt. And it was while I peeked into that room that I heard Zac's voice. I passed by a big media room with four large recliners and a projector. It also looked brand new.

I found him in what had to be a master bedroom, or at least one of the master bedrooms in a house this big. I'd be surprised if there wasn't one downstairs too. One day when I was bored at work, I'd looked up plans to a new development I'd driven by, and some of those houses had not one but *two* suites. F-a-n-c-y.

Zac had my phone against his ear, and there was a suitcase sitting open on top of a king-sized mattress. A plain white comforter and sheets were balled up at the foot of it. A random pair of socks were lying right next to stained blue and gray sneakers. A glass half full of water was on the nightstand closest to the bedroom door... but that was mostly it other than a big black dresser against the wall. There was nothing on the walls in this room either. Nothing personal. No knickknacks.

"Uh-huh, all righty," Zac said, making eye contact with me when I stopped at the doorframe before he tipped his head like he was gesturing me to come in. One hand was aggressively digging through that dark blond hair that was the exact same shade I remembered it, just a little bit longer than I'd usually seen him wearing it through the TV.

I went in. I'd been in his room a couple of times, but I couldn't remember what it had looked like. There were only faint images of a messy, cluttered room that had smelled like sweat and feet and some kind of cologne his aunt had given him for Christmas every year supposedly.

Longing hit me low in the belly for that younger boy I'd loved as a brother figure and then as a fantasy, even though he'd let me down by moving on with his life and leaving me behind. But it was in the past, and I understood.

I watched as Zac turned to the dresser, pulled out some clothes, and tossed them into the suitcase.

But I saw it. Saw him.

His hands were shaking.

They were shaking big-time.

Shit.

He said "okay" and "uh-huh" a couple more times as he dumped more clothing into his suitcase. And yeah, I listened the whole time. "I'll be there as soon as I can. Love you, Mama."

His mom.

He was clutching my phone hard as he ended the call and stood there. He'd pulled his cowboy hat off at some point—this plain brown thing—and his hair was tossed all over his head, messy. I could see in the bedroom light that he was really tan from all his outdoor training, and he looked more muscular than I'd ever seen him. His torso was lean and endless, his shoulders so broad in person, those strong arms lined with ropey muscles; it caught me off guard.

But his face....

It reminded me again of how long it had been since I'd last seen him in person. He was about to be thirty-five in a few months. I could faintly remember his seventeenth birthday when Mamá Lupe, my grandma and the person who had babysat Zac for years, had surprised him after football practice with his favorite tres leches cake—cake made with three different kinds of milk. She'd kept the picture of him blowing out the candles on that day, with an enormous smile on his face, on her mantle for the rest of her life. You could barely see me right beside his shoulder, all cheeks and chins, peeking at what I'd known was going to be some awesome cake, with Boogie on Zac's other side.

I had kept the picture after we cleaned out her house years later. I had it sitting in a drawer in one of my night-stands. Me with one of my favorite people and a childhood friend who had grown up to be a superstar. I could tell my kids about it someday. *I saved his life once*, I could tell them too.

Well, for now, my job was done. I could go home, watch some more of the Turkish romance, and brainstorm my chocolate and banana recipe some more. I could call Boogie tomorrow and see how Paw-Paw was doing.

"Zac—"

"Could you drive me back home?"

I froze.

He wanted *me* to drive him? When he had a house full of people?

Blue eyes met my own, filled with worry and distress and probably a dozen other emotions I didn't know how to clas-sify or what to do with.

"Please?" Zac asked in a quiet voice that snuck straight into the place inside of me that had managed to hold on to the love I had for Zac even after so long.

The memory of him surprising me at my high school grad-uation, holding up a Mylar balloon and waving at me like a lunatic while I'd approached my family, hit me right then. He'd been living in Dallas at that point. I had been staying with Boogie's parents for a couple months. He'd warned me via text that he wasn't positive if he'd be able to make it or not, but he had.

It had been one of the last times we'd seen each other, but that was beside the point.

He had come when he didn't have to, and now....

"Sure," I told him, only a little reluctant, watching his face. I was surprised he still felt comfortable enough around me that he would ask *me*. And if I wondered again why he didn't hit up one of the many people at his house—or whatever this place was—I kept the question to myself. It wasn't my business, and he wouldn't ask me unless there was a good reason.

His hand went up to his face, and he dragged the back of it across his forehead. How he could still look like an innocent boy and a full-grown man at the same time was beyond me. He swallowed hard as he quietly zipped his suitcase, giving me a tight smile afterward before gesturing toward the door.

He wasn't crying, so that was a good sign, right? That meant nothing could be so bad. Maybe I should text Boogie and ask him once we traded phones.

I headed down the hall in silence, down the stairs the same way too. At the bottom of them, I stopped and glanced over my shoulder at the tight, strained face that was busy focusing on the floor. His cheeks looked hollow, that light pink mouth thin. "Do you need to talk to anyone before you leave? Or kick everyone out or something?"

The man I had known looked up with eyes that were more distressed than kind at that moment, his forehead furrowed. "No."

All right. He knew what he was doing.

I nodded before handing him his cell, which I'd stuck in my back pocket while he'd been talking to his mom. He took it with a dip of his chin, then handed mine over. We kept going, and I couldn't ignore the stares from the strangers in the house as they watched Zac carrying his carry-on suitcase around and through them. If I'd expected some expensive luggage with initials and designer logos all over it, I would have been disappointed. His suitcase was black and looked like it had been around the world a couple of times.

Maybe it had.

"Hey, man, where you going?" one guy asked him as we walked by.

He looked familiar....

"Out. See ya," my old friend responded distractedly.

I really did need to know if there was any news on Paw-Paw.

Neither one of us said a word—in my case, I didn't know what the hell to say—as we left through the front door, a couple more people calling out greetings to Zac that he answered vaguely and in that weird voice that sounded like it belonged to another human being—a human being that was weighed down by a concrete block attached to his feet.

Down the street and at my car, I popped the trunk so he could drop his suitcase in it. He closed it as I watched him, those high cheekbones straining against his skin. *Upset* and *worried* were stamped along the surface of them. Years ago, I had known just how much he adored his grandpa. The same way I'd adored my mom's mom, my Mamá Lupe.

Completely and totally, because that was exactly how they'd loved us.

I could never forget how I'd felt when she'd had her heart attack. Helpless. Desperate. Like the world had been kicked out from under my feet.

Maybe Zac hadn't been my friend for almost a third of my life, but he had been there for me time and time again for the first two-thirds. When Mamá Lupe died, he had hugged me while I'd sobbed against him, worried about what I was going to do from then on. And I could never forget that he'd cried too. He'd cried over the woman who had babysat him for a decade. Who had kept on making him birthday cakes even after he'd gotten so busy with after-school activities that he didn't need another set of eyes keeping tabs on him. I couldn't forget that he'd promised me then that I'd be okay.

I knew what my grandma and my cousin would want from me. I knew what they would want me to do for someone they loved so much. This wasn't about me and what I wanted and needed.

So I did it. I offered the only thing I could then, what they would want, but braced myself to get rejected just in case.

"Hey," I said to him, telling myself again to prepare for a *hell no*. "You need a hug? You can say no."

The lean, beautiful man in front of me—with the weight of an entire solar system bearing down on his shoulders it seemed—stared at me for a moment.

Then he nodded.

It was me who cut the distance between us until I was staring up at him, like I had so many times while I'd been growing up. I would have smiled if this had been any other circumstance, but his grandpa was in the hospital, I wasn't sure what his mom had told him, and he may or may not know what he was doing with his career now that his NFO—National Football Organization—team had signed someone else to his position. On top of all that, I was confused and hurt and relieved all at the same time. So I settled for looking right into those eyes that were and weren't familiar anymore.

I went up to my tiptoes and slid my arms around his neck. He was a stranger and yet not a stranger, and I pulled in his heat and the strength of his chest against my own that, in a way, felt almost frail right then.

And it just made me hug him even tighter.

Yes, he had hurt me. His distance had wounded me. But that wasn't what this was about. This was about further back than that, back when things had been good between us. The best.

Zac waited a few seconds before wrapping his arms around the middle of my back, and then it was him pulling me in even closer to that body of his, like I wasn't some girl he hadn't seen in forever, like time hadn't passed and it had just been yesterday when he'd spot me after his high school football games and introduce me to whoever happened to be around as Peewee. When he'd come home to visit from college and lay around the television at Mamá Lupe's, throwing pillows at me when I was being a pest.

I wanted to ask him what his mom had said, but I didn't.

As I felt his chest expand with one breath after another, hearing a sigh here, followed by another one there, I let this moment be enough for right then. I hesitated for a second before sliding my hands up and down the muscles along his back like I would have done to any of my friends or loved ones if they needed comfort. Because a third of my life ago, I would've given him a kidney if he'd needed it.

All right, I'd still give it to him, but I'd give it to just about anyone if they really needed it and only had me.

Things changed. People changed. Life changed. I knew it and accepted it.

His phone started ringing then, and he broke our connection and stepped away.

I met his gaze. "Let's go. You can take your calls while I drive."

Zac, who had seemed so happy to see me thirty minutes ago, stuck to nodding as a response, the rest of his features totally sober.

I sent my sister another text real quick before I got back into the car.

Me: Driving to Austin and back. I'll let you know when I get home.

The man in my passenger seat talked, but only on the phone as he spoke to who I guessed were his agent, his manager—who was some guy named Trevor that I'd met once and thought he was a jerk, who was also the man who had texted him, now that I thought about it—and my cousin Boogie. He'd basically relayed to the first two that his grandpa was in the hospital and that he was going back home to be with him.

"*I'm not sure when I'll be back,*" Zac had told Trevor, who, from what I had gathered, wasn't very happy with his decision to leave Houston. I managed to hear bits and pieces of him replying to Zac using a sharp voice and saying words like "time" and "can't afford to" and "what are you doing?" To which Zac responded by gritting his teeth and replying to him in an annoyed voice that "*this was Paw-Paw*" and "*family comes first, Trev*" and "*yeah, he's at the house; don't worry about it.*"

Their conversation had interested me the most, honestly. But I reminded myself again that it wasn't my business what happened and I just wished Zac the best, like I always would.

Then he called someone who lived with him, based off the clues.

"*Hey, I left the house. My grandpa is in the hospital, and I gotta get home to see him.... Yeah.... Look, kick everybody out when you're ready. The cleanin' crew will be there tomorrow; I called them this mornin', so you're gonna be good.... Yeah. All right. Sorry, Ceej.... Sure. Bye.*"

After those calls, Zac hardly said anything, even when I stopped at a big gas station with a beaver logo on the way out of Houston. He just sat in the car and waited for me while I went in. I bought two sausages on a stick and a couple drinks, intending to share one with the man waiting in the car, but when I tried to hand him one, he gave me a tiny smile and shook that dark blond head of hair. He did take the bottle of water I'd got him.

The Zac I had known would have never turned down a sausage on a stick—or any food really. It was just a reminder that, in some ways, he wasn't the same person. Even my cramping stomach agreed.

That or he had a really strict diet that didn't include processed meats. Who the hell knew? I was going to go with option B to make myself feel better.

I drove with my wrists, hands full while I ate both the sausages because they weren't about to go to waste, and we— at least I—listened to a podcast about affirmations and the history of beans.

But, yeah, the entire ride was spent without us saying a word to each other. When before we both would have run our mouths nonstop about everything and anything. He was a talker, and so was I.

It was just another reminder we were different people.

Luckily, I hadn't expected anything, especially not this— driving him a couple hundred miles back to the area where we'd grown up. At least I was off work the next day. I contemplated staying at Boogie's, so I wouldn't drive home in the dark, but immediately decided against it. I needed to film tomorrow, and Deepa had warned me she had something to do in the afternoon, so we had to start early.

The hours went by fast at least, and Zac eventually mentioned what hospital Paw-Paw was at once we got close to northern Austin and had to use the navigation app to get there since I couldn't remember.

"We're here," I told him when I pulled in front of the medical center.

Zac lifted his head off where it had been resting against the window for the last hour and sighed. It made my heart hurt a little. All right, maybe more than a little.

Reaching over, I set my hand on his shoulder, giving it a quick pat for what would more than likely be the last time in a very long time. "Do you need anything else before I go?" I asked him gently as I tried to take in that familiar-not-familiar face one last time.

You know, for old times' sake.

He really had gotten better looking. If I closed one eye, he'd look like he could've been the muse for one or two Disney princes. Good for him.

The edges of his mouth turned down as he frowned at me and asked in that same quiet, pained voice from hours ago, "You're leavin'?"

Well... yeah. I had been. But now, with him looking at me all strange and sad....

Maybe... not?

Shit.

"I can stay if you want me to," I offered hesitantly before I could overthink it or make up an excuse for why I needed to go. I wasn't sure why he would want me, of all people, to stay, but....

I definitely didn't expect the nod he instantly answered me with, that was for sure.

He really wanted me to stay?

O-kay. I could. For a little bit. Just long enough to leave him with someone and say hi to my cousin. We texted a lot, but it had been almost two months since we'd seen each other in person. Traveling for work had eaten up a lot of his time lately. So had his girlfriend.

I nodded back, giving him a little smile that was mostly uncertain—while inside I was pretty much surprised as shit and just as confused—and drove around to find the parking garage, pulling into the first open space big enough that I could easily pull out of. I sucked at parking. And reversing. Everyone teased me for parking a mile away everywhere.

Zac didn't make a comment when it took me two tries to pull in decently.

I thought about the plain black suitcase in my trunk and figured I'd bring it up once I knew what was going on since he had other things to worry about. Zac and I walked side by side into the hospital, and I couldn't help but glance up at his face a couple times. His brows were drawn low, and he looked tired. I hoped again, more than anything, that Paw-Paw was all right.

No one paid much attention to us as we walked through the hospital. Subconsciously, I had expected everyone in the world to recognize him, especially in the Austin area, where he'd been everyone's hero for most of his life. Zac had been an icon here back in his college days. On the occasions that I had been invited to go out to eat with them back then, someone had always recognized him and tried to pay for his food or buy him a drink.

It had been weird, even though it had been the same way, on a smaller scale, back when he'd been in high school.

But as we passed the employees at the front desk and the random people sitting in the waiting areas, no one looked twice in our direction. Then again, Zac was tall but not too tall, and lean and muscular, but not overloaded with bulky muscles like the giants he played alongside. There was also the fact that his hair wasn't eye catching at his shade and length. His face was very handsome, but there was nothing about it that would *force* someone to look in his direction. There definitely wasn't anything outrageous about his clothes either.

Really, he just looked like an attractive, everyday guy.

Except he wasn't, not really, cracked phone or not. I wasn't going to forget that.

Zac's butt cheeks had been plastered to the cover of TSN's Anatomy Issue—a special edition The Sports Network released once a year that featured professional athlete's... anatomy. AKA, they were all butt naked but with their crown jewels angled away. I had bought a copy for support. So had millions of other people. I was pretty sure it was still tucked away in my nightstand drawer too.

At the elevator bank, we got in with a couple just as Zac's phone started ringing once more. He pulled it out of his pocket, took a peek, and then put it right back where it had been.

He caught me looking at him, and I smiled. He smiled back, but it wasn't anywhere close to being on the same level it had been on when he'd first seen me hours ago. "An old teammate," he explained in a voice I had never, ever heard from him before, even on TV with people shoving microphones at his face and asking what went wrong, all while hinting that losing had been all his fault. He was that worried.

I just settled for another nod as I wondered if it had been an "old" one from Oklahoma or from before.

One of his cheeks hitched up a little higher in a smile just a millimeter bigger than the one before. "Thanks for bringin' me, darlin'," he said in a tired, distracted voice.

"You're welcome."

When the doors opened, I walked out ahead of him, following the signs. I stopped at the desk and signed my name in, sensing Zac still behind me. Then I filled in James Travis for him, deciding his first name was too much. You never knew who might read the sign-in sheet. I knew I did.

"I put you down too," I said as I turned around.

Those familiar-not-familiar blue eyes slid to me, his chin tucked. "Thank you," he repeated, voice still off and flat.

We were just walking by a glass-encased waiting area when someone called out, "Zac! B!"

I knew that voice. I *loved* that voice.

I turned around, already grinning because I couldn't help it despite the circumstances. Sure enough, Boogie was waving at us as he got up from the seat he was in. In his fitted pants and tailored shirt, he had to have come straight from work. But one glance into the waiting room told me that he wasn't alone. A woman was sitting in the seat next to the one he'd been in. She lifted her hand, and I lifted mine. His girlfriend.

Bleh.

Looking away from her, I got to watch as Boogie and Zac clashed in a hug.

The thirty-five-year-old and the thirty-four-year-old. They'd been best friends since third grade when Zac had moved to Liberty Hill to be closer to his grandparents, who happened to employ Boogie's dad at the time. His parents had never married, and I wasn't sure if Zac knew who his dad was.

Boogie and Zac had met at Mamá Lupe's house when she'd started keeping an eye on him after school while his mom worked. They'd gone to the same middle and high school. Even when Zac had gone to college in Austin, and Boogie had gone to San Antonio, they had still seen each other at least one weekend a month. When Boogie when to Zac's games, he would always come pick me up and take me with him. Then he'd go back after dropping me off and hang out with him... and whoever else they were with.

Unlike my relationship with him, I had never doubted how much those two cared for each other, especially in situations like this, where I was pretty sure Boogie had come straight to the hospital to be with Zac's family. But that was just the kind of guy my cousin was, and it was one of the many reasons I loved the shit out of him. He was one of the most selfless, loyal people in the world.

As his dumb girlfriend had already learned.

"He's conscious," I heard Boogie say as the two men hugged. "The doctor thinks his blood sugar levels dropped. We'll find out more soon. He got really lucky."

Zac's head dropped forward until it was resting on my

cousin's shoulder, and I didn't miss the huge relieved breath he let out. I didn't miss his "Good Lord" either.

My cousin patted him on the back, hard. "Your mom is with him. They have a two-person limit for visitors. He was asking for you earlier. Go on in there."

Zac nodded, and after another pat on the back, I watched him take a step away from my cousin. He must have glanced into the waiting room like I had, because a second later, he raised his hand the same way I had and dropped it almost immediately.

Maybe Connie and I weren't the only ones unsure about Boog's girlfriend.

That made me feel like a little less of a hater.

Then I watched him glance over his shoulder at me and say the last thing I would have expected for the second time in a day. "You comin', Peewee? Say hi to Mama?"

Did he think I hadn't seen her in years too?

And how could I say no to telling Ms. Travis hi? Especially when he still drawled *mama* out all sweet and with that accent? I couldn't, that was the problem. Two-person limit be damned. I'd leave if someone complained.

I nodded at Zac for probably the twentieth time and gave Boogie a quick hug and kiss on the cheek. We'd talk later. I even raised my hand up one more time at the fake redhead too because it would hurt Boogie's feelings if I didn't.

Zac and I headed down the hall to Paw-Paw's room, following the digits posted on each sterile white door. A man and a woman were standing at the nurses' station, and I saw the woman glance at us, look down, then do a double take. Well, it wasn't me who made her look twice. She elbowed the man in the scrubs standing beside her and whispered something.

I was about to say something to Zac, but then realized getting recognized was probably old news for him.

I closed my mouth and kept it that way when Zac happened to look over and see his audience. He lifted that big hand again as he said in a tired voice, "Evenin'."

The woman greeted him back. The man said nothing.

That must have been enough, because Zac glanced at me with stress clouding those baby blues. And I'd be a freaking liar if I said that a wave of tenderness didn't hit me right then. "Thanks for comin' with me," he said in an eggshell-thin voice that sounded seriously exhausted, his audience forgotten. "Hopefully Paw-Paw is awake. He'll love to see you."

I didn't hold back a little smile. "That's what he always says."

Zac was looking straight forward as he asked, "How long's it been?"

"Mmm, not that long ago," I admitted, looking forward too because I wanted to, not because I didn't want to make eye contact.

Silence.

Then, "When was the last time you saw Mama?" my old friend drawled in a tone that might have had me glancing at him if I'd had some balls... but I'd dropped mine along the way somewhere. Probably outside of his house.

"Same time. At Boogie's birthday party." Back in March. "They said you were in the Bahamas." That and I'd seen the pictures he'd posted on his Picturegram account. There was one of him on a yacht surrounded by greenish blue water with two teammates and five women. Boogie claimed he'd been invited to go but hadn't been able to take the time off.

Looking over, I noticed Zac made the slightest, tiniest face. I turned away at the same time he full-on glanced over.

I pointed at the door we were looking for. "Look, this is it." Not waiting for him, I knocked lightly and pushed the door open slowly, gesturing for him to go in first.

A familiar woman with dark blonde hair was sitting in a

recliner turned toward a small television on the wall with her arms crossed over her chest. But it was the elderly man lying in the hospital bed with his arms at his sides that I focused on. He had a few tubes hooked up to his arms and one into his nose, and most importantly, his eyes were glued to the television too.

I guess they hadn't heard me knock, because the second Zac took about four steps into the hospital room, Paw-Paw Travis gasped and followed that up by smiling so big, it took up the majority of his lined and weathered face. At eighty-nine years old, his hair was all white and fluffy, where usually he had it all combed and nice looking.

"Zac," the old man crooned as he lifted his head and flashed his mouthful of dentures. I knew they were dentures because he'd let me see them once when they'd gotten loose. Paw-Paw Travis must have caught sight of me hovering behind his grandson because he breathed out, that big smile still on his face as he gasped my name in that thick drawl that even put Zac's to shame. "Bianca."

At least he recognized me.

"Hi, Paw-Paw Travis," I greeted him just as Zac made it to the bed and instantly bent over, slipping an arm under his grandfather's head effortlessly, his free arm curling over to hug him. I smiled and didn't miss the harsh hiccup that took over Zac as he said who knew what kind of words into the older man's ear. I glanced over at Ms. Travis, Mr. Travis's daughter, and caught her sitting up and smiling tiredly over at her father and son as they embraced. "Hi, Ms. Travis."

Ms. Travis got to her feet with an exhausted sigh, and we hugged. I'd known her just as long as I'd known her son. We hadn't been all that close while I'd been little—she'd been a mom figure that worked a lot, and she'd kind of intimidated me once when she'd literally grabbed Zac by the ear and dragged him out of Mamá Lupe's house—but over the years, we'd grown closer through Boogie. "Bianca, thank you so much for bringing him," the woman said.

"It was nothing," I replied, still in the middle of a hug. "Any news?"

She pulled back and lowered her voice just enough to whisper, "We're waiting for some test results. We were lucky I found him so soon."

"I'm so glad he's fine. I'm sure it scared the hell out of you. Do you need anything? Can I do anything?" I asked the blonde-haired, blue-eyed woman who towered over me. I'd asked her once how tall she was, and she'd laughed and said five-ten.

"No, no, I'm fine. Boogie ran out and got us some supper earlier." She squeezed my hand and lowered her voice even more. "Has my baby boy eaten anything?"

Her baby boy. Pfft. I almost laughed.

We both glanced toward the bed and found Zac stretched out on it beside his grandfather, facing him, head cushioned on his biceps as they whispered to each other. This grown-ass man on the bed with his equally long grandpa *was* pretty freaking adorable; they looked like time-lapsed twins.

And despite how cute Zac looked with Paw-Paw, I was about to rat him out to his mom anyway. I wasn't sure I'd ever done that before. That was one of the main reasons why he and Boog had always let me hang out. Well, that and the life-saving thing, I guessed. *Snitches get stitches, bitches*, Connie had taught me when I'd been like... five.

I'd been around when Connie had taught her daughter the same saying—minus the bitch part—and had impressed my sister by dragging my thumb across my throat while she'd done it. We'd had a good laugh over it later when my niece hadn't been around. I needed to go visit them again soon.

"No, not with me. He's been really worried."

"Like he should be." She sighed, attention still focused on

the two generations of men. "Thank you so much for going to find him for us. Boogie said he had to call and get you out of work to go get him."

"It's not a big deal. I was almost done with my shift when he did. It was no problem."

The same milky, light blue eyes as Zac's, but on a much more feminine face, slid in my direction. Ms. Travis was beautiful. A thinking and judging beautiful woman who knew from our last interaction that I still hadn't seen her son in years. I bet she hadn't forgotten that part.

"It's hard to keep track of him nowadays. If he could find it in him to settle down and stay somewhere, buy a place of his own, we wouldn't have to be searching for him all the time. God knows I send him lists of houses every other week close to Paw-Paw and me, but he just won't set up roots with anything or anyone," she told me quietly and with an exasperated expression.

The only thing I could do was smile at her and nod like I understood.

And I guess, in a way, I did.

And if that comment about settling down with *anything* and *anyone* wasn't my cue to get the hell out of there, I didn't know what was. "If it's okay, let me give Paw-Paw a hug, and I'll get out of here before you get in trouble for having too many people hanging around."

Ms. Travis nodded.

I made my way over to the bed as Zac and Paw-Paw continued talking to each other. As soon as the older man spotted me though, he stopped talking and gave me a tired but somehow bright smile. His deep, sweet voice was weak. "You came all this way to check on me?"

"You know I did." I smiled at him before eyeing Zac and feeling a small part of my expression drop off. I glanced back at the older man. "Did you like the present I brought you, Paw? He was pretty hard to find."

Mr. Travis's hand, connected to tubes, slid across the bed and patted his grandson's denim-covered hip. "Best gift anyone has ever found for me. Bless you, sweetheart."

I leaned forward and kissed the older man on the cheek. He still had the faintest hint of cologne clinging to him. I liked it. "Do you need anything?"

"To get out of here."

I grinned. "I'll put in a good word for you with the doctor, okay? Maybe he'll let you out of here sooner. We'll smuggle you out if not."

"That'd be real nice, sweetheart. How's work?" he asked on a sudden yawn.

That was my second sign to bounce. "I've got a new boss, and he's a jerk, but I'm hanging in there." I reached down and combed his hair to the side with my fingers as he yawned again. "I'm going to get out of here before they kick me out. They don't want your fan club taking over the whole floor. If you need anything, give me a call or have someone else give me a call, okay?"

His smile turned soft, and I did my best to keep ignoring the set of eyes that had been aimed at me from the moment I'd approached the bed. "I will," he assured me.

I stroked Mr. Travis's hand, his veins big and blue and purple, as Zac sat up a bit.

Right. Time to say bye. And I was going to do it right, because Mamá Lupe would haunt me in my dreams tonight if I didn't.

And also, life was fucking short, and I wasn't harboring any resentment. Just some melancholy and bittersweetness in there. That was it.

Zac was sitting up by the time I got around to his side, and I didn't hesitate to put my arms around the parts of him I could reach, hugging him too—not very tight but just enough.

Those long arms that I knew had to be so strong went around my back instantly.

I wasn't going to lie to myself; I almost sighed. I really had missed this guy, despite everything. But there was a reason why amputees survived and thrived; you learned how to live without.

I pulled away and smiled a little as I told the handsome man looking at me, "I have to head home. You'll be fine getting back?"

"You're goin' back right now?" the man I hadn't seen in nearly a decade asked, startling me. *Yet again.*

I nodded.

"You can't spend the night?"

He was on a freaking roll with the surprises, huh?

It was nice to know I could cherish the friendship we'd had for the rest of my life and keep being proud of it. My friend was a good man to the people he loved. Being famous and wealthy were just the cherry topping on the sundae. That knowledge lifted me up and kept me there, just far enough away to not be sad.

Things happened for a reason.

"No, I'm sorry. I have to get back home. I'll get Boogie to get your bag from my car though so you can stay up here," I told him quickly before going up to my toes and kissing him on the cheek, just like I'd done to his grandfather. Then I gave him another small smile as my eyes took in his face one last time.

Tenderness and nostalgia filled my stomach for a second as I took in those suntanned features that were aging so gracefully, and I couldn't help myself. I really couldn't as I touched his thigh with my fingertips for a second and busted out the nickname I hadn't used in forever and ever.

"Take care of yourself, Snack Pack. I'm super proud of you."

A slight, slow smile took over the lower half of Zac's face as his gaze locked on to mine, but it was Paw-Paw who chuckled at what I'd called him.

Before he'd been "Big Texas," he'd been "Zac the Snack Pack."

Right.

Time to go.

I took a step back and waved at the three of them. "Do whatever the doctor tells you, Paw-Paw Travis. Bye!"

"Bye, Bianca," three different voices called out. Or it might have just been two of them. I wasn't going to wonder about that too much. Zac had seemed genuinely happy to see me at first, and that was good enough.

I was out of there, opening the door and closing it behind me, and then instantly stopping.

Because directly across from Paw-Paw's room were what seemed like ten people.

And they were all watching the door like hawks.

Yep, that lady had recognized Zac.

I decided to tell Boogie to warn them about the crowd outside the door—though that might work in their favor. Maybe they would be nicer to Paw-Paw if they knew who his grandson was. They should be nice to him because he was wonderful, but whatever worked.

I found my cousin in the waiting room beside his girl-friend. They were both hunched over typing on their phones. "Boogie Baggins, I'm leaving."

My cousin got up with a yawn. His white button-up was wrinkled, and his pants were even worse; the only thing still put-together about him were his shiny black shoes, equally shiny belt, and the fancy-schmancy expensive watch he'd bought himself for his thirtieth birthday. Draped across the free chair beside the one he'd been sitting in were his jacket and tie.

Behind him, his girlfriend stayed in her seat.

"You don't want to spend the night?" he asked, giving me another hug when he was close.

I shook my head against his shoulder for maybe the millionth time in my life. "I'm filming tomorrow," I explained when we let each other go. "I'll come visit when I have another weekend off if you're not busy."

I wanted to side-eye his girlfriend but didn't. I had promised myself not to be an asshole. Mostly though, I didn't do it because it would only hurt Boog if he saw it.

My cousin-brother sighed but nodded. He'd been letting his facial hair grow in, and it looked nice. "You going to be fine driving back?"

"Oh yeah. I'm not tired yet; it'll be okay."

He kept on frowning, so I nudged his fancy red-soled shoe with the tip of my sneaker, careful not to scuff it. I'd teased him for like ten minutes the first time I'd snooped through his closet and seen all of his expensive shoes. It had been back when the *what are those* thing had been going on, and he'd been rolling.

"Go down to the lot with me though. Zac left his suitcase in my trunk."

From behind him, his girlfriend said, proving she'd been listening, "I'll wait here."

Boogie glanced over his shoulder. "You sure, babe?"

"Yeah, baby," his girlfriend of the last two-ish years replied.

I knew it was mean and didn't care, but *thank God*. The less time she was around, the better.

My cousin slung his arm over my shoulder after saying something back. I wiggled my fingers at her briefly, getting a tight smile and a nod back, and then we took off. I kicked him in the back of his leg, and he kicked me back. I poked him, and he poked me back. When we got into the elevator, he turned to me and frowned. "What's wrong?"

"I've been holding in a fart for the last hour and a half, and my stomach fucking hurts," I told him, pressing my palms down on my lower stomach. "I've been trying not to think about it."

Boogie burst out laughing, slapping a hand over his face. "What is wrong with you? Wait until you get in your car to do it."

"I'm trying," I groaned. "But it hurts."

I really was trying. I'd overdone it eating both sausages and not just one.

My cousin was still laughing and still had a hand over his face as he said, "Try harder."

"You used to fart on me and around me all the time, you hypocrite. It's a totally natural bodily function. There'd be something wrong with me if I didn't need to pass gas, Boog. It's just as natural as a burp. As a period. But it comes out of your butt instead."

My prude cousin closed his eyes, shook his head like he always did, and changed the subject. I loved him. He really was the best. He never wanted to talk about periods or bodily functions or fluid—unlike my sister who would give me an in-depth report on her period and any unusual bowel movements she might have—but I knew if I needed a tampon, he'd go and buy me ten boxes for every flow. He just wouldn't make eye contact with me afterward. *"Changing the subject.* Thank you for going to find him. He said someone had his phone and he'd forgotten all about it."

For one second, I thought about the nice, pretty blonde who had known where his bedroom was. Then I stopped thinking about it. Good for him. At least she'd been nice and not like the last girlfriend I'd had the unfortunate luck to meet. Because fuck that girl still, even ten years later.

"Yeah, there were a bunch of people over at his house when I showed up," I said. "I let myself in and had to walk around to find him. *Awkward.*"

He snorted. "Did you surprise the hell out of him?"

I shrugged against his side just as the doors opened and an older woman stepped inside the elevator too. "Yeah, he didn't recognize me. I told him my name, but it didn't click until I used yours."

That had Boogie glancing at me. It hadn't been the first time someone hadn't recognized me. We'd had a good laugh about it before, especially when our aunt had gasped and just about lost her shit years ago. It had been after I'd been in North Carolina for a couple years.

Then she'd said some other backhanded compliment and ruined it, but oh well.

"Anyway, I'm glad I got to see him." I was glad. It was one thing to see him on TV, but it was totally different in flesh and blood. Better. He had seemed happy and fine, despite his thing with the Thunderbirds, before I'd given him the bad news. What more could you ask for?

"I told you he'd be happy to see you."

He had. Years ago. But I still lifted my shoulder. "Well, you know, it's been forever." I fought the urge to clear my throat.

He knew part of what happened. A very, very small part. He'd known I had a crush on him that had sprouted out of nowhere—even though that wasn't really true—and that I'd struggled with it. I'd pleaded with him not to say anything and to just let me get over it on my own. But that was it.

It wasn't like I had ever doubted that my cousin loved me the most, but he'd proved it to me that day and every day after when he'd respected my wishes.

Boogie made a face I could have probably seen from down the hall. "You know we've both had to work on keeping a friendship after all this time, and it hasn't been easy, especially not when I was in London for a while. I'm busy. He's busy—"

"I know," I cut him off, not needing—or wanting—him to make excuses. Not wanting to hear them, honestly. What was the point? "It's all right."

I understood. I really did. I couldn't imagine how many people he'd met. How many people wanted something from him.

And I was just... his best friend's cousin. The girl known as Peewee back in the day. The kid who had "saved his life" like he'd reminded me about a thousand times over the years, even though I couldn't remember doing it. And I was his fan because I didn't know how not to be. I was a lifelong fangirl, even though he'd forgotten about me.

Because I understood.

I knew what we'd had as kids had been real. He had loved me like a little sister, and I had loved him in more ways than one. I would always have that.

And I hoped he felt the same way.

Selfishly, I knew it helped that I hadn't spent the last ten years pining away.

I didn't need to glance over to know my cousin was sliding me another look.

I scrunched up my nose back at him, and fortunately, that seemed like the right thing to do because he dropped it. At least for now. Maybe always. You never knew with Boogie. He'd let me get away with not contacting Zac for years after I'd insisted.

"You look really tired, B. You getting some sleep? Or is the g-a-s getting to you?"

The older woman in the elevator glanced at us, obviously

because she knew how to spell, and I shook my head at Boogie with a grin on my face.

"No, it's not the g-a-s. And I am getting some sleep. If four hours a night, six days a week counts."

His mouth went flat, and I knew I was in for it when he put his hands on his hips like the overprotective cousin-brother he was. "Four hours isn't enough. We talked about this already. You need sleep. Get some sunshine while you're at it too. You can't be cooped up at the gym or at your apartment all day. Get some sun on those pale arms."

I wrinkled my nose at him.

He just kept on making a face at me. "I'm serious. It's important. I know you're only working part-time at Maio House now, but I bet you're still doing your Lazy Baker stuff every minute you're not there. I thought that was why you cut your hours back."

He wasn't wrong.

"Please, B. From one workaholic to another, you need to make time for you. Go ahead and quit now that you settled things with that shithead," my cousin said. "And take a probiotic or two to help with the g-a-s."

I stopped wrinkling my nose and nodded, smiling a little... and pressing my hands down on my lower stomach again. The thing was, Connie had told me pretty much the same exact thing a couple days ago. And I'd seen my face in the mirror lately. I was tired. I couldn't remember the last time I'd left my house to do something that wasn't grocery shopping or going to work.

He had a point. They both did. These two people who loved me.

But I did genuinely love working and having a purpose so... I'd figure it out.

Boogie kicked me again in the back of the thigh like he knew exactly where my mind had gone. "I need to go down to

Houston for a couple meetings coming up. Want to get some wings?"

"With you? Nah, I'm good."

Boogie kicked me once more, and I laughed. Like I would ever say no to spending time with him. Please. "I saw one of your short videos, the one-minute long ones; it popped up on my timeline the other day. Someone shared it. It was the one of you and Connie trying to make s'mores using an electric grill. It made me crack up."

"You liked when I burned myself and yelled?" I snickered, pinching him on the back of the arm lightly. "I'm making zucchini cookies for my next 'healthy' recipe. I saw a recipe for zucchini bread, and it got me thinking."

Boogie, who was used to the food I had made a little bit of a name for myself creating, tried not to show his disbelief but failed. Big-time. And he couldn't hide the vague disgust in his voice. "Zucchini cookies, B? Really? You can't just make chocolate chip?" my cousin asked, totally letting another potentially uncomfortable conversation go.

Thank God.

I nodded slowly and then reached up to try and jab my finger up his nose for maybe the millionth time in our lives. "I'll mail you some. You'll eat them, and you'll like them."

Boogie dry heaved as he ducked away with a laugh that made me miss him so much in that moment, that I couldn't help but wonder if I should move back to Austin to be closer to him.

Or move closer to Connie again.

It wasn't like there was really anything keeping me in Houston now after all. I'd kicked that reason out of my life and hadn't regretted it for a second since. But that was the only thing I'd done right in that whole situation.

I needed to keep moving forward, because I sure wasn't planning on moving backward.

CHAPTER FOUR

I had only been waiting for a couple minutes by the wrought iron fence that surrounded my apartment complex when a familiar, sleek, silver car pulled up behind a big black truck at the gate to go in.

It was my neighbor, the hot one who I'd heard through the grapevine had broken up with his girlfriend two months ago. I knew a couple of the neighbors had made bets on who was going to be the one to keep the apartment when it'd been clear things were going downhill for them. Apparently, he'd won.

I wasn't exactly disappointed, even though I rarely got to see Santiago.

And I was suddenly a little grateful that, if I were going to be waiting by the visitor's lot for Boogie to come pick me up, at least I was looking about as decent as I usually managed to get. Nothing got me to put some effort in like hanging out with my cousin, who didn't know the meaning of "hot mess." Plus, it had been a good day off. I'd gotten not one but *two* new vlogs filmed for my WatchTube channel and Picturegram account. And when I'd talked to Deepa *again* about quitting

Maio House, she seemed into it. Between videos while we ate lunch, she had even started going through online ads for businesses hiring, and I'd watched her send a couple emails out for more details. That was more than she'd done the last few times I'd brought it up.

So, because of my good day and because I'd already put on makeup and done a little extra with my hair because of filming, I kept my "work" clothes on, which consisted of a skirt and a tucked-in loose blouse even though we were going to eat wings.

Right then, I was mostly just worried about my skirt flying up at a random gust of wind and showing everybody driving by my maroon underwear.

Specifically Santiago, who was two months single and possibly ready to mingle.

Maybe that wouldn't be such a bad idea.

I was just thinking about my underwear and Santiago when the black pickup pulled through the opening gate and his silver car stopped at the keypad instead of piggybacking like everyone did.

The window rolled down right before I heard a "Bianca!"

I thanked God in that second that I'd never gotten all flustered over hot guys. The only things that had ever made me sweat was tres leches cake and lime sherbet.

And sometimes certain male body parts could hypnotize me, but not for long.

So I was able to lift my hand up and wave at the black-haired man leaning out of his car window with his forearm resting along it. "Hi, Santiago!"

"You locked out? Need a ride in?"

A ride. The jokes I could make with that.

"No, I'm okay. I'm just waiting to get picked up. Thank you though."

"You sure?" the man I'd seen a couple times without a

shirt on when he got home after a run hollered, making me imagine his six-pack for a second.

I gave him a thumbs-up and replied, "Yeah, no, it's fine. He's on his way." I only slightly regretted not going into detail on who "he" was, but oh well. It had been a few months since I'd last gone on a date.

A memory of Boogie telling me to get out more crept through my head. I hoped he didn't remember that conversation, because he wasn't going to be happy if I had to tell him the truth. *Does going to Target count?*

The way-too-good-looking sheriff's deputy smiled a smile that would have made a lesser woman throw her panties at him. "You sure?"

I smiled back, and right as I opened my mouth, a car pulled into the driveway for the complex and quickly turned left to stop directly in the visitor's lot, right in front of where I was standing. It was a car I definitely recognized.

A four-door black sedan. Boogie's car.

The passenger side window rolled down, and something else familiar appeared, even though it wasn't what I was expecting.

Zac's freaking smiling face. Zac's freaking smiling face with its tan skin and high cheekbones and perfect nose. And he looked so happy.

"Hop in, we're starvin'," the man I'd seen weeks ago said.

What?

My old friend's smile grew a little wider, flashing me more of that immaculate row of white teeth highlighted by the dark sunglasses protecting his eyes and making his skin look even more bronze. Back when we'd been kids, he'd been pale, but year after year of practices and working out under the sun nearly year-round had given him an incredible base coat. He was tanner than I was now.

"Get in, Peewee," he said like I hadn't heard him the first time.

I couldn't see my cousin, but I heard him from the driver's seat. "Let's go, B. We're hungry."

Zac was in the *car*?

And he was coming *with us*?

It had been over a month since I'd dropped Zac off in Austin to see Paw-Paw. It had been weeks since the last time I'd even thought about him, much less talked about him. When I'd asked about the Travis family, Boogie had only brought up the older man's status, stating that he'd been discharged from the hospital, which was normal. Over the last few years, he only mentioned his best friend if I brought him up or if they'd seen each other.

And I hadn't asked about him lately. I had purposely changed the channel every time someone put The Sports Network on, and I'd been too busy lately to browse any other sports news websites for updates on his career. For all I'd known, he was still in Austin or in a different city working out with a new team. I didn't even know if he'd signed with someone.

What I *did* know was that camp—the training they went to before the season started—had already begun.

And he was here. In Houston. Again.

When my cousin had texted me during his lunch break earlier to confirm that we were on for wings, he hadn't said shit about Zac coming with us.

And now he was here.

In the car.

And they wanted to go eat.

With me.

It took me another second before I managed to nod. What was I going to do? Say no? Claim I had a migraine? And then I remembered who I'd been talking to a second before.

Glancing over, I could see my neighbor at the keypad to the gate, attention still focused in my direction. He looked curious... and I was pretty sure he might have looked at my butt when I'd bent over a little to make sure I wasn't imagining that it was Zac in the passenger seat. Hm. I lifted a hand and waved at him. "My ride's here. See you, Santiago! Thanks for checking on me!"

My neighbor nodded, and in the time it took me to reach for the handle to Boogie's car and open it, the gate into the complex was opening and the window to his car was up. Ducking into the sedan, I closed the door and smoothed my skirt down my thighs—at least as far down my thighs as it would go—and turned to the two men in the front.

Leaning over, I wrapped a forearm around Boogie's neck, pretending to choke him at the same time, and he squeezed my forearm. Then, because I was an adult and because I wasn't going to flip out that Zac was in the car, I only hesitated for about a millisecond before patting him on the shoulder, totally *not* noticing how muscular that part of his body was.

Or how he smelled like some subtle, expensive cologne.

"Hey. I wasn't expecting both of you." I shot my cousin a look, but he was facing forward, putting the car into Drive while I put my seat belt on.

He could've given me a warning, and we both knew it, but okay.

Zac turned in the seat enough to give me a good view of that blondish brown stubble along his jawline and the sliver of the smile he had aimed at me—this pretty, friendly thing that was about as second nature to him as breathing probably was. He was just being himself. And it wasn't like there was some invisible person beside me that he was happy to see, as surprising as it was that he was here in the first place. "Boog said you wouldn't mind me taggin' along," he stated.

Something that wasn't exactly guilt settled right inside my chest, and I remembered, and reminded myself just in case, that this was no big deal. We'd seen each other not long ago, and that it had been fine. We were both adults now, so going to eat was nothing either. Just two friends catching up. A two-for-one kind of deal—seeing his best friend that he didn't see enough of and being forced to see me too since we were all in the same city and I already had plans with said best friend.

Right. Moving forward. No moving back.

And that helped me. It made it not so hard to say, "I don't mind. It's nice to see you again."

That sounded forced as hell to my own ears. Probably to Boogie's too since I used the same voice every time I talked to his girlfriend.

Zac smiled even wider though, oblivious to my half lie and how iffy I sounded, and Boog glanced back at me for a second, his own tiny smile on his face.

It was fine. It was good. No big deal. I was sure it had to be a relief for my cousin after so long of existing in the middle between us.

"I was just surprised. I thought you were some random stranger about to ask if I wanted some candy." Apparently, I decided to try and joke, but there was still a little hesitation in my voice. Could I joke with him? Should I joke with him? Damn it, this was complicated. It didn't need to be.

Everything was fine.

Zac faced forward again, giving me only the smallest view of his ear and the back of his head. "No candy, but I've got some beef jerky in my bag up here," he said in return.

"I'm good," I told him, cringing. I folded my hands in my lap and stared at the side of Boogie's head, debating whether or not to kick his ass later. Technically I was fine, so he didn't deserve an ass kicking.

But he still could've warned me so I could've mentally prepared myself.

"Did you get everything done that you wanted to today?" my cousin asked, like he could read my mind.

I was still staring at his profile. "Yeah. It went fast." Glancing at Zac's head again, I changed the subject. We didn't need to bring that up in front of him. "Your meetings went okay? Did you have to deal with that guy you don't like?"

Boogie nodded, attention still forward. "No, it was my lucky day. He called in sick. I got one more tomorrow morning, and then I drive home in the afternoon."

The sound of my cell ringing had me sighing.

MAIO HOUSE

I hadn't gotten around to altering its name to **MAIO HOUSE SUCKS NOW**, but I would.

"Sorry. Hold on a sec," I muttered to Boogie, before saying, "Fuck," under my breath as I hit the answer icon.

He nodded just as my boss's voice answered with "Hello?"

I shouldn't have answered; I knew I shouldn't have. No smart person answered their phones when work called on a day off. I was hourly, not on salary. That's what I told myself at least to justify not being a "team player."

"Hello?" Well, if we were going to get into this, I didn't see a point in farting around. If Gunner called, it was only ever for a specific reason. "Do you need something?"

I was pretty sure it wasn't my imagination that he seemed to pause, and then he asked in a tone that I knew was aggravated because that was basically the only one he had, "I was calling to see if you could come in and close tonight."

Not a question, a statement.

Did I need my job? Not anymore.

Did I want it? Nope.

Did I feel obligated to keep it because my friend still

worked there and I felt super guilty leaving her there alone? Yes.

But he couldn't fire me for not coming in on my day off, riiiight? Especially not after I'd already stayed late twice last week. And he'd bitched at me yesterday for talking to a member for too long.

"Hi, Gunner. I can't make it. I'm not home and don't have my car on me, but I'll be in tomorrow." For my scheduled shift. Sucker.

I almost asked what happened with whoever was supposed to work; I was pretty sure it was one of the new girls, but... well, I wasn't walking into that shit. I didn't care that much.

"There's no way I can get you to come in?"

Wow, someone was desperate. This was after he'd gone on a rant about us not working a second over our schedule because he *wouldn't* pay us a dime over our allotted shifts. Then literally twenty-four hours after that, Asshole #2—another one of the owners—asked me to work an extra shift. They made no sense.

"Yeah, no. Sorry. I'm really not at home and won't be for a while." I made a face at my lap.

Gunner responded with a gruff huff, but whatever. You reap what you sow. Be an asshole and you get treated like one. He said, "Bye," and hung up on me.

Ahh, the sweet taste of always being right. I made a face at my phone before dropping it back into my purse and focusing again on the two friends in the front. They were talking about... Trevor? Zac's manager?

"...still pissed about havin' people over. He made it seem like I burned the house down," Zac told him with a chuckle and a shake of his head. "My ear is still ringin'."

I kept on eavesdropping, but the wing place was really close to my apartment, and it only took about five minutes total until we pulled into the lot. We all got out, and maybe it wasn't nice, but I made sure to move fast before Zac got out of the car. I went straight for giving Boogie a hug.

"Damn, B, did you do your hair for me?" my cousin asked as he pulled away.

I groaned at him as I took a step back too. "I straightened it for work." And then I wondered why I usually put some effort into how I looked when we went to do things. "Are your socks matching today?"

My cousin chuckled as he slipped his hands into the pockets of his perfectly dry-cleaned slacks. The only thing not absolutely perfect about him were the sleeves of his blue button-down that he'd rolled up to his elbows, one was slightly higher than the other one. I'd bet he'd fix them as soon as he noticed they weren't even. "They always match."

"Overachiever," I said with a snort just before a hand that wasn't mine or my cousin's landed on my shoulder.

I had to remind myself for just about the hundredth time that this was all fine. That I hadn't invited myself to be here. That I wasn't an inconvenience and that some people genuinely went out of their way to hang out with me because they liked me.

And I needed to get over myself. I really did.

"I still can't get over that you're an adult," Zac told me a second before his arm—heavy and muscular—draped over my shoulder like it was second nature, like he'd done so a thousand times years ago, and his hip came into contact with my side. I was pretty sure even his cheek came to rest on the top of my head, and I'd be lying if I said I didn't tense at his touch. At his familiarity. He'd been so happy to see me at his house a few weeks ago, but... it still didn't make sense to me. Unless it was an act, but.... "How have you been?" he asked, with this expression... with this tone....

Was he asking about the last two weeks or the last ten years?

"Good, you?" I answered, certain I could hear the tension in my voice, so I sure as hell didn't look at my cousin who knew me too well.

"Pretty good, kiddo," the tall man replied, affectionately squeezing me into his side once more. Catching me off guard as well. Confusing me too, if I was going to be totally honest with myself.

But all it took was one peek at my cousin's smiling face— something about his eyes looked a little off, but I ignored it— to remind me about my priorities. About who I was and what Mamá Lupe would want for me: to be nice and kind to someone she had loved very much even if he hadn't loved me very much—or at all—in a long time.

I waited a second, then lifted my arm to wrap around the middle of his back, fingers curling over his lowest ribs before giving him a side hug for a second.

And that was my cue to get us in to eat and back out. I'd let him and my cousin do most of the talking. That was good with me. I could catch up with Boogie another time.

"Well, I'm hungry," I said, trying my best to keep my tone light.

I didn't miss the side look Boogie shot me as I slid out from under Zac's arm like a fish, flashing him a brief smile before we headed inside the chain restaurant. The place was small, and we'd been there together a bunch of times in the past. The hostess didn't do much more than glance at my cousin in his work clothes, Zac in his dark jeans and plain white T-shirt, and me before leading us toward a booth. I slid in to one side first, Boogie following, and Zac taking a seat across from us.

I could do this.

And Zac, fortunately, decided to pick on my cousin as he

opened his menu and asked, "What's that dumb look on your face for, Boog?"

I glanced over. He did have a weird expression on his face as he took in the menu like he wasn't going to order the same thing he did every time. Was he looking weird because I was being weird? There'd been something in his eyes when we'd been outside....

My cousin didn't glance up as he shot his best friend the middle finger.

Zac snickered.

Worried it was me causing him to make that strange expression, I nudged Boogie. "I like that dumb look on your face."

And one of my favorite people in the world nudged me back in a way I was pretty sure said I wasn't causing anything before lifting his other hand and shooting yet another middle finger at the man across from us.

And that made Zac laugh, the sound rich and familiar still. Like old times. But not like old times.

Focusing down at my menu, I reminded myself again that this was all fine, that I wasn't going to stare at Zac's face or, much less, bring up anything from the past. I wasn't going to ruin dinner with my cousin. I was going to go about the rest of my day and my week and—

"I was going to wait until after we finished eating, but the dumb look on my face is because I was planning on asking you two to be in my wedding, and I wasn't sure how to ask."

Yeah, both of our elbows dropped off the edge of the table—mine and Zac's—and for whatever freaking reason, we looked right at each other. Light blue to my very dark blue. Just like in the past when we'd be on the verge of ragging on Boogie over something.

And that was when he raised his head.

Busted.

His facial expression wasn't a hurt one or even a sad one. He still had too much of a babyface to really be good at mean-mugging, but it was more... resigned. He knew us both well enough to have an idea of what we were thinking. Which was: *you want to marry* her? *Of all the people in the world... of all the women he'd dated over the years...* her?

But he didn't say anything. He didn't explain or apologize. He'd made a decision, and everybody else had to live with it.

My cousin—the man who was basically my brother, who had been there for me more often than my own dad—was going to get married.

To someone who didn't deserve him.

Shit.

"Congratulations?" I said, trying not to let it sound like a question and failing because... well, because I still couldn't believe he was going to get married, period, much less to someone I didn't like. If I'd ever fantasized about it, I'd figured he'd marry someone I liked as much as I did my sister's husband.

"Congrats," Zac said, sounding only slightly more convincing than me.

At least it wasn't just Connie and me who hated Boogie's girlfriend. Future wife. Whatever she was now. It made me feel a little more justified in my dislike to see Zac didn't seem all that stoked about it either.

"Thank you," Boogie replied.

I scratched my nose, and Zac just sat there. Neither one of us had the balls to make a face, probably because we were both being watched.

Boogie's tongue poked at the inside of his cheek, and he continued making constant and complete eye contact with one of us the whole time as he kept on talking. "I'm doing this, and you're both going to be in the wedding, bitchfacing or not," Boogie let us know before bringing the menu back up to his face and hiding most of it. From the other side, he said, "We're planning on doing it in February, on our anniversary. Mark it in your calendars." He rattled off a specific date at the beginning of the month.

They'd already planned this far ahead? What the hell? And in *February?*

And I should've been surprised, but wasn't, when Zac echoed, "February?"

"Yes, February. I haven't told my mom yet, or anybody," he ended, still focused on the menu.

And *that* got my thoughts to stop in their place.

As much as I disliked his girlfriend, well... Boogie *was* my favorite. Favorite cousin. Favorite male. Favorite Pictionary partner. He was my brother from another mother. And there was no way in hell he was going to be getting married without me close by.

Even if I thought he was about a million times too good for the woman he was marrying.

But most importantly, Boogie had been there for me from the moment my parents had moved into my abuela's house and every second since.

Even if this was a mistake, it was his mistake to make. He'd let me make a handful of my own. It was just another reason why I couldn't say anything to him about getting married.

Been there, done that, fucked it up, and regretted it.

Plus, more than anything, my cousin was a good man. One of the best. And I knew his heart. If he said he'd forgiven what's-her-face, he really had. Down to his bones.

So, it was either isolating my cousin or rolling with it. If things didn't work out... well, I was going to be there for that too. Through thick and thin. Like he'd always been with me. The little cousin he'd always treated better than a sister.

Just as I opened my mouth to tell Boogie I was in, Zac leaned forward across the table.

"Look, if you wanna marry Lauren, then I'll be right there next to you." The long man stretched his spine as he lifted an elbow and settled it on the back of the booth, spreading out across it. My God, when the hell had he grown those muscles on his chest? I didn't remember seeing them so clearly before, even in the pictures he posted on Picturegram of himself at some beach around the world. I forced myself to focus on his Disney prince face though as he kept going. "You already know why I feel the way I feel, but you know I want the best for you." Those blue eyes then slid toward me, and the tiny lines at the corners of them crinkled as he took in my face, slow and lingering on me in a way that made me wonder why he was taking so long looking at me. "*We* want the best for you because you are the best. Same as you'd want for us, right, Peewee?"

I felt my nostrils flare as I glanced back and forth between the two longtime best friends. Two nearly complete opposites in every physical way. Tall and not as tall. The athlete and the... whatever it was he did. He'd explained it to me a dozen times, and I still didn't get it. Managing wealth, whatever the hell that meant.

Two people who loved and valued each other very much.

Who wanted the best for themselves and always had.

In a way, it was like me and Connie. We made no sense on paper but made total sense in person.

Because people who loved you really did want the best for you, and that was why I had supported Zac throughout the years even though he'd hurt me and had no idea I'd been rooting for him all along. So.

"Right," I agreed, nudging my cousin again. "We love your dumb face, Boog. As long as you're happy, that's what matters." God, that had been hard to get out. I *really* didn't like Lauren, but I wasn't the one marrying her, and fortunately, she had never made it seem like she hated how close Boogie and I were, so I'd give her that.

Boogie, though, exhaled in relief. He was all dark, short hair and a forever baby face with his grown-up clothes of a button-up shirt only missing the tie he wore for work. And my cousin said, in a voice that I could hear was tight, "Yeah, that's what I want. You know it."

Of course it was. Nobody wanted to get married and have loved ones upset over it. He deserved to have us cheering, but considering the circumstances... this was better than nothing? I was sorry that I wasn't sorry I still wanted better for him.

Zac and Boogie both nodded at each other, and I just sat there and watched.

When my cousin's dark eyes moved toward me, I gave him a smile I knew was faker than I would have wanted, but I hoped it was genuine enough. If Zac could do it, so could I. Even if he couldn't, I would, because I could do anything for Boogie. And being in his wedding was the least of it. I'd survived three months working for Gunner. I'd made it five years in a relationship with someone I didn't actually know. I'd read mean comments about myself. I had goals and a few dreams. I could handle anything.

Including but not limited to this. So I poked him. "I'm too old to be the flower girl, by the way," I told him. "So I'm a little disappointed you've made me wait this long."

That got my cousin shaking his head, a big grin settling over his face. "I'm sorry, B."

I smiled back at him, settling back against the booth and peeking at Zac who was still sprawled on his side of the booth with a lazy grin on his face... looking at me.

Still looking at me.

I glanced at him and kept a small smile; he gave me a big one right back that might have made me feel just a little bad for not being nicer and trying to ask him a thousand questions to make it seem like I wanted to catch up with him.

The reason I didn't was because I figured I already knew most of his business. There wasn't much for me to wonder over, except what he was doing, but that had to be a sore subject.

"Is Zac going to be your best man? Am I going to be your assistant best woman?"

My old friend snickered, but it was Boogie who said, "Assistant best woman?"

"Yeah. Maybe you two already had a plan worked out. I don't know if you spit into each other's hands and shook on it to make a deal. Maybe it's just a girl thing."

That had my cousin sliding me a horrified face. "What? You and Connie spit in each other's hands and shook on it? To be a maid of honor?"

"Hell yeah, we did. I thought you knew. That's why I was her maid of honor when I was thirteen. We made a deal."

"I don't know what's wrong with you two."

I snorted before deciding on what I was going to get. It was what I always got—wings with honey barbecue sauce. *Yum*. The stain-removing spray was ready by my washing machine. And I'd worn a shirt that wasn't that big of a deal if it did end up with sauce all over it. Because it might. I dropped my menu and smiled at my cousin. "The same thing that's wrong with you. Ahhhh, bitch."

Boogie groaned.

I poked his shoulder, keeping my gaze on him instead of the man across from us. "So, tell me, I mean us, more about this wedding."

"Did you say you're doing it in February?" Zac asked again.

My cousin tensed up and made another dumb face that had me squinting at him. "Yeah. We thought about doing it earlier, but we want to do it on our anniversary to keep the date the same and...."

And I saw it, because I was looking at Boogie, I saw his eye do this weird little twitch thing then, and *I knew it. I KNEW IT.*

So I whispered, because I couldn't fucking believe what I'd just seen and what that twitch implied, "Boogie, *is she pregnant?*"

His eye did the twitch thing again.

Even Zac dropped his menu. He was so dramatic. And maybe I would've smiled under any other circumstance.

My cousin cursed under his breath. "It's a secret. You can't tell anyone."

I set my hand on top of the table and felt my eyes widen. *HOLY SHIT.* "I can't promise that. You know I can't keep secrets from Connie."

Boogie rolled his eyes as he groaned. "Fine, you can tell Connie." Then she would tell her husband, but I wasn't going to bring that up.

"Oh, thank God," I muttered, relieved and something else I wasn't totally sure how to process yet.

Then he said the words I'd known to expect from that little eye twitch. "I thought she'd want to get married soon, but it was her idea to do it on our anniversary. Lauren's expecting around late March."

Zac and I both looked at each other again, eyes wide, like we'd practiced it or something, and I wasn't sure how I felt about it. So I wasn't going to feel anything.

"You're already doing that again?" my cousin asked, and that reminded me of when we'd been so much younger and had always done that—just looked at each other at the same time. It had always made me feel special, or at least it had reminded me that what we'd had had been real, that we'd been friends.

I wouldn't forget that had been a long time ago.

"I haven't told my mom," Boogie admitted, and that had Zac and me focusing back on him with a blink. He frowned. "Not yet. Later."

I was watching him with wide eyes as I raised my hands and curled my index and middle fingers into quotation marks. "Later."

As much as I loved my aunt and appreciated everything she had ever done for me—including letting me live with her while I'd finished high school and then a little while after that—I couldn't say I didn't understand why he hadn't told her yet. I'd never met anyone more Catholic than my aunt. She was either going to faint at hearing that her precious baby was having a baby himself, or she was going to beat him with a chancla at the fact he had gotten someone pregnant *out of wedlock*. Sound the alarms.

"Your mom knows how to add, Boog, you know that, don't ya?" the light-blue-eyed man asked, his mouth twisted up on one side in amusement.

Boogie made a face just as a waitress arrived at the head of the table. She smiled at me because I smiled at her. "Hi, my name is Clary, and I'll be your server today. Would you like to get started with any drinks? We have—holy motherfucker."

Yeah, her gaze had moved over to Boogie as she spoke and had ended on Zac, so had her speech.

The woman gaped at the man on the other side of the booth. The man who was smiling up at her, all innocence and friendliness.

"How's it goin'?" he asked cheerfully.

"Can I...?" She cleared her throat and brought a big smile onto her face as her eyes brightened and she seemed to shake for a second in excitement or nerves or whatever it was. "Hi, I'm so sorry. Could I...? Would you mind...? Can I have a picture, Zac? I'm such a fan. I have been since your days in Austin."

He nodded, lifting a hand to brush his dark blond hair to the side. "Sure can, but can we wait until I'm done with dinner?" He winked, and I watched the unsuspecting woman instantly swoon.

"Yes, yeah. Thank you so much," she rushed out before turning around and taking two steps away before coming to a stop. Then she turned around and walked back, shaking her head. "I don't know what I was doing," she admitted in a rush, and I smiled at her again. "What can I get you to drink? I'm sorry."

I went first when neither one of them made a move to speak. "A frozen house margarita, please."

My cousin rattled off some craft beer, and Zac said, "Water for me, please and thank you."

But the reality of what Boogie said really sank in then. Not the marriage to a woman I felt didn't deserve him. Not the fact that he'd asked me not to tattle to his mom who was going to lose her shit either way, but the part before that. The part about why he was getting married—maybe in the first place.

His girlfriend—fiancée, whatever—was pregnant.

With my Boogie's child.

My Boogie was having a mini Boogie. A girl Boogie. A boy Boogie. Who knew? Who cared? The point was, it was a mini Boogie.

And just like I'd felt when Connie had been pregnant with my niece and nephew, joy, this pure, pure joy, filled my entire soul. And I could barely make the words sound louder than a whisper as I said, "You're having a *baby*."

And it said everything about Boogie that he hadn't gotten initially hung up on the fact that we hadn't cried out in happiness the instant he'd implied that his lady was pregnant. That now that we—or I—had really realized what he'd said, it felt like the greatest gift I'd been given in a while. Someone with half his genetic makeup was going to be born!

"Boogie!" I whisper-hissed at him before clapping my hands right in front of my boobs. "Holy *shit*!"

My wonderful, amazing cousin instantly beamed. Happy. Nervous, I could always tell he was nervous. But mostly, he was happy. Very happy.

"I know," he agreed.

I reached for his forearm and shook it.

Oh my God, I mouthed.

Oh my God, my cousin mouthed back.

"Is it a boy? Is it a girl? Do you know?"

He shook his head. "Not yet. Soon."

I put my palms against my cheeks and opened my mouth again in a silent scream, and he grinned back.

"Ya know, it took me a sec, but I just realized what you said. I didn't think about it," Zac muttered, sounding like he was in a daze at that point too. "I'm gonna be an uncle again?"

Again? He didn't have any siblings, not that I knew of.

His dad had never been in the picture, period. It was why he had Travis as a last name. No one ever talked about him.

"Yup," my cousin replied, still smiling wide.

Zac slid out of the booth like freaking water and bent at the hips before suddenly swooping down and hugging Boogie, who moved to the side after a split second and hugged him right back.

They were so cute, it killed me.

All hugging and loving and making these happy guy noises as they gave each other affection.

The waitress arrived just as Zac slid back into the booth, giving me another big, beaming smile that I returned for about a second before looking back at my cousin instead.

"Would you like to start with an appetizer? Or do you know what you want?"

I rattled off my order, and so did the other two as she set our drinks down, all the while sneaking glances at Zac literally every other second. I had to give her props though. She hadn't told any of her coworkers, even though she knew damn well who he was. So they wouldn't stiff her out of serving him? So she could be the only one to get a picture? Maybe just to be nice and give him his privacy?

I nudged my cousin as the waitress said something to Zac. "Psst."

He glanced at me.

"I'm just throwing this out there, but Connie said doing Kegels before giving birth was the best thing she could've done, so maybe that's something Lauren should look into," I whispered.

Boogie frowned. "Do what?"

"Kegels," I repeated. How the hell did he not know what Kegel exercises were?

"What's that?"

I blinked at him.

"Am I supposed to know what that is?"

I nodded.

Boogie turned to his best friend just as he put his glass of water to his lips. The waitress had walked away. "Do you know what that is?"

"What is?" Zac asked before taking a sip.

"Bianca said Lauren should start doing Kegels—"

Water sloshed over the rim of the glass a split second before a big laugh shot out of Zac and made its way through the tiny dining area.

I smiled a little; then I smiled even more at Boogie's confused face.

But Zac's eyes were on me as he asked, "You said that to him?"

I nodded, feeling my smile drop a little. I hadn't meant for Zac to hear, but....

"Should I do a search to figure out what that is?"

Zac and I both said, "Yes," at the same time, and we smiled at each other right before I looked away again.

———

We spent the rest of dinner talking about Boogie's wedding and *his baby*.

After he'd moaned and groaned following his search to find out what "Kegels" were—pelvic-floor exercises. Even me explaining quietly that men did them too didn't make him groan any less. It probably didn't help either that Zac cracked up the whole time Boogie and I bickered over it. "Everyone should do them" wasn't legit enough for him.

Anyway.

If I thought I was surprised about the baby and the wedding, Zac seemed to be even more surprised over it. His smile never faltered, I noticed, even when I cut my own smiles short when they met his.

Thankfully, it wasn't until we were back in my cousin's car that the conversation moved to something other than a baby and a wedding. What never got brought up, I'd realize hours later, was what was going on with Zac and his career.

"B, have you thought up anymore recipes?" Boogie asked randomly, about three seconds after we all buckled in.

"Yeah, a couple," I told him vaguely, staring at the back of Zac's head. He'd been looking at me a lot while we'd been eating—these long peruses of my face—and a couple times, I let myself wonder what he thought. Then I tried to be an adult and reminded myself that it didn't matter. "Did I tell you that Connie's driving down next month, and she's bringing Guillermo with her?"

Guillermo was my favorite nephew—my only one—and one of my viewers' favorite guests. They were visiting so he could film a couple videos for my channel with me. More than a couple if we could fit it in, but I wasn't holding my breath. Things always went wrong when they came over. It was part of his appeal, besides being adorable and great.

"They're coming down for the weekend?"

"Yup."

"I haven't seen him in forever. Tell me when, and I'll see if I can make it work with Lauren."

It took a lot of effort not to sneer at her name. But I was going to try my best. Because: Baby Boogie. I wondered what he or she was going to look and act like. I hoped they liked me.

"Are you a chef or something, Peewee?" Zac asked, turning slightly in his seat so he could kind of see me behind him.

"No, I'm not," I answered him before glancing out the window. I wasn't sure how much he knew but was pretty certain he didn't know anything about my life. And to an extent, I'd rather keep it that way. It wasn't like we had time, anyway, to go into what I'd done with my life in the five minutes we had to get to my apartment. So I changed the subject. "Hey, Boog, are you going to Lola's quince?"

My cousin groaned. "I don't want to, but I'm sure I'll end up there. You want to stay at my place?"

"It's all right. Connie and I are probably going to split a hotel room," I answered him, still looking out the window.

Guilt was a bitch though.

And I felt bad for barely answering Zac's question. And for barely speaking to him. The problem was that I didn't know what to ask him or even how to treat him even though he had done nothing but smile at me. *How are things going?*

Maybe terrible. *Do you know what you're doing?* Great job reminding him he'd basically been released from a team he'd been with for five seasons. *How's your grandpa?* Let's remind him Paw-Paw had been in the hospital and he'd been worried sick.

None of it seemed like a good topic.

And we really, *really* didn't have time.

Before I could think something up, my cousin turned his car into my apartment complex and put in the code to go inside. The only reason I'd offered to meet him outside was because I'd been hungry and had just wanted to go instead of waiting for him to get through the gate. In no time at all, he was in front of my building.

Unbuckling my seat belt, I scooted toward the middle of the back seat and gave my cousin another choke-hug. "Bye, Boog. Thank you for dinner. Have a good meeting tomorrow. I'll text you about Connie and Guillermo coming."

He patted my elbow. "Text me when you get in."

"Make sure to tell Lauren about the Kegel exercises. Oh hell no, don't make that face at me."

He made some noises that didn't make me all that confident he would, but whatever.

I held my breath and turned to the right to see Zac angled in his seat just enough so he could look at me with those light blue eyes and that perfect face. His grin was wide. I gave him a little smile as the guilt ate me up. Reaching toward him, I set my hand on his forearm. "Bye, Zac. It was nice seeing you again so soon. Take care of yourself, okay?"

The hand not resting on his thigh cupped mine between his forearm, and his gaze locked on me, his forehead slightly furrowed like he was confused or thinking about something. But the corners of his mouth still tilted up a bit in that forever Zac smile. "I'm really glad I got to see you, kiddo," he said, seriously and slowly.

For a second, I thought he was going to say more.

And in that next second, I decided I didn't really need to hear him say anything else.

I pulled my arm back, patted him and then Boogie once more, and threw the door open. "Bye! Drive safe!" I slammed it shut before they both finished telling me to be safe too.

And like the coward I apparently was, I ran up the steps to my apartment and kicked myself in the ass for being so mean.

But it really had been for the best.

CHAPTER FIVE

"...don't pay you to talk to each other."

I stared at Deepa, my coworker, employee, and friend and saw that it wasn't just my nostrils that were flaring. Hers were too. We'd been staring dead-ass into each other's eyes for the last two minutes.

Two minutes I would never get back.

Two minutes that consisted of us looking at each other so that we wouldn't have to look at our boss while he chewed us out. *Again.* You'd figure I would have gotten used to it after two months, but nope. Neither had Deepa by how easily her expression had gone blank the second he'd started talking.

The man chewing us out was leaning against the counter, continuing to freaking ramble on and on and *on*, all because he'd happened to come out while we'd been talking about this member—one of the MMA guys—with the biggest, roundest booty either one of us had ever seen. Every time he came in, we talked about how majestic the thing was... and whether it was real or not.

So yeah, of course we discussed it. Everybody noticed that

thing. I'd even go as far as to say it was mesmerizing. Implants or not, it was something special.

And of course, that was when Gunner walked by and caught us.

Because we'd been too distracted talking—and staring—to notice the side door opening. We'd gotten really good at keeping an eye out for him and immediately making it seem like we were busy so that we wouldn't get caught. Like we had. Like fucking rookies.

"We've talked about this before," Gunner kept going, oblivious to the fact we were both tuning him out as much as humanly possible.

We'd gotten really good at this in-one-ear-and-out-the-other thing.

Deepa and I had hit it off from the moment we'd met right after I got hired. She was my work best friend, and she helped me out a few hours a week at my apartment when I filmed. We'd met when she was eighteen, and she had reminded me a lot of myself at her age—young, alone in a different place than where she'd grown up, and just trying to get by. But she was an only child of a single parent who lived too far away to visit regularly. I felt protective of her, and I wanted the best for her.

She was the only person at Maio House who knew about my "side business." But as friendly as we'd been before—because she really was the only reason now why I hadn't walked out of the gym like so many of our coworkers had—nothing had brought us together more over the last couple of months quite like our mutual hatred for the same person: Gunner.

"You get paid to work, not to stand around chatting," our new boss complained. "If you need more things to do, let me know. And if you don't want to work, then that's fine with me too. The McDonald's down the street is hiring. They posted a sign."

I hated him.

And I wished I knew Morse code so I could tell Deepa that with my eyelids.

"Have I made myself clear?"

Had he made himself clear that we were paid to work the front desk—and in Deepa's case the juice bar—and couldn't exactly walk away from the counter to go do other things?

I didn't trust myself, so I just nodded, and so did my friend.

"It's business, ladies. Don't take it personally. One day, if you're lucky, maybe one of you will be a business owner and understand where I'm coming from," the asshole went on.

If this dickwad only knew.

He could suck on his condescending advice.

I *was* my own business. And the only reason I was still around was because of the dumb decisions I'd made in the past—financial and personal.

A few days ago, after I'd gotten home from eating dinner with Zac and Boogie, I'd laid in bed and thought about my future more than I had in a while. I thought about what I wanted. Mostly though, I thought about what I dreamed of—after I'd beat myself up for being so cold to Zac and not answering his questions or asking my own.

For not telling him what I'd been doing with my life the last few years.

I hadn't exactly started filming videos of myself cooking on purpose. It had just kind of... happened.

As far as I could remember, I had always loved making things in the kitchen. It was something I'd inherited from all the time I'd spent with Mamá Lupe. It had been our bonding time. Our happy time. Even our sad time. Some of my absolute favorite memories had been in her house, making empanadas and cakes and mole and guisado. She'd even bought an Irish cookbook so I could make some things that my dad's family would have liked... if he'd still had any of them. And when we hadn't been cooking, we loved watching talk shows with cooking segments. We'd binge Emeril. She had made it fun and TV show-like when we made things together, and it had sucked me in and turned into a place of comfort and love.

When there were a ton of other things in my life I couldn't control, I had always been able to pick and choose what I made; that was something I didn't have to rely on other people for.

And later on, being in the kitchen made me feel closer to the woman I had adored who I missed so much. She had left me with a legacy. With a way to still feel her.

So yeah, I loved making things I could eat. I always had. I *loved* eating.

One night, about seven years ago, after I'd had a bad day at the restaurant I'd been waitressing at and only had a couple things in the fridge to make for dinner and no money to go buy more groceries until payday, that's when it happened. That was when that first seed of an idea had been planted in my head. Looking back on it, I'd only been brave enough because Connie and her family hadn't been home to watch me. They had been on vacation visiting Richard's family.

Before I could talk myself out of it, I'd done it. I'd uploaded a video to WatchTube just for the hell of it. For fun. Pepperoni pasta, I'd called it, because all I'd had was pasta, pepperoni slices, and leftover parmesan cheese in packets. It took a month to get five views. A month later, I uploaded another one on Mamá Lupe's birthday, just for her. That time, it had been her favorite tres leches cake, a recipe I'd known off the top of my head for years. I got twenty views and twenty thumbs up from my family members after sending

Connie and Boogie the link. My boyfriend at the time—that idiot—had suggested I keep doing them.

No one told me I sucked or that I was awkward or an inconvenience, so I kept going, because I got a thrill from seeing nice comments, even though they had been from relatives and my ex. They had made me feel good. The people pleaser in me liked making people happy and enjoyed making them laugh even more. I'd struggled with my self-esteem for so long that it was nice, *for me*, to feel... nice.

And slowly but surely, those views went up and up and up over the years.

I wasn't an Emeril or a Rachel, but I was a Bianca. A Lazy Baker. *The* Lazy Baker.

I had gone from posting a video whenever I felt like it, to a video a week, and after time, to two a week. I had done it for fun until I'd finally started to see it as a business, which was a stupid decision I realized years later because I could've been making some serious money. It was a potential future. My future. A bright one that I enjoyed doing despite the drawbacks.

Then my dickwad of an ex had tried to take it away from me.

But it was still mine.

Maybe I wasn't in the ideal situation I wanted to be *yet*—thanks to all his bullshit—but I was trudging ahead, slowly but surely. With plan B, plan C, and plan D. And none of that meant I got to take time off with my finger up my butt. Plan B, plan C, and plan D were waiting for me.

And I was finally going on vacation to Disney World because *I* was taking myself there.

Plan B: have a better website. (I hadn't decided some minor details on the layout yet.)

Plan C: release a cookbook. (I had more than half the recipes I planned on sharing done.)

Plan D: branch out into more than just posting videos online. (But this was the scariest plan and the one I wasn't so sure I was brave enough to go after.)

There were more plans, but for now, those were the most important.

I was going to do this, for me.

Yet... none of that mattered in that moment while I was busy.

Busy listening to this butthole of a human being.

Gunner knocked on the counter eventually when neither one of us said a word to him, and I hoped he knew we were both calling him an asshole in our heads. It wasn't like we didn't do what we were paid for. We did. It had literally been two minutes of checking out a big butt while we hadn't been busy. I'd bet he checked it out too every time that guy walked by.

On top of that, I knew for a fact Gunner hung out in his office and played Tetris. I'd gone in there twice early on while he'd been in the bathroom and spotted his computer screen. Hypocrite.

"Get back to work," he had the nerve to call out over his shoulder as he walked away like he hadn't just spent five solid minutes trying to kick us in the ass with his words.

"God, I fucking hate him," Deepa muttered when he disappeared through the rows of machines.

I kept watching to make sure he didn't come back into view. "I hope he steps on a Lego."

She snorted, and I grinned at the girl a few years younger than me. "I started working on my resume like you said. I'm going to email a couple more of those businesses we found. Fingers crossed."

"Good. Before we quit, we can sprinkle a bunch of Legos all over his office and pray for the best," I told her quietly.

We both snickered, and she went back to work a second

later when a gym member came up to the counter and requested a drink.

Irritated, I slipped my hand under my keyboard and pulled my cell out. There was a message. But it wasn't Connie's name that appeared on my screen.

There was a text from a number I didn't recognize. From half an hour ago, apparently. I made sure Gunner wasn't around and then unlocked the screen and read it.

512-555-0199: Hey

O-kay.

I didn't reply. But when my phone vibrated five minutes later when I still wasn't busy, I took another peek. There was another message from the same number.

512-555-0199: You ignoring me?

Ignoring? I texted the number back.

Me: New phone, who dis?

Thirty seconds later a reply came in.

512-555-0199: Snack pack

Snack Pack?

Zac?

It had been three days since Boogie had picked me up and we'd gone out to eat. Three days since I'd been living with the regret of not being very nice to my old friend when he'd tried to ask about my life. And two whole days since I'd scrolled through his Picturegram account while sitting on the toilet.

It wasn't like I didn't follow Zac online and hadn't been following him for years. I saw all of his posts. But I'd still scrolled and lingered over some of his pictures, especially the ones where he carefully cropped out whatever woman was sitting beside him. It was always obvious. It wasn't any of my business, and 99 percent of the time, it didn't twist up my stomach like it had back when I'd been a kid who had been in love with the last person in the world she could ever have a shot with for a million different reasons.

Then I'd exited out of the app, reminding myself that I was glad I'd gotten to see him and that I was so happy for how successful he was. Despite the setbacks but everyone went through those.

He deserved all of it. He had motivated me to follow my own heart, even if my dream was about one-hundredth the size of his. But if every person weighed their dream against someone else's, nobody would ever dream at all.

Anyway, other than a text from Boogie about him possibly coming to visit when my sister was here, I hadn't thought much about it—okay, Zac—since.

So the last thing I freaking expected was for him to text me.

And *that* was exactly when another message came through.

512-555-0199: Zac, peewee

Did he think I'd forgotten who Snack Pack was? The thing was, I hadn't had his number in my phone in probably five years, if not longer. I'd dropped my cell in the toilet and had to start all over again with my contacts. I sure as hell hadn't been about to ask my cousin for his number. There hadn't been a need for it.

I made sure no one was paying attention to me and texted him back. I might not get a response but... it wouldn't be the first time, and at least I'd know I had tried. It was my choice, and I knew the worst that would happen: I wouldn't hear from him again.

Been there, done that, and I had the bumper sticker.

Plus, I still felt like an asshole, and I hated knowing I'd acted that way. I'd thought I was better than that. And I just wanted to know that I *had* always tried. Unlike him.

Me: Hi Zac

There we go. That wasn't needy or inconvenient or too familiar.

My phone vibrated a minute later, and if my heart skipped a tiny beat, well, it was dumb, and I didn't need to be paying attention to it anyway.

512-555-0199: Hi darlin

512-555-0199: You free after work?

I didn't know what it said about me that I noticed he used "darlin'" enough so that it was saved on his phone instead of "darling."

Most importantly though, how did he know I was at work? And now that I thought about it, *had he had my number or had he asked Boogie for it?*

You know what? I didn't need either of those questions answered.

Because regardless, it had taken ten years for him to remember I existed.

But at least this time, I was prepared for what could happen next. It wouldn't be a shock to my system again. I knew where I stood, and that would be the difference between now and before.

Mostly though, I didn't want to be a jerk.

Me: Yes. [smiley face emoji] Need something?

That was good, right? I thought so. Hoped so. Maybe a *little* cold and blah, but oh well.

He replied five minutes later, but it took me twenty more minutes after that to read it because someone came in and signed up for a month-to-month membership.

512-555-0199: I just wanna see you if you have time for me.

Okay. So he wanted to catch up? All right. I hadn't been very nice to him, but he was still trying, which was so like him—or at least how he used to be. And that made me feel a little worse.

But....

He was asking for it, not me. The fact was: I didn't cry

myself to sleep at night because he'd stopped caring about me. And if he wanted to come back into my life, even if it was just for a couple of hours?

That was all right too.

Expectations.

And he loved my cousin. And maybe I'd see him again during Boogie's wedding. Might as well get used to the idea.

I peeked again to make sure the coast was clear and replied.

Me: I get off at 4. Let me know when you're free. [smiley face emoji] No pressure.

No pressure. A smiley face. Passive aggressive much?

It took three minutes to get a response.

512-555-0199: Come over when you get off work.

What?

Me: Today?

512-555-0199: Yeah

Yeah.

For one brief second, I thought about all the things I needed to do at home. Laundry for sure. Meal prep for a couple of days. Respond to some emails. And brainstorm some more ideas for upcoming recipes. Watch another episode or two of the Turkish show I was hooked on....

But an image of Mamá Lupe settled into my brain right then—specifically an image of Zac standing beside her on his twenty-first birthday with his arm over her shoulders, slouched over so much that his cheek rested on her head. She had loved the hell out of him.

And I knew what she would want me to do.

I also knew what would keep me up at night and what wouldn't.

Shit balls.

———

Four hours later, I was pulling up to a house that looked even bigger without three hundred cars parked in the driveway and in front of the street. There *were* cars in the driveway but only two, a newish Mercedes and a red Jeep.

Parking on the street after pulling a U-turn, I headed up the pathway and shot off a text to Zac letting him know I was there. I wasn't nervous. My stomach didn't hurt in any way either. I'd had hours to come to terms with the fact that I was going to hang out with him—as in physically drive to his house and spend some time with him one-on-one. Because he'd asked me to.

And I was planning on apologizing for how I'd acted.

Okay, maybe I was a little nervous, but just a little.

And really, my nerves came from me not wanting to talk about certain things. But that was it.

At the door, I rang the doorbell and waited, glancing down to see if he'd replied; he hadn't. But not even thirty seconds later, someone approached the glass and iron door. Someone that couldn't be Zac from how much shorter and beefier he seemed to be built.

I remembered during his days in Dallas, he had lived with some big-name player for a couple years. Toward the end of that living situation was when he'd been released from that team, the Three Hundreds. Boogie had told me he'd struggled during that time a lot; that had been when he had been working in London long-term. It had been before Zac had been picked up to play in Oklahoma.

The door swung open, and the guy who had called Zac's phone, the one with the bleached, platinum blond dread-locks, stood there, dark eyebrows already up and aimed at me.

I lifted my hand and offered him a smile, a real one. "Hi again." I held my hand out. "I'm Bianca."

The muscular guy looked down at my hand. He looked at

it for so long I was more than halfway expecting him to just keep on looking at it, but he finally took it, giving it the slowest shake as he said, in the deepest voice I'd probably ever heard other than on those insurance commercials, "CJ."

CJ, *right*. "Is Zac here?"

"He's upstairs."

My phone pinged at that exact moment, and I looked down to see it was a message.

512-555-0199: Gimme 5. Sorry.

I showed him the screen—regretting for a second that I hadn't saved his phone number and more than likely wasn't going to—when I glanced back up at him and found him still looking at me funny. "He said he'll be done in five minutes. Can I wait for him inside? Mosquitoes really like me."

CJ nodded, his expression still careful and almost wary, but he stepped aside.

I went in, taking in how clean the place was, and waited for who I was pretty sure was a football player too to head back into the main part of the house before I followed after him, taking everything in now that I wasn't looking through a mass of people for Zac to give him bad news.

Sure enough, the house was just as bare as I remembered.

There was only the most basic of furniture. Nothing on the walls. It was all so... vanilla. And so unlike Zac and his hoarder ways from what I could remember. His car had been a mess. Then again, this was probably just a rental he was sharing during the off-season, so why would it have personal touches in it?

Maybe one day I'd ask Boogie about the situation.

I was going to do this right. I was a—mostly—grown woman, and I could handle this... friendship. I knew what I was getting myself into. He had asked me questions. He had been happy to see me. I was ready and willing to be the kind of friend to him that I was to everyone else, for however long he was around.

Well, to an extent.

The past had happened, and it was where it belonged: back in the day. You live and you learn, and all that jazz. Once I was done here, I was going to go home and live my best life.

Like I had been.

One fortifying breath later, I clutched the bag in my hand when we got to the very white kitchen. I didn't hesitate before asking the man I'd briefly met weeks ago, "CJ, would you like a scone?"

The man paused in the process of settling onto a stool that had already been pulled out around the kitchen island, and I didn't miss the way his eyes flicked down to the canvas bag in my hand.

I held it up a little higher. "I promise they aren't drugged, and they have blueberries in them. Coconut oil too. They're mini-sized." This wasn't my first rodeo with skepticism. My nephew had acted like I'd been trying to feed him arsenic the one time I offered him scones with rosemary in them... and he'd ended up eating four once he gave them a chance and stopped gagging before he'd put anything into his mouth. He never doubted me again after that.

Yep, CJ's gaze still narrowed anyway.

So I kept going. "I give them out to my coworkers, but I forgot, and by the time I remembered...." My favorite coworkers were already gone, and I hadn't felt like sharing anymore, mostly because I didn't want Gunner to have any, so everyone was going to miss out. But I stopped talking because this CJ guy didn't need to hear all that.

He narrowed his eyes even more, and I made mine go even wider to keep from smiling. Jesus, he was making me work for it. All right.

Well, luckily, I was a chicken, but I wasn't a quitter. The

scones *were* good. They only had six ingredients and took about ten minutes to make, which were two of my most important requirements for recipes I attempted. And it was one I'd nailed years ago and had just tweaked a little more so they were even better than the original version. The blueberry scones were going in the book I wanted to publish one day in the near future, AKA plan C. "They're mini scones. Almost cookies. Scookies, I guess. I'll eat one if you—"

The way the man's very handsome head reared back, with his eyes going wide, was what shut me up.

Then his next words kept me silent.

He snapped his fingers. "I know why you look familiar," CJ said, his gaze sharpened.

Uh... "We met a few weeks ago for like a second," I reminded him. It wouldn't be the first time someone forgot meeting me, but....

He instantly shook his head, and he said in that deep freaking voice that seemed at odds with the fact he wasn't even six feet tall, "You're The Lazy Baker, aren't you?"

The Lazy Baker.

I don't know who the hell was more surprised, him or me, because I was pretty sure I squeaked, "You've seen my videos?" at the same time the narrowed-eyed expression fell off his face *like that* and he jabbed his finger in my direction. "It *is* you."

I nodded because, *yeah*, it was me. I was The Lazy Baker, or at least that was my WatchTube channel. And Picturegram. And website, which was okay for now but would soon be even better.

I had my hands over my heart as I gaped at him, with my mouth open and everything, because that was how classy I was.

He knew my channel!
HE KNEW MY CHANNEL.

"I thought you looked familiar the other night." He grinned all of a sudden, all bright white teeth and a smile that turned his face into the opposite of the serious man who had let me in.

"You did?" I'd only been recognized in person maybe like... five times. Five times in more than six years.

It was my hair. I always wore it up and straightened it when I did videos instead of down and curly like in "real life." And I wore a lot more makeup in them. That, and as one viewer had said, I didn't exactly have a memorable face. "*She's hot, but I don't get why???*" another viewer had written after that first comment.

So that was cool. A real boost to the ego the internet was. But anyway.

"I just watched the one with you and your sister trying to make the honey walnut shrimp knockoff a couple days ago," this maybe-football player admitted, still grinning in a way that totally threw me off as his hands went to his hips and he shook his head in what seemed like disbelief again. Disbelief! At me! "I tried to make your banana bread recipe a week ago."

He'd made my banana bread?

I shit myself anytime anyone told me they did that, but *now?*

My face already fucking hurt from smiling, and I was going to ignore the tears trying to bubble up in my eyes in reaction. *I'd been recognized. He'd made my recipes.*

This might be one of the best moments of my entire life.

"You just made my whole month," I told him, pretty sure I croaked the words out, still holding my hands up against my chest as I tried to keep my shit together. I wanted to give him a hug, but you know, maybe next time.

If we ever saw each other again.

"Do you want a scone then?" I whispered, still hung up on him having made my banana bread.

That time, the nice man didn't hesitate to nod as he kept on basically beaming at me.

I shot him another smile that probably had me looking like a crazy person and walked over to the island, popping the lid off the glass container and holding it out toward him.

There was literally glee in his eyes. I almost fainted.

I soaked up his face like a psycho as he chewed thought-fully. *He knew who I was!* I shook the container at him, feeling light as a feather all of a sudden. I couldn't believe it. "Have more. I brought them for Zac, but you can have half."

He didn't wait. My new best friend, who didn't know he was my best friend, grabbed three more blueberry scone/cookies and held them in one hand while he fed himself with the other in neat little bites that had me smiling like a moron on the inside—all right, and the outside. But it was called for, and I had no shame.

I could feel myself going up to the balls of my feet again. Still happy. So freaking happy I was going to be happy for the rest of the month, at least. Maybe my whole life. "Do you play football too?"

CJ bobbed his head while he chewed his scone. "For the White Oaks. Receiver. Damn, these are good. There's really rosemary in them?"

The White Oaks were Houston's professional football team. They weren't the best, and most of the time, they weren't the worst either. The majority of what I knew was that they were a newish team and their quarterback was young. I couldn't tell how old CJ was; he had a face that could have been twenty-two or thirty-four. What I did know was that I liked him.

"Yes. Thank you. Where are you from?"

"Philly, originally. Then I spent four years in Austin."

That had me perking up. Was that how he'd met Zac? Some kind of alumni something?

I didn't get the chance to ask though. "Can I ask you something?" the other man said, still eyeing my tiny scones.

I held the container out toward him again. "Sure."

He took two more as he seemed to think about it for a second before he went for it. "Do you really make up the recipes on the spot?"

I got that question a lot, and I mean *a lot*. I had built my viewers up on the idea that I went in mostly blind to each episode, specifically so they could see me fail. I came up with something I wanted to make and tried it with the camera recording the whole time. Some days, they were original recipes. Some days I tried to make healthier versions of fast food and restaurant dishes, with fewer ingredients, and followed my gut. Some days, I made things that weren't exactly healthy but were homemade. I'd tried just about everything. When Guillermo, my nephew, came to visit, we did kid-friendly cooking episodes, and it worked. Making things without a plan, using less than ten ingredients, and trying to make it as easy as possible was my *thing*. "If it isn't broke, don't fix it," was my motto most of the time.

"I brainstorm it a lot in my head, but I wing it in the end. Subscribers like it when I bomb something. Those videos usually do the best, especially if I have someone in them with me."

I didn't have a whole lot of "guest stars." Almost all of the people who joined in during my episodes were family members. The small percent who weren't consisted of other video bloggers who contacted me, and the rest were friends and family who asked. I would have done more people, but the idea of letting total strangers into my apartment kind of went against every lesson I'd learned watching *Law and Order*. It was another reason why I wanted to eventually rent a studio apartment where I could film separately. That was plan E. A plan for the distant future.

CJ grunted around the tiny scone he'd popped in his mouth. "Those are my favorites." He eyed me with a grin as he ate another cookie. "Zac doesn't talk much about anyone other than his mama or his Paw-Paw, but he never said anything about you."

Of course he hadn't.

"I'm pretty sure he doesn't know about... it. The other day was the first time I've seen him in ten years," I admitted.

CJ made a thoughtful face but pulled the stool out between the one he'd been planning on sitting in and the one I was standing beside. He gestured to it.

I had to use the supporting bar at the bottom to boost myself into it, facing him. I was going to have to ask Connie if she knew who CJ was and rub it in her face I'd met him, if she did.

"We grew up together. We were from the same town. He's best friends with my cousin," I explained so he wouldn't think I was **BIANCA BLACKHAIRGYM HOU** on his phone. I would rather not be anything on his phone, which was more than likely the case based on how the last decade had gone. Not that I was upset about it.

And now I wanted to change the subject. "How long have you played here in Houston?" I rarely watched football, and when I did, it was only when Zac played. But I was never going to admit that out loud.

"Since the White Oaks joined the organization. They recruited me." CJ scratched at the back of his neck, biceps flexing under his T-shirt and everything. "You're smaller in person than you look."

I snorted as I set my palm down flat on the white granite shot through with swirls of gray and brown. It was a nice countertop. Durable. If I ever got a studio just for filming, I'd want something like it. The one at my apartment was plain white, but I still loved it. "At the beginning, when I first started posting stuff online, people said I looked like a munchkin. That they could barely see me, so I wear heels now. Big old platform ones so I don't look like I'm still in middle school." Honestly, I'd gotten used to short jokes since I'd been like... eight. They were nothing new. They weren't even annoying anymore. I wasn't *that* short.

CJ lifted an impressive eyebrow at the same time he raised another scone to his mouth. "How tall are you?"

"How tall are you?"

His big, unexpected laugh made me grin a second before the sounds of Zac's voice carried into the kitchen. Stretching to the side, I glanced around to find him standing in the doorway that I had learned the week before led to a staircase. The same staircase that led upstairs.

He was on the phone, looking in our direction. I could see that much. And he was arguing. I could hear that much.

"*...is the problem? I'm doing what I have to do,*" his low voice spat, irritation in every inch of his tone. In jeans and a light brown T-shirt, Zac stood there with one hand on the doorframe and his other one at his side balled into a fist.

When we made eye contact, I waved at him.

He gave me a small nod before that fisted hand came up and he held up an index finger.

Someone was on an important call. Okay. No problem.

"*No, we agreed on it. No.*" He ducked his head again to grumble into the receiver. He had it pretty much pressed against his mouth. That's how I knew he was mad. I'd had conversations like that with my ex. I saw him dig a hand through his longish dark blond hair as he griped, "*That's not my fault!*"

Yikes.

Turning back around to face CJ, I smiled at him. He gave me one right back.

"*Why should I have to—*" Zac's voice carried for a second, but when I glanced back in the direction he'd been in, he wasn't there anymore. But I could still hear him.

"Trevor's still mad at him about the party," CJ said out of nowhere.

What party? The one here weeks ago?

"I hope someone signs him. He's got a lot left in him."

I glanced up to find my new best friend eyeing the container of scones in front of me. I nudged them toward him again and watched as he pried the lid off and plucked two more out. I wanted to ask him if he knew anything I didn't— but when you knew nothing, which was exactly the amount of knowledge in my brain regarding Zac and his career, everything was information—but kept my mouth shut.

If Zac wanted me to know, he would just tell me himself, right? Not that I was expecting anything. And hadn't I literally just told myself to mind my own business like fifteen minutes ago?

Luckily and unluckily, I didn't have to wonder about it too much because CJ's phone started ringing. The ringtone must have meant something, because the next thing I knew, he was shoving his stool back, saying, "I need to take this. Thanks for the scones, Bianca."

All I managed to do was say, "You're welcome, CJ," before he was heading out the doorway and up the staircase.

Well, that had been interesting.

It had made my whole day.

I twisted again to glance where Zac had disappeared to. I couldn't hear him anymore. Maybe he just wanted some privacy to finish up a conversation that didn't sound all that pleasant. Made sense. I could wait.

As I sat there, I pulled out my phone and opened my

email app, figuring I might as well get some work in while I waited. Random people messaged me all the time with various cooking questions, especially when they were trying to tweak one of my recipes, and I tried my best to write them all back. Most of the time I did it while I was on the toilet, but there was no point in sitting around not doing anything, was there?

I answered one email. Two. Three. Four. Five, six, seven, eight, nine, ten, and after the fifteenth one—from two days ago—had been replied to, I glanced at the clock on the microwave across from me... almost an hour had gone by.

Disappointment shaped like a sledgehammer hit me right in the center of the chest.

Did he forget I was here?

Something hot and uncomfortable layered itself over my sternum, and I turned again to see if he had come back and was just... being quiet. Wishful fucking thinking, and I knew it was. I knew it.

Quietly, as freaking quietly as I could, I scooted off the stool that my butt had molded itself to and crept toward the staircase.

Unless he had an invisibility cloak on, he wasn't there. Something that could have been his voice floated down the stairs. He'd given me the finger to ask me to wait for him...

But that had been an hour ago.

Who the hell talked on the phone for that long? Okay, maybe me with my sister, but I'd get off the phone with her if I had something to do or someone was visiting.

It's probably something really important, my brain tried to reason.

But....

I did have things to do. And apparently so did Zac.

Things that didn't include me after all.

CHAPTER SIX

I spent the entire ride to the grocery store trying my best not to be disappointed about what happened at Zac's place.

More like... what *hadn't* happened.

But like most things, it was easier said than done, like when my New Year's resolution was to wake up at five in the morning every day to work out before my shift. I hadn't taken into consideration that I rarely went to bed before two in the morning.

The truth was, I was disappointed in how disappointed I was.

I knew better.

I had gone there with the intention of apologizing, and I hadn't done that.

Because I'd been forgotten. For not the first time in my life.

My stomach felt off no matter how much I "understood" that Zac was "famous" and probably had a ton of things going on. He was busy with his own life. *I* was busy with my life, and of course he was even busier than me. He'd invited me when he'd thought he had a moment and didn't I know things came up? Of course I got it. There had been plenty of times when I'd had to pull over or go straight home from work because something had happened to my website, or if I got an email about a mistake someone had found on a video or a post and I had to do damage control.

I told myself that Zac had asked me to come over because he'd wanted to see me.

And I was disappointed because I'd literally seen him for maybe five seconds from a distance.

If something wouldn't have been happening, he would have come down. But I'd met CJ, and he'd known who I was and had even made one of my recipes. That should have been enough. It would have been more than enough in any other situation.

But my stomach—and my heart—didn't give enough of a shit.

Because that molasses-like layer of "my friend had bailed on me" didn't really go anywhere on the drive or during my shopping trip.

Telling yourself something and believing it were two totally different things.

But the call that came to my cell while I was in line at the checkout counter had helped. Some.

I'd been surprised as shit when my phone started ringing while I was loading my groceries onto the conveyor belt and taken a peek at the screen to see **512-555-0199** flash across the screen.

I looked at the number for a second and thought about not answering it. But I did it anyway, because I wasn't an asshole. Because I *had* wanted to try.

I just wasn't going to put much weight into any of my interactions with Zac, mostly because I wasn't going to expect anything.

If you didn't have expectations, you couldn't be let down.

Before I could second-guess myself, I answered the phone... and kept loading my groceries.

"Hello?" It wasn't like I didn't know it was him, but my feelings were a little hurt regardless of knowing better.

"Aww, darlin', I'm so damn sorry," the voice that was only still familiar because I'd heard it on television piped up over the line just as I set my vanilla creamer onto the conveyor belt.

I made a face to myself and glanced up to see the cashier watching me. I forced a smile.

"Are you close? Can you come back?"

Go back to his house?

Some part of me was tempted to say yes. I would have liked to talk to him. Listen to that voice that had felt like a warm hug back in the day. Watch a face that had smiled at me what felt like a hundred thousand times. Maybe hear a laugh that I'd heard almost as much. And say I was sorry for being so weird at dinner.

But what would you really have to talk about? What's the point? My brain tried to whisper... and I couldn't exactly ignore it.

My heart gave this painful little twist I tried to ignore, but failed at doing so.

He'd left me downstairs alone for almost an hour. After inviting me over. I had shit to do.

I smiled at the employee behind the register once more as I finished loading the rest of my heavy stuff: milk and a bag of potatoes. "I'm not by there anymore." I *wasn't* bitter he was barely getting around to noticing I'd left. "And I'm checking out at the grocery store now. Can I call you when I'm done?" I had to blink my eyes as another swell of disappointment went through my chest at having been forgotten. *Again.*

It was my own fault for feeling this way, and it was up to me to dig my way out of it. I had gone over there with the best of intentions, wanting to make up for how I'd behaved, and goddamn it, I was going to go through with it. To an extent.

"By the way," I said, "I left some scones on the counter for you. They aren't full-sized, but... if you don't like them, just give them to CJ."

There, no pressure on him. If he didn't like them, at least his roommate had. He wouldn't have to feel bad about not enjoying them. Also, I told him about them instead of letting them rot away on the counter. Look at me trying to be mature.

There was a beat of silence, and then another, and I frowned as I handed over my grocery bags to the bagger and asked, "You there?"

"Yeah," my old friend replied after a second. "I'm real sorry, honey. You sure you can't make it back? You can put your things in the fridge...."

I didn't want to be this person, did I? The one who got all upset when I knew better, when he didn't owe me a freaking thing. I could be polite and still watch out for myself. Do what was best for me. *I had tried*, and that had to be enough. If anything, this was all just another sign of how this friendship between us hadn't been meant to be.

I could read the signs. I'd closed my eyes to them a bunch of times in my life, but I'd learned my lesson by now. Just because you close your eyes and pretend something isn't there, doesn't make it go away.

"Thanks, but I have something I need to do." Make dinner and watch TV. I hesitated for a second. "Take care of yourself, okay?"

There was another pause, then, "I thought you were gonna call me when you got home?"

Yeah, I'd been lying out of my ass when I offered to. But it was for the best. For me, and probably for him too. He didn't need to be wasting time. From the sounds of it, he had enough shit to deal with.

So even though I didn't want to, even though it hurt a little, I still said it because I was going to be nice, because I didn't harbor resentment over the past anymore. "I'll talk to you later, Zac."

Later. Right. Maybe we both knew what I really meant.

There was a soft exhale I only barely managed to hear before, "I'm sorry, Peewee."

Peewee.

There came that squeeze again, and that time, it did hurt. Just a little, but more than enough. "I know. It's all right. See ya."

There was a sound in the background I didn't know what to do with before I heard, "Bye, Bianca," and *then*, I hung up.

There wasn't much else for us to say to each other, was there?

We'd both tried. Some things just really weren't meant to be.

———

"You did what?"

On the screen of my phone, I could see my sister lean into her camera and flash her teeth at me. "I got some of those whitening strips. What do you think?"

What I *really* thought was that Connie's mouth could now light up a glow-in-the-dark mini golf course. "Con, I think that stuff wears away at your enamel, but your teeth look nice," I told her as I finished chopping the white onion I'd bought about an hour ago. "They're not going to be as nice as the dentures you're going to end up having to get though if you keep using those things."

"That's what I said!" my brother-in-law, who had been sitting beside her on the couch, right on the edge of the screen, piped in. I could barely see his knee right then, but earlier he'd leaned into the camera and asked when I was planning on visiting.

I watched as my sister's head turned slowly to the right, to where he was. She stared at him.

"Punkin, we're just watching out for you," the man who had married my sister fourteen years ago—the father of their two children—tried to backtrack. I already knew exactly what placating face he was giving her; I'd seen it in person way too many times. "I'd love you with three teeth, but please don't ask me to. I might laugh if you start whistling through them."

I snorted. My sister kept on staring at him.

At twelve years older than me, Connie had been more like a mom figure to me than a sibling for the majority of my life. Tied with Boogie, she was my best friend.

Despite the age gap between us, we had cemented our bond over the dozens of times she'd knock on my window in the middle of the night so she could sneak back in. I'd earned her loyalty by never ratting her out—mostly because I had always thought she was the coolest human being, but also because, according to what our mom had said a couple of times when she'd been around, I'd come out of the womb, and we'd fallen in love with each other.

We'd stayed in love with each other. Not that long ago, Connie had said something about how she'd raised three kids and wasn't planning on having any more. She had given birth to two of them, and I knew I was the third. The first. Her practice baby. For as long as I could remember, she had always been my rock.

Even shorter than me—and really, basically a hobbit if we were going to throw words around, because I was below aver-age, but she took it to a whole new level—she was also a regular source of entertainment. And she was very lovable, nuts or not.

On the screen, she blinked at her husband.

He did something that made it seem like he squirmed.

She blinked again.

And again he seemed to squirm.

I missed her. And her husband. And their kids.

"Do you hear that?" my brother-in-law said suddenly, getting to his feet. "I think my phone is ringing. Let me go look for it."

I snorted, "Liar!" at the same time my sister muttered, "Chickenshit."

And then we both laughed and gave each other a thumbs-up through our cameras when the microphone picked up my brother-in-law's, "I'm not lying! I'm pretty sure I heard it!"

He was totally lying.

And it just made us laugh more.

Richard did some dumb shit every once in a while, but he was awesome. After my sister and cousin, he was probably my third favorite person. Chickenshit or not.

He'd won me over from the start. It wasn't every man who would be crazy about his sister-in-law moving in for years, but he'd been the first one to bring it up after Mamá Lupe had died. Not once in the years that I lived with them did he ever make me feel bad or weird or unwanted.

There was a reason why my sister stuck around with him and all their moves over the years while he was active in the army.

On the screen though, Connie almost instantly sobered as she faced the camera again and asked, "Now that Nosey is gone, are you going to tell me what upset you, or am I going to have to guess?"

Damn it. I knew I should have waited to video chat with her. What else did I expect?

Luckily, I finished chopping up the onions at the same time as she'd thrown her question out at me, so I had an excuse to set my knife down on the cutting board. I knew better than to try to lie to her. But I also didn't want her to have the full story. *Zac Travis invited me over and then blew me off. But it's no big deal because it seemed he had an important call!* Yeah, like that would fly with the psycho living in Killeen, hours away. God forbid anyone ever hurt me, mentally, emotionally, or physically.

My sister had never given me a reason to doubt that she would come straight to help me if I ever needed her. And even when I didn't need her. Kids in tow at three in the morning and everything.

She was my hero.

And maybe Zac had inadvertently hurt my feelings, but I wasn't about to throw him under the bus when part of me understood he had apologized and whatever had happened hadn't been planned.

She had seen him a few times over the years, and I didn't want to make things awkward. She had never been as close to Boogie or him as I'd been, but they weren't total strangers. She had lived with our abuela for a few years before moving away once she had finished her basics at the local community college.

"I was supposed to hang out with a friend, but they kind of left me hanging. It's not a big deal, but I just overreacted and got annoyed."

Eyes lighter than mine stared at me through my tablet as she narrowed them. We didn't totally look alike. Her hair was straight; mine was about as curly as humanly possible. Hers was light like our dad's, and mine was dark like our mom's. She had always been all cute and small, and I gained weight if I just looked at a single Chips Ahoy. Connie had always been pretty and popular and had boys all over her. Me? Not so much. At least not until my early twenties.

But she wasn't totally believing me; I could tell from her facial expression.

"It's no big deal," I insisted. That got me an eye roll that made me want to change the subject ASAP. "Say, have you talked to your parents lately? They haven't emailed or video messaged me in over a week."

That had my sister sliding me a look before grunting. She let the "your parents" thing go, fortunately. "Yeah. Mom emailed me yesterday—"

"Mom! Mommy! I think I super-glued my fingers together!" a voice hollered from somewhere in the background. *"Oww! Mom! Help me!"*

My sister instantly sighed, lifted a hand, and pinched the bridge of her nose for a second before shooting me a flat look. "I want you to think about this moment if you ever decide to have kids, Peewee. Think long and hard." One side of her mouth went up in a half smile that meant nothing good was about to come out of her mouth. "Long and hard are what got me into this situation."

I scrunched up my nose and covered my ears with my palms. "Nope. You're crossing the line. I've told you before, Richard is in the Never-Want-to-Hear-About-It category."

She cackled. "Let me go deal with this. Love you. Bye," Connie said before ending the call only after I'd said bye too.

I was still trying to shake off her TMI as I opened my pantry and pulled out the cans of beans I was going to need for the soup I was making for dinner—because I could eat soup for lunch and dinner and be happy for the rest of my life —when the doorbell rang.

Ah, hell.

Even though the complex I lived in had a gate that required

an access code to get in, and even though solicitation was banned according to the signs posted at every entrance, every once in a while, people still managed to sneak through. Just last week, someone holding pamphlets and offering to speak to anyone who would listen about our Lord and Savior Jesus Christ had rung my doorbell. The only reason I'd checked the peephole ahead of time was because I'd heard voices outside the door—specifically my neighbor Santiago's voice—and had been curious. And I wasn't even embarrassed to admit that I'd laid down on the floor for a solid five minutes afterward.

Then again, I pretended I wasn't home anytime anyone I didn't know knocked. Even when Girl Scouts came around and tried to sell cookies. I had no willpower.

So, you could say that I knew better than to call out to whoever was ringing the doorbell.

I set my can down beside the Dutch oven I had been about to use and crept as quietly as I could toward the door. Boogie had tried to tell me once you could see shadows move across the peephole from the outside when they were used, but I didn't totally believe him. I'd stopped believing everything he said when I was thirteen and he'd tried to tell me that kissing boys made babies.

Yeah, I'd found Connie's condoms two years before that and had had *that* conversation with her. My sister had taught me about the birds and the bees using a carrot and a cinnamon donut. There was a reason we were so close. She could tell me anything.

Anything that wasn't related to her husband, because I saw him too much and just didn't want to picture things.

Anyway, one quick glance through the peephole had me dropping to my heels from my tiptoes, then going right back onto them to make sure I hadn't imagined the face on the other side tipped up toward the ceiling.

I wasn't seeing things.

It was Zac.

How the hell had he—

That was a stupid question. Obviously there was only one person who could or would have given him my address. *But why had he asked for it? And what was he* doing *here?*

Through the peephole, I saw him lean forward, and not even a second later, the doorbell went off again.

Okay.

"One second!" I called out, frowning to myself before undoing the deadbolt and then the bottom lock and opening the door carefully to face the man who had been my friend a long time ago. A man who was very, very busy. And that I was very happy for.

I'm not going to take anything personally. I'm not going to be hurt. I'm not going to be more disappointed than I've already been, I reminded myself as I halfway forced a casual smile onto my face.

"Hi," I told Zac, wincing on the inside at how almost half-assed my greeting sounded.

The dirty-blond-haired man with his freshly shaved face shot me a smile that seemed wary as his eyes, a nearly perfect baby blue, locked onto my own. I couldn't help but notice his clothing—jeans, a T-shirt, and worn cowboy boots. "Hi, darlin'," he drawled.

What the hell was he doing here?

He must have known I was surprised by his presence, because he kept right on going, aiming those eyes at me. One corner of that pink mouth hitched up—he didn't have the fullest mouth, but it was well-shaped and just pretty—and he lifted one of those broad shoulders too as he asked, "Got a minute for me, honey?" He tried to lay it on me, I'd give him that. "Pretty please?"

A sudden flashback of my abuela complaining about letting Zac get away with everything came out of nowhere.

And I understood her completely. Now. So many freaking years later. It was that smile and the earnestness in his face—but mostly that freaking smile—that tugged at me despite everything.

He was here, and he was Zac, and maybe he'd hurt my feelings for forgetting about me, but....

He was here. Being all... himself, or at least showing me the bits and pieces that had made up the person I'd known.

The important parts.

Damn it.

I was going to be fine. I wasn't going to show him he'd hurt me, because I knew... somehow... he hadn't meant to do that.

The world was a heavy place, and I had a finicky back.

Plus, if anyone had to feel bad, it was me for how I'd behaved in the first place.

His eyebrows went up. "So... yeah?"

So... yeah?

I stood aside and gestured Zac in. "Sure. Come in."

That smile of his went wide.

Yeah, there was a reason Mamá Lupe had loved him and why I'd been so in love with him, both as a friend and more, back in the day.

"I was in the middle of making dinner," I told him, waving at Zac to follow me toward the island that separated the kitchen from the living room. I had two stools lined up along it. "Do you want something to drink? I have water, Pepsi, and pink lemonade powder."

When I'd first moved in about a year and a half ago, I hadn't bought too many things for the living room because the deposit on this place had been so pricey. There was a sofa bed, a chair that was only there because I thought it was cute, because it sure as hell wasn't comfortable, and a TV that my sister and her family had bought me, claiming it was my birthday and Christmas present for the next two years. She hadn't been joking either. For Christmas, she'd given me a card with a picture of the television in it. I'd cried from how hard I'd laughed. I had old movie posters of *Mulan* and *The Lion King* framed on my wall that a friend had gifted me.

The kitchen was the whole reason that I'd moved into this expensive complex in the first place. I'd taken one tour of it and known that *this* was what I wanted. With white cabinets, pull-out drawers, white granite counters, light blue subway glass tile backsplash, stainless steel appliances, and a cute little island in the middle, I'd immediately envisioned filming video blogs in the small but perfect kitchen. It had been love at first sight.

One day, maybe, I could buy a house with a beautiful, big kitchen. But I'd settle for renting a studio to film. Someday.

"I'll take some water," Zac replied, bringing me back to the present and getting me to stop admiring my kitchen.

I nodded as I grabbed a clean glass and filled it up through the tabletop water filter I'd spent an arm and a leg on as the sound of him pulling out a stool told me what he was doing. Getting comfortable. Sure enough, he was sitting on the other side of the counter, giving me another tight-lipped smile when I set the glass in front of him and pushed it just a little closer.

Zac looked... off. His light brown eyebrows were drawn tight, his forehead was scrunched, and the lines along his mouth were deep, and I didn't like it. I only partially disliked that I didn't like it.

"You okay?" I went right out there and asked, taking in his strong, tan face.

He really did still look like some kind of fairy-tale prince.

A fairy-tale prince who a lot of women wanted to do dirty, dirty things to, according to some of the comments on his Picturegram posts. I'd read some of them after his TSN

Anatomy Issue had come out—the one with his naked butt cheeks on it—and *woo-wee*. I thought I liked dirty shit. Not compared to some people.

"Apart from feeling like a shit about what I did, sure, honey," he answered back, bringing me back to the moment, those baby blue eyes locking on me as he lifted the glass and took a sip out of it.

I mean... if he wanted to feel terrible....

I didn't miss the way he glanced down at it before he took another sip and licked those cotton candy pink lips. "Is this water delicious or am I imagining it?"

Of course he was going to make this hard.

I snorted, and that earned me half a smile from a handsome face. "It is. It's a reverse osmosis machine-thing. It filters everything out."

That blue gaze flicked back down to the glass. "You gotta write the name down for me," he said after taking another sip, and I'd swear on my life he smacked his lips a little. "This is good stuff, Peewee."

Talking about water filters was fine and safe. That worked for me. "I will. It's worth every penny."

"How much was it?"

I'd lied to everybody else about the price, but... I'd seen pictures of his last car. What car he drove now, I had no idea. You'd figure the same one, but some of the MMA guys at the gym bought a new car like every three months for shits and giggles. You never knew. Plus, I could only imagine how much money he probably spent feeding himself, or more like having other people feed him. "Three hundred bucks, but I can get you a discount code." He didn't need to know I had a discount code I promoted all the time that the company had given me. I kept the water filter on the counter so it could be seen in just about every video I shot. Publicity wasn't free. For a long time, I'd stopped including sponsors—people who paid me to advertise their products—in my videos. I was trying to make up for it now.

"Did you say *three hundred dollars?*" the freaking millionaire penny-pincher choked on his sip.

I gave him my back as I turned around with a snort that I hadn't been expecting ten minutes ago, or an hour ago, or five years ago.

This man had been my friend despite our age gap. He had cared for me. I knew that, for a long time, he had loved me.

And that was why his distance had hurt me so bad.

But, even after all this time and... everything, he was still the same cheapskate who waited six months to replace his car window because *"the tape is working fine."*

And so I surprised myself when I muttered, "You can afford it," like I would have if we'd stayed friends.

If we'd stayed friends.

I needed to stop and just... take this for what it was. I really did. A quick, friendly visit like mine was supposed to have been. We were reconnecting.

"Jesus H. Christ," Zac croaked, making me focus on him. "For three hundred bucks, I'll drink out of the hose," he claimed, even as I heard him taking another sip.

I grabbed my can opener, shaking my head as I hooked it onto one of the cans I needed. I could do this. I could talk to him like I would any friendly person who came into the gym. I wasn't shy. I never had been.

I could do this for the people I loved.

"You live here by yourself?" Zac asked.

"Yeah." He didn't need to know the whole story. I opened one of the cans of cannellini beans, the word *here* bouncing around in my head some more. "I really liked the kitchen," I explained, like that would mean something to him. For a split second, I wondered if CJ had mentioned my WatchTube channel to him, but it wasn't like it mattered. I wasn't going to bring it up.

Unless he asked, I guessed.

"It sure is a nice kitchen."

"For what I'm paying, it should be." Peeking over my shoulder, I didn't have to force myself to smile at my old friend who was sitting there with his elbows on the counter and his chin resting on one palm, those light blue eyes on me, striking against his handsome and—now that I really got a good look at it—tired face.

Had he not been sleeping? Or was he just tired and stressed? I hadn't heard a word about what was going on with his career since that first day.

One corner of that cute mouth went up, reminding me again of the boy I had known and loved who had always been nothing but kind and good to me... until he'd basically disappeared. "No roommate?"

"No," I explained as I dumped the beans into a strainer and moved toward the sink to rinse them. "This is the first time I've lived by myself, but I like it." I cleared my throat, wanting to change the subject. "Your roommate, CJ, seemed nice."

"Yeah, he's a good guy." It was Zac's turn to blow out a breath that he didn't even try and muffle even though I had my back to him. "I'm so damn sorry I left you hanging, Peewee," my old friend said unexpectedly, direct and to the point, in a clear voice that managed to sound genuinely apologetic.

I could do this.

"It's okay," I started to say, turning back around to him. He was shaking his head. The lines at his eyes creased deeply as he frowned.

"No, it ain't. It was a real dick thing, darlin', and I'm sorry as hell. Mama would've tanned my hide for doin' that to anybody, but especially to you. I was on the phone with my agent. I got in trouble for ignorin' his calls there for a while, when I was in Liberty Hill, and he got all bent out of shape. It's no excuse, but I'm sorry I couldn't get off the phone with him sooner," Zac said in a rush of words, like he had to get it out. "I already had Trevor breathin' down my neck, and I couldn't put my agent off much longer anymore."

He'd gotten in trouble? Because his agent was trying to get him on a new team or something and he hadn't been answering his calls? Or what?

He kept on going, showing more and more pieces of the boy-man who had earned my loyalty and love so long ago. "Will you forgive your old Snack Pack?" he asked in that Zac way that was all sugar and earnestness and that smile that could slay a dragon as he glanced up at me from beneath his eyelashes.

My old Snack Pack.

Ah, *shit*.

He wasn't done either. "Next time, you can listen to me gettin' reamed, if you want. My agent's a pro, and Trev's real good at it too. He could teach some classes on rippin' folks new ones when they're already down."

I blinked again.

I'd never been the type of person who held crazy grudges. Even Connie let go of things pretty quick. It was probably our parents' fault, honestly. Their soft hearts were the reason why they were good doctors. Our grandma, on the other hand, had remembered everything and didn't let you forget it.

But everything about that long body here at my apartment, because he was so tall and all of his muscles were as endless and ripped as his bones were, seemed apologetic and honest. Sincere. Those eyes of his were kind and *real*.

I never listened to what those TV anchors said about him,

about how he was immature and unreliable, about how he'd never reached his max potential.

The thing was, my cousin wouldn't still be best friends with an asshole.

And Zac wouldn't be here if he hadn't given a shit about leaving me hanging.

All that said something to me.

This was my choice—to forgive or not. I hadn't lived my life waiting around for him to remember me. And whatever reasons he'd had... well, he'd had them.

So, it was up to me, and I knew what my heart was telling me. A heart that could hear my grandma's quiet whisper in it. A heart that recognized what my eyes could see.

"Yeah, I forgive you," I breathed out, meaning it completely, down to the bottoms of my bare feet. "Thank you for explaining."

It was the truth, and it made me feel so much better; it was kind of annoying how much better. I glanced at him over my shoulder again and saw that he'd dropped his hands and was sitting upright in the stool, his features serious.

His gaze was slowly roaming my face too.

I turned back to the counter. I could do my part too. "Hey, speaking of things to apologize for, I'm sorry I wasn't being very nice when we went out to eat. I was just... surprised to see you." And being petty. Mostly that. That didn't come out of my mouth though. "I'm sorry."

"There's nothin' in the world for you to apologize for, kiddo."

That made me feel more like shit. But since I didn't want to talk about it any longer than we needed to, I'd take it and run. So I changed the subject, because I was trying, damn it. "So... did you work things out with your agent at least?"

"Kinda," he answered. "He's still pissed, but we're gettin' it sorted. I just can't be leavin' unexpectedly anymore."

Before I could stop myself, before the rest of my body could catch up with the distance—no, the *expectation* to not expect anything—my mouth went for it like it always did around people I knew, or at least felt comfortable with. "You gotta tell Paw-Paw to quit BSing and make sure he doesn't fall again, huh? So you don't have to leave randomly?" I asked, peeking at him over my shoulder.

That got him cracking a smile that had his elbows coming back up to the island counter. His square-shaped chin landed in the cradle of his broad palm too. But it was those sneaky, subtle, calming eyes that lit up. Familiar and old and natural. Like it hadn't gone anywhere in forever.

Lord, how was I supposed to hold a grudge when he was looking at me like that? I wasn't. So it was a good thing that hadn't been the plan.

Then he nailed me with another smile that might have made someone else weak-kneed. "I know, darlin'. He needs to stop actin' like he's a fragile old man."

I smiled, and Zac gave me a huge grin—a full grin that made the rest of his face light up even more when he laughed.

Yeah, there was a reason why I had missed him. He had always been so nice, and we'd always gotten along so well.

And if that had been the case because he'd felt like he'd owed me for something I couldn't remember doing... whatever. I wasn't going to overthink it too much. I was forgiving, and I felt... right about it. Good about it. For however long this lasted, right? I turned toward the food I'd prepped and said, "Boogie told me he's home now and doing fine."

"He's good. They kept him overnight as a precaution," Zac replied. "He sure was happy to see you."

I tore open the bag of kale I'd bought and shook some of it out to stick under the tap to rinse in the colander. "I hope he knows I love seeing him. And your mom. I swear she looks the same as she did back when we were kids." I held back the joke about our age difference though just as it was about to come out. It had been a long time, after all.

There was a beat of silence while I was focused down on the leafy greens, but Zac cleared his throat and piped up again, sounding just a little different when he did. "You doin' anything the rest of the day? I thought you said you had plans or somethin'."

Well, that came back to bite me in the ass real quick. "Plans to do stuff here. I've got to work tomorrow. You?"

Fortunately, he was either too polite or felt too bad about leaving me hanging to point out I'd lied.

"No. My only plan was to catch up with you, darlin'," he drawled. "I still can't believe you live here. Nobody said a word to me." There was a pause and then, "I can't get over that I didn't recognize you. How old are you now? Twenty... seven?"

I knew why no one had. Because in ten years, he had obviously never tried hard enough to see how I was doing, because he could have just asked and hadn't. *If he'd cared.* And *that* was the wrong thing to think about.

I was letting that shit go.

He was here now. I tried not to hold on to stuff like that, especially when it was obvious he was trying *now*.

And if he could try, so could I.

Expectations.

This man had picked me up from school a time or ten.

"Well, if you want soup for dinner, you're welcome to stay. I don't know if it fits into your meal plan though. It has sausage in it," I offered up, mostly expecting him to decline because he had plans, like a date or something... maybe with that nice blonde.

So I was surprised as shit for maybe the hundredth time since we'd seen each other weeks ago when Zac said, "I love soup."

He'd loved everything back in the day.

"Sausage, beans, and kale?"

This fool said, "Mm-hmm," and I couldn't help but glance at him again. He was taking another sip of water, peeking into the glass as he did so like it looked weird or he was trying to figure out if there was magic in it.

Being cute just came naturally to some people.

"I figured you'd have plans," I let slip out, only partially regretting it as I turned on the burner beneath my Dutch oven.

But Zac didn't hesitate to answer. "I told you. Spendin' some time with you was my only plan, Peewee."

There he went again.

And maybe that made me feel nice enough that I was able to keep trying to joke around with him, trying to go back to that ground we had built a fourteen-year childhood friend-ship on. It rose up inside of me like a wave I had no chance against. It was too second nature, and I'd already repressed it enough during the day at work and the last times we'd seen each other.

"Well, la-di-da, lucky me then," I told him sarcastically, like I would have if he were Boogie or Connie.

Zac laughed, the sound raspy and thick and bright and *familiar*. "You used to be so excited to spend time with me."

Yeah, that was nice. So I took it and ran with it. "Well yeah, because all of my friends lived far, and it was only you, Boogie, and Connie nearby," I deadpanned as I waited for the pot to heat up. It was going to take a few minutes. "Then Connie bounced, and it was only you two left."

That got me another one of those raspy, bright laughs that felt like an old pair of comfy undies. "You tryin' to tell me some of my fondest memories were a lie?"

I really had loved spending time with him and Boogie back then, and he knew it. I didn't need to confirm anything.

I glanced at him. "You don't want me to answer that. I'm not going to break your heart today, but I probably wouldn't ask your mom any questions about the tooth fairy or Santa anytime soon either, m'kay?"

It was this fool's turn to blink. And he even went as far as to raise a hand and set it right on the center of his chest. "Are you tryin' to say...."

It was so freaking hard to keep from snorting, but if he wanted to joke around... well, that was second nature to me too. I kept my face even. "I think this is a conversation you need to have with her. I'm sorry."

My friend of such a long time ago freaking hooted. He shook his head like... he was so happy. To be around me.

And I liked it. I liked it a lot more than I had any business doing so.

"Ah, darlin', I missed the shit out of you, and I—" Zac cut himself off.

But I knew what he'd been about to say. At least my gut did.

I missed the shit out of you, and I didn't even know it. That's what he'd caught himself about to say. You know, because he'd forgotten about me. Otherwise he would have asked or gotten back in touch at some point over the years. All it would've taken was a phone call. A "hi" via text.

I faced the stove and dropped some oil into the Dutch oven, biting the inside of my cheek as I did it.

He'd been busy.

And it was fine. I'd been busy too. I had a life.

But none of that changed the weird silence that filled that sliver of a second before Zac started to say, "Bianca—"

I didn't want to hear it. I was going to focus on the good. On the *here.*

"So, did they put Paw-Paw on medications? Boogie didn't say," I cut him off.

———

"So... whatcha been up to?" Zac asked me half an hour later after spilling all the beans on Paw-Paw's health and throwing in a couple more stories about him that I'd never heard before that had me cracking up.

And most importantly, skirting around our past.

What have I been up to? Instead of *how's life been the last ten years?* I wasn't the only one on strange ground, and that was all right. I hadn't wanted things to get awkward after his last comment about not realizing he'd missed me.

I knew he wasn't trying to hurt me by reminding me again that we hadn't seen each other in so long—and definitely not why that was—but... I was choosing not to let it bother me.

And if it was still just a little bit of a sore subject, that shit was on me.

But honestly, *really,* it was the easiest thing in the world to forgive Zac for just about anything when talking to him was like slipping into a favorite pair of matching socks that had been separated by a magical dryer for months. If I wanted to be less technical, like riding a bike. He was so likable and dumb and talking to him was too...

Natural. Hanging out with him, talking to him, was just... easy. Somehow that was annoying and nice at the same time.

"You workin' at a gym? I think that's the last place Boogie told me you were at." He'd kept going with the questions after telling me about Paw-Paw Travis calling him at six in the morning to ask how to buy some sunglasses he'd seen on the television that would help his night driving.

It had been six years since he should have given up driving, but that hadn't stopped him, apparently. Paw-Paw claimed he only wanted to drive around the ranch.

Wait.

His question took me a second to process. Boogie had

told him where I worked? I couldn't remember mentioning anything about it in the car when we'd gone to dinner.

Had he *asked* Boogie?

He knew about the gym but not my WatchTube channel?

"Yeah. I work a few hours a week at the front desk at Maio House," I told him as I scooped a load of sausage and greens from my plate and pondered that over. That was enough information without being too much. "It's a gym in one building and the building next door is for MMA and stuff."

From the corner of my eye, I could see him glance at me as he swallowed his food. We had moved to sit in the living room on the couch, but the television wasn't on. I had a glass of pink lemonade sitting beside me on the tiny side table.

"You do MMA? How long you been there?"

I shifted, angling my butt into that corner to face him a little better. His profile was sharp under the overhead fan lighting, but he looked relaxed, slouched and sunken into the coffee brown couch I'd inherited from a friend of my cousin's, all long limbs and skin that had gotten tanner and tanner each year. He had an elbow propped on the arm of it and was holding his own bowl in the air on his palm. "No. Not at all. I've been there about three years now, but the original owners sold it not too long ago, and I don't like the new people much." Or at all. "Hopefully I won't be there too much longer."

Why had I said that out loud?

Unfortunately, he was paying attention. "What's the plan after that?"

I ate another spoonful of sausage and waited until I swallowed it to tell him vaguely, "I don't know. I was playing around with the idea of moving, but I just started thinking about it. We'll see." I hadn't mentioned it to anyone, but if he brought it up to Boogie, it wouldn't be a big deal. I'd probably talk to him about it sooner than later anyway.

Zac's eyes had flicked up to me when the "m" word had come out of my mouth, and they were still there when I finished. Those light brown eyebrows knit together; they weren't really thick, but they weren't thin either. They were just kind of perfect for his face. Honestly, everything about him worked together in a pretty boy but somehow still manly way. "Move to another apartment or somewhere else?"

"Away," I answered, pulling my legs up onto the couch so my feet were planted on it too and I could balance my bowl on top of my knees. How much should I tell him? "I like Houston, but I don't really have anyone here anymore other than some friends. And I used to like my job, but now I don't. Connie lives in Killeen. Boogie's in Austin...." I trailed off. "Anyway, we'll see. I've still got a few more months left in my lease to decide. Are you... okay in Houston for now? Are you planning on going somewhere else? Back home?"

Maybe I should have shut the hell up and not asked anything about his future.

His smile was strained, and it made me feel bad. "It's all right so far. I'm still workin' with a trainer here." The shoulder he shrugged said everything else though, I thought. "You heard, I'm guessin'?"

About not continuing on with the Thunderbirds? What the hell else would he be asking about? I nodded, leaving that in his court.

He tipped his head to the side in silence. Long enough for me to expect him not to want to talk about his career anymore, and I couldn't blame him. I wouldn't. I'd bet everyone wanted to talk to him about it. It had to be annoying. "We're sortin' things out," he stated after a while, spoon still scraping along the sides of the plain white bowl.

Huh. It wasn't my business to ask.

"I don't know, darlin'. Between us, maybe I'll retire."

I just about spit my food out. I knew for sure I choked because the sausage went down the wrong pipe, and I had to take a sip of my lemonade before I got out, *"Retire?"* the same way I used to say cooties.

Zac leaned over, hand going to the cushion between us, a concerned expression on his perfect face. "You all right?"

I nodded, coughing a little even after a big gulp of tart lemonade, which he'd declined.

He kept on frowning, and I was pretty sure he leaned over a little more. "You sure, honey? Your face is all red. Want some of my water?"

I gave him a thumbs-up even as I coughed a little more.

He didn't look convinced, but he eased back into the couch and picked up his bowl again, setting it on his lap, but he didn't start up eating again. He just looked at me all worried.

So even though it wasn't any of my damn business, I asked again, without choking up half a pound of sausage that time, "Did you say you're thinking about retiring?" I hadn't imagined it, right?

His blue eyes flicked to me. "Heard that part, huh?"

"Yes." He wanted to fucking *retire?* Just thinking the word in my head felt disgusting.

His response was lifting both those broad shoulders and peering down at his dinner. "I'm thinkin' about it."

This is none of your business, Bianca. This is none of your business.

"Why?" I asked before I could stop myself.

"Things aren't goin' exactly the way I planned, darlin'," he stated calmly, evenly. Almost in... resignation? "It's July, and I don't exactly have a team waitin' on me, you know?"

A memory of that damn segment on the sports show a

month ago ran through my head. *Is it over for Zac Travis as a starting NFO quarterback?*

Bitches.

I had a choice, and I knew I did. Keep my mouth shut and commiserate with him. Tell him he had his whole life ahead of him to do whatever he wanted. Say that football wasn't everything.

Or... not.

Because *how the hell could he be considering dropping his dream now?* After so long? *How?*

It's none of your business, Bianca, my brain tried to tell me for about the millionth time.

And sure, maybe it wasn't—definitely wasn't—but how could he seriously be considering retiring?

Was he out of his mind?

Had he told anyone else? That was a stupid question, of course he probably had. Why would Boogie tell me if he had? There was no reason. I could see Boog though telling him everything would work out.

But it wasn't fine.

And before I could stop myself again, I asked, "Is that what you want?"

Those broad shoulders of his went up.

I could take that as a no, right? "What do your agent and your manager think?" I kept going with the questions like I had some right to know the answers.

That blue-eyed gaze moved to me as he scooped up some more beans and kale in a way that seemed pretty distracted. "They're... concerned."

Lord, he was making me work for it. "About...?"

This is none of your business. This is none of your business. This is none—

I saw his hesitation, saw the way his eyes flicked to the side for a split second, and saw as that blond-and-ash-brown-dusted jaw did this weird little grind, but he answered me anyway. "They're worried I'm too old."

Too old?

He made a sound I didn't know what to think of. "I'm not done yet. Least I don't feel like I am. There're other things.... It's just been other shit with the head coach in Oklahoma. We got off on bad terms. We weren't clickin'."

Ohhh.

"But not everyone gets it or sees it that way. It wasn't the right place for me." He buried those long fingers through his hair, flipping those multicolored strands back, away from his forehead. "Now... I'm here. Trevor and my agent think other teams would rather get someone young," Zac finished. "Somebody to build a team around and all that."

I blinked, tapped the handle of the spoon against my nose, and I stared at him. At that Disney prince nose and the silhouette of his mouth and the rest of his handsome face....

What in the hell was wrong with him?

"They're concerned because you aren't 'young' anymore? They think other teams wouldn't want you because you're old? And decrepit?" I mean... he was asking for it, wasn't he?

He blinked. Zac's bottom lip dropped into a literal gape, and he sat up straight on my couch. Offended. Or maybe it was hurt? Shocked?

Jesus, help me. Maybe all three.

"I'm only thirty-four," he basically said in a tone that might have hurt my feelings a decade ago. Eyes wider than usual, or at least what I considered "usual" based off the faces I usually saw him rocking on camera. Yep, he was insulted. "Why are you makin' it sound like I'm in a walker?"

I blinked again, fighting like freaking hell to keep from laughing, because he really was making this way too easy. *Way too easy.* And way too fun, even though he'd lost his mind with his retiring talk. "I'm just working off what you said."

His mouth was still open a little as his eyebrows knit together, 100 percent offended/shocked/hurt.

But not sad at least.

So I couldn't help it. I snorted. "Hey, you're the one throwing yourself a pity party for one. It felt like an invitation. You're the one implying you're an old man and all that." All right. And there we were with us going back to young Bianca who had treated Zac just like Boogie, teasing and messing around and normal.

But he deserved it. He was asking for it.

I hadn't exactly planned on jumping right into it, but old habits die hard. And there were worse things in the world to do than picking on Zac Travis when he was being dramatic. I could be on drugs.

Zac blinked again, thinking. I could tell he was freaking thinking.

And then, *then,* I looked at him with an expression that said *you're an idiot.* Because that was younger Bianca too. Okay, and teenage and adult Bianca, especially around people I trusted and felt extra comfortable with.

My heart was on a different page from my brain, and that was okay.

Then and only then did his mouth curl up. *Then* he shook his head with a laugh that sounded like it surprised him. "All right, all right. You made your point, kiddo. I'm not old. I know I'm not. Other teams might feel that way, but I don't feel like it. That's what I was tryin' to say. I'm not done yet."

"You're not *that* old," I clarified, trying to goad him out of his little world a little more, inch by inch.

"No. I ain't old period." He gave me a side-look that had his cheek twitching. "Not really."

But it was too late. We were too in this now, and this was too familiar. Too easy. "You're sure you can still handle throwing a ball a few feet?"

He laughed, and it was light and awesome, and I couldn't have expected how glad that made me. "*A few feet?*"

My response was to shrug at him.

That lopsided smile of his released itself into the world. "I don't remember you bein' this much of a pest."

"I don't remember you being such a negative little Nancy." I spooned some more beans and greens onto my spoon before adding, "Seventeen-year-old Zac would be telling Old Fart Zac right now that he should quit crying because some people might not believe in him. You remember how much grief people gave you in college? How they told you that you were too skinny back then? Young Zac would tell you to suck it up and take advantage of every opportunity you're given, even if that means going back to being second string again. Or third string. Who knows, maybe one of these young bucks will get hurt and they'll call you and ask you to take over. Just saying.

"If teams think they don't want to even consider you in the first place because you're in your thirties now, don't give them a choice but to notice you. Post your workouts on social media. Take advantage of your Picturegram platform. Show everyone you still got it, and even if nothing happens, at least you'll know you tried. Seventeen-year-old Zac would be snapping his fingers at you to get to it, and you know it," I told him with a smile.

He didn't laugh or even smile at my comment like I'd hoped.

Maybe I'd pushed too far based on the expression he had started giving me before slowly turning his head toward the blank television screen. He didn't say anything for so long, I got just a little bit worried he was going to be mad now.

I mean, we weren't *really* friends. Not anymore. We had been.

And I wasn't the same person who used to be able to joke

around and talk shit to him because I'd been so secure in our friendship, or at least in the affection he'd felt toward me because of what I'd done for him.

But I told him the truth, and I wouldn't take it back. If I never saw him again after tonight, at least he'd have the memory of me calling him out in the future if he started to feel sorry for himself. Mamá Lupe had thought he'd walked on water, and in Paw-Paw's eyes, Zac could do no wrong.

I thought he was pretty great too, but that didn't mean I was going to sit back and blow smoke up his butt so he could float around longer or make him think that quitting was okay. And if you wanted something, you didn't quit when you came up to a hurdle, not if it really meant something to you. You pushed it over and jumped over it. I didn't care what anybody said. I didn't have the biggest audience on WatchTube, and that didn't mean that I didn't try as hard or didn't try my best with every video I posted. I wasn't *less* than someone else because they had more than me, and I wasn't any better because I had more than other people. I hungered for myself. For my future.

And just as he opened his mouth to tell me to mind my own business, or who the hell knows what, his cell phone rang.

My old friend, who had come by to catch up with me, cast me a quick look I didn't know what to think of before he pulled it out of the pocket he'd stashed it in and grimaced at the screen.

Is it a girl? my brain asked, knowing I had no business wondering that, fully aware I didn't need that question answered.

"It's my agent again," Zac blurted in the time it took for his ringtone to start up all over again, even though he didn't have to explain anything. "Hope this ain't embarassin'," he muttered, sounding distracted.

"Remember that time you threw up funnel cake all over yourself because you got on a roller coaster right after eating it? That was embarrassing. Not getting chewed out."

His gaze flicked to mine, and that mouth of his tilted up on one side. "You remember that?"

I nodded. How could I forget? Boogie and I had cracked up about it a couple years back when we'd gone to a carnival with Connie and the kids and seen a funnel cake stand. We hadn't even needed to say anything to each other. We'd both just burst out laughing out of nowhere.

"Forget it happened," he said with a sneaky little smile that made me feel better about his reaction to my shitty pep talk before tapping on the screen and bringing the phone up to his ear. "*Yes, sir?*"

Facing my blank TV to give him a little bit of privacy, I took a couple more bites while he said nothing. Scoop, chew, repeat. This soup was *good*.

I'd shared the recipe a couple years ago on one of my vlogs. The beans, sausage, and greens were a recipe from Grandma Brannen that I'd adapted and tweaked a while back from memory. I'd never met Grandma Brannen, my dad's mom, but he'd given me her recipe cards for my birthday when I was sixteen. I had a lot of my own too that I screwed around with when I didn't have all the ingredients to other recipes I liked. I had a ton of Mamá Lupe's as well, but most of those always felt too personal to share.

Maybe I could mess with a couple of the ingredients a little and post an updated recipe for it? Like a variation if you had different things in your fridge?

"*You don't say*," Zac replied in a way that had me glancing toward him. He was staring at my television screen. Correction: through my television screen. His stubble-covered chin was locked and resembled something on a statue. "*Is that right?*"

Uh-oh. I could think about my stuff later.

He kept on staring forward, and I kept on staring at him, at that perfect silhouette of a face, trying to pick up on any hints he might drop because I wanted to know what his agent was saying. Bad news? Good news?

"*Yeah*," Zac went on, giving me *nothing.*

I glanced at one of his big hands to see his fingers tapping along his thigh.

It was bad news, wasn't it?

Then he sucked in a breath, nodded at no one, and said in a strained voice, "*Course I am. I'll be there.*" He took a massive breath that made me want to take a deep breath too. "*Got it. Yeah. Thank you.*"

He hung up.

I'll be there?

I stared at my old friend and chanted, "*Tell me, tell me, tell me,*" in my head, hoping to project the message into his mind without having to verbally request it. Because I wouldn't actually ask him. If he wanted to tell me, great. If he didn't, that was okay too. I was toeing the line carefully.

That beautiful, sculpted jawline turned until his baby blue eyes locked in on mine. The giant breath he sucked in worried me though.

But his words didn't as he asked in a strange, almost distorted voice, "Peewee?"

I set my plate on the side table to give him my full attention, ready to give him a hug if he needed it. And wanted it. And not be hurt if he didn't. "Yeah?"

His Adam's apple bobbed as he took another deep, deep breath through his mouth before releasing it through his nose. He was still squeezing his hands into fists. "Either somebody doesn't think I'm too old or you're my lucky charm. I got a workout with the Miami Sharks."

CHAPTER SEVEN

"Did you hear?"

"Hear what?" I asked as I scrolled down the spreadsheet that Gunner had practically thrown at me five minutes before. It was full of names of past members who had cancelled their memberships for one reason or another. He wanted me to call them when I had a chance.

You know, because I stood around all day with my finger up my butt.

I was pretty sure that if Deandre, the gym's last manager, or Lenny or Mr. DeMaio, the previous owners, had asked me to make random phone calls, I would have done it even if I felt awkward, but since it was this asshole asking, my brain wanted to hate it on principle. He'd been an extra ass since the day I hadn't taken him up on his request to come in and close on my day off. Just two days ago, he'd gone through the drawer beneath the computer I worked at and thrown away all the colored pens I loved to use because they "weren't professional."

It had taken everything in me not to throw his lunch away that day.

"They're filming some commercial next door today." By next door, Deepa meant the MMA building beside the one we worked in. "The camera crew got here while you were on your lunch break," she explained in a whisper. I didn't need to look at her face to know she was trying not to move her lips.

You know, so we wouldn't get in trouble. Because that's what life around here had come to. Having your boss toss papers at you and being hesitant to talk because you didn't want to get griped at.

I just barely managed to hold back rubbing at my eyebrow and sighing.

"Bianca? Did you hear me?"

"Sorry. What did you say? They're filming a commercial?"

"Yeah, in the building next door. I saw the camera crew and heard Gunner on the phone. Maybe it's not a commercial for TV, but it might be for some online promo. I thought you'd want to go scope it out, but you-know-who is over there."

"That's neat." I wondered what kind of equipment they were using. Maybe I could find a reason to sneak over there real quick and peek at it. Not like I needed any new equipment since I'd just bought a new 4k camera not too long ago, but it would be interesting to see what they were using. Something out of this world expensive, I'd bet.

"You okay?"

I made sure not to look at her as I said, "Yeah. I just don't want to call these people. If they wanted to join the gym again, they would. They're just going to be annoyed, you know?"

Out of the corner of my eye, I saw her nod, and I was pretty sure she peeked at me too before saying quietly, "Bianca, you don't need to stay here if you're just doing it for me. I know you don't need this job."

I glanced at her and made a face. She had said the same thing to me last week at my apartment. "Don't start again—"

The sound of the front door opening had me standing up straight, ready to scan someone's keychain to give me an excuse not to start going through the stupid list.

But just as soon as the smile came onto my face, it fell back off.

And it stayed off as the four men approached the desk I was working behind. The one on the left was a bulky, buff man with a tiny mohawk. The guy in the middle towered over the one beside him, in height and size. He had a buzzcut and the whitest teeth I'd ever seen as he laughed at whatever the big, buff guy had just said. But it wasn't either of the two fit men who wiped the smile off my face. Or the older man with salt-and-pepper hair and in a suit that screamed expensive.

It was the man on the right who had me staring blankly as the group stopped in front of my desk.

That dark blond hair.

Those eyes that could be described as baby blue.

A face that was so lean, it highlighted the high cheekbones, defined jaw, and a chin that had only gotten cuter over time.

A mouth that had an incredible smile.

A smile that was currently taking over all the rest of those features that made up a face that was striking.

Unforgettable.

But mostly, it was familiar.

And I couldn't freaking help but go up to my tiptoes, lean forward, and say a name I had just spoken out loud not even a week ago when he'd left my apartment. "Zac?"

Fucking Zac, in sweatpants and a white T-shirt, and most of all, a surprised—but happy—expression on his face. "Darlin'?"

From her spot down the counter, Deepa gasped, and I was pretty sure she whispered, "Is that...?"

But I couldn't process the fact I knew she was a football fan—and that I hadn't told her about Zac—because I was too busy being surprised he was here.

I waved at him and then smiled at the men with him. Leaning forward against the counter, I tipped my chin up. What were the chances? "What are you doing here?" I asked.

He'd left my apartment a week ago in kind of a trance. Distracted. Maybe shocked? He'd finished his food, offered to help me wash the dishes—I'd said no—and then left after giving me a quick hug, saying he needed to make some plans and calls. I'd made sure to tell him again to take care of himself and to wish him good luck with the workout he had scheduled in Miami. I mean, I'd been surprised and elated for him. Of course, I figured he'd feel the same way since we'd literally just been talking about it, about his chances and his future.

I had gone to bed that night thinking that I was glad he had come over and shown me those pieces of him that I had hoped were still there. It had been easy to resign myself to the idea I'd see him again in the future. Maybe for Boogie's wedding. Not just days later.

"What are you doin' here?" he asked with a big smile on his beaming face.

"I work here."

Those light brown eyebrows went up, his pleased and surprised expression getting even brighter as his gaze strayed to the counter in front of me, lingering over the logo painted onto the front of it. He had to be reading the MAIO HOUSE spelled out across it. "You sure do work here, huh? I forgot all about the name 'til now."

What was he still doing here in Houston? Had he had his workout in Miami already?

Before I could wonder over it too much, my old friend dipped his chin and extended his arms out at his sides in a universal gesture. "You don't wanna be seen with me in public?"

Umm... not really?

But how mean would it be for me to not welcome a hug from him?

I thought about Gunner for a second. But... fuck it.

Heading around the counter, I walked right up to the man with the familiar face and wrapped my arms around his neck while he hugged me over my shoulders, all warm and freshly showered from the smell of him. He hugged me tight right back, basically shoving me into the expanse of a chest that felt as hard as I'd imagined it would.

He smelled pretty nice too.

But I still stepped away quickly and asked again, "What are you doing here?"

"We're doin' a video for a charity." That gave me no news on what had happened with the Miami Sharks, and that was fine.

"Zac," the older man who had walked in with him sighed in exasperation. I peeked at him in his tailored gray suit, white shirt, and light pink tie. He wasn't even looking at Zac, but instead at the phone he was busy tapping away on.

Zac made a face at me that I couldn't decipher before turning us both around to face the other men. He winked at me. "Bianca, this is Dwight and this is Kevin," he said, referring to the two bigger guys. "And this is Trevor, my manager. You can call him Trev. Y'all, this is Bianca." His attention came back to me at the same time as his hand landed on the top of my head in a way that reminded me of how he'd done it a ton while I'd been growing up. "We've known each other twenty somethin' years."

Twenty-four, but okay, no need to be technical.

I was pretty sure Deepa made a little gasp, but I didn't look at her. I was going to have some explaining to do after this. I'd get there.

I held my hand out to the biggest guy because he was the only one smiling at me. "Nice to meet you."

"How's it goin'?" the man replied, taking my hand in one that was three times the size of my own. And that was saying something, because I wasn't a huge person, but I had pretty big hands.

"Good, thank you." I turned to the other guy and shook his too. It was big but not as large as the other one's had been. "Hi."

"Hey."

Then I turned to the older man, Trevor, and held out my hand to him as well because I highly doubted he'd remember meeting me years ago.

He glanced down at my outstretched palm, and then so did I. Was there something wrong with it?

And that was when Zac reached over, grabbed his manager's hand from where it had been hanging loosely at his side, and held it out toward me.

It took everything inside of my soul to keep a straight face when I slipped my hand into his mostly limp one, only held up because of Zac who was still supporting it and who moved it up and down jerkily as he shook mine back. I looked at him and could see how thin his mouth was... because he was trying to keep from laughing too. I'd seen him make the same expression a million times back in the day.

We shook some more, way longer than what was necessary or normal, until the other man finally gave my hand a gentle squeeze, and I tore mine away from his with a glance at a Zac with laughing eyes.

And he thought I was a pest.

I guess I'd been right about Trevor not being pleasant from the memories I had.

"Hi," I told him, fighting for my damn life to not smile. "So nice to meet you." Except not really.

"Do you need me to move your mouth too or...?" My friend trailed off, and I didn't know until then just how much harder it was going to be to not crack up at how rude this man was being and how it wasn't unheard of from the way Zac was acting. That was the only reason why it didn't hurt my feelings.

Something told me this was normal for him. That and Zac had already told me about this man being capable of not being very nice. Why the hell was he still with him? Maybe I could sneak the question into a conversation with Boogie one day. He would probably know.

The older man slid Zac a disgusted look that would have insulted me if I didn't sense that he was like this with everyone. "Hello," Trevor said with all the enthusiasm of someone about to get a colonoscopy without the use of drugs. "We've met. You're the one who saved his life."

He remembered that?

Zac turned back to face me then, blue eyes bright and that freaking mouth twisted to the side like he was surprised Trevor remembered me too. Maybe he didn't remember we'd met? I wasn't sure and didn't get a chance to think about it much because the funny face he was shooting his manager wiped my memory.

"Zac, this is my friend Deepa," I said, gesturing behind me.

She squeaked and waved.

Zac did that polite smile of his and greeted her briefly before turning back to me. "What time you get off, Peewee?"

"Four." I almost asked him what time he would be done

but decided against it. I didn't want him to assume I was asking because I wanted to hang out.

Before either one of us could get another word out though, the side door leading outside opened. My heart skipped a beat because I didn't want to get caught and bitched at. Fortunately, a face I didn't recognize appeared. The woman stopped at the sight of the four men standing there and said, "Oh. You're here. Great, come on. We'll get started."

I smiled up at Zac and took a step away from him as Trevor said something to the woman that I couldn't totally hear. "Well, have fun. It was nice meeting everyone."

Zac smirked, and I freaking failed to keep from smiling. "I'll text you later, kiddo," he told me.

I shrugged, not wanting him to feel forced to if he forgot or had other plans. There was no way in hell he'd think I assumed we'd see each other regularly. I was already surprised we'd seen each other as much as we had. Three times in less than two months? I didn't even get to see my own family members that often.

Plus, I had no idea what was going on with him and football.

But that must have been the wrong way to respond because I didn't miss the way his eyes narrowed, just a little, but enough. I got saved from whatever thoughts were in his head when his manager called out, "Zac!"

Those blue eyes settled on me, still thoughtful, as he took a step back. "I'll text you later."

Sure he would, but I still gave him a smile that time. "If you have time and want to. Have a good day."

The pensive face he was making went nowhere as he turned around and headed toward his friends and manager, slapping Trevor on the back. They all followed the woman through the door and into the building adjacent to the one I worked at. I thought Zac might have glanced over his shoulder one last time, but I wasn't positive since he ended up in the middle of his friends, or whoever the hell they were.

Turning around, telling myself not to expect shit, I found Deepa standing in the same spot she'd been in at the juice bar, her lips parted.

And in front of her, there was a regular member I recognized doing the same thing.

It was him who asked, "You know Zac Travis?"

And it was Deepa who asked, "How do you know Zac Travis?"

Well, I'd walked right into that shit. I headed back over to the front desk before my luck ran out and Gunner reappeared. "We grew up together." Or at least as together as two people with a seven-year age gap could grow up together.

Luckily—kind of—the same door that Zac had walked through opened, and we both instantly tried to look busy. I picked up the work phone and glanced down at the list Gunner had given me, and out of the corner of my eye, I saw Deepa drop to her haunches and make it seem like she was looking through a shelf. For what, I had no idea, but she looked busy, and it took everything inside of me not to make a face.

I knew she was going to load me up with questions later.

"I understand," I started saying into the receiver even though there was no one on the other end. "Thank you so much for your time. I hope you keep Maio House in mind if you ever move back."

Man, I was good.

And lucky, because just as I finished my bullshit spiel, I spotted Gunner in my peripheral vision, stopping just in front of the desk the second I set the phone back down into the cradle.

The jerk knocked on the counter, and it took a lot of

patience not to roll my eyes and instead look at him blankly. "How are the calls going?"

"Fine." I kept my face even. "Do you need something?"

"Can you stay late today?"

"No, I can't."

His jaw moved to the side a little. "There's no way?"

"No." He'd offered me a full-time position right after people had started quitting, and I had told him it was a hard no for me. Because it was.

His jaw moved a little more. "You know, it's really unfortunate that you can never seem to stay late when you're needed," the jerkface tried to say, picking at my mood, and blatantly ignoring the fact that I had stayed late recently.

Just not on days he asked.

"I stayed an hour late yesterday and three days ago...." I trailed off, calling him an asshole with my eyeballs.

"What good does that do me today?"

And folks wondered what drove nice, normal people to first degree murder.

I had always been a team player, but he was such a pain in the ass, I just couldn't find it in me to do him a solid. The two days I stayed late had been after he'd already been gone, otherwise I would have said no to that too. The new assistant manager, who had been hired after everyone else quit, was an all right guy, but none of us had any confidence in him protecting us from Gunner's wrath.

Then again, it wasn't my problem that they hadn't hired enough new people. I'd seen some come in to interview, and I wasn't sure why hardly any of them came back. Or maybe they had sensed the evil in him and not accepted the positions they'd gone in for.

"I'm sure I can find someone willing to get some overtime if you aren't."

Here we went again.

I kept my face blank and said, "I'm sure you can."

Asshole.

That freaking settled it. Come hell or high water, I was going to get the hell out of this place.

I was going to find Deepa another job somewhere else. If I got bored at home, I could learn a hobby. Maybe I could learn a language. Volunteer.

Gunner grimaced, clearly irritated, and pointed at the sheets I had in front of me. "Make sure you get through that list before you leave."

I didn't even bother giving him a fake sweet smile, instead settling for a nod. Just one. He didn't deserve more than that.

And, fortunately, about three seconds after he finished bitching at Deepa about keeping busy, that was when my phone vibrated with an incoming message.

I peeked at it the second he'd moved far enough away.

It was Zac. Again.

512-555-0199: You free tonight?

Tonight?

Me: Yes.

Why?

He answered my question with his next text.

512-555-0199: Can I pay you to take me to a dealership?

Frowning, I looked up to make sure no one was paying attention to me and then texted him a response.

Me: Pay me??

And why would he ask me and not Trevor or CJ or one of the other three hundred people he apparently knew?

512-555-0199: With money.

I made a face at my screen and thought about it for a minute.

Me: Get real. You're not paying me. I can take you. Let me know when you want to go.

512-555-0199: You sure?

I mean, I wasn't but... I was.

I could do it, so I would. If you could do something for others—at least decent human beings, not counting Gunner because he was a shithead—then you did it. It was that simple.

Me: Yes.

The snapping of fingers had me glancing up.

Deepa was glaring. "I think you've got some explaining to do."

Shit.

———

"Hi, CJ."

CJ full-on smiled at me as he opened the door. "Hi, Bianca." His gaze went straight to my hands.

My empty hands.

"I didn't bring any snacks. I haven't filmed yet," I told him. "I'm planning to at the end of the week."

Because it was true.

After that last conversation with Gunner, I knew I needed to get out of the gym. I needed to get *Deepa* out of there. She had a good heart, and she was smart and detailed, but there were a couple people who I didn't trust or like that she was too friendly with. She had moved to Houston for school, but I knew she hadn't registered for this upcoming fall semester. I kept on top of her because I knew no one else other than her mom did, but....

I had to pick my battles, like I was sure Connie had to do with me plenty of times.

I knew how lucky I'd been that, even though my parents hadn't been very active in my life, I'd had other people who stepped up and held me accountable. That rooted me. The older I got, the more I realized how important things like that were.

That was partially why I wouldn't just leave her knowing her only family member was a few hundred miles away.

If anything, I was just so much more grateful to have something waiting for me outside of the gym.

Hating my boss was exhausting. There were good parts and bad parts about focusing all of my time on The Lazy Baker, just like with every job. People talked a lot of shit in the comments section and in social media, it was *a lot* of work since I did just about everything myself, and it was a hell of a lot more stressful now. It hadn't been years ago. But that was before I'd started to see it as more of my future and less as a fun hobby I did on the side.

"There was no such thing as a perfect job," Boogie had told me one day when I'd gotten one of the first ugly comments on my videos and he'd found me crying.

But if I was going to get pissed off, at least it would be on my own terms.

And even though I had never started vlogging with any real expectations, it didn't mean I wasn't going to take it to the next level if I could. You didn't squander opportunities in life—at least I wouldn't.

So I was going to do this shit and do it right.

Part of that was to finish putting together my recipes and finally hire a photographer for my cookbook. I also needed to see about revamping my site so I could have more space for ad revenue on it. Lastly, I needed to make more business-conscious steps too, because I hadn't taken advantage of my reach until almost too late. I hadn't taken it seriously enough for too long.

But that was shit to think about at work or at home. My plan B, C, D, and all the ones after that. My future.

Anyway.

I was pretty sure the man who, now that I got to see him again without nerves, had to be around my age with big, brown eyes, and a couple of cystic acne scars on his cheeks, nodded once. "What are you going to make?"

I walked in and waited for him to close the door behind me. "I'm tweaking an old soup recipe, and I was thinking about trying to make brownies."

"Brownies?" Zac's roommate asked as we headed toward the kitchen. He had to be five-ten, maybe five-eleven, max.

I spotted a male figure dart from the kitchen in the direction of the corner where the stairs were. Who the hell had that been? I was pretty sure I'd seen gray pants and a white shirt. Hadn't that been what Trevor was wearing earlier? I wondered but focused back on CJ's question. "Yeah, but I don't want to use eggs."

CJ genuinely "hmmed" beside me. "What are you going to use instead? A flaxseed egg?"

A flaxseed egg? How many of my videos had he *seen?* I didn't use them that often. I glanced at him. "Nah. I was thinking bananas could work to hold everything together. What do you think?" I asked when we stopped in the living room and kitchen area. Zac wasn't around. I had messaged him on the way over, thinking it was better to give him some notice in case he was busy and needed to bail on me before I got here. But he had texted me back and hadn't said anything about being busy.

It was fine. It was cool. Maybe he was taking a crap.

The football player—I'd forgotten to look him up or ask Connie about him—planted his butt against the back of the straw-colored couch and aimed his dark brown eyes at me. "You didn't use eggs with your banana bread recipe either, and it held up okay in the video at least. It didn't work for me, but I bet it would hold your ingredients together."

"It didn't work for you?"

"I'm no good in the kitchen," he said, seriously. "You should try bananas."

How many things had he screwed up before? "I think I will. And I want to try not to use flour either."

"No flour for brownies?"

I smiled at him. "Everybody uses flour for brownies. I gotta try and make them different somehow."

"For a reason," Zac's roommate stated, sounding skeptical as hell.

"Yeah, but I don't want to.... Aww, don't make that face. I was thinking about using peanut butter or maybe almond butter for some healthy fats... but probably peanut butter because more people have that in their pantries."

"I like peanut butter." Some of the skepticism fell off his face, and his eyes stopped being so narrowed. "You're not going to use chocolate chips then?"

I shook my head. "No. I want to keep it to less than four or five ingredients." All of my recipes were as hassle-free as possible. That was part of my "thing" with my recipes.

He wrinkled his nose, and it made me smile again. "Cacao powder is going to be too bitter if you were thinking about using that."

Cacao powder. Look at this guy. He was going to make me swoon. "Yeah, I know. Cocoa powder might be all right though, and it's easier to find."

CJ gave me a thoughtful and disbelieving face, but he nodded after a moment.

"If they're decent, I'll bring them over," I offered.

"What are you going to bring over?"

I turned to find Zac crossing the living room, freshly showered and smiling at me. He was in his normal outfit, his face clean-shaved. "Flourless brownies, but only if they're decent." I slid his roommate a look.

CJ grunted, straightening off the couch he was leaning

against. "With bananas and no chocolate chips," he reminded me, making it seem almost like an accusation.

Zac stopped in front of me, and I only froze for a second before reaching up and putting my arms around his neck, his wrapping around the middle of my back as we hugged each other tight. Taking a step back after a second, I smiled up at Zac's face even as I told CJ, "Maybe it'll be pretty good. Who knows?"

That had CJ making a noise with his nose. "Like the first time you tried to make Funyuns?"

I stopped laughing.

The other man cracked a smile. "You smoked out your kitchen the first time, and then the second time, you spit out what you did make."

I could feel Zac's gaze on my face as I muttered, "There are some things you should leave to the professionals." I'd forgotten all about smoking out the damn kitchen. That homemade Funyuns fail had been my first screwup at my apartment. To be fair, even the second time, it had still been pretty disgusting, like sandpaper sprinkled with garlic and onion powder. I'd given up after that. Whatever magic they put into the chips was a secret and should be kept that way.

CJ snickered at the same time that Zac asked in a confused tone, those light blue eyes bouncing between his roommate and me, "You two already knew each other?"

It was CJ who replied. "No." The pause he took gave me enough time to glance at the other man. "You didn't watch that video?"

Hadn't I told CJ I was pretty sure Zac didn't know about my vlog? Well, it had been bound to happen eventually, especially with how much we'd been seeing each other. I scratched at my cheek and carefully crouched, pretending to tie my sneaker while I gave myself a couple seconds to figure out how the hell I was going to explain this.

"What video?" my old friend asked.

I grimaced at my black tennis shoe, but his roommate beat me to it again. "The Funyuns one."

"What Funyuns one? Like the chip?"

Yeah, he had no clue.

I took my sweet time finishing the knot that hadn't needed to be tied in the first place.

"On her vlog," CJ answered for me. "The Lazy Baker."

Shit. Well, there was the truth. I stood up straight and instantly caught the blue eyes that had swung toward me.

Zac was frowning a little bit. "What? Like on WatchTube?"

"Yeah."

All right, this had definitely not been the way I had hoped this would happen, but I guess it could have been worse.

Okay, I wasn't sure how it could have possibly been worse, but I was sure there was a way.

I had, on purpose, not told him something big when he'd specifically asked me how life had been going. To be fair, I hadn't thought we'd see each other again so soon. But none of those excuses mattered right then because I was busted in the worst way.

Then Zac glanced down at me, and I felt about three inches tall.

For what had to be about the twentieth time since we'd seen each other, I shrugged again, like *no big deal,* even though some part of my gut realized... well, that he might not think it wasn't a big deal that I had purposely skipped around a big part of my life.

Or maybe it was just my guilt for purposely not telling him when I'd had plenty of opportunities to do so.

I'd had good intentions, but they were hard to explain.

Lying had this ability of making a person feel like a piece of shit—sometimes a little piece of shit, sometimes a giant piece of shit, but a piece of shit nonetheless. And now my small piece of shit ass had to own up to what I'd done: not told him something that *was* important to me. Very important to me. Because I'd been an asshole. "I have a WatchTube channel, Zac. I film videos and upload them," I tried to explain to the confused man looking down at me. "I try to make things—food—for fun."

Okay, that was all a stretch. I had a schedule. I posted videos at the same day and time every week. They were all just about the same length. I picked my clothes out and ironed them before filming. Did my makeup with care. Straightened my hair. Spent hours editing each video. Answered hundreds of emails and comments a week. Worked on my website regularly. Haggled with sponsors who wanted me to promote their products in my videos.

I'd made money from it and a little bit of a name.

And I'd almost lost it at all. Keeping it had come at a really high cost. I'd wiped out my bank account for it. It was why I hadn't thought about quitting the gym until recently.

That handsome face swung toward me even more, eyebrows furrowing, and I could tell by the look in his eyes that he was genuinely thinking about what I'd just explained. "Why didn't I know that?"

Because he hadn't asked about me in years, but I didn't say that. I just shrugged. Again. "I don't really tell anyone about it unless they bring it up. Only one person at my job knows—the girl I introduced you to." I scratched at my nose again. "It's not a big deal," I tried to insist.

Out of the corner of my eye, I watched CJ's face screw up. "Don't you have a million subscribers?"

He wasn't helping, he wasn't helping *at all*, and the expression I shot him conveyed that. "Somewhere around there." It was more than that now, but....

Zac's frown got even deeper, and there was something in

his eyes that made my stomach clench. "You bake in the videos?" he asked.

"Bakes, makes meals, snacks, but the recipes are all off the top of her head, and she messes them up every once in a while," CJ explained for me, still not helping, but probably thinking that he was.

Bless his heart.

Well, I had brought this upon myself, and I had to own up to it.

"I make them up as I go along, and I don't write anything down until I'm in front of the camera," I confirmed. It always annoyed the shit out of me that people assumed I butchered recipes on purpose. "Messing up is part of what viewers like though. People like to watch other people fail." My most viewed videos were of my screwups without a doubt.

Zac's face was still twisted into a frown as he pulled his phone out from his pocket. "You're on WatchTube?"

Did he have to say it like that? All surprised? "Yeah, and Picturegram, but it's no big deal. You really don't need to look. Most of the videos are really short and have me cursing when I mess up. You're not missing out on any—"

"What's it called again? The Lazy..." my longtime friend cut me off as he focused on his phone.

"The Lazy Baker," I piped up, but my heart still clung to the fact that I'd been doing my videos for years, and if Zac had *genuinely* asked about me... well, Boogie would have probably told him all about it. He'd told other people about it, and apparently, he'd told him a couple other things.

Damn. That hurt a little. I could admit it.

All right, maybe more than a little bit.

Those blue eyes met mine, and I suddenly hoped he couldn't tell by my expression what I was thinking. *How could you not have asked about me in so long, Snack Pack? Huh? How?*

But if he could, he didn't zone in on it, because the next thing I knew, he asked, "You're called The Lazy Baker?"

Good. Fine. Good. I forced a little smile onto my face as I nodded. "I don't make anything that's too complicated or has too many ingredients."

And fortunately, *luckily*, one of my oldest friends—my oldest friend honestly that I wasn't related to—looked back down at his phone as he poked away at the screen, typing in who knows what. "I got it... Jesus Christ, Peewee. No big deal? It says you've got over four hundred videos uploaded on here!" he stated with a jerk of his head and enough surprise in his tone that I couldn't help but feel pride in what I had built, in what I had made and fought for. Maybe he hadn't cared enough to wonder about me, but I'd tried. For myself. For Mamá Lupe. I had done my best, and I had people who were proud of me and happy for me the entire time along the way.

Maybe I got embarrassed talking about it—bringing it up, mostly—but I was proud of myself, and I wasn't going to let him forgetting about me make me feel small now. I wasn't. Life was good despite the tiny shit I could change to make it even better.

Steadying that ache in my chest and forcing it away, I leaned over him and peeked at his phone. There were six million views on the first one. "Eh, they don't all have that many views. That one just went viral because my mom lit my hair on fire when we tried to make crème brûlée."

It had been a bittersweet day that one. My mom had been so happy... and then I hadn't heard from her for a month after that. I couldn't even say it was the first or the last time it happened. Same old, same old.

Those blue eyes slid to me.

And CJ *still* didn't help any. "The one you did with your cousin, I think you were making some no-bake cookies, that one had a lot of views too."

I knew exactly what video he was talking about, and even more pleasure filled my body.

There was nothing for me to feel sorry about. There really wasn't.

Zac blinked, oblivious, and I smiled at him, trying to get myself to move past this ache once and for all. *It is no big deal*, I repeated to myself, hoping I'd believe it the more I said and thought it. "Yeah, because he spit them out." Holding my breath and struggling to keep ahold of the not-ache I was still shying away from, I tried to get Zac's attention. *It isn't his fault. He didn't mean to hurt me.* "You know how dramatic Boogie can be."

But the expression on Zac's face—surprise mixed with maybe confusion or something close to it—kicked me in the back of the knees. "He never said a word," he admitted in a voice that had gone quiet. "He'd tell me he saw you or say you were doing okay, but that was it."

He had? Boogie had never said shit about Zac asking about me. Not once. Then again... he knew me better than just about anyone and would've known I didn't want to hear it. Actions spoke louder than words every day of the week.

He had every opportunity to find out for himself.

I lifted the shoulder farthest away from him, steadying myself some more. "It's really not a big deal. I'm sure you have better things to do with your time."

CJ made a noise as he got up. "I caught Amari watching one the other day between sets while we were working out."

Aww. That had me perking up. "Is that someone else you two know?"

It was Zac who answered in that still-funky voice. "Yeah. A rookie. He's a receiver that's been catching for me. He got drafted by the White Oaks."

Yeah, I had no clue who he was talking about. I'd only watched the draft—where each NFO team picked new players for their organizations—one year. The year Zac had been in it.

"Which video should I watch first?"

I said, "None of them," at the same time CJ piped up with "The no-bake chocolate chip cookies."

"Goddamn it, CJ," slid out of my mouth before I could stop myself. "I'm sorry, CJ. I meant it, but I'm still sorry."

The man laughed for the first time since I'd met him, and it was just as deep as his speaking voice. "We're good. But that one is my favorite. You should watch that one."

Beside me—and basically on top of me—Zac tapped on the fourth video down as I said, "You really don't need to."

His index finger paused on the screen, and I wasn't sure if I imagined the hurt in his tone as he asked, "You don't want me to watch 'em?"

"It's not that." It kind of was, and I was pretty sure we both knew it. "They're just goofy videos, and didn't you need to go to the dealership or something?" I wasn't sure what he needed to do. He wouldn't be buying a car when he wasn't sure where he would end up, right? I hadn't even seen proof that he *had* a car here either.

He ducked his head, his blue eyes moving from one of mine to the other and back again before he gave me a small smile that looked a lot more hurt than I would have expected. Or wanted. "How about one and we leave?"

Did he have to go off and make me feel bad? "Okay." Damn it. "All right... just one."

He slid me another small smile that was definitely off as his finger tapped on the Play button of his screen.

And inside, I cringed big-time. "*Hi, friends! It's me Bianca, The Lazy Baker, and I'm here today with a very special guest, my cousin, Boogie!*"

Oh God, I wanted him to stop it, and I had to force myself to peek at his face.

Zac was smiling faintly.

"*Hi,*" Boogie's voice came over the speaker.

"*We're going to be attempting to make no-bake chocolate chip cookies today. Wish us luck! Like with all my recipes, we're going to try and make this with the least amount of ingredients as possible to start. Our first ingredient is going to be—*"

"*Salted cashews,*" Boogie butted in.

"*One cup of salted cashews, and... drumroll, Boog....*"

"*Dates?*"

"*Yes, Boog, Medjool dates. Trust me. I'm thinking... 8 ounces. Might as well use the whole package so they don't go bad.*"

And it all went downhill after that.

But what made me smile was the laughter that bubbled out of Zac during the four-minute, *long version*, video. There was a quick one-minute long video I had uploaded to Picture-gram shortly afterward that was more of a highlight reel.

By the time the final product came out of the freezer fifteen edited minutes later, there were tears in Zac's eyes, and most surprisingly, at one point he slid an arm around my shoulders and was pretty much holding me hostage against his warm side as Boogie choked, "*Goddamn, B, this tastes like ass.*"

I didn't need to look at the screen to know that I had been turning red then as I replied, embarrassed like I always was and always would be when something came out freaking atrocious, "*How much ass have you tasted?*"

But as Zac wiped at his eyes, well... I didn't mind at all, especially not when he glanced at me with sparkling baby blues and shook his head. "Kiddo, I forgot about that mouth." One corner of his mouth went up. "You're adorable."

Oh.

Well.

I gave him a little smile. I was going to let the "adorable" comment go. "I mean, it all goes downhill from there, so don't think the rest of them get any better."

"I fuckin' doubt that, darlin'." Zac looked right into my soul then, his arm around me still. "I highly doubt that."

———

Zac acted kind of weird the entire ride over to the car dealership. I couldn't put my finger on exactly what he was doing that was strange, especially since I didn't totally know this adult version of him, but there was a tension there that was similar to the last time we'd seen each other at my apartment. And I was way too much of a chicken to ask what he was thinking.

Instead, I'd settled for asking him what he was going to do at the dealership... but kept the question about why he'd gone to me for a ride instead of someone else to myself.

"I dropped it off a couple weeks ago to have it checked out. There was a problem with the electronics," he answered. "I need to get it back just in case I have to move last minute."

Move last minute. Because he signed with another team, I guessed.

"Oh," I told him, trying to make it seem like I wasn't nosey as hell about details. "They didn't give you a rental?"

Out of the corner of my eye, I saw him shrug. "They offered me one, but Trev's never around, so I use his car when I need it."

That still didn't explain why he didn't ask for a car to get him, or why he didn't ask CJ or anyone else, but... maybe it was because I seemed like I had the least busy or important life? That was a bitchy thought.

"So...." I trailed off, telling myself for about the thousandth time that his career wasn't my business, but I was going to ask anyway. "Can I ask how your tryout in Miami went?"

He was staring out the window as he answered. "Fine."

Fine.

That was what I fucking got. I should have just shut the hell up and put two and two together.

Zac sighed and scrubbed at his forehead. "They weren't gonna sign me. Knew it the minute I got there. They were just usin' me as a threat to get their current QB to take less money. It was a waste of damn time."

I winced, regretting bringing it up. "I'm sorry."

The shoulder closest to me went up. "It's all right. At least they paid for my travel expenses, and I got to see some people I know."

"Well, I hope they suck this year for doing that to you."

I was pretty sure I heard him snort a little, but that was all he gave me.

So for the rest of the ride, I kept my questions and jokes to myself and instead turned up the radio. The dealership wasn't close enough for me to bother starting a podcast. It wasn't until I parked and looked at him expectantly, thinking he was going to get out and I could go on with my day, that he said, "Will you come in with me in case it isn't ready?"

Well... okay. I nodded.

We parked and headed in. Zac hadn't even taken three steps inside the service building when a man beelined straight for him. "Hello, Mr. Travis, thank you for coming in. Like I told you over the phone, we would have been more than willing to bring the car to you."

So then why...?

My old friend took the man's outstretched hand. "That's not necessary, but I sure do appreciate it. Is it ready?"

"Yes, sir, we just need you to sign off on the repairs. If you don't mind, our general manager is going to sit in while I review the paperwork with you... for customer satisfaction purposes."

For customer satisfaction purposes. Sureee. I'd bet that was normal.

The man introduced the general manager to Zac, and they started leading him to one of the closest offices before Zac stopped. "C'mon, Peewee."

He wanted me to go in with him? "I need to pee, but I'll wait for you out here." I had emails to respond to.

"You're sure?"

I nodded and returned his smile after he gave me one as he headed into the office, and I didn't miss how the show-room floor was suddenly filled with employees when a minute ago there hadn't been anyone. And they were all casually looking in the direction that the three men had disappeared into.

Problems of the rich and famous.

One bathroom break later, I spotted a snack station and crept over to it, grabbing one of the complimentary bottles of water just as I heard, "Hi."

There was a man and a woman standing a few feet behind me. "Hi."

It was the woman who smiled and went right for it. "Do you think Zac Travis would mind taking a picture with us?"

The fact they called him by his—mostly—full name made it really hard for me not to smile. It was weird. "I don't think so."

They nodded, and I smiled at them, waiting for them to say something else, but they didn't. And it got awkward. So I pulled my phone out and opened my email app, totally aware that they were both watching me and whispering to each other.

They probably thought I was his assistant, considering the women he'd been seen with in the past.

Pretty blondes.

Pretty redheads.

Pretty brunettes.

Yeah, he didn't have a type as long as they were pretty. I was still in my work clothes with makeup that had gotten rubbed off from how irritated Gunner made me, and I'd gotten about four hours of sleep last night.

I wasn't exactly his type.

This tiny ache pulled through my heart, but I ignored it.

Short girls with black hair were some guys' types though. I'd had five guys ask me to marry them over the years. Four of them I'd never met, and one of them I had actually considered marrying.

And it was right then that the tall Texan came out of the office, leaned to the side like he'd spotted me across the building, and called out, "Peewee!"

Yeah, Peewee. That was me. The girl of men's dreams.

I frowned as I headed over to him, the two nosey employees following behind, whispering to each other.

"That was fast."

His smile was knowing. "They made it really easy."

I raised my eyebrows at him and got two light brown eyebrows raised back at me. "I bet they did, Mr. Special. Excuse me," I joked, feeling pretty halfhearted about it.

"You're excused."

We smiled at each other, and it was nice. Familiar. Okay.

More than okay.

"Hi, Mr. Travis?" the woman I'd been speaking to earlier chirped up.

Zac turned to her, offering her a polite smile, the same one he'd given me before he'd figured out who I was weeks ago. "Yes, ma'am?"

The woman flushed red at the "m" word. "Would you mind taking a picture with us, please?"

"Sure will," my friend replied. "Both y'all or just one?"

"By ourselves," the man said as the woman replied with "Both." They both made a face at each other before the man said, "Both."

"I can take it," I offered.

By the time I handed the two people their phones back, there were more employees around who wanted one too, so I took more for them. It was a nonstop photoshoot there for a second. I might have peeked at Zac's butt a time or two while I was at it, wondering....

The instant he got done though, after saying bye to just about everyone he'd met with waves, handshakes, and a few winks thrown in, he walked over, smiling steadily.

I smiled back at him. "I like how nice you still are to people."

He stopped right in front of me. "Why wouldn't I be, darlin'? They're all good folks. Least I can do is take a few pictures. It don't cost me nothin'."

"Well, I'm sure there are people out there who wouldn't be so nice about it." I tilted my head back to take in that extremely handsome face giving me a little lopsided smile as his eyes moved over mine for the second time that day—like he was trying to remember it or something. "Can I ask you something personal?"

"Sure can."

"It's pretty personal," I warned him.

Zac tilted his head to the side. "I doubt you'd ask anything I haven't already been asked a million times, kiddo."

Okay then. "Did they have to tape your nuts up when you did the Anatomy issue?"

Zac's mouth dropped open, and I'd swear even his cheeks went instantly pink, and for a moment or two, he literally said and did nothing other than stare at me.

And then he hooted out a laugh that made me laugh too. "Bianca Brannen, my God—"

I was laughing so hard I wasn't sure if he understood me. "I asked! I warned you!"

Zac sputtered the entire walk back out of the dealership, torn between laughing and looking at me in disbelief before laughing some more.

He never did answer my question.

CHAPTER EIGHT

"Folks, it's official! Bryce Castro is OUT! The Houston White Oaks released a statement late last night. Castro reportedly suffered an elbow injury in an accident inside of his home. He's expected to be out at least six months. *This is devastating news for such a young team—"*

"Fucking hell, we're cursed," the man leaning against the counter a little to my left muttered to his friend as we all read the closed captioning on the television screen closest to us. My guess was that the juice bar employee had changed the channel while I'd been in the bathroom.

"How does somebody hurt their elbow inside their house?" the member's friend replied with a shake of his head.

I watched them carefully while I reached for the remote, which had been put back in its place, ready to change the channel if commentators started talking about Zac. I wasn't positive they would in the first place, but I was prepared. Just yesterday, I'd walked into work after lunch to see that the commentators on TSN were talking about him trying out for a team in San Diego.

I was overjoyed for him and for his next shot.

And I still felt really, really guilty that I hadn't just told him about my Lazy Baker business on my own. He hadn't said another word about it as we'd walked to where I'd parked my car. Instead, all he'd done was keep laughing about my question regarding tape and his nuts, and then he'd given me a big hug and invited me back over to his house. I had things I needed to do and declined though.

He'd texted me twice since, which had honestly still surprised the shit out of me. But he hadn't mentioned anything about another workout.

The first text had been:

512-555-0199: Saw your almond cake video. Is it as good as it looked? And was that Maw Maw's flamingo you had on?

It had made me smile... and made me a little nauseous. Him watching my videos was nice, but it made me feel self-conscious. Really self-conscious.

I'd texted him back that the cake *was* really good—the recipe was going in my book—and that if I had time, maybe I'd make him some the next time we saw each other. I also confirmed that the flamingo pendant I'd had pinned to my apron had belonged to his grandma.

He hadn't texted me back after that.

Two days later, I got another message.

512-555-0199: Paw-Paw told me to tell you thank you for his puzzle and card. Said to call him when you get a chance.

The text had come through while I had been busy at work, and I'd forgotten to text him back. But I had called Paw-Paw on my way home from work the day after that, and I'd heard Zac in the background telling him to tell me hi. Apparently, he'd gone back to Liberty Hill.

And that had been the last I'd heard from him. At least until yesterday when the news of his workout was reported.

So now all I knew was that he was in San Diego, hopefully getting another shot. Chances were, he wouldn't be coming back to Houston if things worked out. And that was good. It was great. The preseason was set to begin in about a week. It was crunch time for everyone. He needed to sign with someone, and he had to do it soon. I wanted that for him, even if it meant... well, whatever it meant. That we wouldn't see each other again for a while.

No pressure on him or anything. It was just his whole life hanging in the balance of a workout—a tryout, whatever it was called.

"What the fuck are they going to do now?" the voice of one of the members snapped me out of my memory of the day before.

I glanced at the guy with his back to me before plastering a smile on my face as a totally different member came in through the doors, scanning her pass with a quick, "Hey, Bianca" that I managed to return, distractedly.

After that, I glanced at the digital clock on the wall. I didn't know what time his workout was supposed to start, but....

I hesitated for a second... thinking about it... then decided just to go for it. I peeked around the gym, making sure Gunner wasn't visible, and then pulled my phone out from underneath the keyboard. It only took a second to type up a text.

Then I deleted it and wrote another one.

He had come over. He had apologized. He had asked enough questions about my past to seem genuine. For some strange reason, he'd asked me to take him to the dealership instead of his manager or his roommate or one of his hundreds of friends in Houston.

Friends were supportive, and I really did want to try and do better, at least this one last time.

Especially since, from the way things had gone the day I'd taken him to the dealership, I wasn't the only one who thought our friendship was like riding a bike. Some things were easy. And there were some people in life that you just... clicked with if you had the chance. It just so happened that Zac was one of the most likable people I'd ever met. I just wouldn't forget that he got along with everyone.

And so did I, for the most part—minus Gunner, but nobody liked him.

So I was going to keep cheering my friend on, I decided, and sent him the message.

Me: You still got it, old man.

See? It wasn't worded to where he would feel obligated to respond, and if he didn't, I wouldn't get disappointed. I hadn't the second to last time he didn't text me back. It was good enough, and I was pleased. I had tried.

Freaking luckily, I managed to stash my phone back under my keyboard about three seconds before the side door opened and Gunner the Micromanaging Butthole stepped inside with one of the other new owners trailing after him.

I grabbed a stack of flyers sitting on top of the counter and started straightening them so it wouldn't look like I was just standing there. You know, because organizing and restacking things was time consuming. Right.

I was going to get out of here. One day soon, damn it.

Just as I started straightening up the next stack over— pamphlets for personal training—out of the corner of my eye, I saw Gunner and the Other Asshole Owner steer straight toward the desk. By some miracle, the two members who had been busy talking about the White Oaks said something about the team that caught Gunner's attention at the exact second he and Asshole #2 stopped in front of the counter.

He didn't even look in my direction before turning around

to face the television that the members were watching; Asshole #2 did the same thing.

"No fucking way," Gunner muttered, eyes glued to the screen.

"He's out?" Asshole Owner #2 asked him, like he couldn't read the headline on the screen where it said *Castro Suffers Elbow Injury, Out 6 Months.*

"What the hell? Fisher is all right, but he's no Castro," Roy muttered, referring to someone whose name was Fisher. The backup quarterback? Years ago, Houston had a team called the Fire, but they moved to North Carolina. Luckily, before anyone could miss them too much, the White Oaks had been born.

I kept my gaze forward, hearing the slight vibration of my phone and trying to zone out the two jerks who I hoped weren't around in case the commentators started talking about Zac. And that was how I spent the next fifteen minutes: trying to keep my face neutral as they talked about quarterbacks and the White Oaks.

If anything, I was going to consider myself lucky that the injured quarterback was enough of a distraction that Asshole 1 and 2 forgot whatever it was they were coming over for, and they left when one of the MMA guys came in and got their attention. They followed him into the next building. Thank God.

That was when I snuck my phone back out, in between members, and saw a message that had come in.

512-555-0199: That vote of confidence...

512-555-0199: Thanks darlin

I thought about what else I wanted to tell him for a second before actually sending it.

Me: I'd say good luck, but you don't need it. XOX.

There. More messages that weren't pressured at all. And I'd carry that XOX on my shoulders with pride. I meant it.

Part of me figured it wouldn't be unwelcome either based on the number of hugs he'd given me the week before. If this was the last time we messaged for a while, at least I'd put my love and support out there for him.

In a world where people lived for criticizing the shit out of each other, at least I'd hope he knew that there were some people out there who were always proud of him. Who would always root for him. Maybe we weren't perfect people, but nobody was. We had both tried—now—and that was something.

My job, as his friend, was done.

I just really hoped he got signed.

———

"Do you need my help finding you a date or what?" my sister asked me hours later, just as I managed to finally plop down in the middle of my couch with a plate of leftover beef, quinoa, and potato soup. Crossing my legs under me, I flexed my toes to get my feet to ache just a little less after a twelve-hour day. The employee who was supposed to come in after me had called in, and since it was Deepa working the juice bar, I'd offered to stay so that she wouldn't be totally screwed over.

But now I was tired and partially regretting my decision; my feet, shoulders, and lower back were aching me good. I wasn't used to working long days anymore, just a few hours here and there. The good thing was, I was off tomorrow.

Squirming deep into the couch, I scooped some food into my mouth, and with it full, grumbled, "I really don't think I need a date. It's a freaking quince, Connie, not.... I don't even know what the hell you'd need a date for. Nothing. I can go anywhere by myself."

"Bianca," my sister muttered, something banging in the

background. She had to have pulled the phone away from her face because her yell was muffled. "*Yermo! What the hell are you doing up there? Breakdancing? Don't you dare break the sheetrock again!*"

I snorted into the phone and waited until I could hear her breathing before asking, "He broke the sheetrock?"

She huffed something that sounded like *fuck* under her breath before coming back onto the line. "I didn't send you a picture? He did it last week. Stuck his whole damn foot in the wall."

I laughed. "I love that kid. Tell him to record himself and send it to me."

That got me a groan. "He kicked Tony in the face a week ago when they came over and gave him a black eye."

Imagining my little cousin Tony with a black eye made me snort again. Tony was a pain in the ass and always had been. "He could be into crack, Con, and Tony probably needs another kick to the face. *Anyway*, I really don't think I need a date. I might be there for an hour or two max before someone gets on my nerves and I sneak out."

My sister didn't say anything for a second before saying, "My money is on Tía Licha."

"So is mine." A memory of the last time I'd seen that aunt came to me all of a sudden, and I snorted again. "What did she tell you when we saw her last time? That you needed to start using under-eye cream?"

My freaking sister growled. "No, that was the time before, two Christmases ago. Last time, at Maggie's wedding, she came up to me, touched my chin and asked if two weren't enough."

I had to grip the shit out of my bowl so that I wouldn't topple it as I started laughing my fucking ass off. *Yeah, that was exactly what had happened.*

"Shut up."

I didn't. "Don't forget she came up to me and pinched my stomach and tried to hand me some fat-burning pills she'd smuggled," I tried to tell her... knowing she'd definitely still had it worse. I'd been standing across the room from her when the aunt we both had always dreaded had cornered her, and I'd left her to suffer through it.

Mostly because she would have done the same thing if it had been me she'd gotten.

At least one of us had gotten away unscathed.

Still.

I fucking laughed at the memory of Tía Licha poking at Connie's chin while she bitchfaced her, trying her hardest to be polite and not whack her hand away like she had really wanted.

"So you want Tía Licha to get all judgy about you getting old and not having a boyfriend?"

I laughed as I chewed my food. "She's just jelly I'm single and have my whole life ahead of me."

"She is. I saw Tío Rudy in his underwear that one time, remember? She's been missing out. Like... big-time."

We both cracked up.

"*Mooooooom! I forgot! I need to take cupcakes to school tomorrow! Can you make some?*" my niece yelled from somewhere in the background.

Connie growled into the line. "Holy fuuuuu... Peewee, let me call you back."

We both knew she wasn't going to call me back.

But I laughed. "Okay, be nice to my girl. Bye."

"Bye," she said. I heard a slice of a "*Luisa, what the—*" before she hung up.

I was smiling to myself as I hit Play on the remote and settled in to watch another episode of the Turkish drama I still hadn't gotten through.

As soon as I finished eating though, I grabbed my laptop

and went through the list of recipes I had been slowly working on for the book I was hoping to release. Someday.

No, not someday. One day soon. I'd publish it myself since none of the agents I'd sent queries to had responded, I'd decided months ago.

And that *one day* was what kept me working on my computer, rewriting a couple of summaries at the top of the recipes I was planning on using because I didn't feel like doing much else.

At least until I passed out on the couch with my laptop. I woke up with a jolt and checked my screen, telling myself that I wasn't hoping Zac had sent a text with an update and that was mostly true. I wasn't *hoping*. Just wishing that he had good news.

But there wasn't a message. He hadn't updated his Picturegram account either, I learned after I'd scrolled through my feed. There was nothing about him or San Diego or anything.

Fingers crossed.

Then I went to bed.

———

Three days later though, I found myself pulling my car into an open spot in front of the house Zac was living in. I didn't want to park in the circular driveway. There were three cars parked in it, including the BMW that he had gone to pick up, and I didn't want to block anyone in.

Grabbing the big insulated bag I used when I bought cold stuff at the grocery store, I hefted the weight of the four containers inside of it: two were for the frozen yogurt I'd made the day before, and the other two were of cake. Two for Zac and two for CJ. No pressure.

I'd been surprised as shit when the night before, I'd been

tweaking the almond cake recipe I'd sort of nailed in a video a couple years ago—the same one Zac had asked about—when my phone had beeped with an incoming message. Like fate.

512-555-0199 had stared back at me on my phone screen. Along with a message of: **You free?**

And that was how I found myself walking across a front lawn to get to the pavestones that led up to the front door before ringing the doorbell and taking a step back to wait. I wasn't surprised to see a familiarish figure approaching. I waved.

CJ's slightly smiling face greeted me right back as he unlocked and then opened it.

"Hi, CJ."

"How's it going? Come in." He tipped his head toward the inside of the house.

"I'm good. How are you?" I asked, stepping in and holding my hand out.

CJ dipped his chin as he shook it. "All right." He closed the door. "Zac hollered down, said to give him a minute."

I followed after him down the hall into the main room. "Okay." Unzipping the bag in my hand, I pulled out the two containers I'd brought just for him with "CJ" written on a note at the top of them and held it out when we stopped in the kitchen. "Here. I brought you some frozen yogurt I made. It's strawberry. The other one has strawberry almond cake in it." I smiled. "They had frozen strawberries on sale, and I went a little apeshit."

Those brown eyes lit up, and he didn't waste a second before plucking them out of my hand. I was pretty sure I wasn't imagining the fact he pulled them toward that wide chest hidden beneath a gray college T-shirt and held it there either. "Is it as good as your nice cream?"

He'd made my nice cream too? How else would he know it

was good? I'd ask him later. Maybe. If there was a later. "It's different, but it's good, I think. But I'm biased."

I was pretty positive he really did pull the containers in even closer to his chest. "Thank you." Brown eyes flicked down to his frozen yogurt. "You made it for a vlog?"

"Yeah. The almond cake is one I made before; I just changed a couple things to the original recipe."

"By yourself?"

I nodded. "I don't have anyone who can do one with me any time soon." And because I had no shame, I grinned at him. "If you ever want to do one, let me know. But no pressure."

The buff man blinked. "Serious?"

"I'm for real, if you're for real. Anytime you want, but you don't have to."

CJ nodded, but I could tell he was thinking about it.

Or maybe he was thinking I was out of my damn mind.

"Sorry about that, Peewee," echoed through the living room and into the kitchen.

Feeling high from CJ hinting that he'd made my recipe and sounding so interested in guest starring in a video, and also a little bad because I figured Zac hadn't gotten good news about the team in San Diego since he was back here, I glanced at Zac who was walking across the living room from the direction of the back staircase and gave my longtime friend a smile that was even bigger than any of the ones I'd given him before.

Here. Now. Trying. That was my motto with this guy from now on. The past was mostly still in the past.

"It's okay," I called out to him, sucking up the bright expression on his face and trying not to notice how his old college T-shirt fit him, showing off that long, muscular torso.

He was smiling as he came up to me, and we both reached for each other at the same time. My arms went for his neck, going up to my tiptoes, and those long, strong arms of his wrapped around my back, pulling me into his chest, letting me get a solid feel of all those lean, hard muscles from his throat down to his hips pressed against me. I was pretty sure even his cheek went to the top of my head.

He squeezed me just as tight as I squeezed him, and I knew I didn't imagine the deep breath he let out right before saying into the top of my head, "You sure do give the best hugs."

"You do too." Because he really did. They were so warm and tight.

It was me who pulled back then, but it was him who flashed those pretty white teeth as he looked down at me. "I was running late and popped into the shower real quick. Sorry 'bout that."

"No big deal. CJ was—"

Settling onto my feet, I turned. CJ was gone. So was his frozen yogurt and his almond cake.

Okay.

I snapped my fingers. "I brought you a few pieces of that almond cake you asked about and some homemade ice cream. Well, it's kind of ice cream, it's frozen yogurt. If you want it. But if you don't want it, or you don't like it, it's okay. CJ might eat it. I brought him some too, but he took off with it, I guess."

Zac had started frowning about halfway through me talking, and it was full-fledged at the end of it, wiping off every trace of the beaming face he'd been shooting at me when he'd first come into the kitchen.

"What?" I asked him.

His frown was only a little subtle. "I've been meanin' to ask, what's up with you?"

"What do you mean?"

Zac lifted both hands in the air, index and middle finger up and formed into quotation marks. "*If you want it...*"

What?

He kept going with the air quotations. "*If you want to... you have better things to do with your time*," he repeated, throwing out words I knew I'd used on him over the last few times we'd been around each other, but hadn't realized he'd actually noticed.

Shit.

Zac's head tipped to the side. "What's up with all that, darlin'?" he asked, sounding very, very careful all of a sudden.

Double shit.

CHAPTER NINE

"Meant to ask you the other day when you said somethin', but it slipped my mind," he drawled on, definitely thoughtfully, looking at me real close in this way that was too observant.

I'd been that obvious?

Those light blue eyes got even more watchful, and I couldn't trust the way one corner of his mouth slid a bit to the side.

I scratched the tip of my nose. "Nothing."

Yeah, that lopsided smile totally dropped like a freaking fly in the blink of an eye, and I wasn't ready for what came out of his mouth next. "I've been thinkin' a lot about it, you know."

Thinking a lot about what?

"I saw you follow me on Picturegram."

Yeah, he went for it. In a too-still voice with that piercing gaze aimed straight at me.

How did he know I followed him online? Had he finally looked me up?

"Why didn't you tell me you lived here? Last I heard, you were in North Carolina with Connie," he kept going, but for some reason, even though he was looking at me, it didn't feel aimed in my direction... more like in general, like it was the first time he'd really thought about *that*. "Why didn't anybody else tell me either, kiddo?"

And that didn't exactly hurt my feelings. If there was one thing I'd learned over vlogging the last few years, it was my limits for the things that could actually hurt me. I didn't flinch over people picking apart my looks or personality anymore, but it had hurt me for weeks back in the day. A lot of comments had robbed me of sleep. People being mean had made me want to quit a time or ten. Fifty. A hundred. A thousand.

So now....

Well, now, Zac taking ten years to question what had split up our friendship had the ability. To an extent. Only because I'd beat the reality into my heart over the years.

All I managed to do was give him a wonky smile, mostly because I didn't know how to answer him.

Nah, I just didn't want to answer him.

The easygoing man who had just been smiling at me minutes ago raised those tawny eyebrows, his expression wary, voice careful, trying to sound easygoing but just... not. "Why's that?"

I scratched at my temple, hoping to play this off. "Because we hadn't talked in ten years?"

God, I was the worst.

But what did he want me to say? Did he want to pretend the past hadn't happened? Did he want to pretend he hadn't ignored my texts for nearly two years until I'd given up?

And why was I starting to sweat?

I thought I was over this. I just thought we were both going to move forward from the past and pretend it hadn't happened. That had been fine with me. Better than fine with me. It was easy.

Zac's eyes narrowed. "I've known you since you were three, Peewee. Your cousin's the closest thing I've got to a brother," he stated steadily like I didn't know all of this. "Why wouldn't he tell me we were in the same city?"

Because you hadn't asked about me in forever. Because you hurt me when I was seventeen and forgot about me. But mostly, because he knew I didn't want to see you, and maybe Boogie loves us both, but he loves me more.

But I swallowed my words, swallowed my heart, and figured I was an adult and had nothing to hide. I knew how things had gone, and if he wanted to bring this up? Well, he was a grown man too, and we could both take responsibility for our actions.

"I didn't want to bother you after so long."

So long. Nearly a decade ago, and didn't that freaking still sting no matter how much I told myself that it didn't? I didn't want to do this. Didn't want to talk about this.

But Zac wasn't on the same page. "Bother me?" he asked slowly.

"You're busy."

His eyes narrowed. "*Bother me, Bianca?*"

Did he have to say it like that? And did he *really* want to do this? With that tone and that expression and everything?

"You're serious?" he asked like he could read my freaking mind.

Okay, apparently he did want to do this. All right. "Yes, bother you. I know that you're busy. I know that you have a lot on your mind, and that you're always meeting people and people are always wanting things from you...." And *holy shit,* that *did* sting. "I did know you were here, and I didn't want to bother you. I didn't see a point when you have enough other things going on."

And maybe, just maybe he might have asked about me a time or two, but he could've tried to find me on his own. Find out how I was doing on his own. He could have just… texted me. That part was on him.

The man who had smiled at me so wide a second ago was gone.

He wanted this, right? Maybe I wouldn't—couldn't—give him everything, but I could do some of it. Half of it. "I wouldn't want you to feel obligated to see me or anything like that." All right, that wasn't so bad. "We haven't seen each other in ten years, Zac. I didn't want to just barge back into your life. Everyone knows you're busy—they know I'm busy—and that we hadn't spent time together in forever. We hadn't talked in so long I'm sure Boogie didn't think you'd care that we were close by. And he was out of the country when you got here."

Apparently, he only listened to part of what I said. "You think seein' you would be an obligation?" he asked, still speaking slowly, and frowning.

Well, when he put it like that…. He wanted the truth, right? I wasn't going to take the entire blame. "Yeah," I confirmed. "Yeah, I do. You've felt obligated toward me ever since the snake thing." It didn't hurt me to admit it. I'd come to terms with it.

But he blinked. "No. I mean, yeah, but no…."

I just looked at him and watched his eyebrows drop down into a harsh, hard expression.

"I've asked about you."

It took everything in me not to snort. How hard had he really tried? He could have looked me up at any freaking time. It wasn't like I hid my existence.

"I've asked about you a bunch of times since you stopped textin' me back."

Since I stopped texting him back? What kind of alternate reality was he living in?

But I had to answer because we were in this, and I wasn't

going to hide. I'd messed up in a way. I had bothered him too much when he'd been busy; I could take responsibility for it. But that was the worst I'd done, and I'd go to my grave thinking that. "Since *I* stopped texting you back? That's not how it happened. I didn't just disappear, Zac. I've been around." I tried to smile at him, but I failed pretty miserably because this hurt a lot.

"I see Paw-Paw once a year, and I've only seen your mom a few times." I didn't know why neither one of them had never mentioned it to him. But they hadn't. I snuck in and out of conversations that revolved around him, avoiding them so that I could avoid talking about seeing him. More like not seeing him. I didn't want to talk about it or make it seem like a big deal.

At the end of the day, it had been Zac's decision not to get in contact with me.

Not in years.

He'd been busy. I understood. Why would he have worried and sat there and wondered how his old friend was doing when he had so many new ones? It wasn't like I ever wondered what my friends from elementary school were up to.

But that had been different, the voice in my head whispered. And I knew she—that voice—was right. But....

This wasn't what I had wanted or why I had come over. I didn't want to talk about it. All I wanted was to move on, to be fine with where we were now.

But apparently Zac did want to talk about it after so freaking long.

"Why *haven't* we seen each other?"

You're just a little kid. Zac has better things to do, honey. Do you understand? He's in the NFO now. He has more important people to spend time with. Don't take it personally.

The words echoed in my head once and then twice as Zac's Adam's apple bobbed again in front of me.

But that hadn't been totally it, had it? It had just been the beginning. The tip of the iceberg.

Him ignoring me had happened afterward, after the seed had been planted and watered and germinated.

I couldn't help it; I got defensive. For the younger Bianca who had loved her friend a little too much. That was the most she had been guilty of. "You're asking me why?"

That blond-bristled chin dipped.

"Because we hadn't been in the same city at the same time in years," I told him, which was also part of it, and also not the whole of it. I'd just made certain we weren't. Whenever he played in Houston, I made it a point to go visit Connie so that I'd have an excuse not to be around if Boogie came into town to watch. I knew my sister was fully aware of what I was doing, but that was just because she knew me too well.

But that excuse wasn't enough for him apparently. "But why? I know you had to have come visit." He took a deep breath, and I could tell, I could tell he was thinking, thinking, and thinking—thinking about me and him and how ten years had gone by somehow and he hadn't realized it. "We used to see each other all the time," he said, like I didn't fucking know that. "Then, one second to the next, you dropped out of my life, moved across the country, and I didn't see you or hear from you in forever."

Uh.

Something hot and spiky appeared in my throat, but I ignored it. At least I tried my best to. Because this wasn't what I wanted to talk about now or ever. "Yeah, back when things were less complicated we saw each other a lot. I've been busy. You've been busy. I moved to North Carolina because I didn't have anywhere else to go after I graduated high school, Zac."

Because my parents had decided to leave just as quickly as they'd arrived, and my grandmother had been buried, and I hadn't wanted to live with my aunts and uncles long-term.

Unlike him, I'd never forgotten him; I'd just kept going with a Zac-shaped hole in my heart.

And it had been the other way around. He'd dropped out of *my* life. None of this had been my fault.

But his "So?" cut me straight down the center. Deep and unforgiving. "Before you left, I texted you, and you never wrote me back. Then you stopped comin' over with Boogie, and I know I asked, but I don't remember what he'd say. I did ask about you. *He* told me you moved. Not you."

More like, he *thought* he'd texted me, but he hadn't. And if he had asked about me, then maybe Boogie had given him some bullshit answer he'd accepted, and he'd moved on with his life. Not wanting details. Not caring about more.

Dear God, that kinda hurt. But it was bullshit. Straight-up, stinky bullshit.

And it sure as hell didn't belong to me.

"I tried reaching out to you. Over and over again. Friendships go both ways," I told him in a voice that sounded so small it hurt me even more.

I could see it on his features. In his eyes. Him still thinking. Processing. Trying to remember what? If I was lying? Or trying to piece together his fault in all this?

Why couldn't we just... move on? I'd fucking talked myself into it. I'd told myself this was fine the way it was. That I could go forward, but all this was doing was hurting me. Making me feel small and forgotten—two things I hadn't ever wanted to feel again. Like I hadn't mattered enough, and maybe I still didn't... even though the reasonable part of my brain knew that wasn't true.

But the happy, smiling man was still totally gone as his eyes roamed mine, searching and searching. "I tried." He cleared his throat. "I tried textin' you. I swear, darlin'. I know I did. I—"

Whatever was in my chest blew up, taking up more and more space, and this wasn't what I had *wanted*... but that was life. Giving you what you wanted and didn't want without a single shit.

"You didn't." Ah, shit. Well, here we were. "You didn't text me back for years, Zac. You never answered my calls either. I never got anything from you, and I tried." And it was a lot harder than I ever could have imagined to lift my shoulder and make it seem like when it had happened, it hadn't bothered me. But I wasn't lingering on this, damn it. I wasn't. I wasn't forgotten. I did matter. "Look, it was a long time ago. It's not important anymore."

"No." He stood up even straighter, making our height difference that much more apparent when he had to tip his chin down to look at me. "This does matter. I know I texted you. I wouldn't have ignored any of your messages."

I raised both my eyebrows at him as my chest ached. Because I had missed him. Because I knew without a doubt that I had tried. I hadn't been the one to disappear. To forget.

He had, and he was reminding me. Hurting me.

Without meaning to.

But he was still doing it.

I had loved him, thought the world of him, and he'd left me behind—to follow his dreams, sure.

But he'd still forgotten.

After all the times he would roll his eyes at my parents when they would barge into mine or Connie's lives once a year, acting like they were so happy to be around and that it didn't matter they never were... he had done the same thing in a way.

"No," he repeated himself, staring at me with those soft blue eyes. "I wouldn't have. Maybe I would've taken a minute textin' you back, but I would've—" His mouth opened and closed. Even his nostrils flared. Pink tinged his cheeks, and he shook his head aggressively. "I would have gotten back to you, darlin'. I wouldn't have forgotten—"

He shut his mouth.

That instant, he shut his mouth.

Because he realized it then. He *had*. Maybe not ten years ago, but along the way he had.

Because he had stopped asking about me at some point.

Maybe in his imagination he'd texted me back or messaged me. Maybe once, maybe twice. But it had happened. Maybe he'd had every intention of calling me back, but that hadn't happened either. I had stopped reaching out but only after he had.

And yeah, that stung. It stung a lot. So much that I had to suck in a breath and hold it and stare into his eyes because I wouldn't let myself do any less. I was Bianca. I was The Lazy Baker. And I made my own destiny. I made my own choices.

Maybe some people forgot about me, outgrew me, or never had room for me in the first place.

But I had fucking *tried*. With all of them. With every single person, I'd put in effort.

And it was by some freaking miracle, my phone rang right then.

I didn't hesitate. I didn't wait. I reached into my purse and pulled out my phone, looking at Zac's thoughtful, disturbed face as I did it. **BOOGIE IS MY FAVORITE** flashed across the screen, and I met those baby blue eyes as I hit the green icon and pulled the phone to my face.

I had tried with him, with Zac, and I'd take that to the grave with me.

"Hey, Boog," I answered cautiously, meeting Zac's gaze head-on.

"B, I'm driving, but I have a quick question for you," my

cousin replied. There was so much background noise, I could tell he was driving. "Do you know any videographers in Austin?"

Relief filled my stomach. I was worried something bad had happened for him to actually call again.

"Um, no. But I know a few people in Houston that could do a great job if they're willing to drive up there," I told him. "For what? Your—" I almost choked on the word. I had purposely tried not to think about him getting married since he'd dropped the news on our asses, but being reminded of it —of him marrying someone I had no fondness for even though she was expecting my future niece or nephew, and I realized I needed to get over it—soured my stomach.

But this was my cousin, who was the closest man I had in my life, so I was going to suck all kinds of shit up for him.

Even if a part of me died inside.

This was his life, and he knew what he was doing. Marrying a cheating asshole. A cheating asshole who he'd forgiven.

So.

"For your wedding?" I finally got out.

Either I did a great job hiding the strain in my voice or he was pretending not to hear it. "Yeah, for the wedding." He said something, but it didn't sound like it was meant for my ears, and I was pretty sure he was talking to his fiancée. "Let me call around here then, and if I can't find anybody, I'll hit you up for those numbers. We called this one company, and they're already booked that far ahead."

I caught Zac's gaze. He was staring at me, his forehead lined, lips pinched tight. "The good ones always are. Let me know though," I told him.

There was more whispering, then, "Okay, thanks, B."

I paused. "Hey, did you tell your mom about the baby yet?"

He made a sound that nearly came out as a snort. "*Yes.* She smacked me upside the head and then gave me a hug. She's excited."

"I hope she smacked you hard."

My cousin snickered. "I bet you do. I'll text you later, all right?"

"Okay, love you, bye."

"Love you too. See you," my cousin said just as Zac held out his hand.

"Uh, wait a second, Boogie," I muttered before slowly handing my phone over.

Zac took it, meeting my gaze dead-on as he said into the receiver, "*Boog? It's Zac.... Yeah, we're hangin' out. I've got a question for you that's buggin' me. Why didn't you tell me Peewee lived in Houston?.... What?.... No—*" He stopped talking, pulled the phone away from his face, and said, "He hung up on me."

"Boog hung up on you?"

Those light blue eyes flicked up to mine. "Yeah. He said he wasn't gettin' in the middle of this and we both needed to sort it out ourselves and hung up."

I blinked.

He blinked.

Well.

I guess I should have seen that coming. I couldn't even say I blamed my cousin. This was between Zac and me, and he didn't deserve to be caught up in the middle of it more than he already had.

Shit balls.

My hand went to the back of my neck as I looked him in the eye again, resignation pumping through my blood steadily. "Look, Zac, I don't want to fight with you. That was all a long time ago and—"

Why the hell was he shaking his head?

"What?"

Zac took a step forward, that frown back on his smooth face. "I don't wanna fight with you either, darlin', but that's not what we're doin'."

"I was pretty sure that's what we'd been doing."

Those tawny eyebrows went up. "No, we were *discussin'* what happened."

"Discussing?"

"Yeah."

"Zac—"

"Bianca."

I rubbed at the back of my neck some more. "Look—" I tried again, but again he cut me off as he stepped forward and locked his gaze on mine, face intent.

"Is that why you've been actin' like yourself sometimes and like we're strangers the rest of the time?" he asked quietly. "Why you didn't wanna tell me about your Lazy Baker? Why you've hardly wanted to tell me anything?"

Acting like myself? What? Joking with him? And did he really need to point out the fact that I had been cagey and he'd noticed? "Is what why?" was what I decided to pick at first.

That cute chin angled upward just a little as he stared at my face way too closely. I had to fight the urge to tuck my hair behind my ear as those light blue eyes roamed over my face like they had been since we'd started seeing each other again. "You thinkin' I never texted you back."

My chest hurt.

"Is that why you're so tense around me, darlin'? Why you're always sayin' bye like it's the last time you're ever gonna see me?"

He'd noticed that too?

The arched eyebrow he was aiming at me said, "*Yeah, I noticed.*"

And my face said, "*What do you want me to say?*"

And there we were. At a standstill. Because I hadn't done anything wrong, and in his head, the only thing wrong he'd done was forget about me. *Eventually.* Because he had pretty much sworn he'd texted me and that I hadn't responded. Because he'd asked about me, supposedly, and no one had given him details.

Yeah, that still stung. Thinking it over and over again didn't help ease it. Not really.

Not at all.

Zac took a step closer, and I felt something light brush my forearm. "Peewee, I don't know what the hell happened, but I know there's no way I wouldn't have texted you back eventually. And I swear on Paw-Paw's life, I reached out to you too and never heard back. I thought you were busy, thought you were grievin' Mama Lupe too since you had moved to be with Connie after you finished school and were settlin' in. I *know* I texted you to check in with you. It hurt my feelings real good when I didn't hear back from you either, kiddo, but I thought maybe you needed some space. Maybe you didn't want a reminder like me...."

Yeah, it was *still* stinging.

"But I swear on my Maw-Maw's grave, maybe I would've taken my time if I was busy or somethin', respondin' to you, but there's no goddamn way I would've done somethin' like that for long."

Why was it hurting worse with every word out of his mouth?

"You sure you were messagin' me and not somebody else? You sure you didn't just forget about me?"

And that had me staring back at him. "Unless you changed your number back then, I had the same one I was always reaching out to you on, Zac." But that suddenly got me thinking. Had he changed his number and he'd forgotten to tell me? It wasn't like I had gotten some message back saying the number wasn't active anymore... but that had been so long ago, had that even been a thing back then?

Did that make sense?

"I've changed my number a few times, when somebody's figured out it's mine, but I don't remember doin' it that long ago," he kept going, nailing me with that intense expression that felt like looking at an eclipse. "I know I would've told you if I'd changed it and your messages would've been on it. *I know it.*"

But he hadn't.

I knew without a doubt in my mind that I'd texted him. If he'd forgotten to tell me, or Boogie, that was one thing, but it just didn't make sense. We had texted once a week back then. I wouldn't have been all the way at the bottom. He wouldn't have forgotten about me in a month if I'd kept blowing up his phone.

And *oh my God* that really did sting like crazy.

I didn't want to do this. I didn't want to bring this shit back up. I didn't want to talk about this anymore. It was done. There was nothing we could do to go back in time.

"Look, I don't know what happened, but I know I messaged you. Over and over again. Not like every day or anything, but like we used to, you know?"

He looked like he wanted to believe me.

"And you never texted me back, Zac. I wouldn't lie about that. I literally have no reason to," I said, because I didn't want him to think I'd been desperately reaching out to him. He could do whatever he wanted to, even if that included not having time for me. But I wasn't going to get blamed for shit. "Even moving in with Connie and Richard, I wouldn't have been *so busy* that I wouldn't have texted you back. You were my friend, and I loved you. That was a bad time for me after Mamá Lupe passed away and I had to go live with Boogie's parents for a couple months before finishing school, but... I'm telling you the truth. I tried. I just thought...."

That time in my life, after I'd had to move out of my abuelita's house two months before my high school graduation, when Connie had been living in North Carolina, Boogie had been crazy busy with work, Zac had been in Dallas, and my parents... my parents had been gone again, had been the hardest time in my life. I had loved my aunt and uncle, but they hadn't been the woman who had raised me, or even my big sister. Moving so far away to be with Connie had been scary, but it had really been my only option then. I could've stayed with my aunt and uncle, but I hadn't wanted to stay longer than I needed to.

And then everything with Zac had happened, and it had just felt like the right thing to do.

I'd hit my limit on loss and grief then.

I glanced up at the ceiling for a second when I felt my eyes get watery and my nose started to get a little funny as well. I sniffed and forced myself to drop my gaze as I told him another thing that was partially the truth. "I thought you didn't want to be my friend anymore."

His features slackened, and I was pretty sure I saw him bite his bottom lip for a second before his forehead was lined all over again as he shook his head. "At no point in my life have I ever not wanted to be your friend," he told me in a stricken voice, "and I know you wouldn't lie, kiddo." His gaze was solid and steady. "But you've gotta believe me that I wouldn't have ignored you, and I wouldn't lie about that either. I wouldn't lie to you period."

Well, I could believe it, because it had happened.

But...

"You don't believe me."

Ah, shit. "I think you believe you wouldn't have done

that, but—" *You had.* "—I texted and called you, and that's the truth."

"I would have texted you, Peewee," he insisted.

But he hadn't. Because I would have responded.

"I was busy back then. Everything was crazy, but I—" He swallowed, and again, I knew what he was thinking. What he wanted to say but didn't want to say. *I wouldn't have forgotten you,* but he had.

Otherwise, he would have tried harder to communicate with me over the years.

Maybe he *had* asked Boogie about me.

Maybe he had thought about me from time to time at the beginning, when he was imagining messaging me back, but after a while, he'd forgotten.

And we both knew it.

And in a way, I was glad he wasn't forcing himself to get that claim out.

It would have just been worse.

So when he aimed strained, light blue eyes at me, I didn't know what to tell him, how to comfort him, because honestly, I needed a little bit of comforting too. Mine wasn't out of guilt though; it was just at the reality. At the loss.

"Look, it doesn't matter anymore, okay? There's no point in... pointing fingers." Because we both knew who had the biggest finger pointed. It wasn't freaking me.

Zac stared. "No, it does matter, darlin'. It matters to me. I haven't seen your face in ten goddamn years, and I don't understand why, and the more I think about it, the more it's pissin' me off."

I raised my eyebrows at him.

He kept going. "You used to hug me all the time, mess with me all the time." His mouth went tight and flat. "Now, you treat me like we barely know each other; you barely joke with me."

"I joke with you." That sounded weak even to me.

He shook his head and blew out a breath that made his lips do a raspberry. "Peewee, I've got my heart up to here." He gestured toward his neck. "And I'm gettin' pissed off."

"At me?"

"No, honey, not at you. At... everything. Myself." His gaze strayed upward, and he blew another breath. "How the hell did that happen? I don't understand."

What did he want me to say?

Those blue eyes moved back toward me, and that time he sighed, his shoulders going down in the same way they had back when I'd told him about Paw-Paw, like just, *down* and *sad* and unsure.

And honestly, I hated it.

"No wonder you look at me like that," he stated quietly.

My heartbeat was in my throat, but I asked anyway, knowing I shouldn't, knowing it was mean to make him feel worse. "Like how?"

His Adam's apple bobbed. "All nice like a stranger. Jokin' with me and then rememberin' that you don't wanna do that." Zac looked away for a moment. "I missed ten years of your life, kiddo. I didn't even recognize you at first. I didn't think I could feel like more of a piece of shit than I did that other night, but I do."

He had missed ten years, but I'd missed ten years out of his too.

And that had been my choice.

I sighed and took a step closer to him, closer to that tall, lean body that I was sure had to be a wallpaper on hundreds of women's cell phones. To that face that really did deserve to be on the cover of magazines far more often. I reached over to grab his warm forearm and said, "I could've reached out to you too, but my feelings were hurt." It was the truth. But I didn't want him to focus on that too much. "I'm sorry, Zac. I

honestly thought you just didn't want me around anymore."
That was the truth too, even more so than my first statement,
and that was enough drama for me. Enough sadness. I didn't
want to talk about the other shit; this was exhausting enough.
And there was even less of a point in bringing that up
than this.

I knew that.

So I gave him more of my honesty. I gave him a tiny piece
of me that I knew I'd been suppressing around him. For my
safety. "I missed your big, dumb face too, Snack Pack."

His eyes widened. Those dark, nearly blond eyelashes fell
slowly over them. And that mouth of his parted slightly.

In surprise?

I gave him a little smile in return. A smile that I wanted
to be bigger, but I was holding onto it for a second longer. To
make sure. To not overstep myself.

And then he blinked and gave me a little piece of himself
too.

"You coulda just said 'dumb face.' You know I'm sensitive
about my big head," Zac deadpanned, quietly, almost hesitant.

I couldn't help it; I nodded at him. "You grew into your
big head, if that makes you feel any better."

His mouth quirked just a little bit more. "It does. Thank
you, darlin'."

My grin went wide despite the warning alarms going off in
my head that tried to remind me of what this was, of what my
expectations should be.

But Zac's smile was like one of those slow-motion blos-
soming flowers on the nature channel.

I only partially hated myself for loving it—not because I
loved him like *that*, but because I still cared so much. And
sometimes it was easier not to care about people—at least
people who weren't as invested in you as you were in them.

"We can be friends when we both have time, if that works

for you," I told him gently, trying to give him a smile. "Because I wasn't kidding about your big head."

Something in him faltered for a moment—it was in his eyes, I could see it—but a split second later, he opened his arms.

I took the step into them. As an adult, as grown-up Bianca.

He drew me into him, into his chest, into his life, I guess.

Zac Travis hugged me and said, "I sure did miss you, Little Texas."

Something in me unraveled at the name he hadn't used in so long.

In so, so long.

With my cheek against his chest, I told him the truth. "I really missed you too, Big Texas."

CHAPTER TEN

What had to be one of his million-dollar hands palmed the back of my head, and I liked it. I liked it a lot. "Ah, honey. It's gonna take some time for my heart not to be crushed that you didn't want me to know we live so close to each other."

I pulled back a little, taking in that blond and light brown dusted chin and lifted my index finger. I booped him on the nose, just like old times, and I wasn't surprised that it didn't feel wrong. I still did it to Boogie, Connie, and my niece and nephew.

I kept on telling him the truth. "I just didn't want to be a nuisance or somebody else that wants something from you. That's all." At least that was 99 percent accurate.

All right, 90 percent, but who was keeping track? Only me.

His nose wrinkled, and I wasn't sure how to take his watchful gaze. I wanted to fidget, wanted to be self-conscious about having him so close he could see all of my imperfections. The eyebrows I was a week overdue to get threaded. The upper lip past its prime too. The bags under my eyes from sleep that I only caught up on once a week.

Zac had been around beautiful, pretty, cute women his entire life. It wasn't like that reality was new to me.

I wasn't ugly—well, not that ugly anyway. I could date when I wanted to—*had* dated when I wanted to.

So it made it easier to have him right in my face, sucking up my features because he either wanted to see if I was lying or because he was still trying to remember what I looked like. "I worried about you all the time after I left for school, you know that?"

He was killing me.

"I worried about you too, you know that? I still worry about you every time you play. I loved you—I still do." *Shut up.* "But you got busy and had other things to worry about. I don't hold that against you." I winced. "Much. I knew that, when you left, the world was going to open up to you. Or at least, I understood that once I got older." After I'd cried at first, but he didn't need to know that. I'd only been eleven back then.

Plus, I didn't want to touch down on the years after that too closely. I hadn't wanted to bother him, that part was absolutely true. I didn't want to be the person who his ex-girlfriend had accused me of being. But there had been a reason why the thought that I could even be a bother to my longtime friend had even formed in the first place.

For one split second, I thought about that girl with the long brown hair who had given me this pitiful little fake smile, right before making me feel a foot tall. The girl who had plucked my self-esteem out and poked at it with the tip of her shoe. Doubt was a terrible thing for anyone.

Hopefully she'd gotten crabs at some point over the years.

Zac didn't say anything to me for so long, I wasn't sure he was going to despite his big hug. He just kept right on watching me and watching me a little more until eventually his shoulders seemed to relax.

I waited, not sure what the hell was going through his head now since I'd already gotten it wrong. Or maybe I'd gotten it right, and then he'd changed his mind.

This was confusing.

Fortunately, he didn't exactly confuse me anymore. "I still love you too, Peewee," Zac told me with a sigh, still watching me way too close and carefully. One corner of his mouth hitched up just a tiny, little bit.

In another lifetime, I would have killed for those words meant in a different way.

But I would take them now, wrap them up in tissue paper, and store them somewhere safe.

I smiled at him, and it took a second for the other side of his mouth to hitch up as well, all reluctant and uncertain. Too careful.

It had taken my ex a year to tell me he loved me. I hadn't seen Zac in ten years, but it took him weeks to say the same words to me—under a different meaning, but they still meant what they meant. Loyalty. Friendship. Affection. Those three things were basically engraved into his DNA.

How could I not love him? Even if this crap was confusing.

Zac reached up to scrub a hand over his right cheek. "Ten years flew by, kiddo." He sighed again, his soft blue gaze lingering, unmoving and unflinching. "Still can't believe it was that long."

"It's okay."

"No, it's not." He sighed once more, brushing a hand over his face again before his index finger came up and he pressed the tip of it to the beauty mark right off the edge of my mouth. "I really didn't recognize you." That dirty blond head tipped to the side, and he wasn't looking at anything other than my eyeballs as he asked, "When'd you get to be this cute, huh?"

That would have been a dagger to my freaking heart as a teenager, but now... now I knew what cute was.

It wasn't like I still thought there was some alternate universe where Zac would ever like me in any other way than how he currently did—because even that, at this point, was kind of a miracle. And it was fine. It was totally fine.

I was pretty proud of myself when a smile slid over my mouth, relatively easily, and I lifted a shoulder. "I stopped using so much gel in my hair, and I learned that I wasn't supposed to brush it. Exercise, four years of clear retainers, makeup. Connie says I can't thank puberty for it either since it kicked in like five years late."

That jerk. I almost laughed thinking about the way she'd said it too, now that I thought about it. But I didn't.

Zac's expression got a little funny then, but that gradual little smile stayed in place. "Nah, you were always cute, darlin'."

Cute. Again. I still smirked though, taking his compliment for what it was. This man had dated models—Boogie had whispered their names to me when he'd showed me pictures of them—and an actress or two. I couldn't forget those either.

"You and Boogie were the only ones to ever say that," I admitted to him. My sister and my grandma—and even my parents when they were around—had always told me I was pretty, but beauty was in the eye of the beholder. I knew it firsthand from some of the guys at the gym. Most of the hot ones were really nice and normal dudes, but a couple of them had turned out to be enormous, cocky assholes who had me cheering for the guy they were fighting because I wanted them to learn a lesson in humility.

Nice, I was not—or half the time I wasn't. But that was everyone. At least that's what I was going to tell myself.

This man who was trying to be my friend again gave me a

slightly brighter smile than the one before. "I told you back then boys were dumb."

I snorted, and it felt natural. Right. "They still are."

Zac's smile turned lopsided in the blink of an eye, and I could see the affection flare back up behind his eyes. And that was natural and right too. Familiar. "When'd you lose it, Peewee?"

Why my virginity was the first thing that popped into my head, I had no fucking clue. Then I got it. It. The weight. The "baby fat" as I'd clung to calling it.

"It took a few years, but... ta-da." I snorted and shrugged. "I'm happy."

That very white smile that had been a product of three years of braces according to Boogie—because in my head it felt like he'd only had them for a couple months—went full beam on me. "Happy looks good on you." His nostrils flared a little. "You're somethin', kiddo."

Something.

Considering all the women he'd seen, the actually beautiful women he'd seen, I was going to take his compliment for what it was: he'd cared about me, and what I looked like had never mattered to him. It was a compliment from a wonderful man who had told me not to let dumb boys get to me. Who had gone to school to pick me up with Boogie when I'd been sixteen, scowling the whole time because Boogie had told him I'd been upset that this boy had called me an ugly name since I wouldn't let him copy my homework and it had gotten to me.

"Thanks, Snack Pack," I told him sincerely, clinging to that memory, him demanding I tell them who'd made me cry. I never did tell him, but he'd really tried to get it out of me. Him and Boogie. "So," I shrugged for about the eightieth time, "you want some frozen yogurt?"

He gave me a side look that said, *What do you think?*

I smiled at him and handed it over. "Hey, was that Trevor I saw run upstairs when I got here?"

"I'm sure it was. He's here this week. Most of the time he's in LA, sometimes he's in New York, and every once in a while, he makes some house calls to the couple other players he manages just to make sure they aren't screwin' up."

"You and CJ let him stay here? Or is this CJ's house and he lets you stay here?" I finally asked, trying to figure this shit out.

"This is Trevor's place. His 'Houston' house." He used quotation marks and waggled his eyebrows. "He's from League City." That was a suburb on the outskirts of Houston. "He's only here a week out of the month, if that. He lets me and CJ stay here."

Ohhh. That kind of explained things. The bare minimum furniture. The fact the house looked brand new, because no one really lived in it.

"No use wastin' money stayin' somewhere when I won't be there for long, you know?"

Something slender and sad slipped over and into my chest slowly. *God, I hoped things went well for him. I hoped he could settle down for the remainder of his career and be happy.*

I understood what he meant. I'd followed him closely enough to get it. He'd been released once back in Dallas, and now Oklahoma had said, "See ya." I had a tiny memory of overhearing Zac tell Boogie years ago about how much he and his mom had moved around Texas before they'd moved back in with her parents.

I kept my mouth closed and my thoughts to myself.

"Not so bad, huh?" he finished, but I didn't like the way he asked it.

I should bring it up to Boogie, have him make sure he was really fine. That was best friend territory, not person-I-haven't-seen-or-remembered-in-ten-years territory.

I was going to stay in my lane. I knew my lane and felt comfortable in it. I still hadn't even gotten around to asking him about his tryout in San Diego. Part of me hoped he'd bring it up on his own, but I'd give him a chance. Or at least a little while.

"I'm glad you think living in this big-ass house isn't so bad," I told him with a straight face, hoping to lighten him up a bit in the meantime. "I'm sure it's hard to slum it in the master suite."

He stared at me for a second. Then his laugh drawled out of him, all slow and lazy. But even his features lit up.

"I mean, these hardwood floors aren't marble, old man. I don't know how your sensitive feet can stand it."

He straight-up groaned, but I caught a peek at those flashing white teeth, and it was nice. Real nice. "All right. I deserved that." He glanced up at the vaulted ceiling, those lean cheeks pulled wide with the smile still on his face, a big smile. "This place is bigger than five of the houses we grew up in, huh?"

"Yup. You know I'm just messing with you. I know you're used to the finer things in life now. Boogie showed me some pictures of the house you were living in in Oklahoma. You've worked hard for everything you have. You don't need to apologize for being able to afford buying nice things, or for not wanting to buy a place. If I could afford it, I'd live somewhere this nice too."

"That house in Oklahoma was just a rental." His smile got a little smaller as it kept on being aimed up at the ceiling with its wooden beams, so I wasn't totally expecting his next question. "Why didn't you ever come visit with him, Peewee? You really thought I didn't wanna see you?"

And we were back here. He still wasn't totally letting this go. Shit.

I didn't want to lie to him though. "Pretty much."

I didn't appreciate the face he made.

So I made a face right back at him. "You know, you're putting this all on me when your ass could have visited me too." *If you'd remembered I'd been alive.* Luckily, there wasn't much bitterness in the thought. Just a little. So that was good. "I didn't change my name or go into Witness Protection or anything, you know."

I was in a good mood. I was moving forward. I wasn't going to let this affect our friendship.

Not anymore.

Zac instantly shut his mouth, blinked, and then reopened it. His gaze totally settled on me then, and it took him a second, but he finally got out, "You know, nobody talks to me like that to my face except Boogie and Trevor." He paused. "And Mama."

Ah. More familiarity.

I went up to the balls of my feet, reached forward, and tapped his still-straight nose. "I don't know about Trevor, but the rest of us knew you back when you wore tighty-whities, so...."

Freaking Zac laughed again, and it made something warm pop up in my stomach. "I still do."

I snorted. "Please tell me they still have little Spiderman on them."

Zac shook his head. "They're big Spiderman now."

This idiot.

We both laughed, loud, and he was still cracking up as he added, "Goddamn, I missed you, Peewee. You and that mouth."

I missed you, Peewee. Warmth and not a small amount of sadness filled my chest. I couldn't help but tell him the truth. "I know. I missed you too. I hope we don't go another ten years without seeing each other."

Maybe it wasn't the perfect thing to say, but most of Zac's

smile didn't wither away afterward, at least. Apparently, he was trying too. "No way that's happenin'," he told me, looking straight into my eyes as he did so. "So, you got plans today?"

"Big ones." I met his gaze dead on. "I have to go grocery shopping. You?"

"I could do some grocery shopping."

"You buy your own groceries?"

It was his turn to blink. "What? You think I pay somebody to do what I can do myself?"

"Well, yeah. It's like five dollars. I'm just picky with my produce." I watched him closer than before and whispered, "Are you having financial trouble? Because a few years ago, I got in really bad credit card debt, and it took a while, but I got out of it, and—why are you smiling like that?"

Yeah, he was smiling and not even bothering trying to hide it. "Smiling like what?"

"Like an idiot," I told him.

Zac freaking hooted, and it made me laugh. "I've got plenty. Promise."

Well then. "So? Are you serious? Do you really want to go?" The idea of him going grocery shopping period pretty much blew my mind. The idea of him wanting to go with me grocery shopping blew it into another state.

Not that I minded or cared.

That big, quick hand came out of nowhere to boop me on the nose before I could dodge out of the way. "Count me in, darlin'. A boy's gotta eat too."

———

If someone had told me two weeks ago that I was going to be heading into a grocery store next to Zac, who had my reusable bags thrown over one of his shoulders as he tried to be inconspicuous with a burnt orange and white baseball cap pressed low over his head, I would have thought they were full of shit.

Mostly because I still couldn't believe this cheapskate wasn't willing to pay a couple bucks for someone else to buy his groceries.

I had made sure to bring that up no less than three more times on the drive there—a drive that consisted of me behind the wheel because apparently someone didn't "want to drive" and because my car had "a bigger trunk." I mean, I didn't care, but if I had to choose between my Honda Accord or his luxury vehicle, I would have chosen his. Mostly because I'd never been in anything more expensive than Boogie's Audi.

And if he wanted to risk his life getting kidnapped by hanging around the rest of us plebs, I sure hoped his manager had access to his bank account for ransom money, because I wasn't going to risk my life saving him from a hostage situation. He'd been alive longer than me. I had a lot left to live for.

I told him that too, which made him laugh. "Nah, nobody ever recognizes me," he'd claimed.

"So, do you have a list or are you just picking up random stuff along the way?" I asked him later on as I pulled out a full-sized cart at the entrance to the store. Zac had teased me about my shitty parking job the entire walk inside.

He was busy grabbing a half-sized one with two baskets, a small one at the top and a bigger one at the bottom. He winked at me. "No list. It'll all come to me."

"Uh-huh." Because that always worked out. I was playing with fire coming without eating something beforehand.

Hearing the sarcasm in my voice, that nearly thin mouth drawled up into a smirk. "I got this, kiddo. Whatcha gettin'?"

I pushed my cart toward the produce first like I always did. "I've got a pretty big list." Turning over my shoulder, I held up my phone to show him my notes app and watched his eyes widen.

He pushed his cart forward to walk beside me. "The last person I knew who used that many groceries was a two-hundred-and-eighty-pound defensive end."

"I don't eat out much, and someone is always dropping by and eating at my house."

He looked at me. "Who?"

I shrugged as I started grabbing celery, falling right into that comfortable trap of I-know-you-and-I-feel-comfortable-with-you-so-I'm-going-to-joke-with-you. He didn't need to know I was talking about Deepa. "People."

It took a second for Zac to snicker, but he did as he ditched his cart and came over, picking a bag of baby carrots I hoped he had a plan for so that they wouldn't go bad.

I waited until he stood beside me, picking up avocados and testing how hard they were, to gently ask, "So... can I ask you about..." I turned to make sure no one was standing close. There wasn't. "How things went in San Diego, or would you rather not talk about it?"

I could feel the surprise coming off him. It only lasted about a second, but it was there, and then it was gone. "You can ask, darlin'. Nobody else ever checks." He lowered his voice. "It went all right. Another guy was there too, but I didn't get a good feelin' about it. I'm not expectin' a thing."

Those motherfuckers. I hoped they lost every game this season. I peeked at his face, but he caught me, and I forced a smile. "That stinks. San Diego is expensive to live in anyway."

"Yeah, you're right." I didn't really like the way he ticked his head to the side. "I still got some time."

Not much, I'm sure we both knew, but neither one of us admitted it. The season was going to start in no time.

I wasn't surprised he went straight into changing the subject back in my direction. "You have a good day at work?"

"I only thought about quitting twice. That's about as good as it gets for me now," I admitted, setting four avocados into the cotton bags I used for my produce.

He leaned over and plucked the bag from my hand, taking out two and setting them bare into his cart. "What's goin' on with your boss again?"

I stared at him, leaned over just like he had, grabbed one back, and said, "Let me show you how to pick them."

So I showed him how to pick them, pointing at the nipple and telling him all about my paper bag trick to get them to ripen. Once he'd gotten three of his own that were just as good as the ones I'd found, I answered his question about my bosses.

"They're new, three of them. They bought the gym I work at, but two of them are basically silent partners. The other one is just an asshole, but he's like that with everyone, so it makes me feel a little better that it isn't just me. I still pretty much hate his guts."

"Don't you make enough money off your WatchTube channel?"

I glanced at him as we pushed our carts toward the onions, but I was the only one who grabbed one. "I do. Now. I have for the last two years, but before, it fluctuated too much, and I didn't want to quit until I knew for sure I could keep making a living off my sponsors and ad money," I explained. There was still so much other stuff I hadn't told him about that my gut knew was going to come up eventually. "Some other stuff happened right around then, but it's complicated and a long story. I'll tell you about it some other time. Anyway, I want to quit now, but my friend Deepa that you met—"

"The young one?"

I nodded. "I feel bad leaving her there, so I'm just waiting for her to find another job so I can leave too. She works for me too, helping me out with things when I film my videos, but it's not enough to pay her full-time. I do all my own editing." I'd had to teach myself two years ago, but that was more than he needed to know then.

He raised an eyebrow. "You have an assistant?"

"Sort of." I nudged him. "Just for little things. I do almost everything myself." Because I didn't trust other people anymore to help, but that was part of the story that was too complicated to explain at the grocery store. "So, I'll get out of there sooner than later. I'm not too worried about it. I think I'm just too excited about my trip I have coming up in a couple months to worry about the gym too much."

"What trip?"

"I'm going to Disney World in October."

"With Connie?"

"No, by myself," I answered him. "It's my redemption trip twelve years late. I'm so excited."

"I remember you always talked about goin' someday." He slid me a warm smile before he seemed to think about something that made him go thoughtful. "Kiddo, where are your parents now?"

I wasn't really surprised it had taken him this long to ask about them. Of course he'd remember the basics of my relationship with them. Or at least, he had an idea of how they had always been, which was fine with leaving their daughters with their abuelita while they went off and did their own thing. "They're in Nicaragua right now on a missionary trip. My mom sent me an email a couple days ago and said she thinks they'll be down there at least another two or three months."

His fingers drummed across the handle of the cart, and I could only begin to imagine what he was thinking. "I wasn't sure if they were still travelin' all the time or not" was all he said... in a tight voice that lifted my heart just a little.

"Yeah, they are," I replied. I'd gotten used to them being gone all the time. Then again, I'd gotten used to it by the time I was six.

Well, for the most part.

I didn't want to talk about them anymore, and I was sure he probably didn't either. "I'm done here, old fart, do you need anything else? Want to split up?" I offered in a voice a lot cheerier than I was genuinely feeling.

"I'll follow you."

Okay. "I'm getting some shrimp next."

Zac nodded back and followed after me. I spotted the familiar man behind the counter and waved at him when we made eye contact.

"Hi," the employee greeted me back, coming around the bar behind the coolers lined up with fresh fish and meats. "How's it goin'? What you need today?"

"Two pounds of that peeled shrimp, please," I told the employee, flashing him a smile. "No Anthony today?"

The older man grinned at me as he slid the cooler door open and reached in. "Nah, it's his day off. It'll make his whole week if I tell him you asked about him."

I snorted as Zac came to stand beside me. "Aww. Leave him alone."

The employee's eyes slid to my companion, and he made a surprised face. He'd only asked me at least ten times over the last year if I was still single and usually followed that up by trying to offer his younger, but very cute coworker up as boyfriend material. "You went out and got a boyfriend?"

"No." I forced the smile onto my face. "Zac, this is George. George, Zac."

George's eyes narrowed a little, and I had a feeling....

Zac slapped a hand down onto my shoulder. "How's it goin'?"

I had one chance to change the subject, and I went for it.

"George, how are your kids doing? Did your daughter get into that nursing school she was hoping for?"

That was enough of a distraction to get my friend at the grocery store to tell me all about his daughter's latest school drama. People liked to tell me things, and I liked to listen. So thankfully, I managed to get Zac an order of ribeye too, undetected. I told George I'd see him later and pretty much dragged Zac out of there before the other man figured out why he might have thought he looked familiar.

"You sure nobody ever recognizes you?" I asked him when we were far enough away not to be overheard.

Zac picked up a package of spaghetti without really looking at the front. "Well... sometimes. Not often." He arched an eyebrow. "You?"

"Nah. Six times including CJ."

He nodded, and his mouth twitched to the side for a moment before he asked, "I never asked. You got a boyfriend?"

I shook my head. "Nah, I'm my own boyfriend." And since we were on the subject... "Do you have a girlfriend? Was that blonde the day of your party thing your girlfriend?"

"The blonde the day of my party thing...?" he asked and glanced up at the ceiling, thoughtfully.

This fool had no idea who the hell I was talking about. Then he confirmed it by basically reading my mind.

"I don't know who you're talkin' about," he said after a moment, actually looking sheepish. "And no, no girlfriend. No nothin'. I don't have time for that kind of commitment."

I snorted. "'Have time,' okay," I said sarcastically.

His elbow nudged me, and he opened his mouth to tell me who knows what just as his phone started ringing. He pulled it out and read whatever was on the screen, cursing under his breath. Blue eyes flicked up to me right before he muttered, "It's Trevor, my manager," like I didn't know who he was. "One second.... *What's up, Trev?.... He just called you?*" Zac asked with a frown, making eye contact with me.

I smiled at him and turned toward the rows of canned beans a little down the aisle, keeping an ear out.

"*No.... Yeah.... We'll talk about it when I get back to the house in a minute I'm at the grocery store with Little Texas.... Little Texas.... Bianca. I introduced you to her when we did that commercial, 'member?.... No. What? Copyright infringement?*" Zac blew out a breath, and I was pretty sure he rolled his eyes. "*Who do you think came up with my nickname, Trev? She was always Little Texas; then she started callin' me Big Texas.*"

He pulled the phone away from his face, tapped something on the screen, and walked toward me, asking quietly, "Peewee, how old was I when you started callin' me that?"

He knew I was eavesdropping, and later on it would make me laugh. I was holding two cans of black beans when I turned to him and said to Trevor, "I was eight. Zac started calling me Little Texas because I had this T-shirt I wore all the time with the Texas flag on it. For Christmas, I tried to draw a big Texas on a T-shirt for him, and that's when I started calling him that." I looked at Zac and raised my eyebrows. "Why? Do you guys want to start paying me past royalty money for coming up with his nickname?"

Zac tipped his face up toward the ceiling, and I had to pinch my nose when Trevor stuttered, "No. I was only asking. Zac, take me off speakerphone this second."

"I was just kidding about the royalties." I laughed, watching my old friend close his eyes as he kept cracking up too.

"Zac!" the manager hissed before getting cut off by Zac taking him off speakerphone.

But I could still hear Zac respond. "*She was jokin', Trev. It wasn't like we ever made T-shirts with Big Texas on them.*"

"But you should," I called out to him before turning back toward the beans.

"*Bianca just said we should. Maybe once I get on another team—*"

Once he got on another team. I smiled at his optimism. I was glad he wasn't back to being all "*woes is me, I might have to retire.*" I'd be glad if I never met that Zac again.

"*Yeah, we'll talk about that later.... No. I just don't wanna talk about it now. You want somethin' from the store?*" Zac picked up another package of pasta and dumped it into his cart.

Zac spoke into his phone for another minute or two.

I wondered what his manager wanted to talk about and why Zac didn't want to bring it up in front of me.

And I didn't let myself be disappointed when he immediately asked me if I had The Lazy Baker T-shirts.

I didn't.

He asked me why not, and I told him why—because I hadn't thought about it.

He didn't bring up anything else about his phone call with Trevor for the rest of our shopping trip or the journey home.

Boogie was his best friend, not me.

And that was fine.

I just couldn't let myself forget it.

CHAPTER ELEVEN

"Yeah, he's puking again," my sister Connie said into the phone as I finished putting my groceries up about a week later.

I made a face at myself as I elbowed the refrigerator door closed.

"Oh shit, he got some on his shoes. Gross! B, I've gotta call you back! I'm sorry!"

"No, don't be sorry. Hope he feels better! Tell him I love him!" I called into the receiver as I heard my nephew, Guillermo, retching in the background at the gas station they had stopped at.

"K, bye," Connie said before instantly hanging up.

My poor nephew. Apparently, Luisa, my niece, had been saying since the day before that she wasn't feeling well. My nephew had claimed he was feeling fine, but an hour into Guillermo and Connie's trip down from Killeen to spend the weekend with me, it had gone downhill real quick. Yermo started blowing chunks on the side of the road, and then he'd blown some more chunks at the gas station they stopped at. Apparently, Richard, my sister's husband, had called to tell her that Luisa had started projectile vomiting too. So of course, they were turning around and going back home.

It made sense. And if it kind of screwed me on the two videos I'd planned on filming tomorrow, well, it happened. I only hoped for all their sakes they got better soon. I'd figure it out.

It had been about two months since the last time I'd had someone come over and be my "guest," and that was because I'd been pushing it to do one with Guillermo and Connie. Setting my phone down, I thought about my options. Boogie had plans, I knew that. I thought about a couple of friends who were aware of what I did on the side, but they weren't crazy about being on camera. I needed Deepa's help doing other things out of the frame, so she was no help. My parents weren't anywhere nearby either, even though they were backups to the backups to the backups. It was really last minute to try and find someone else, especially when I had all the ingredients I was going to use ready to go. I'd already cleaned the hell out of my kitchen and didn't want to waste that either.

Who else could I ask?

I thought about it as I made a quick dinner of pasta, olive oil, parmesan, red pepper, and some leftover broccoli and chicken breast. And it was while I was eating in front of the television, watching another episode of the Turkish romance I was catching up on, that the idea came to me out of nowhere.

And like with most of the scary things in my life, I asked myself, *What is the worst that could happen?*

It took me two whole minutes to find CJ's Picturegram account and another two minutes to write and then rewrite the message I wanted to send him.

THELAZYBAKER: Hi, CJ! By any chance, do you know anyone (or 2 people?) that might be interested in

doing a video with me tomorrow? I can pay in food or a little bit of money.

Straight and to the point. Perfect. Chances were, he probably got so many messages that mine would get buried, but it was worth a shot. Maybe, worst case, I could recycle an old video? If my nephew was feeling better, I could try to switch shifts with some people and go up to Killeen next week? I knew I had to work on Saturday. Some of my followers would complain, but some people complained about everything. I'd had someone whine once about the color of my shirt; it had hurt their poor, sensitive, little eyes, according to them.

I mean, I couldn't magically make someone appear to be in one with me.

For one tiny second, I thought about Zac…. But he didn't have time. He had messaged me a couple of times since the day we'd been grocery shopping, but from the pictures he posted on his Picturegram, he was busy doing drills and whatever the hell else he worked on during his time off from football. I was glad he was posting more workout stuff on his accounts, like I'd suggested weeks ago.

But I didn't want to bother him or guilt-trip him into doing this for me. Because I knew that if I told him I was in a tight spot, he would offer. And *that*, more than reaching out to CJ, made me feel like I would be taking advantage of him.

Plus, CJ had kind of hinted at being interested in being in one of my vlogs, hadn't he? And if he said no, it was no big deal. He was already busy with his own preseason. But maybe, just maybe, he would know someone who would be interested.

An hour later, when my phone buzzed, I was surprised as shit when I saw the icon for Picturegram on the screen and CJ's Picturegram handle in small letters beside it: **CJDANIELS NEW MESSAGE**.

Worst case, he was going to say no, he didn't know

anyone, and that would be that. No big deal. I opened the app and went to my direct messages.

CJDANIELS: Hey. What time tomorrow?

Oh shitttttt.

I wrote him back immediately.

THELAZYBAKER: 10am? Honestly, I have the whole day. I usually film during the day, but I can make it work anytime. [smiley face emoji]

I was rereading what I wrote him when a reply came through.

Don't get excited. He might still not know anyone.

CJDANIELS: OK.

OK?

Well, it wasn't a "no" at least. What else could it mean? Maybe he was going to ask someone for me?

I waited until the episode of the Turkish show ended and then got up and loaded the dishwasher. I waited until I had it all set, ready for me to start it tonight just in case I used a couple more dishes, and then went to check my phone. The light flashed in the front, and I saw the screen showed I had a new Picturegram message.

CJDANIELS: Anybody can do it?

THELAZYBAKER: Yeah, as long as they want to and are fine with me posting it when it's done.

Beggars can't be choosers. His reply came in immediately.

CJDANIELS: OK

CJDANIELS: Where at?

THELAZYBAKER: My apartment [smiley face emoji]

THELAZYBAKER: [address in Maps]

THELAZYBAKER: Did you think of someone who might be interested?

It was pushy, but... I needed to know so I could plan.

CJDANIELS: Me and Amari. We'll take food. Is that OK?

Him?

THELAZYBAKER: YES! Are you sure?

CJDANIELS: Yeah. OK see you at 10

Holy SHIT. That wasn't what I'd been expecting. That hadn't been my intention... mostly. I would have taken anyone he knew who was interested. I just didn't want to tell anyone else who didn't already know what I did on the side.

He didn't need to do it, and maybe I should tell him not to feel obligated, but...

I'd be an idiot to ruin a good thing. And an idiot, I wasn't. Well, most of the time I wasn't.

————

I was waiting downstairs at the gate ten minutes ahead of schedule. CJ had sent me a message on Picturegram saying he was on his way, and I didn't want him to get lost trying to find my apartment. It was a little tricky the first time, and since he was doing me a huge favor, I didn't want him to get irritated driving around and then decide to leave.

I still couldn't believe he was coming to do this with me—not because he was a professional football player, but because he didn't owe me anything. If I'd learned anything over the last few years, it was that most people didn't usually do nice things unless they got something from it.

And I could literally not think of anything he'd get from doing this. He had way more followers on Picturegram than I did. Apparently, he was one of the most popular players on the White Oaks.

The least I could do was not make him regret doing me such a huge favor.

A red Jeep suddenly turned and pulled into the driveway

to the complex, and I recognized the car as one I'd seen in Trevor's driveway before. Sure enough, the window rolled down and a familiar face appeared on the other side of it. I jogged over and waved. "Hi, CJ."

"Hey." He smiled at me.

Someone in the passenger seat leaned forward and lifted a hand. It was a man I had never seen before.

I lifted a hand too. "Hi," I called out before focusing back on CJ. "I can hop in the back and give you directions if you want."

"The door behind me is open," he agreed, the doors unlocking.

It took me a second to open the back—freezing because Trevor was sitting in the other rear passenger seat with an impatient expression plastered on his face as he looked at me —and hop inside. "Hi, Trevor," I greeted the older man.

"Hi," he replied and then looked down at his phone.

All right. Well, that had gone well. I hoped he wasn't the "friend" that wanted to participate in the video, but I'd take him too if there wasn't another choice.

I leaned forward to give CJ the code to get into the complex. As the doors opened, I patted one of his shoulders. "Thank you so much for coming," I said before turning to the man in the passenger seat as Trevor's gaze seemed to burn a hole into me.

The man in the passenger seat had his body angled toward the center of the Jeep, dark brown eyes locked on me. He was grinning. Big-time.

I shot my hand toward him. "Hi. I'm Bianca."

The man, who I could finally see had a crazy good-looking face—that was almost as good-looking as Zac's—that was covered in light brown skin, heavy dark eyebrows, and a smile that looked almost as friendly as... well, Zac's. Almost. He took my hand and gave it a squeeze.

"I know who you are," he said with a blinding white smile. "I'm Amari," the stranger said, releasing my hand and confirming it was the man CJ had told me about. He *was* another football player, one who had trained with Zac before the season had started, if I remembered correctly.

I smiled, then started giving directions on how to get to the apartment. CJ found a visitor's spot close by, and I waited until we had all gotten out of the car and led them toward my apartment.

"I really can't thank you enough for coming to do this," I called out so that they could hear me. I glanced at Trevor, who today was wearing dark slacks and a light gray button-down shirt with the sleeves rolled up as he stood there with a watchful expression on his face. "If you change your mind, I swear you can back out at any second. You don't have to do anything you don't want to. Asking was a shot in the dark, I didn't expect anything." I smiled at all three of them, and it was only Trevor who didn't return the expression. "Really. No pressure at all."

CJ shifted where he stood, and I noticed that he was in a black T-shirt and dark jeans, his only jewelry a heavy gold watch. He looked nice.

"I can't cook to save my life," he said suddenly.

I had to think about that for a second. "That's okay. I'd probably scream and cover my head if someone threw a football at me. And we're just going to be farting around. It's fine." I turned to the older man, needing to prepare myself. "Trevor, did you want to be in one too?"

The older man yawned before replying, "No. I'm only here to make sure he isn't getting wrangled into doing a porno or something else stupid."

I blinked and had to make sure I heard that correctly.

I had.

"Nope. I promise. No freaky-deaky shit. That's on Tuesdays." I blinked again. "I'm kidding. I have an LLC, an accountant, and a real business bank account. I have a SEP IRA."

He didn't think I was funny, and it wasn't the first time someone didn't. Oh well.

Turning back around, I made my way toward the stairs that went up to the second floor. "CJ, did you end up liking the frozen yogurt?"

"I ate it all that same day."

I smiled.

"Almost ate Zac's too, but he got to it before I did."

That sucker had never told me he ate it, much less if he'd liked it.

"You had frozen yogurt?" Trevor asked out of nowhere.

CJ answered him.

"I have a little bit leftover if you want it, Trevor. It's straw-berry-flavored," I offered the uptight man.

He paused to think about it. "I do love strawberry."

I bet he did. "It's yours. CJ, do you have any requests for what you want?"

He didn't hesitate. "Banana bread. If you make frozen yogurt in the future, I'll take some too."

I'd make him both. It was the least I could do. "Amari?"

"Anything."

We reached my floor; my door was the second one down. Unlocking it, I ushered the three of them in, giving Amari and Trevor an extra smile as they entered.

Deepa and I had already set up just about everything around my kitchen. We had it down to a science. Diffusion paper covered my windows year-round, muting the natural light that came through. Usually I had my shutters down anyway, but I liked the consistency of leaving the paper up. That and I was lazy.

My camera was set up to capture the island and the stove,

highlighted by two soft light boxes set up on opposite ends. One was on the left and one was on the right, tipped down at forty-five-degree angles toward where I usually stood. We'd already checked the LAV microphones to make sure the audio was good.

I'd made sure my camera batteries were charged, and from the look of Deepa standing by my laptop, she was double-checking the memory cards to make sure they weren't full. Even though I'd already warned her who was coming, she still seemed to jump a little bit, and I knew I wasn't imagining that her smile was bigger than normal when I introduced her to CJ and Amari. They were both polite to her. Trevor... whatever. I'd tell her about him later.

I ushered my guests toward the kitchen, realizing how small it looked with both of them in it. We'd roll with it. Knitting my fingers together, I brought them under my chin and said, "I'm so happy you're here. Really. Thank you."

It was Amari who said, "You're welcome. My mom's gonna love it. Can I say 'hi, Mom' on it?"

"Yeah, your whole family. Whatever you want." I bounced up to the balls of my feet. "So, I'm not sure how much time you have, and I can work around you. I don't want to take up more of it than necessary. Do you want to do one with all three of us at the same time? Do you want to do one each? I have four recipes ready we can do. I got the ingredients for all of them. Sometimes we can knock out a video in an hour, but that's really, really rare, and sometimes it takes three or four hours depending on if we have to start and stop."

I'd come up with the idea to have four different recipes ready at nine o'clock the night before and had to make a last-minute run to the grocery store. What if they didn't like peanut butter? The peanut butter Rice Krispies treat idea wouldn't work in that case. Or what if they would rather make a meal? I bought shit to try and wing some crispy sweet chicken. I'd been thinking about a key lime cheesecake bite idea for a while too.

It had gone downhill from there. I didn't want to ruin this happening by asking or being picky, so instead, I prepared. Either way, I was down for whatever the guys said they wanted to do. One video. Two videos. Half a video. Whatever. Peanut butter Rice Krispies treats. Key lime cheesecake bites. Crispy sweet chicken. Or pound cake. My sweet tooth was kicking in this week.

"What do you think?" I asked them both, trying to give them my most easygoing smile. "Whatever works for you, works for me. You can still back out too. My feelings won't be hurt."

"I want to, but I warned you I'm no good in the kitchen unless it involves the microwave," CJ said.

Amari shrugged two perfect shoulders. "I'm not in a rush. Whatever you want to do works for me."

"Whatever you guys want. We already checked three microphones, but we don't need to use them all."

"Say we do one together now and it isn't bad, could I do another one later?" CJ asked.

I didn't even try and hide my excitement. "Any time you want," I told him.

Trevor yawned again as he stood off to the side in my kitchen. He'd been so quiet I forgot he was in there, but he was standing right beside Deepa while she did whatever she was doing on my laptop. "You film cooking videos?" he asked.

If he wanted to simplify it that much... "Something like that."

"For a living?"

CJ sighed, but I nodded. "It isn't my full-time job yet, but it will be. You can look up The Lazy Baker if you want."

The older man raised and dropped his eyebrows, suspicious, I could tell, but he still reached into his pocket for his phone. I wondered what the hell he was thinking. That I was lying? But I would never know because he asked, "Hm. Is there somewhere I can sit and wait?"

"In the living room is fine," I answered him before focusing back on the two men. "So, you guys want to screw up a recipe then? Together?"

Amari grinned. "Let's do one together. If it's bad, I want CJ to throw up too."

My smile melted off, and I squinted at both of them. "Look, that happened one time."

But when we all laughed, I knew this was going to be good.

———

Five hours, several pounds of frozen wings, and eight biscuits from a box later, I was sprawled out on my couch.

Alone.

CJ, Amari, and Trevor had left half an hour ago, thanking *me* for inviting them to participate. Well, at least, CJ and Amari had. Trevor, who I'd caught watching us pretty intently, had muttered a goodbye that sounded almost genuine—especially after I'd given him the rest of my strawberry-flavored frozen yogurt. And after he'd read through the release form that I had asked CJ and Amari to sign.

And they had promised to come back and make another video "whenever I wanted."

Deepa left ten minutes after they did. She'd given me a hug and told me she still couldn't believe they had come over and participated. I couldn't either.

We'd cleaned out my freezer following the twenty minutes it had taken them—because I'd basically stood by monitoring CJ and Amari in action—to mix the ingredients together, drop the "batter" for the key lime cheesecake bites into the muffin pan that CJ had set liners into. Then we'd stood around the kitchen for the twenty-five minutes it had taken to bake them, forty-five minutes for them to cool, and then another hour—that should have been more like four, I realized afterward—to set them in the fridge to chill.

Not bad. Not bad at all.

During that time, I'd heard Amari's stomach grumble and had asked if they wanted to eat. I hadn't been surprised even a little bit when they'd nodded. Deepa and I always took a lunch break while things baked or once we were done if it was something fast. What I had been surprised by was Trevor perking up at the mention of food. I knew there had been a reason why I'd bought the jumbo family pack of frozen wings when they'd gone on sale.

It really had been a good day.

And now I was editing the video of us a little and debating whether or not to try and squeeze another one in. It was a lot more work—and a lot riskier—to film without Deepa helping me, but she'd seemed pretty fidgety, so I'd told her she could go home. Plus, it wasn't like I really had anything else to do. And all the equipment was still set up, so I'd just need to make a few adjustments before I could get started.

I'd give myself another ten minutes before really deciding whether or not to do it despite what time it was in the afternoon. I mean, I had makeup on already, I'd ironed my clothes the night before just in case, and I had the ingredients.

Yeah, ten more minutes. I started the video again from the beginning.

"Hello, Lazy Bakers. We're back at it again today with two very special guests." On the screen, I drum rolled my hands on the light-colored granite counter that was about three seconds away from looking way too small.

That was when CJ and Amari walked right in to the shot

to stand on each side of me, CJ with a stone-cold flat expression that warmed my heart big-time because I had felt his nervousness, and Amari on the other side with the biggest, goofiest expression on his face. I gestured to my left in the video. *"My two new friends, CJ Daniels and Amari—"*

The *oh shit* moment was all over my face in the video.

I had thought about stopping and restarting, but I tried not to do that because it seemed even less authentic. I prided myself on doing things as fluidly as possible. Fuckups and all.

Even when those fuckups included me not knowing someone's name for the first time ever. I guess that was what I got for having someone I'd barely met to participate.

On the screen, my head turned toward Amari, and my face barely managed not to turn totally pink as I put the dumbest smile on my face, scratched the tip of my nose, and asked, *"Eh, Amari? What's your last name?"*

Freaking CJ beside me lost his shit and started laughing. Loud. On the screen, I turned to look at him with a big smile on my face right before I started laughing too.

"I'm so sorry, Amari." I cracked up.

The rest of the video went pretty well; they seemed a little nervous, but they did great, saying a few things here and there as we all did slight alterations to the same recipe to see whose came out better. Key lime cheesecake bites were what we'd ended up with. Mine had been the best. CJ's were pretty gelatinous since he'd opted to leave out the egg, and Amari had added too much sugar to his—CJ and I had complained to his super flat expression.

It was rough, but the potential was there. I just needed another... four hours to finish editing it. Usually I'd wait until another day to start, but the guys had seemed too excited and wanted to see just a little something.

My phone rang. I picked it up and was a little surprised at

the name that flashed across the screen. It made me smile though.

I hit the Answer button. "What's up, old fart?"

His laugh hit me right in the ear. "Peewee. You home? You free?"

"Hey, yes and no."

"Whatcha doin'?"

"Watching porn."

He didn't say anything.

"I'm kidding. I'm editing a video right now. I was thinking about filming another one." Should I tell him about CJ and Amari? I mean, I guess why not? "CJ and Amari... Villanueva just left a little while ago."

I mean, it wasn't like we'd had a threesome.

From the slight pause on his end, I wondered if that's what he was thinking. Or maybe he was thinking about my porn joke.

Nah.

He probably didn't even think I had a vagina.

"Why? What are you up to?" I asked when his moment of silence felt like it went on for a second too long.

To give him credit, he didn't hesitate that time or ask what they'd been doing over. He said, "I was callin' to see if you were hungry."

Should I... invite him over? I didn't *have* to do another video. I could take the rest of the afternoon off. "I ate a little while ago. I might be able to scrounge up a sandwich or two for you if you want. Or did you want to go somewhere to eat?"

There was another pause on his end before he said, in his usual happy voice, "I'll eat a sandwich."

"Then head over. The gate code is 321125, Snack Pack." Even though I realized now that my cousin had already given it to him the other time he'd come over.

"See you in about ten, darlin'."

"K, drive safe," I told him before he said bye and we hung up.

Not even fifteen minutes later, a knock came at my door. Sure enough, it was Zac on the other side. I smiled as I let him in. He kissed me on the cheek, catching me off guard for about one second, and I managed to plant one on his own cheek right back.

"Where the hell were you, down the street?" I asked as I closed and locked the door.

He laughed lightly, looking down at me with those baby blue eyes. In a white button-down shirt, a black vest, black dress pants, and shiny dress shoes... he looked pretty damn amazing. A very good-looking friend.

Had he been on a date? This early?

"About two miles down. The owner for the White Oaks invited me over for lunch," he said carefully.

"The *owner*?"

He nodded, his expression serious.

"Is that a good thing?"

"Could be."

I grabbed his forearm. "Fingers crossed then?"

His smile was stretched small, like he was trying to keep it that way on purpose, like he didn't want to get too excited. "Yeah, *yeah,* we'll see. The whole team is young like Ceej...."

I lifted both hands and crossed both sets of fingers for him. If he didn't want to talk about it much or jinx it, I got it. Then I thought about what he'd said on the phone. "I thought you said you were hungry?"

"I am," he replied. "Had some fancy chef and all, but it was finger foods. Swear on my life the fish dish he had was the size of a silver dollar with some brown stuff on it that looked like deer droppings and tasted like them too."

"I don't know how you survived."

"I don't either," he said before following me into the kitchen. I'd cleaned it up while we'd been baking the cheesecake bites. I got it from Mamá Lupe, the need to keep things cleaned up. I couldn't sleep knowing there were dirty dishes in the sink, but the good thing was, I was the only one who usually ate, so it wasn't much. There weren't three hundred dishes that came from having a big family. "His wife—his fifth wife, he'd claimed—said some pretty disturbin' things to me every time she got the chance."

"Like what?" He couldn't just leave it open like that.

Our eyes met as I pulled open the door to my oven and pulled out the four slices of bread I'd put in there the moment after he'd called. Zac made a face as I set the cookie tray on top of the potholders I had spread out on the counter. "She mentioned some masquerade party they were havin' comin' up where *anything goes*."

I made a face at him over my shoulder, and he nodded, eyes wide and goofy.

"Said I should go. Then she mentioned later on how he goes to bed at nine most nights."

I blinked. He blinked right back.

I couldn't help it. I really couldn't. "Is it hard being handsome?"

And this idiot was totally stone-faced as he answered, "Very."

Yeah, I couldn't help it. I snorted. "What a burden you have to live with."

Zac laughed. "I'm objectified daily."

"I believe it."

"Hey, it's hard sometimes gettin' taken seriously," he said. "You know how shitty it makes me feel when some women tell me how pretty I am? I've had a few tell me out of nowhere how I'd look—" He stopped talking.

I pulled out a bag of sliced roast beef and eyed him. "How you'd look what?"

"It's graphic," he warned.

I rolled my eyes again as I opened the bag and pulled out a slice and rolled it up like a cigarette. "Please don't make me say it." I took a bite and chewed. He flicked his fingers at me to approach, and I did.

"Say what?" he asked as he plucked the slice out of my hand and put the rest of it in his mouth.

All right, so we were back to this point in our friendship. Sharing food. That was fine with me too. "You know what," I tried to hedge, still chewing on my bite. "I know how babies are born."

Zac blinked.

"They come out of buttholes."

He burst out laughing, choking on the roast beef in his mouth. His face went red and everything. That's what he got for stealing my deli meat. "I can't believe he tried to pull that on you," he gasped.

Once, after he'd tried to tell me about babies occurring just from kissing, Boogie, my dear, beloved Boogie, had tried to tell me that babies came out of buttholes. Word for word. If my memory served me correctly, Zac had been rolling on the ground laughing afterward.

But Connie had already told me the truth, so I'd just rolled my eyes and walked off.

"He's so dumb." I laughed. "If we see him together again, remind me to ask him if he got Lauren pregnant doing butt stuff."

Zac howled, leaning forward and setting his forehead on my shoulder as I stood there.

I took a sniff.

He smelled nice, like expensive cologne.

Actually, knowing his cheap-ass, it was probably something his mom bought him for Christmas or his birthday every year.

"Who the hell have you been hangin' around the last ten years?" he asked against my shoulder, his head a nice, comforting weight on me.

"People into butt stuff, obviously."

His warm puffing laugh hit my neck for a second, and I had to hold very, very still as he cracked up some more.

After a second, I ducked out from under him and went back to finish his sandwiches, adding meat, some mayo, a little horseradish, and a slice of cheddar cheese to both of them. Damn, they looked good. My stomach grumbled in appreciation. Then I carefully set the plate on the counter and shoved it close to the man who was still cracking up.

But not cracking up enough to not notice he had food in front of him. He took a huge bite. "Mmm, this is good." Those blue eyes hit me as he took another bite. "What'd you do today?" he asked, sounding casual.

I grabbed his other sandwich and took a little bite of the corner and put it back, waiting until I swallowed it before answering. "I filmed today."

I was pretty sure it wasn't my imagination when one of his eyebrows arched up a little. "A cookin' one?"

"Yeah. That's why CJ and Amari were here. They were my guest stars."

He dragged his plate closer to him, taking another huge bite, like that would stop me from taking another bite. It *was* good. "CJ didn't say a peep about it yesterday. I didn't know."

"I asked him pretty last minute. My nephew got sick on the drive down to visit for the weekend, and they had to bail on me, so I asked him."

"I didn't know you had his number." He was halfway done with the first sandwich.

"I don't. I messaged him on Picturegram," I admitted. "It

was a shot in the dark, and he asked Amari. They were here up until a little while ago. Trevor came with them to make sure I wasn't trying to get them to do porn. His words, not mine."

"Trev?"

I nodded.

He took another bite.

I reached over to his other sandwich and took one too before replacing it again. "What?" I asked him.

Zac didn't hesitate. "You could've asked me."

"I didn't want to bother you for his number. I didn't expect him to actually say yes."

That head tilted to the side, giving me a view of the sharp line of his jaw. "You're not botherin' me." He blinked. "What I *meant* was that you could've asked me. I would've done it with you."

Oh.

But apparently he wasn't done. "I can do the other one with you," he said as he swallowed. "If you want. You said you were thinkin' about doin' another one, didn't you?"

"I know you would," I told him. "But I don't want to take advantage of you. I asked CJ because he had kind of made it seem like he might be interested in doing it, and he's a fan." A fan. That was literally the weirdest shit I could ever think or say. Me. Fans. It was a trip.

"I'm a fan too."

I blinked.

Zac finally took the sandwich I'd taken a bite out of and ate over the part I had before saying, "I'm a fan of yours. Big one. Your biggest one in Houston." One cheek went up as he ate. "I am. Are you gonna squeeze another one in today or no?"

"I had thought about it," I told him truthfully. "But you're over here. And my assistant left, so it's more time consuming to do things without her. And things always go wrong when I don't have someone constantly making sure the audio doesn't just suddenly cut off or a battery in the camera doesn't die out of nowhere. It can wait until my next day off."

Zac made a thoughtful face as he swallowed what he'd eaten. "Do one while I'm here. I know how to be quiet. If you show me, I can help."

I made a face.

He made a face right back. "I do!" he claimed with a little laugh. "I can sit in the livin' room like a good boy and watch."

"Pssh."

He grinned. "All right, but I can be, promise." His smile melted into a soft one. "I wanna see too."

I watched him for a second before asking, "Are you sure? It'll probably take three hours. I'm not sure how long it'll take the bread to bake."

His eyes lit up. "You're makin' bread?"

"Pound cake."

This fool licked his lips like I did when someone in the family made tres leches. I laughed.

"Are you *sure* you don't mind?"

"I'm sure."

I slid him a look. "All right... if you insist."

He ate a little more and nodded. "Whatcha gotta do?"

"Change, check the LAVs—eh, the microphone—check the lighting, and fix my hair."

"I'll eat while you change, and I'll help. Yeah?"

I could do it all by myself easier, but I nodded. "All right. Let me get dressed then."

Those blue eyes moved from my face down and back again in a second. "Why? You can't wear the same thing?"

"Nope. I did it once and people noticed." I shrugged. "Give me ten. I'll be right back."

Fortunately, it didn't even take me ten minutes to pull my

shirt off and put another blouse on. Bottoms didn't matter because no one could see them on the other side of the island. All I did was blot my face, reapply some eyeliner and lipstick, and I figured I was good to go. My face hadn't gotten too oily since Amari had pulled the cheesecake bites out of the oven.

Zac was standing in the kitchen with his plate held against his chest, his index finger pressing against the surface to catch crumbs. He looked at me and gave me a funny smile.

"What?" I asked him, trying not to be self-conscious.

"Aww, darlin', you look sweet as sugar."

I batted my eyes at him sarcastically. Sweet was nice. It was what a friend would say. "Thank you."

"How long does it take you to do that to your hair?"

"Depends on how humid it is," I told him. He was talking about straightening it. "At least half an hour though. Why? You don't like it?"

"I like it every way you wear it," he said with a smile. "Can I sit in the livin' room and watch?"

I nodded.

"It won't make you nervous?"

"I don't get nervous anymore doing this. I'm just self-conscious about watching my vlogs in front of other people." Lifting my hand, I booped him on the tip of his nose. "And, Snack Pack, I used to fart in front of you. I don't think I could get nervous in front of you if I tried. I'm sorry."

He laughed. "And you used to blame Boogie for it."

It was my turn to laugh. "There's more deli meat in the fridge. Just help me get my lighting right first, would you?"

"You got it. Whatever you need."

Between the two of us, it took about half an hour to get the lighting right. He went poking around at my windows, and I had to explain why there was paper stuck to them. Then we adjusted the camera, and I had him stand at the island to make sure there weren't any weird shadows. If I'd been by myself, it would've taken a lot longer. Zac moved around into the living room, propping himself up on the couch, facing the back of it—into the kitchen area—on his knees, forearms resting on it while he peeked over.

"Are you good?" I asked, giving him a thumbs-up as I hit the record button on my camera and started to walk around the island to get into place.

"I'm good," he called out as he finished settling in.

All right.

I wasn't nervous, I reminded myself as I took a deep breath in and then another one out. It was like stepping into a personality with a lot less baggage than I had. I had built this business up on my own and had to believe in myself. I was capable. I was smart. And I could do this.

I focused on the camera and started. "Hello, Lazy Bakers! I've got a special recipe on the menu today that I'm really hoping goes well. Today, I'm going to be trying my best to make an orange cranberry pound cake right in time for—"

"Ooh," Zac cooed from his spot on the couch.

Shit.

I blinked straight ahead at the camera and could feel my mouth starting to twitch.

Keep it together. Keep it together.

I closed my eyes and snorted, reopening them and glancing up at the ceiling. "Okay, I need to start over."

I was still looking up when I heard my old friend ask, "Could you hear me?"

I snickered and couldn't help but grin at the innocently smiling face still in place, hovering over the back of the couch. "Yeah, you made me laugh. It's fine. I'll start over."

"Oopsie."

"Oopsie my ass. Okay. I'll start over real quick." I walked

around the island and headed toward my camera to delete the recording.

"I like how you start each video," Zac called out while I was busy. "You sound nice, darlin'. Your kitchen looks real great."

"Yeah? One day I'd like to rent a studio to film in, but I think this is good enough for now."

"It's more than good enough to me." There was a pause. "Is that Mama Lupe's apron?"

I turned around to look at him, surprised—when I shouldn't have been—and said, "Yeah. You remember it?"

He nodded, his expression turning pretty bittersweet. "She didn't wear it that often, only on holidays."

"Yeah. It was always my favorite," I admitted, suddenly missing my abuelita a ton. "Like... magic was going to happen when she put it on." I looked down and smoothed my hands down the front of the checkered orange apron that had three colorful stitched flowers right on the corner of my chest. I washed it by hand when it needed it. "It makes me feel like she's close to me when I do this, like she'd be proud." Glancing up, I found Zac's mouth edging upward into a little smile.

He nodded. "Yeah, Little Texas, she'd be real proud of you. She'd love knowing you wore it." He sighed. "She'd be real proud of you with all this."

Lifting a shoulder, I smiled at him. "Thanks, Big Texas."

"I sure do miss her."

His words squeezed my damn heart. "I miss her so much too," I admitted. "All the time." Then I turned around and hit the record button again. "All right, I'm going to cry. Let me start over again first."

"Got it. I'll be quiet."

I gave him another thumbs-up and headed around the island to stop in place. I took another deep breath, closed my eyes, and then reopened them before pushing my shoulders back and starting again. "Hi, Lazy Bakers! Today I've got a special idea I want to try. Orange pound cake!"

His voice came from the living room. "I thought you were makin' orange cranberry pound cake?"

I stopped talking and lifted my gaze to land on Zac's smiling face around the edge of the camera directly in front of me. "I am. Damn it. Okay, screw it, let me start again."

"You can do it," he cheered me on.

I smiled, shook it off, and then focused again. I could do this. Okay. *I'll just go with it. Delete it later.* "Hello, Lazy Bakers! I've got a real special idea I want to try today. We're going to be making cranberry pound cake!"

"Orange cranberry pound cake," Zac piped up again.

I closed my mouth. "Shit!"

"You know you're real good at this, darlin'. It's a long name. A whole mouthful. Orange cranberry pound cake," he tried to appease me while I wanted to smack myself for screwing up the name of it again.

"Last time, damn it. I'm not starting over again," I claimed, going back around the island and deleting the recording and starting again. "You're distracting me. I can't remember the last time I had to start over this many times."

"Mama's said the same thing plenty of times."

"I'm sure she has. I'm sure she hasn't been the only one either."

His silence told me he was thinking about it. "Yeah, you're right. She's not."

I snickered. "Okay, I'm starting again." Behind the counter, I stopped. "All right. No stopping. I can do this."

"You can do anything, Little Texas," my friend said with a serious nod from where he was still on the couch. "One take, you got this."

"One take, I got this." I shook my shoulders, pressed my

lips together, held my head up high, and went back into it. "Hey, Lazy Bakers! Today, I've got a special idea I want to try just in time for the fall! Orange cranberry pound cake!"

"Nailed it," Zac whispered.

Shit. I started laughing. "Damn it, Zac!"

"What'd I do? Was I that loud? Could you hear me? I'm gettin' real into this. You're so professional. Everything is so nice. I think I'm a little jealous CJ got to do this before me."

His words hugged my heart, and I had to pause. I'd genuinely thought he'd offered to participate just to be nice. "Zac, do you want to be in it?"

He didn't even hesitate. He said, "Okay," instantly, and in the time it took me to blink, he was up and heading over.

All right.

Okay.

No more starting over, right?

I stared dead at the camera. *No more starting over.* "Well, we're having a special guest today after all."

The tall, lean man came to stand beside me, freaking hip bumping me an inch over.

I snorted and tried to keep my shit together. "My long-time friend—"

"And number one fan," he piped in.

I blinked at the camera and then blinked at him. "And number one fan, excuse me, Zac Travis."

"Hi," he greeted the camera, forcing me back to focus on what we were doing.

"And today, right after I get a microphone and an apron on Zac, we're going to be making orange cranberry pound cake."

"Just in time for the fall," Zac added loudly, looking down at me at the same time I glanced up.

We grinned at each other.

"For our ingredients today, we're going to be using...."

CHAPTER TWELVE

If I was ever going to wonder how the hell I ended up in Zac's car on the way to Austin for my cousin Lola's quinceañera....

I would have been in the shitter, because I wasn't sure how the hell it had actually happened. One minute, I'd been packing my bag and someone had been knocking away at my door. The next minute, Zac was in my apartment, in damp workout clothes, wondering what I was doing and *did I want to have lunch?*

Then an hour and three sandwiches later, he was dumping his carry-on bag into the back of his car while I'd talked to CJ downstairs about his claim of being a terrible cook. Apparently, his mom hadn't been a great cook either and it was inherited.

Anyway.

Now, hours, two podcasts, a classic hits playlist, and some K-pop that Zac had whined through, later... he was parking his car in the lot of the hotel I'd booked weeks ago. A hotel I'd had to book because apparently there was so much family in town, no one but my cousin had bothered to invite us to stay with them. I had two aunts and three uncles, and they *all* had full houses. Even then, Boogie only had a one-bedroom apartment so....

Truthfully, I was relieved we were staying somewhere else instead of sharing a bathroom with eight other people who had no sense of privacy or personal space. I was sharing a bed with Luisa, and Connie was going to share a bed with her son. Her husband was staying home because he had to work.

Zac was going to rent his own room... to go with us to a quinceañera.

Zac Travis was going to a fifteen-year-old's party.

"You sure you want to do this?" I asked for about the tenth time as we walked from the car toward the entrance to the hotel. He'd parked in literally the furthest spot away from the entrance. His reasoning was because he didn't want anyone to park close to him.

Zac huffed, pulling his suitcase along. He'd tried to take mine too, but I'd taken it from him. "Kiddo, how many times have I been around your family?"

"A lot. But that was back in the day, before you turned into Mr. Hot Shit," I explained, pulling my suitcase along too.

He grunted. "I'm not exactly on a team right now."

"So?" I didn't need to egg him on into feeling bad for himself. He could do that pretty well on his own. "For *now*. It doesn't mean you're not still Mr. Hot Shit to some people."

I just happened to glance over and see a little smile crack his face. "But not to you?"

"Nah." I elbowed him. "But on a serious note, I'm worried you're going to get harassed. Did you tell Boogie you're coming? And are you sure you don't want to go stay at Paw-Paw's instead?"

He elbowed me back, lightly. "I told him. He offered to let me crash on his couch, but...."

"How the hell could you sleep on his couch? He has that

dumb short one he bought because he liked the way it looked."

"I haven't seen it."

"Well, you're not missing out. I slept on it one night and woke up the next morning with shoulder and back pain. You'd probably need a realignment afterward." I nudged him again. "You know? Because you're old?"

That got him to look at me. "I get it. And, yeah, there's no point in stayin' at Paw-Paw's because they're all in Lubbock for the weekend. Mama's gonna kill me for not tellin' her 'til the last minute I was comin', but it's fine."

She probably would kill him for it. He'd told me he tried going back home once a month, if he wasn't staying there with them long-term during the off-season. I was sure he had to be at least a little disappointed his family wasn't in town, but I hadn't thought about inviting him because... well, he probably had things to do. He hadn't said anything else about the White Oaks, and I hadn't had the heart to bring it up.

"Why aren't you staying with family anyway?" he asked. "I remember that one time we went to Corpus Christi with Mama Lupe and she stuffed eight of us in one room, 'member that?"

I laughed. "No one invited us, and no, I don't remember that. Did Boogie have to spoon you all night on the floor?"

"Only half the night."

I snorted. "Well, if you change your mind and don't want to see everyone, run. I told Connie you were coming, but that's it."

It was his turn to laugh right as we hit the sliding doors to the lobby.

"You know what? Do you want me to book your room under my name? You famous people usually do that, don't you? So your fans don't know where you're staying?"

"Us famous people? Cut it out," he groaned. "But yeah,

that's what's... done. Or you get your assistant to book it, or your manager's assistant."

"So see? Give me your credit card."

Zac slid me a look as he reached behind him with his free hand and pulled out his wallet—a crisp newish looking navy blue one—and bopped me on the top of my head with it before I plucked it out of his hand. Then I tried to wave him away. "Beat it, kid, otherwise it'll defeat the purpose if someone recognizes you."

His eyebrows went up at the same time as a grin spread across his mouth. "Beat it?"

"Scram? Skedaddle?"

This fool laughed.

"Go. Don't show anybody your face. I don't need you getting kidnapped."

He booped me on the nose before taking a step back and grabbing my suitcase to take with him.

It only took a second to check in with my reservation and a second more to get another room two down from the one I'd be sharing with Connie and the kids. With four different keys in hand, I trudged toward Zac and handed him his. "Here you go. It's on the same floor as ours, just a couple doors down."

"LITTLE B!"

My shoulders dropped, and I turned slowly around, excited and irritated at the same time. Then again that pretty much described my relationship with Connie completely. I couldn't live with her, and I couldn't live without her.

One glance toward the door had me finding my big sister hauling ass through the sliding glass doors in what had to be five-inch heels like she was trying to win a gold medal. Connie could run faster in heels than flat-footed, that was a fact. An impressive one too. At least I thought so.

As soon as she was close enough, I told her, "Not in

public, Con. Word for word, that's what I thought we agreed. No calling me Little B in—"

"No one's listening!" the four-foot-eleven body claimed a second before she threw herself at me, arms around my shoulders, legs circling my thighs. "I've missed you."

I grunted. "Oh my God, get off."

She didn't.

She just squeezed me tighter, and I felt myself start to lean back with her weight. "Zac, please help me," I gasped, past the point of trying to get her off because I knew she wouldn't.

There was a laugh behind me before two hands slipped beneath my armpits. Then something that had to be his chest came up right behind me too. "I got you," he said above my head, actually supporting me. The warmth of his body pierced through my shirt.

"I miss you too, you heifer. Can you get off now though?" I groaned, hugging her back just as tightly and feeling my back protesting her weight. She was a small person, but my God she was heavy.

Well, that and the most weight I lifted was a cast iron Dutch oven.

"Hi, Aunt Bianca," a familiar voice said from somewhere behind my sister.

I instantly pushed her away and turned toward my nephew, pulling him in close as he hugged me back. He'd grown a couple inches since the last time we'd seen each other.

"Hi, Tía B," another voice said.

I hugged my niece too, oohing and aahing over how cute her clothes were and hugged them both all over again. Connie had hugged Zac while I'd greeted my niece and nephew, and I found them watching us. They were both smiling.

While Zac hadn't been as close to Connie even though they were only five years apart in age, she had still been around long enough, rolling her eyes and talking shit to him and Boogie in the periphery. Basically, he'd witnessed or overheard all kinds of stuff. And I knew he'd seen her at least a couple times over the years.

"Are you getting hungry? Want to drop off our stuff and then go to Tía Meche's for food since it's the least they can do for being rude?"

"Did they buy food, or did someone make it?" I asked, wanting to make sure I wasn't going to put myself into a situation that going to a restaurant would save me from. I loved this side of my family, but sometimes they brought up stuff that I really didn't want to hear. It was why I had warned Zac that I would more than likely not stay at the party for longer than a couple of hours.

"Everybody was bringing something," Connie explained. "Except us."

It took me a moment to process what she was hinting at. "*No,*" I gasped when I did.

My sister nodded. "She's bringing tres leches."

Well, *shit*. That settled it. I could listen to anything for a little while if it meant tres leches cake. "Okay, let's do it."

"Who made tres leches?" even Zac asked suspiciously, hung up on it.

I'd forgotten he loved it as much as I did, or at least he used to. "Rico's wife."

"Rico with the neck tat?"

The neck tat that was a set of lips that made me laugh every time I saw them? "Yup."

He blinked. "Let's go."

We piled into his BMW... after I ran for the front seat before Connie tried to steal it. Since she didn't know what he even drove in the first place, it wasn't a competition.

"Fucking cheater," she gasped for breath as she slid into the back seat.

"I wondered if you two were the same... and it's nice to see y'all haven't changed a bit," Zac said in a cheery voice as he turned on the car at the same time the kids slammed the doors shut.

I peeked at my sister in the back seat, and we both shrugged.

We hadn't changed much. Her husband, Richard, had sighed over us nonstop during the time I'd lived with them. Connie might be hitting forty, and I might be close to thirty, but when we were together, it was like we made up for the fact we hadn't been little kids together so we were going to do it from here on out.

"Uncle Boogie says they're stuck at twelve," my nephew piped in. "Then Mom says he's eleven, and he laughs."

"What have I told you about Uncle Boogie?" Connie asked.

"I'm not saying it!" Guillermo claimed.

I turned to Zac and could see him staring ahead, pressing his lips together.

"Tell me," I whispered to my nephew, who shook his head. "Will you tell Zac?"

He shook his head again. "It has a bad word," he tried to explain.

"Please. Tell me. I won't tell Boogie you said it."

The ten-year-old seemed to think about it.

"I'll give you five dollars."

Out of the corner of my eye, I saw my eight-year-old niece shift forward and blurt out, "Mom says Uncle Boogie is a punk-ass. Can I have the five dollars?"

Zac choked, I started cracking up, and Connie laughed even after she said, "That's the only time you can say that word, Luisa." Then she glanced at me and said, "Tell me I'm wrong."

"Yeah, you can have the five. You are wrong," I laughed. "And he's only a little bit of a punk. Not a total one."

Zac snickered as he drove, and we listened to Guillermo and Luisa bicker the entire ride over to our aunt's house. Of course, there were about a hundred cars parked on the street. He found a spot a few houses down. We piled out, and I spotted Boogie's car as we headed over to the two-story house I'd been to about a hundred times over my life. The same one I had lived in while I'd finished high school and decided what I was going to do afterward.

At the front door, Connie rang the doorbell once and then threw the door open, not bothering to wait.

"I want to get food first and then go tell everyone hi," I said over my shoulder. "Want to come with or are you going to look for Boogie?"

"Food," Zac answered immediately, making me smile.

Except for a couple of kids hogging the living room who waved at us instead of actually getting up to give us a hug, there was hardly anyone in the house. Score for us. From the sounds of it, everyone was outside. My aunt and uncle had set up a trampoline in the back... even though they didn't have a grandkid yet. In the kitchen, I grabbed a stack of paper plates and passed them around.

Connie followed after her kids, watching what they picked at and adding more to their plates. Zac followed behind me getting food. Just as I went to put a slice of cake on a small paper plate, a blur of a dark head came out of nowhere. A boy I recognized as Tony ran up to the tres leches and stuck his hand into the pan, scooping out a big mound of it and shoving it straight into his mouth.

"Eww, Tony, don't use your hand. I'll help you if you want some. Put it on a plate," I griped, figuring I could cut the part out where his dirty little fingers had been. Seriously, they were dirty. Last time I'd seen him, months ago, he'd been digging boogers out of his nose and eating them.

The boy, probably nine-ish, sneered at me as he started to back up. "Mind your own business," he said before running off.

I gasped even as my nephew said, "Mom!"

Staring after the little jerk, I could only shake my head. "I'm gonna fight a child today. I can feel it."

Something warm landed on the back of my neck, and I knew without looking it was Zac's hand. "You're about the same size as one, so go for it."

I looked up at him with a straight face. "You know what, Zac?"

Those blue eyes were locked on mine as he drawled, seriously, way too seriously for the sparkle in his eye, "Tell me, darlin'."

"You're a pain in the ass."

His laugh filled my ears as he squeezed the back of my neck again. "Want me to pay your niece to trip him?"

I thought about it for a second before nodding. "If not, maybe my nephew can kick him in the face again."

An amused eyebrow went up. "Do I wanna know how that happened?"

Connie chimed in as she spooned food onto Luisa's plate, using her fingers as quotation marks. "Breakdancing."

"Mom! It was breakdancing! I swear!" my nephew insisted.

Connie winked at him. "You keep telling yourself that. I'm not even a little mad at you."

"But you were mad at me for the hole in the wall."

"That was different."

"Whose kid is that?" Zac asked.

"Do you remember Chuy?"

He made a thoughtful face and then shook his head.

I rolled a shoulder back. "Eh. It's his kid."

"Squinty eyes? Fat head? Little body?" Connie offered before screwing up her face. "Never mind, that's like half our cousins."

"What is?" a familiar voice asked from out of nowhere.

It was Boogie. I turned around to find him coming in from the living room, holding a stack of empty, used plates.

"Squinty eyes, fat heads, and little bodies," my sister replied.

He groaned as he came forward, dropping the plates into a big, black trash bag first before making his way over. He hugged me, then Zac, and finally headed for the kids.

Luisa was in the middle of giving him a hug when she said, "Uncle Boogie, I called you a punk-a word, but I love you, and Tía Bianca paid me five dollars to say it."

My cousin blinked, and I caught an edge of his smile before he held out his hand. "Give me half."

"No!"

"Give me a kiss then?"

She sighed but slapped her little hands on his shoulders and pecked him on the cheek. But I didn't miss how Boogie snuck another hug in. He was going to be such a good dad, I could feel it.

And that reminded me that I needed to start trying to be nicer to his future wife the next time I saw her, which was fortunately not going to be today because she was working in New York or something.

We made our way outside, and I had barely gotten through the sliding glass door that Boogie had shoved open for us when I heard, "Ah, shit! Las güeras are here!"

Connie and I looked at each other.

"Zac? Is that you?" the same person called out. I was pretty sure it was my cousin with the neck tattoo. No matter how many times Boogie told him to stop calling us las güeras, the white girls, because we were half, he still did it. Fucker.

And in true Boogie fashion, he muttered, "Shut the hell up, Rico."

I loved him.

But I still called out, "Don't be jelly my Spanish is better than yours, Rico." You'd figure after this long he'd stop pointing out our dad was Irish, but nope. He still said something about it every time we saw him.

He didn't say anything in return.

"Bianca!" one of my little cousins shouted from out of nowhere, and I barely had time to set my plate of cake and tamales down before a small body banged into the back of my legs. "Will you come jump on the trampoline with me?"

Glancing down, I found my six-year-old cousin with her arms wrapped around me, blinking up at me with deep brown eyes. She had pigtails, one was higher than the other, and she was missing two front teeth. She was fucking adorable, and I had no idea how she was related to the cake-eating demon inside.

"Please?" she begged.

Well, shit. I looked down at her and knew there was only one answer. "Yeah. Give me one second, okay?"

She nodded, and I looked up to find Zac watching me, a little smile on his face.

"I'll protect your food, don't you worry."

I was pretty sure I heard Connie snicker under her breath as she went around me.

I told everyone hi really quick—even annoying Rico—as my cousin tugged me toward the trampoline, and once I was done, I chased her to it, thanking God I'd worn tennis shoes. There were two other cousins already on it, sweaty and laughing. But the six-year-old, who I'd played with on it the last time we'd come to my aunt's house, kept on pulling at my jeans, saying, "Do it again! Do it again!"

It.

The backflip.

"I don't know...," I told her as I jumped a little. "Can't we just jump?"

"No! Please!" she begged.

I had literally done gymnastics for like three months twenty years ago.

"Please," she begged some more.

I knew I was going to regret it, I really did. "Okay, let me try," I told her, already hating myself but not sure how I could get away with it when she was shrieking.

So I did, with a seven-year-old, a six-year-old, and a five-year-old cheering me on.

Well, I tried to do a backflip.

And my back said *nope*.

I landed it.

But *nope*.

"Oh my God," I whispered to myself as I rolled to lay flat on my back, gasping for air because somehow tweaking my lower back had me unable to fucking breathe.

"Are you okay?" my little cousin whispered as she stood over me.

"Are you dead?" the older cousin asked.

"I want to be," I told them with a groan.

"Want me to get Connie?" my same older cousin asked.

Oh hell no. She was the last person I wanted to come see this and laugh at me for trying to do a backflip I had no business or enough experience to do. "I'm fine, just give me a second," I grunted, still lying there, flat on my fucking back.

"Peewee?" a familiar voice came out of nowhere. "You okay?"

Well, Zac was marginally better than Connie. I moved my

head to the side to see him standing on the opposite end of the trampoline from where we'd entered. He didn't have a worried expression on his face, but it was something.

"Yeah, you know, just threw my back out a little, I think."

I could tell the corners of his mouth went up. "Just a little?"

"Yeah, just a little."

His lips were still trembling from trying not to smile or laugh as he asked, "Need some help?"

"That would be nice."

Then he grinned, and before he told me what he was doing, his hands went for my ankles and he was dragging me across the trampoline toward the edge. I sat up as much as I could once my butt hit the metal edge, but his arms slid under the backs of my knees and shoulders, and he hoisted me up into his arms, smiling the whole time.

Well, at least until he turned, kneeled, and lowered me to the grass right there, where the majority of the trampoline blocked us from being seen by everyone on the deck.

"Lean forward," he said the second I was down.

I did and grunted the whole time. I was pretty sure I whined too.

He chuckled. "You're all right; you tweaked it. Happens to me all the time. Relax."

Relax?

His fingers dug into my lower back a second later, and I straight-up grunted as he kneaded my muscles.

"That was a pretty impressive backflip," he said from behind as he dug some more into my back and I groaned again. It hurt, but it felt kind of good at the same time. But mostly it hurt.

"I hope it was if I'm not able to walk tomorrow, damn it."

"You'll be fine," he assured me a second before his hands went under my shirt and touched my bare back.

I only froze for a second before I relaxed and let him keep doing it. I mean, he got massages all the time. What was a little bare skin? It wasn't like he was touching my butt or anything.

"Thank you," I told him with another grunt.

"You're welcome," he said, still working those incredibly strong fingers right above the band to my jeans. I hoped my butt crack wasn't peeking out. "You gotta be careful so you don't hurt yourself."

I waited until he changed the motion he was doing and moved to a slightly different spot. "Thank you for coming to save me," I told him, trying to ignore the feel of his warm fingertips.

And the urge to shiver over them.

His thumbs pressed deep along my spine, and I winced. "I was more worried about you flyin' off the side and breakin' an arm."

"I just broke my back, no big deal."

His puff of a laugh was low as he kept on massaging me.

"Zac?"

"Hmm?"

"Who's watching our tres leches if you're here?"

———

I felt a warm weight wiggle in behind me, hot breath blowing against the back of my neck.

"Are you awake?" the voice whispered.

I was on my side, holding my phone up to my face as I replied, "No."

Connie dug her knuckle into a spot on my spine, and I squeaked when she got me right on a nerve. "You awake now?" she giggled inches from my neck.

Reaching behind me, I tried to aim for her arm, but she

was too close and grabbed my fist with both hands, holding it in place so that I couldn't get her. "Oh my God, why would you do that? My back still hurts, you monster. What are you doing?"

"Ah, you're fine. I saw you ice it. Luisa's taking a shower," she whispered. Her son was passed out on the other bed. He'd been the first one to jump in and shower and had been out like a log by the time I'd gotten out.

"You all right?" I asked her, turning off my screen and rolling onto my back carefully, with another grunt, to get a good look at her. Zac had worked on my back for at least five minutes, assuring me the whole time that I'd be fine later, but it was still achy. I'd walked back to his car like I needed a cane... and gotten teased the whole time for it.

With her hair wet and all over the place, and no makeup, she looked like a version of Connie I hadn't seen since before she'd been too young to put on makeup. Our parents hadn't let her until she'd turned sixteen. Well, Mamá Lupe hadn't let her until she'd turned sixteen was more like it. "I'm good." She let go of my hand and tried to knuckle me again, but this time, it was my turn to grab her hand and make sure she couldn't get me again. She raised her eyebrows. "What's up with you?"

"Nothing, I'm good. Work sucks, but everything else is good." I smiled at her.

"Are you going to make me ask or are you telling me on your own?"

I blinked. "Tell you what?"

She sighed. "What's going on with you and...." She made her eyebrows go up and down.

"Who?" I tried to think about what I'd done that evening.

After going outside at my aunt's house and nearly throwing out my back, we'd all hung around the table and talked—mostly talked shit. In a good way, not the way our mean aunt tried to get away with saying things.

One of my cousins had brought his friend over, but the guy had sat across the table and I hadn't done more than greet him. I'd been too busy talking to Zac, Boogie, my sister, and the kids to do more. And we'd talked so much crap during that time, even the kids adding in their own quips, it had been a ton of fun.

So... I literally had no clue what the hell she was talking about.

And it was apparent she didn't believe me.

But then I realized she had to have been doing drugs in the bathroom when she said, "Zac."

"Zac?" I looked at her. "You on something?"

"Not in fifteen years."

I snorted and poked at her face.

She grabbed my hand and tucked it under her chin. "I'm not joking. What's going on with you two?"

"Nothing."

Had I... done something? Looked at him weird? I liked Zac. I liked him a lot.

But that was it.

But she wasn't going to drop it now. "You two have been hanging out a ton."

I kept my face even. "Because we're friends and we live in the same city. We've always been friends."

"That was ten years ago."

"What's the difference now and then?"

"Exactly. That was ten years and a few hundred girls ago."

Well, that felt shitty, and I could have gone without the mental picture. "Yeah, but he hasn't known any of those girls since they were three like me."

She scrunched up her nose. "Yeah, that's not what I mean, and you know it."

"Yeah, but you know we've always gotten along."

"And it was cute when you were younger, but now...."

"Now what?"

"Now it just seems a little fishy."

I didn't like where this was going and knew I needed to shut it down as soon as possible. "You seem a little fishy," I muttered.

Connie rolled her eyes. "Just tell me the truth."

"Nothing is going on," I whispered, lifting up a little to glance over her shoulder and make sure my nephew was asleep.

He was.

"He's just my friend." I swallowed. "And I know he doesn't see me like that, Con. I think he's just lonely or something. He probably still feels like he owes me since I 'saved his life' a million years ago. And he rarely talks to me about football stuff. I don't really ask about it much either. He probably just likes getting away from it sometimes."

That had my sister's face softening.

"We're just friends. I'm not following him around like a puppy. He calls me. He invites me to his house. I leave him alone. He comes over sometimes," I told her in another whisper just as the water in the shower cut off. "And we just get along really well. Like we always have."

"B, I wasn't putting it all on you. Him too. I know you would've told me if you invited him, but I know that you wouldn't have."

"Well, yeah. He invites himself. I like it; I miss him. You know I have some friends, I know a lot of people, but it's different with Zac. It was just like putting on old shoes that fit really great."

"You're sure?"

It was my turn to roll my eyes. "Yeah, I'm sure. I'm not his type, Con. I was just reminding him about when I used to fart around him not too long ago. I love him, but I only dream about things I can make happen on my own now."

"Or with me."

I smiled. "Or with you."

"I don't ask because I worry about your feelings, B. You know that, right? I just want to know if there's something going on you didn't want to tell me about."

"Nope."

Her face got thoughtful again.

"Nope," I repeated.

She sighed. "You get along so well though…. I don't know, B. I guess it'd be cute if things were different." I wasn't sure what she meant by different. What? If Boogie wasn't his best friend? If I was older or prettier? Or he was different and wanted something serious?

"Well, we're just meant to be friends, and there's nothing there like that. I doubt he would ever do anything to ruin the longest relationship he's ever had."

"Well, whatever. It'd be nice to get some tickets in the box if you know what I'm saying." She elbowed me.

I laughed. "I'm sure if you just asked, he'd get you tickets."

"He probably would, right?"

"I think so."

"Club tickets would be cool."

I looked at her.

"Box tickets would be nicer."

"You're a monster."

"Your mama's a monster."

CHAPTER THIRTEEN

We were inside the event hall when Boogie stopped in front of the double doors that led into the ballroom and lifted his arms to block us from going any further.

I was trailing at the end of our small group—the kids, Connie, Zac, my cousin, and I—

trying not to limp over my stupidity. I'd decided to wear brand-new shoes without breaking them in, like a newbie, and was going to need a Band-Aid ASAP. As in, the second we sat down, I was kicking these bitches off and stealing one or two from Connie. She always had a bunch in her purse. Just earlier in the day, before the mass for Lola's quince, we'd gone to the outlet mall and Guillermo had busted his ass in the parking lot, requiring two.

"What are you doing, Boog? I need to take these shoes off before my toes start bleeding," I whined the second I saw what he was doing.

"Yeah, Boog, what are you doing?" Connie echoed as she held her phone against her face. "No, Mom, I'm talking to Boogie," she backtracked into the receiver.

I'd been side-eyeing her and eavesdropping on her conver-

sation the entire ride to the event hall. I'd tried to call my
mom while we'd been at the mall, but she hadn't answered.
All I'd wanted was to check in with her. She hadn't called me
back either, but she had randomly called Connie. I'd yelled
out a "hi" in the car and gotten a "hello, my love" back.

I hadn't rolled my eyes. I'd stopped doing that a long
time ago.

"I thought food was going to start getting served soon?"
Zac piped in as he hovered at my side, bringing me back to
what the hell Boogie was doing.

I tried my best not to look at Zac, especially after the
conversation I'd had with my sister the night before.

And especially not when he was dressed in a sleek dark
blue suit that hugged his body like it had been tailor-made for
him—which it more than likely had been—and a white shirt.
The worst part was that he'd brushed his hair at some point
since we'd had breakfast that morning; he'd gone over to
Boogie's afterward and spent hours playing *Call of Duty* or
something beforehand. When my niece had opened the door
after he'd knocked and he'd strolled into our small, messy
room, I'd felt something in me stutter for a second. But I'd
sucked that shit up even though I'd whistled at him and asked
if Mama had packed his clothes for him.

The truth was, he looked great, just like a prince but
better.

And, unfortunately, I had a bunch of distant relatives with
no shame that I was mentally preparing myself to have to put
up with, coming up and fawning all over him. I mean, they
could do whatever they wanted, and so could he.

"One second," Boogie told us before dropping his arms. "I
need you to promise me something."

After looking around like there was someone else he
could be talking to, Connie asked, "Who?"

Our cousin flicked his finger at us—at me and Con.

I blinked. "What? Why me?"

"The dancing—" he started to say before Connie scoffed.

"You're not doing that again. Let's go sit down," she muttered, shoving him to the side and then saying something to our mom on the phone.

I pointed at Boogie and stuck my tongue out as we passed him, heading toward a table close to one of the four beautiful, curtain-covered walls, right at the edge of the hall. Luckily, we were early and there weren't that many people already in the salon. Most of our family were pretty shit at getting anywhere on time, but we had all wanted to take advantage of the free food. Well, at least, some of us did. I couldn't speak for Zac, but I was pretty positive I'd spotted a package of beef jerky in his jacket pocket.

We sat around the table, Zac taking a chair on the other side of Boogie, right by me. My nephew was on my other side.

"No, listen to me," our cousin started up again as he scooted his chair in. "There are certain things nobody wants to see, especially me. So the two of you need to keep it together."

"I don't know what you're talking about. Bianca, do you know what he's talking about?" Connie asked as she pushed her chair in and folded her hands on top of the sequined, lavender tablecloth. She was already done talking, I guess. That had been quick.

I shook my head as I scooted my chair forward too and grabbed the napkin that had been folded into the shape of a swan, ready to use that shit the second the food started getting served, any minute now, I figured. "Nope, I have no idea what he's talking about."

Actually, I was pretty sure I did—mostly because I did actually remember what had happened the last time Connie and I had been to a family party that had booze and a dance floor. I regretted nothing.

"Bullshit," Boogie muttered before he cringed. "I'm sorry, kids."

Connie and I both snorted. Like they hadn't heard worse just about every other hour of their lives. *Oh, Boogie.*

"B.S.," he corrected himself and kept going. "You've got to keep it PG tonight. There are kids around; this isn't a wedding. No tootsie rolls—"

I don't know what it said about me and my sister that we both gasped.

Zac slid right in, turning that soft blue gaze toward me with an amused expression on his face. "You're too young to know how to do the tootsie roll," he said with a chuckle.

I gave him an innocent smile. "Am I?"

Boogie ignored us and kept going. "I'm still scarred from Chato's wedding. None of that tonight."

Zac hadn't stopped looking at me with his curious face, like he didn't believe what my cousin was saying, so I shrugged at him.

"Why do I feel like you're not listening to me?" Boog asked.

"I am." I patted my swan towel. "Was it the hammer dance? Was that what scarred you? Because I told Connie that it was too much."

Connie burst out laughing just as Boogie rolled his eyes and Zac asked, "I missed out on you doing the hammer dance?"

My niece sighed out of nowhere. "Uncle Zac, at Uncle Rico's and Tía Maria's party, they did this song about backing that—"

"What have I told you about telling everybody all of our business?" Connie asked her daughter, shaking her head like she couldn't believe her own kid would rat out her secrets.

"And Mom tried to show Aunt B how to do the sprinkler," Guillermo put in as he picked up a little mint that had been set by the plate in front of him.

Boogie groaned.

I was too busy laughing just remembering that evening and Boogie trying to drag us both off the floor, especially after we'd tried backing our asses up into each other, then into him even as he tried pushing us away.

"You joined in, so don't even start." I snorted, pointing at my cousin.

"It's less embarrassing if I'm involved," he tried to defend himself but started cracking up too because he was full of shit. He'd stayed on the dance floor just as long as we had after that. We'd made a little circle that had family members coming and going all night.

"Mom, what was it that Uncle Boogie did? You remember? He hurt his back?" my nephew asked. "The dolphin?"

Zac sat up straight, those baby blue eyes swinging toward me. "Was it...?"

"Yes." I cackled, knowing exactly what he was referring to. "He tried doing the worm."

"I *did* the worm!"

Zac threw both hands up to his head. "Didn't you learn your lesson the first time, you ass?"

"I have a bad back!"

I mouthed "*holy shit*" to Zac.

His mouth was open, and those white teeth were out as he nodded in agreement.

"You know what? I hate all of you. Not you Yermo and Luisa, but you three...."

Connie sniffed as she plucked her own swan napkin. "Haters gonna hate."

I was too busy snorting as servers started coming out of

nowhere with trolleys full of food, and I was pretty sure my niece clapped in excitement.

"Aunt B, they should have asked you to make the food and the cake," my nephew announced.

Dropping my palm over my chest, I told him I loved him. Then I asked him when he was going to come over to do another video with me.

It didn't take long at all for the food to be served, with baskets of bread being left in the middle of each table, and we were all too busy eating to do more than make faces at each other. I met Zac's eyes at one point, and we grinned at each other. Right around the time we were finishing, the lights in the ballroom dropped, and pink and white lights around the outskirts of the room illuminated the walls as our cousin strolled in to some pretty majestic music that seemed totally over the top. We clapped, and Connie hooted. Lola danced with her dad, then her brothers as the servers came around and picked up all the plates.

Then the music started.

I only fought Connie for about three seconds when she got up, grabbed her son with one hand, gestured to her daughter with her chin, then went for my hand.

"I just ate. Give me a second," I moaned even as she tugged at my arm.

"You need to work off those calories," she replied, really putting some weight into it. "Quit being a heifer. You know you want to."

I did want to.

Ah, fuck it.

I gestured to Boogie as I stood up. "Come save me if I'm not back in thirty."

He had a breadstick in his mouth that looked like a cigar. "Okay. Uh-huh."

He was useless. I knew it. "Save me, Zac," I called out to my friend as I followed my sister and her kids.

"I got you, darlin'," he called out after me even as he reached for a breadstick too.

I was pretty sure I saw him tap it against Boogie's like they were swords before I turned back.

But... he didn't have me. He didn't have me at all.

I lost count of how many songs played while we danced in a circle, my sister, me, and her two kids, with a couple more cousins coming to join along the way. A few times, I grabbed my niece or nephew for some one-on-one, and at least twice Connie backed her ass up against me, and I was pretty sure I heard Boogie's voice over the music... probably telling us to stop.

Finally, at some point, I ran off and went back to our table, finding Zac there... surrounded by four different women. I knew one of them. I could only see his profile, and it looked like he was smiling at them.

And that was fine. Good. At least he wasn't bored and miserable.

Where the hell was Boogie?

Somehow, Zac must have sensed my approach because his eyes instantly swung toward me the second I got close enough, and I saw the truth. He was smiling, but it was his polite smile, not the real one that was so bright it lit him up from the inside out.

I smirked.

One corner of his mouth hooked up higher than the other.

His new companions must have seen him stop paying attention to them because when they spotted me making my way over, two of them pushed their chairs back and got up, which was weird, but okay.

"There she is," Zac called out as I stopped behind the

chair that I'd been sitting in and sucked back my leftover watered-down lemonade.

He held his own glass up toward me, and I took it and drank it all too. I was thirsty.

"Sorry, ladies," my friend said as he got to his feet as I set his glass on the table. "I owe someone a dance."

He did?

"She's so busy I had to schedule it in," he lied as he shoved his chair under the table.

He was using me as an excuse to get away. All right. My feet hurt, and I wanted to sit down, but I wouldn't leave him hanging.

I made eye contact with my second cousin, who had been one of the people surrounding him and the only one I recognized, and waved.

I didn't like the curious face she made back at me, but whatever, she still waved in return. I looked back at Zac as he got to my side, grabbed my hand, and led me out to the floor as—like it had been freaking planned—a country song came over the speakers.

Zac grinned as he reached for my free hand once we were on the edge of the dance floor and set it on his shoulder. "Still remember how to two-step?"

A blurry memory of him teaching Boogie—and me—how to dance a lifetime ago filled my head and made me smile. "*Shit.*"

He beamed down at me, his hands warm and mine probably even hotter, as he led me straight into it, moving around the floor, spinning me around from time to time, and thankfully not stepping on my toes a single time. "Kiddo, you're better at this than I am," he called out loudly, his pink mouth wide with laughter.

"I'm better at a lot of things than you are," I joked. "You're rusty."

"Rusty?" he had the nerve to ask. "I've been doin' this since you were in diapers, Peewee."

"Eh."

I wasn't sure if he specifically pulled me in or if it just kind of happened as we moved, but we were right up in there together, our thighs constantly brushing together. Zac twirled me around right at the end a few times, and he made a face to warn me as he dipped me back right at the end, with a laugh that had me choking one out too as blood rushed into my nose.

When another country song started right after that, he spun me around the floor some more, putting it all into it like I'd offended him or something during the first song.

If he'd expected me to trip over my own feet or step on his toes... he would have been in for a real surprise.

I knew he was impressed when his gaze caught mine, fore-head furrowing as he asked in a voice that I barely just caught, "Who you been dancin' with like this?"

I caught a glimpse of my sister's face as he spun me around, and I waited until we were facing each other again—well, I was facing his chest more than his face until I lifted my head—and answered back loud enough for him to hope-fully hear, "People."

I'd spent a Saturday a month going to country clubs with one of my old coworkers. My ex used to hate me going, but since he didn't like to dance, I didn't listen to him. My favorite partners had always been the older men whose wives were so busy dancing with other people that they were pawning their husbands off on strangers. *Those men* knew how to dance.

Just like Zac did.

Fluid and almost sinuous, a lifetime athlete who knew every movement of his body. Strong and secure.

I wondered for a second how many partners he'd had that he'd gotten so good at it with.

Whatever.

Apparently, my answer hadn't been enough for him because the second we were facing each other again, he ducked his head to speak into my ear, his breath a tickle along the sensitive skin there, "What people?"

My mouth was inches from his chest. I could smell the sweet, clean scent of his cologne. "People at the club, buster. Good teachers, huh?"

His breath was still in my ear. "What club?"

I told him the name, imagining him going for a moment —imagining him dancing with any of the hundreds of women who went to it—and then forced myself to stop that mental image.

He waited so long to say anything else, his next words surprised me more than they should have. "I'll dance with you anytime you want."

"Oh yeah?" I asked, lifting my face.

He was focused down on me, on my face—eyes, whatever. "Yeah" was his simple answer.

"You don't mind the height difference?" I'd kicked off my shoes and put Band-Aids on after we ate.

"Nuh-uh, shorty," he said with a smile that lit me up completely, all affection and love and comfort. "You move real well with me."

I waited until he'd spun me around again to say, "That's Miss Shorty to you, and you still got it, old man."

I felt his laugh in the way his chest puffed against mine more than I heard it.

We moved toward the right and then the left, the hand that had at some point moved to span the center of my back sliding a little lower over my gold wrap dress. I could feel the pressure and weight of every single one of his fingers on me.

That was when I glanced over and saw Connie and Boogie moving across the floor... arguing.

"Look at these assholes," I muttered, gesturing toward them with my chin.

Zac's laugh brushed my ear again, and it made me smile when he lifted his head and peeked at them. The hand he had on my back flexing for a second before he moved us around. "Did I tell you how nice you look today?"

"Nope."

His breath tickled my ear again. "Well, you look real nice, kiddo. I like your hair like this."

I squeezed his hand and smiled up at him. I'd just left it curly and tied it loosely back with a couple pieces sneaking out because my hair didn't like being restrained unless I'd straightened the shit out of it. "Thank you, Snack Pack. You look real nice too."

He winked at me, his smile that lopsided one that was my favorite.

We danced another song, this slow thing that had us moving together in a circle with my arms on his shoulders and those big, big hands light on my waist. It could have been romantic and sweet... if we were anyone else. Instead, we cracked jokes the whole time.

And that was when the DJ called everyone to the floor... to do the hokey pokey.

Zac's hands loosened, and he took a step back.

I grabbed his forearm. "Where are you going?"

His face was a little bit pink under the lights, but he was grinning. "To go sit this one out."

"What? Why?"

One corner of his mouth went up, and he gave the table we'd been at a side look. "'Cause. It's the hokey pokey." He drew his forearm across his forehead before blasting me with another bright, white smile.

I blinked at him. "You're gonna make me do it by myself?"

He was still smiling even as his head lolled to the side. "All right. Come on, I'll do the hokey pokey with you then."

And he did, his expression nearly pained, but he was laughing the whole time he turned himself around along with the two hundred other people at the venue.

Afterward, Boogie came over and asked me to dance, my sister gesturing to Zac to come over to her.

One line dance and another song later, my aunt came over and stole my cousin, and I took the chance to put my shoes back on, with a groan, and go get something to drink and pee. Zac was spinning Luisa, my niece around, and my sister was talking to Boogie's dad.

That was when I got cornered by the one person in the family everyone tried to avoid. The one person who I had purposely kept an eye on to make sure we didn't get close enough for her to feel the need to come over and say hi. We'd chosen our table by the wall on purpose.

Shit!

"Hola, Bianca," the older woman said as she purposely blocked the exit to the bathroom.

I pasted just about the fakest smile in the universe onto my face—one that rivaled every expression I'd ever given Gunner—as I finished drying my hands. "Hi, Tía Licha," I said, taking my time to turn around and give her a hug—the most half-assed hug in the history of hugs, but it wasn't like she deserved more. She'd always been mean, especially to my mom, Connie, and me.

My mom's cousin raked her gaze up and down my body as she stayed exactly where she was standing. "I like your dress."

Wait for it.

"Did you gain weight?"

She'd gained weight, but okay. I tried to smile at her, but you try and form a smile when your damn face is made from granite. It was a grimace. It was definitely a grimace that I made at her, trying its best to disguise itself as a smile and failing big-time. Because I knew all about respecting my elders. I could remember the one and only time my abuelita called for me and I answered with ¿que?—what—instead of ¿mande?

I don't think I'd ever backtracked so fast in my life.

But even my mom had lost her patience with her cousin a long time ago. I wasn't sure what was said, but I did know that my dad had to grab Mom by the back of her pants and carry her out of the room like she was a bowling ball. That was after years of little cutting comments she was known to give to everyone.

So I knew I was going to be polite, but not an inch more than I needed to.

She was so mean, it honestly surprised me she still got invited places and that everyone hadn't just had a meeting where everybody agreed to keep family get-togethers a secret so she wouldn't go.

I settled for shrugging at her. If I didn't say anything, maybe she'd get bored and stop talking to me faster.

It didn't work.

"Where are your parents?"

That's where she was going with this from the get-go. I should've expected it. "They're in Nicaragua right now."

Her "Hmmph" said everything. "Where's your boyfriend?"

And she went there too.

I blinked at her; then I blinked at her some more. I couldn't exactly call my aunt a nosey heifer, could I? As much as I might fucking wish I could. Knowing I didn't have time, I smiled at her. "Which one?"

She blinked.

I hoped she got a bunion.

"It was nice seeing you, byeeee," I called out over my

shoulder as I sped toward the door and got the hell out of there.

Turning around, I gave the door both middle fingers. Fucking hell, I was going to have to tell Connie all about that shit. That woman was something else.

"What are you doing?"

I jumped and found a figure leaning against the pillar in front of the bathroom door with a big grin on his face.

It was Zac, and his face was flushed.

"Escaping my aunt and flipping her off," I told him as I stopped in front of him, tucking my fingers back into my fist, ready to fight another day. "What are you doing, creeper?"

He snickered and ignored my question, throwing out one of his. "Which one?"

I reached forward and slipped my hand into the crook of his elbow, trying to pull him away. The last thing I wanted was for her to come out and see us talking and make some other dumb comment or question. Luckily, he let me. "Licha. She only managed to ask if I'd gained weight and then ask about my ex, so it was kind of my day in a way."

He followed me toward the doors to the hall, his inner elbow cupped in my palm. "Your ex?" he asked.

"Uh-huh. She made it seem like she didn't know we had split up when I know she damn well knew about it," I explained.

Out of the corner of my eye, I saw him glance down at me, but I didn't look up. "What ex?"

Well, it wasn't like it was some secret, and okay, maybe I'd purposely avoided mentioning him, but it was just because I liked to pretend that stage in my life hadn't happened. A whole five years. "Kenny. I don't like to talk about it. We split up almost two years ago." I didn't want to tell him the rest, but knowing him, he was going to ask. "We were together for five years. He's why I moved here. We met when I lived in North Carolina with Connie. His job transferred him here, then eventually Richard—that's Connie's husband—got moved to Texas, and they came back too."

"Five years?" he asked slowly.

"Yeah, we were engaged for a minute and everything."

Under my hand, his arm tensed. "I didn't know that. What happened?"

Of course he was going to ask. "At first, it was the same old shit. He told me he was going out of town for work, but surprise, my coworkers invited me to go to the movies and I said yes, and he was there with his ex-girlfriend, who I guess had flown down to see him. He had his arm around her and everything. How about that, huh?"

There. Done. I glanced up at him and instantly met his eyes.

He was frowning. "What'd you do?"

We stopped just outside the doors to the event hall, and I let go of his arm. "I went to his condo, left the ring and the key on his kitchen counter, then spent the next two hours texting everyone that we both knew what he'd done and to please not tell him anything about me, and I blocked his number. Connie drove down that night with the kids and stayed with me. It just so happened that my lease was almost over with my roommate at the time, and I moved out two weeks later and got my new one." I had originally been supposed to move in with him, but....

The lines across his forehead got deep.

I smiled at him. "He went to my job a couple times, and I pretended not to know him. He made excuses, tried to say nothing happened, then said it was the first time. Whatever. I should have known he was a dud when he said he'd rather get a vasectomy than go to Disney World with me." Shrugging, I said, "Then he tried to sue me. So that's that. Next time I'll listen to Boogie when he tells me he doesn't like someone."

"Boog didn't like him?"

"Nooo. But he was already dating Lauren and things were already awkward between us, so we just didn't talk about them in front of each other." I thought about the women Zac had supposedly been with and decided not to ask about his dating life.

I didn't want to know.

He stopped suddenly and turned. "Hold on, darlin'. Did you say he tried to sue you?"

I'd been waiting for that. This wasn't where I wanted to talk about it, but I knew he wouldn't let me put it off any longer. "Yeah. He claimed he was entitled to part of my Lazy Baker business. That he helped me come up with it. That he helped me run it, even though all he did was edit my videos and help with filming. Dickhead. I ended up having to settle with him so he'd finally drop it."

Zac's head reared back, and his forehead was furrowed. "You settled with him? For how much?"

I bit my lip. "I've never told anyone before the right amount." And then I told him.

And Zac blinked slowly. "US Dollars?"

"Unfortunately."

Even in the poor lighting, I could tell his face went pale. "Where the hell did you come up with that kind of money?"

I poked him. "My piggy bank, where else?" I grinned at him, pleased with myself for doing well enough that even he couldn't believe it. It made me feel extra proud of myself. Just for a moment, before I remembered how much of an idiot I had been. "He knew everything. How much money I was making, how much I had in savings. Everything. So he went after me for all of it." Anger stirred my chest, and I forced a tight, uncomfortable smile on my face. "That's why I didn't quit my job at the gym. We just settled six months ago. I'm barely getting my feet back under me. I stopped accepting sponsors while all of that was going on because I was genuinely worried that the more money I made, the more I'd have to give him, and I didn't want him to end up with more of my hard-earned work. But he still got so much of it. I feel like an idiot."

His mouth parted, and his gaze was intense on mine. "That's why you never said nothin'?"

"Yeah. How stupid was I, Zac? I considered marrying that asshole. I didn't see that he was capable of something like that. I wasted so much time and energy. And he got almost all of my money. Honestly, between us, it really fucked me up for a while. I still have trust issues. It took me almost a year after we split up to finally break down and hire someone to help me film because I didn't want to let anyone in."

"I can't believe you paid him."

"His family had money, and I know he would have fought me forever. I had to tell myself that it wasn't worth it to me, to stunt my business for so long. And at least I'll never have to see or hear from him again. That was what I added to our agreement when I paid him off. That he better never contact me again. I regret all of it, but I learned a valuable lesson."

"What's that?" he asked in a flat voice with his forehead still wrinkled.

"Never date anybody Boogie hates." I forced a smile and tried to shake off what we were just talking about. "Anyway, I'm thinking about sneaking out pretty soon. I'm tired."

He was watching me pretty damn carefully as he replied, "I'm feelin' a little tired too, darlin'. I'm thinkin' I'm gonna get a car back to the hotel. You wanna ride back with me?"

My feet hurt, and inside, I could see Connie still dancing her ass off. She was going to go for hours. I knew it. "You know what? Yeah. I'll make sure no one kidnaps you, and I could get a little work done so I don't feel guilty for taking the whole day off."

He smiled, but he was always freaking smiling. "You're so thoughtful."

"I know. Lucky you, right?"

That made him smile even more and got me a boop me on the nose.

Back inside, we told everyone bye, with Connie shouting, "Are you sure you don't want to stay? After party at Tío Chato's house!" There was only one answer to that: hell no. It got me a pinch to the ass that I knew was going to leave a bruise before Zac and I busted out of there, right on time for the car he'd requested to pull into the driveway since we'd ridden in Connie's SUV.

The Ford pulled to a stop along the curb, and Zac waved at the driver before snaking around me to open the back door, ticking his head to the side. I slipped in, and he followed right after. I said "Hi" a second before he chimed in with "Evenin'. How's it goin'?"

The driver, a man in his fifties, unbuckled his seat belt and turned all the way around in his freaking seat. The fingers of his right hand went straight to the headrest, his fingers clinging to the leather. His mouth gaped.

Zac was already smiling at him like it was second nature.

The driver startled. "Don't mind my French, but *fuck me....*"

I snorted and pulled the seat belt across my shoulder, clipping it in.

Zac held his hand out, and the driver didn't hesitate to shake it, before gesturing to me. "Mohamed, Bianca, my boss. Bianca, Mohamed."

I shot Zac a look and took the man's hand the second it was free, even though I'm pretty sure he only left it out from the shock.

"Hi," I told him, giving it a quick shake that he didn't register because he was so busy gaping at Zac.

He and Mohamed, a very nice man with three children—two daughters and a twenty-year-old son that Zac signed an autograph for—talked pretty much the entire ride to the hotel.

"Can we get a picture?" Mohamed asked as he stopped in front of the hotel.

"Yeah, sure," Zac agreed as the older man took his phone off its holder and turned it to selfie mode. Zac unbuckled his seat belt and leaned forward. I tried to move to the side to give him room to sneak up and forward, but a big, familiar hand settled on the middle of my back.

He smiled at me as he guided me forward too until we were right beside Mohamed's headrest. He made sure my chin was right there and Zac's cheek was right there too by mine. The tiny bristles tickled my face, and I tried my best to ignore the heat of his skin.

"Cheese!" Mohamed called out before snapping one, then two pictures that had the flash blinding the shit out of me.

After saying bye, we hauled ass through the lobby, and it wasn't until I got into the elevator that I realized what I'd done.

"I left my wallet in Connie's trunk."

Zac held his jacket in one hand and had a hip against the wall as the elevator took us up. His white shirt was unbuttoned at the throat and damp in a few places. "You need money?" he asked.

"No, my room key is in there," I told him, even as I unlocked my phone and sent Connie a text message.

"Oh. Wait in my room 'til Connie gets back. Or you wanna go back and get it?"

Go back? It'd been hard enough to squeeze my feet back

into the death traps called my shoes so that I wouldn't have to walk barefoot outside of the hall and through the hotel.

"I'll wait, if you're fine with that," I told him. "I just sent her a message. When we were at the hall, she said she was going to my uncle's house, but I bet she can drop by first and then go over there."

He was looking down at me. "I don't mind, kiddo. But if I fall asleep, don't take creepy pictures of me."

The door pinged open. "No promises."

He smiled, and so did I.

"Did you have an okay time?" I asked as we walked in the direction of his room.

"Touch my back."

I pulled my arm into my side, not trusting him or this request. "Why? Because you're sweaty?"

"Yeah, from all the dancing. Touch my shirt."

I shook my head, wrinkling my nose. "Thank you, but no thank you. I believe you." Because I did. His hair was dark and matted, and his neck still flushed. And I knew I was sweaty as hell too. I'd been holding my arms stretched at my sides to give them a breeze so they could dry off.

"You sure?"

"Positive."

He winked at me as he slid his keycard into the slot at the door and flipped on the lights before gesturing me in. I went into the room that was pretty much a mirror of the one I shared with Connie and the kids, except that instead of two double beds, there was only a king. I didn't think twice about toeing my shoes off right at the door as Zac flipped the lock and the metal safety bar above it. I sat on the edge of the bed as he flung his jacket aside and began unbuttoning his shirt.

I looked at my phone then, even though it hadn't beeped or vibrated with a response from Connie... or from anyone.

Would they give me a room key if I didn't have my ID?

Probably not. And I definitely didn't want to make Zac go ask in case he could get away with things that the rest of us couldn't.

"I'm gonna take a shower," my friend said as his fingers plucked at the bottom button of his shirt. He peeled it off. The thin white undershirt he had on was clinging to him, and I mean *clinging* to every single spot on his chest and abs, making it nearly see-through.

He was built like a wet dream I had no right having. His upper body was long and perfectly shaped. His waist trim and shoulders wide....

And that was when we made eye contact.

I smiled at him, and he smiled back at me.

Just checking him out. No big deal. He was probably used to it.

"I'll make sure no one breaks in and tries to take naked pictures of you."

He threw his sweaty dress shirt at me, and by the time I plucked it off, he closed the bathroom door behind him. I hung his shirt on the chair in front of the bed to dry and grabbed my phone again, going to the nightstand furthest from the door to plug my phone in to Zac's charger. I sent Connie another text.

Me: I left my wallet in your trunk. Can you come drop it off, pleaseeeee

If she was dancing... fuck. It was going to take forever. One glance at the clock on the nightstand showed 11:15 on it. The party was set to go on until 2 and then... then maybe she'd look at her phone before they went to my uncle's? I hadn't thought this through.

I sent my nephew a text too. Richard and Connie hadn't given Luisa a cell phone yet.

The sound of the water being turned on in the shower had me glancing toward the closed door.

And it had me sighing.

The next thing it had me doing was slapping myself on the forehead.

He was so much fun. We got along great, and he was one of my favorite people even after so long. The episode we had recorded for the orange cranberry pound cake had honestly been the most fun I had probably ever had doing Lazy Baker stuff. We'd laughed our asses off from the moment he'd come to stand next to me until we finished filming. We were always laughing.

And it just so happened he was easy to look at.

I was so lucky to have him around, period.

I wasn't going to fuck this up. Not this time. It didn't matter that his body had been blessed by Greek gods or that he was a wonderful person with a tremendous heart.

He was my friend, and that was it.

Reaching back, I grabbed the remote from the nightstand and turned on the television, waiting to hear back from Connie or Guillermo. I flexed my toes and feet, rolling my ankles from all the freaking dancing. Everything was achy, and goddamn was I sweaty.

I took my time flipping through the channels, leaving it on a rerun of *The Fresh Prince of Bel-Air* as I lifted my arms over my head and tried to stretch my lower back without contaminating the rest of Zac's bed.

"I needed that," my old friend said on a long yawn, scaring the shit out of me because I hadn't even realized he'd opened the bathroom door. "I'm feelin' brand new now."

He was standing at the doorframe in another thin white shirt and... boxer briefs.

Yeah, those weren't shorts on him. Those were boxer briefs. Navy blue ones.

Well, if he wasn't going to make a big deal about it, neither was I.

He stood there rubbing his head with a towel, his legs long and bare. The muscles in his arms bunched as he dried his hair off. That usual smile of his was fixed onto his mouth. I swallowed.

"I bet. I could use one too," I told him. His face. Not his boxer briefs.

"Jump in there. I brought an extra shirt and some boxer briefs you can borrow," he offered, blue gaze on me as he drew the towel away from his head.

I glanced at my phone plugged into his charger. It might be a while.

"You sure?" I asked.

"Long as you don't fart in them."

I snickered. "I won't mark over your territory."

Zac laughed as he stepped further into the room, going straight for his bag and pulling out a dark blue T-shirt and, yep, boxer briefs too. I stood up and took the clothes from him, brushing my finger along the sweet spot of his ribs that had him dodging away from me on a laugh.

I took my time showering, taking advantage of the free shampoo and conditioner that were mounted to the wall. Luckily, I'd shaved before I'd gotten dressed for the wedding and nothing had grown back in that aggressively over a few hours. My hair was going to be a wreck without my usual hair products, but I'd rather it be clean and frizzy than sweaty.

Plus, Zac had known me back when I hadn't done anything but put ass-loads of gel into my hair and it had still been a mess.

I eyed his tube of toothpaste and put a little on my finger, spreading it over my teeth and tongue before rinsing. I felt a lot better once I opened the door. Zac was lying against the headboard, his phone in one hand. He set it aside almost instantly before looking over.

I didn't let myself feel self-conscious about standing there in his boxer briefs and T-shirt. My underwear and bra were damp from the sweat too, so I'd folded them into my dress and figured that was good enough. I mean, if he looked hard enough, he could tell I wasn't wearing a bra, but I couldn't see him doing that. Between football and dating, he'd probably seen more nipples in his life than most people would in several lifetimes.

I smiled at him.

His gaze flick down to my clothes for a second, his lips quirking just a little. "Sometimes I think you can't be any cuter, and then you go and put on my underwear."

I blinked and clung to his joke. "I'm a little disappointed there isn't a giant Spiderman on them, honestly."

"Giant Spiderman? You're gonna make me blush, kiddo."

I groaned and walked around the bed, hoping my boobs weren't bouncing around all over the place. He patted the bed beside him with another one of his big smiles as I crossed around the front of him, taking in his bare feet he had crossed at the ankles. They were nice feet. They weren't milk white like I'd half expected.

I sat down on the other side of the bed and checked my phone. Then I pulled the pillow out from under the comforter and set it on my lap and in front of my chest—because the room felt a lot colder than I'd originally thought—as I pressed my spine against the headboard, knees together and to the side toward Zac.

"Good shower?" he asked, looking so cute, his skin still soft and pink and dewy. For some reason, he reminded me of young Zac right then.

"Very," I sighed before yawning. "Con still hasn't called me back. I tried Yermo too, but he hasn't texted me either." I scrunched up my toes as the air conditioner kicked on. "I can go see if they'll let me into my room so you can go to bed."

His head rolled to the side. "Stay here until she does, Bibi. I'm not kickin' you out."

Bibi? He'd never called me that before, but I could roll with it. I lifted a shoulder. "Maybe you wanted to go to sleep or go do something else...."

Zac full-on rolled onto his side to look at me.

He really was too cute. He'd shaved, and it just made his face seem even more tan.

"Go do what?" he asked softly, sounding serious. "Darlin', I'm asleep by ten every night. And who else would I wanna go out with?"

I did know that. "You know a lot of people here, and I don't want to—"

"Swear on my life, if you use the word 'bother' or 'interrupt' or 'inconvenience,' I'm gonna do something you're not gonna like," he tried to threaten. "I'll put *Titanic* on."

It took me a second, but I laughed. "You remember that?"

He laughed too. "How the hell could I forget? You hated it and wouldn't stop talking about how much you hated it. You made me hate it."

I let my head drop back to the headboard again. "I really did hate it. I still do. She totally could have scooted over. I would have."

All those crinkly, bright features twisted up even more, splendid and shining and everything. "You would've. I know."

I smiled at him with a shrug.

"And I'm serious. There's nowhere else I'd rather be, Peewee. Just 'cause I know a lot of people doesn't mean I wanna see 'em all the time. 'Cause I don't."

My fingers pinched the hem of his T-shirt. "You used to like going out and always doing stuff around other people. I just assumed."

"I do still, but less than before, and only when I feel like it. Which, like I said, is a lot less now than it ever used to be.

Mama said I'm finally growin' up and appreciatin' quality over quantity, and I guess she's right." His eyelids dropped low over his blue eyes for a moment. "I've been up and down so much, I learned who matters and who to take with a grain of salt, and that's most folks."

"Yeah," I agreed carefully. "There are very few people who really matter, and you get to choose them, so you might as well be picky. I wasn't picky enough... and look what happened to me. I just don't want you to think I'm trying to monopolize your time or anything."

"You're not." The long, strong muscles of his thighs flexed as he slid the bottoms of his soles up along the top of the mattress. "If I tell you somethin', you promise not to say nothin' to anybody?"

"Pinky swear," I told him instantly.

His face was even and serious as he said, "My contract with the White Oaks just came in. It's official."

His contract? "Shut up."

Zac nodded, seriously, knitting his fingers together and setting them on his lap, his expression going straight toward the TV. His shoulders hitched up high, and I watched him roll them back with a deep sigh. "Yeah. My agent texted me while we were still at the party that it was comin'. I just got it right now while you were showerin'. One year. Part of me wasn't expectin' it to actually still come through. Can't be stayin' up anymore."

"No, you can't," I agreed before reaching for his arm, pulling his hand toward my face, and pressing the back of it against my cheek. "I'm so happy for you!" I cheered, snuggling his hand since a hug was out of the question because of my boobs.

And if he wondered why I didn't just hug him instead of clutching his hand to my face and then giving it a peck, he didn't say a word. His gaze slid toward mine though, a little apprehensive—I knew his features too well to not recognize what the hell I was looking at—but I was pretty sure there was more excitement in there too than not. "Yeah, I'm excited, but... we'll see what happens. I'm not startin', but I'll take it."

We'll see what happens? "It's a lot of pressure to put on yourself, but if anyone can do it, you can," I told him, still clutching his hand with both of mine. "I'm so happy for you. I won't say anything to anybody. But I'm so, so, so happy. You're going to be incredible. Hopefully the other guy plays like shit and you'll get to start, but even if he doesn't, you're still going to be there, waiting, and that's all that matters. You know how many guys would kill to have that opportunity?"

One corner of his mouth went up, and it was sweet and reluctant. "I'm gonna wait to tell Mama and Paw-Paw tomorrow. They're announcin' it come Monday." He paused. "I hate keepin' secrets."

"Keeping secrets does suck, but it's okay. I think everyone will understand. I know I do." And I couldn't believe he actually told me.

Could I?

His blue eyes moved toward me. "What kind of secrets do you have, kiddo?"

I swallowed and lowered his hand away from my face. "A few of them."

His palm turned, and his long fingers wrapped around mine gently, giving them a light squeeze. "Like what?"

"Well, it's not a secret if I tell you, is it?" I snorted and drew my hand back to scratch at my cheek even though I didn't need to.

He smiled. "But you're only tellin' me."

"So it isn't a secret if I just tell you?"

"You tell Connie secrets, don't you?"

I nodded. "I tell her almost everything."

"Tell me somethin' then."

"You tell me something first."

His mouth went flat, but he got a squinty, thoughtful look on his face. "I almost went to school in Oklahoma instead of Austin. I've never told anybody that."

"No," I gasped.

He nodded and held up his thumb and index finger apart about an inch. "Came this close. I can't remember anymore why I almost went there instead, but it did almost happen."

"Who are you?" I whispered, imagining the devastation Paw-Paw might have felt if he'd done that. He might have cried.

But Zac chuckled deep. "Okay, your turn."

I scratched my nose. "A secret of mine?"

He dipped his chin.

I had to think about it. "I don't really have secrets that are mine. More like, I know other stuff about other people." That was partially a lie but also kind of the truth.

"Nah, I want one of yours."

"My God, you're a nosey son of a bitch."

That got me another deep, throaty laugh that made me smile. "Think of somethin'. A good one."

What...?

I had to think about it.

"It's not really a secret, but... I think you've got really cute butt cheeks?" I offered. "It's like a perfect little peach butt. It was the best one in the magazine."

His smile was playful and smug. "That's not a secret, but thank you. That's why they put it on the cover."

I laughed. "Conceited much?"

Zac grinned. "Only a little. Tell me a real secret, 'cause I'm not gonna forget."

A real one? That was hard. There was one I could think of that I definitely didn't want to share, but what else was there?

I knew it.

Before my brain could catch up with my big damn mouth, I told him the only thing I thought might make him gasp in surprise. Because, and I would tell myself this later so that I wouldn't be embarrassed, it wasn't a big deal. It was a reminder of a life from a long time ago, when I'd been a kid. "I used to have the biggest crush on you when I was a teenager."

Well, I'd done it. There was no going back now.

I got kind of the reaction I'd been expecting. A little bit.

He made a confused face. "You did?"

I nodded, making sure to look him in the eye so that it wouldn't be something really that bad. Nothing could be that bad if you didn't have to hide from it. "Yeah. Huge. Just for like a year..." I hesitated. "Or two, but yeah. I thought you were pretty much perfect. I'm glad you didn't know. You would have been all sweet and understanding about it, and that would have been worse." It was time to change the subject. "What other secrets you got?"

He ignored my question. "When?"

Damn it. "Did I like you? When I was a teenager, I told you. Now what other secrets do you have?"

He continued to ignore me. "But when? I never noticed."

"Oh, not that far back. Hold your horses. When I was like sixteen." I eyed his serious face and smiled. "Seventeen and eighteen too, maybe?" I shrugged. "You gave me a big hug and a kiss, and it all went downhill from there for a while after that. It was a well-kept secret, I guess."

Well, until I realized that mooning over someone like Zac was never going to mean anything because I was me and he was him, and I wasn't anywhere near being his type. I might have wished upon a star and every birthday candle I'd had for those couple of years, hoping and wishing and dreaming of the possibility that one day he would look at me and see *me*.

See that I loved him and that I didn't care about him being some hotshot football player. That I liked *him*. His humor, his kindness, his love.

Obviously, that had never happened, and eventually, after years of sighing from a distance, I had come to terms with it. I would live the rest of my life loving someone who loved me too but like a little sister.

At least he loved me, I had told myself one day after I'd seen him with some girl he'd been seeing. He didn't love them, but he loved me. That made me special.

Over the years, it became easier, especially after we lost touch.

And here we were.

On his hotel bed, both in pajamas that were really underwear, with him being a better friend to me than ever before.

And that friend, my friend who I had just told I'd had feelings for, turned his body to look at me with an expression that wasn't exactly disgusted but completely surprised. "I did?"

That's how little that had meant to him—a little peck on the cheek—but I forced myself to push it back, to not take it that way. I lifted a shoulder and kept the smile on my face. "Yeah. Right here." I pointed right beside my mouth where my beauty mark was, purposely not thinking about how I'd gotten hung up on how his lips had just, just, *just* touched the corner of mine. "I thought of it as my first kiss for a little bit." I flashed my teeth at him, trying to tell him I knew it was lame, but I was not really sorry.

Those big blue eyes blinked at me some more, and I watched his eyes flick down to where I pointed, his face still confused.

I reached over and patted his bare knee. "But that was a long time ago. I promise I haven't thought of you like that in a whole lot of years."

He just kept on looking at me, not moving away, just... there. On the bed. Watching me.

Shit. "What?" I suddenly and instantly regretted opening my fat trap. I should have just stayed quiet and let it go to the grave with me. "I'm sorry for saying something. I didn't think you'd care. I thought you'd laugh."

It took a second, but in the following one, I could tell, *I could tell*, he forced the tight smile onto his face.

And my freaking stomach sank down to my toes.

Past my toes. Straight down through the Earth's crust.

"Zac...," I started to say. God, why the hell had I opened my mouth? *Dumb, Bianca.* I instantly faced forward and figured I might as well try and go downstairs to get a key.

Zac's hand went to my leg, those long fingers wrapping around the kneecap, swallowing it whole. "Hey." His eyes met mine, and there wasn't a hint of panic or disgust on his face. But there wasn't joy or that easygoing expression that came so naturally to him either. His forehead was furrowed, and his lips looked a little tight, but I didn't know what to make of it. "Why you tensin' up?"

I *was* tense. Exhaling, I tried to shake it off.

As I did, I knew I wasn't imagining him scooting over close. His mostly bare thigh lined up to mine, his hand was still on my knee, the tips of his fingers anchored around the bone.

It took a second, but I finally glanced at him, feeling my lips pressed together. "I'm sorry, Zac. I didn't think you'd care."

"Hey." What had to be his fingertip nudged at my chin, drawing my face higher. He wasn't frowning, but he wasn't smiling either.

I looked into his eyes, noticing just how long and pretty his nearly golden eyelashes were, how the area right around the pupil was a shade of bright blue that bled out the further away it got. And when his fingertip slid along my jaw and gently tapped at a spot halfway to my ear, I held my breath. What was he going to do? Tell me he didn't want to be my friend anymore? That wasn't Zac. That would never be him.

It wasn't like I blamed him for not loving me back or even liking me back. I had never and would never hold that against him.

He still wasn't smiling. He just... looked.

He looked and looked and looked.

Right into my freaking eyes. A little over my face. Lingering on the corner of my mouth where I'd pointed.

And he didn't say anything.

A minute passed, maybe two, but it felt like half an hour.

This was up to me. This was just Zac. There was nothing to be scared of. This person was my friend.

I snuck my hand over and was just about to set it on his thigh but detoured it to land on his forearm, and I was going to ignore just how muscular and tight it was. "Hey, I'm sorry. I promise it was a long time ago. You're one of my best friends, and I would never want to ruin this between us. I honestly thought you'd laugh. I'm sorry for making you uncomfortable."

"You didn't make me uncomfortable," he replied instantly, gaze unflinching. "There's nothin' for you to apologize for."

"But there is. I didn't mean to make you feel weird."

That fingertip smoothed its way back down to my chin, and I was pretty sure another finger landed right next to it. The lines across his forehead got deeper. "Bianca, I don't think there's a thing you could do to make me feel weird."

I wasn't so sure about that.

The hand on my knee gave it a squeeze. "You caught me off guard is all. I didn't know. I had no idea. Boog never said nothin'. Nobody did."

"Because it wouldn't have changed anything. Connie

knew. Boogie put it together himself, but you know he wouldn't have teased me over it. He's too nice with that sort of thing." I let go of his forearm and set my hand on top of the one he had on my leg. "I was a kid. It didn't mean anything."

His jaw did this weird thing, and I could see his nostrils flare for a second before he dipped his chin down. "You were a kid."

A kid who had clung to him like a spider monkey. A little sister figure. He was too kind to ever say that to me, but it was the truth, and we both knew it.

"Are we fine? Do you forgive me?"

"There's nothin' to forgive," he said after a second, his words slow.

I looked at him for what felt like a long time. Those features weren't exactly pinched. They weren't even close to being distressed either. They were just... thoughtful.

Too thoughtful.

Any kind of thoughtful was too thoughtful though.

All I had wanted and expected was a laugh, and now we were here.

When he still hadn't said anything after what felt like half an hour but was probably really only about a solid minute, I shifted from one butt cheek to another, ignoring the hand still lingering on my knee, and said, "You're not gonna be all awkward now, are you?"

That did it.

Those light blue eyes that were a perfect mix of bright baby blue and milk, blinked, and in a matter of two seconds, his lips slowly peeled back into a soft and familiar smile. "Me, awkward?"

I ticked my head to the side and couldn't help but smile back at him.

His lips went crooked. "Who you callin' awkward?"

"You're the one sitting there being all quiet and weird, Snack Pack." There, that took us back to our friendship—at least that's what I hoped. "I just want to make sure I don't have to noogie you back to being normal."

He laughed. "You think you're gonna noogie me?"

Good. This was good. "If I have to, Mr. White Oak."

One nearly blond eyebrow went up, and I felt him shift on his butt cheek to face me just a little better.

I raised both my eyebrows right back at him, clinging onto this, wanting this familiarity. "Are we going to pretend this didn't happen or...?"

"Oh, I'm not pretendin' shit, darlin'."

It was my turn to blink.

And this jerk grinned even wider. "What? I'm not. Want me to lie to you?"

I nodded.

He laughed. "I'm never forgettin', so...."

"So what you're saying is we're doing this?"

"Yeah, because I'm not forgettin' you used to like me—"

"Oh hell no." I rolled onto my hip and freaking went for him.

Not for his head but for his ribs. His weak spot.

"What the fuck, Bianca!" Zac literally fucking shouted as he threw his body and head back against the headboard, his arms slamming down into place against his ribs... and my fingers.

I cackled, digging my fingers even deeper into his sides. "You remember now? Who's your daddy, huh?"

Those big, strong arms jerked up and down along his sides, trying to disengage me as he tried to melt into the headboard to get away from me. "You said you were gonna noogie me! What the hell are you doing? Stop it!"

"Duh. Ouch!"

He instantly stopped moving, and so did I in surprise that

he'd actually stopped after his elbow clipped one of the bones on my wrist.

Zac's face was flushed red, eyes bright, and I decided to take pity on him. So I smiled, keeping my fingers where they were but not digging in anymore. "You thought I didn't remember?" I asked him before dipping my face in even closer. Then I whispered, like a psycho, "I remember everything." I tapped my fingers lightly along his sides, feeling him flinch. "Especially you being ticklish."

Those blue eyes bore into mine, and his mouth went damn near flat. Zac's voice was almost a whisper too as he said, "Did you ask me who my daddy is?"

I nodded gravely.

His voice was still a whisper when he went on with, "You're my daddy now, I guess."

Pulling my fingers away, I sat back on my knees and laughed. "Deal. I promise not to use that against you unless I have to."

His nostrils flared, and he stared at me right in the eyes as he said, still quietly, "Bianca."

"Yes?"

"I remember things too."

What?

Before I could process who this man was, what he did for a living, and what talents he'd polished over the years, he came at me with one of those hands that were lightning fast and accurate. Zac licked the tip of his index finger and shoved that turd into my ear just as I started yelling, "Don't you dare!"

He dared.

By the time I pushed him away, we were both breathing hard and laughing, and I had to talk myself into looking at my phone to see if I had a response instead of waiting around for it leisurely.

He was eyeing me carefully, probably making sure I wasn't going to attack again, as I picked up my cell and glanced at it. There wasn't a single reply from her or Guillermo. And I told him so.

"Stay here then until Connie gets back to you in that case. Yeah?"

"If you don't mind."

He picked up the remote, looking me dead in the freaking eye.

"I'm joking! Yeah. Okay. Yes."

The corners of his mouth curled up even more. So I wasn't totally expecting when he pulled the comforter and sheets off the bed and slipped under them. And I wasn't expecting him to lean forward so that his back was curved and shimmy his shoulders. "You can pay me back by scratchin' my back like Mama Lupe used to."

He wanted me to...?

Was it a dumb idea?

Nah.

We were adults, and he was asking me because we were friends, and I would just be touching his back. I mean, he had masseuses and trainers who were always rubbing all over him. With his teammates, he was used to being very hands on. It meant nothing to him.

Fine with me.

"I'll do it for you, if you do it for me," I tried to bargain.

One blue eye aimed itself at me. "Deal."

Before I even moved over, he'd tugged his shirt up along his shoulder blades and he was back to shimmying. I grinned to myself before getting up on my knees, right at his hip, and scratching his back, starting right around his trap muscles and working my way down one side, trying to ignore the freckles along his back... and how soft and blemish-free his skin was.

What I couldn't ignore were his fucking moans though.

And his "Please, right there. *Right there.*" Then his "That's incredible." And a couple "I'd pay you to do this every day."

I shook my head as I did one more pass from the top of his back all the way to the bottom of it, right where the elastic of his boxer briefs started. And before I could talk myself out of it, I sat flat on my butt, so close to him that my thigh was pressed to his through the comforter, and pulled the pillow back in front of me before shaking my own shoulders. "My turn. I'm ready, old man."

He paused as he sat up. I held my breath for a second, expecting him to scratch over my shirt. But that wasn't what happened. Instead, he tugged it up, taking his time to roll it over my shoulders, and in the next breath, his blunt fingernails were there, light and amazing on my skin. Moving from my shoulder blades downward. Taking his time.

I squeezed my arms to my sides to hold my boobs in. It was too good. Way too good.

I only let him get one pass before I sat back, still beside him. "Perfect, thank you."

I glanced at him over my shoulder. He already had his hands in his lap, those light blue eyes on my face. I scooted over a little bit until we weren't touching.

All right then.

He yawned, and then so did I.

"I'm gonna keep my phone right here just in case I fall asleep and Con calls, okay?" I asked him, patting the phone I set on my chest as I leaned back against the headboard.

It was maybe only a second later that he asked, "Bianca?"

"Huh?"

"You really thought I was perfect?"

I made a face to myself. "I said *pretty much* perfect. And that was a long time ago, when I was young and innocent."

"What was wrong with me back then?"

I snorted and shot him a look. He was smiling. "You really want to do this? Yeah? First of all...."

He was already trying not to crack up.

"There were the girls. You dated just about all of them and broke all of their hearts from what I remember you and Boogie talking about."

He groaned. "Never mind. I'm good. Forget I asked."

It was my turn to laugh. "You're sure?"

"Positive."

I snorted.

Then after a moment, he said again, "Bianca?"

"Yeah?"

"You really almost married that asshole?"

My ex. "Yup."

"Why?"

I made a face but didn't look at him. "I don't know. Because I liked him. He paid a lot of attention to me for a while, at least up until the end when he lost interest, and I guess I was lonely. He was cute. I don't know, Snack Pack. I don't mind being alone, but I hate being lonely. Do you know what I mean? I guess I just wanted someone around. Or at least, someone who would come back. That sounds really ungrateful now that I hear it out loud, because I know how many people love me but have their own lives, and I can't expect them to make me the center of the world. I hope you get what I mean."

If he looked at me, I had no idea, because he was only quiet for a moment before saying, "I get what you mean. I hated how much your parents left. I still don't get how they could just stay away so much. And I remember how sad you were when Connie moved away to go to school after community college."

"I didn't get how they could leave so much either, not for a long time. I've tried talking to them about it, but all they said was that they thought I'd do better settled somewhere. That I was safe and in good hands. That I could ask Connie how much it sucked moving around every year. Honestly, even though I was perfectly fine without them, I still resent them a little for just leaving us with Mamá Lupe, even though I know how much they help other people with their work. It makes me feel guilty. Selfish. But you know, everyone has to go and live their lives and fulfill their destinies so... I try to focus on myself too. And I know better now than to expect too much from anyone."

I peeked at him, and he was already looking at me.

"What about you? You've never met anyone you liked enough to think about settling down?" I asked.

His nostrils flared a little, but he shook his head. "Nah. There's a lot of lovely women out there, but in Paw-Paw's words, none of 'em have ever made me feel more than fondness for 'em. And you know, with the way my daddy treated Mama—disappearin' as soon as he found out she was pregnant—I don't want anybody wastin' too much of their time on me if I'm not plannin' on spendin' too much time with them." He shrugged. "And, Peewee, I don't know if I could trust some somebody enough to feel that kinda way about 'em."

I snickered, but I understood his point. "Well, maybe someday you'll meet someone that you do want wasting all their time on you. Maybe it's like football teams; you just have to find the right people, the right person. Someone worth your trust. But if you don't, maybe one day we can be neighbors in a retirement home. We can have the future Baby Boogie come visit us."

He chuckled. "I can already picture you harassin' the male employees at the home, askin' them about their nuts."

I burst out laughing. "I only ask people I trust questions like that."

"Uh-huh."

"But for real... at least tell me, did they put makeup on your butt cheeks because they—"

His whole body was laughing. "You need to go to sleep."

The last thing I remembered before dozing off was both of us laughing over his butt cheeks and why he wouldn't just give me an answer. My cheeks had started hurting, I knew that much.

What I also knew was that sometime later on, I heard Zac whispering, "In here with me. Let her sleep.... Yeah, she's good."

I was fairly certain I felt something brush over my head, over my ear, and touch my cheek.

I must have fallen back asleep, because the next thing I knew, I woke up in a dark room... with my face in a clean-scented armpit.

My arm was thrown over something hard and soft at the same time. My feet were hanging off the edge of the bed. And I was pretty sure I had drooled all over my cheek.

Zac was on his back, with an arm thrown over his eyes. His head was to the side and tucked in, breathing steadily into my hair. Calm and wonderful.

He was smiling even in his sleep.

That was when I realized where his other arm was. Wedged between us. He was holding my hand.

That was when I knew I was in trouble.

CHAPTER FOURTEEN

"He's in a mood today," Deepa whispered to me two weeks later after I'd gotten back from lunch.

The muscles along my shoulders tensed up. I didn't need to ask who she was talking about. I knew. Just like I'd known that he was showing up around noon and that'd I'd have the morning without Gunner's overbearing presence.

You know, because I checked the schedule every day.

"Why?" I whispered back, setting my purse under my keyboard.

"Richie"—he was one of the personal trainers at the gym —"said that he overheard him on the phone. He thinks he was arguing with one of the other owners."

"Over what?" I whispered, standing up.

I didn't need to look directly at her face to guess she was looking around to make sure he hadn't magically appeared out of nowhere. "Something about employee retention."

I snickered and heard Deepa snicker back. "Big surprise."

"Right?"

The side door opened, and we both started trying to look

busy. But it wasn't Gunner. It was one of the MMA guys coming in.

I just about sagged in relief and greeted the guy as he flashed his badge and went ahead with a "Hey."

The second he walked off, we turned back toward each other discreetly, ready to move and change positions if we had to. "Did the nursing home call you back?"

"No, not yet. I was going to call tomorrow morning. They seemed really interested during my interview, but they still haven't called." She grabbed a bottle under the counter and sprayed the surface. "My mom called yesterday and said she isn't feeling well. I'm worried about her. She's going to the doctor tomorrow."

"I'm sorry, Dee. Let me know what the doctor says," I told her.

She nodded as she wiped the counter off. "Are we still on for Sunday?"

I glanced at her. She was talking about filming. "Yeah."

"Are any of your friends coming?" she whispered.

"No, they're busy." They *were*.

"Why didn't—" she started to ask, and it was some miracle that I happened to be facing forward again when the side door open and The Asshole strolled in.

I picked up the phone as fast as I could and pretended to be on a phone call. Right on time.

I could tell from the way he was walking that he was in a mood. I could read his signs, that's how bad it was.

Unfortunately, he came straight for me. Fuck my life.

Holding the phone to my ear, I figured I might as well get this over with and said—to no one, literally no one because it was only the dial tone that could listen to me—"No problem at all. Have a nice day."

Gunner had started watching me from the second he entered, and I was pretty sure he thought I was full of shit and faking being on the phone, but he could never know for sure. Sucker.

"Hi, Gunner."

Yeah, he didn't give a single shit. He just looked at me with his grumpy expression. "Got a sec?"

Nope. "Sure," I said, like he didn't know I *had a second.* Obviously, he could see there wasn't a line of people trying to come in.

He did this weird mouth thing as he glared at me. I watched him take a breath through his nose before saying, "I heard a rumor."

Shit.

"Is it true you're friends with Zac Travis?"

Out of the corner of my eye, I spotted Deepa turning in the opposite direction. Not out of guilt, I knew, but more to get away so she wouldn't get dragged into the conversation.

Now I could handle this a few different ways. Actually, there were only two ways. I could say yes, or I could say no.

Yes. We were friends.

No. We weren't friends.

Mind your own business wasn't exactly the angle I wanted to take. It was rude, and I wasn't going to be outright rude. That didn't change the fact it was none of his business.

I looked him right in those asshole eyes and said, "Yes."

I wasn't going to ask why. I wasn't going to introduce or give a segue into making this conversation longer. If there was something he wanted to ask, he could do it.

He wasn't surprised by my answer. "Good friends?" he had the nerve to ask.

All right, in this case, there were three different ways to handle this.

A smart person would say, *"Yes, sir."* Then wonder how they could use it to their advantage.

A decent person would answer *"Yes"* and leave it at that.

A person who wanted to just give enough of an answer to not get in trouble would reply with "*No.*"

An idiot would say... well, they would answer the way I answered. "I'm not sure how my answer has anything to do with my job."

Because it wasn't any of his business. I knew that. He damn well knew that too.

I was pretty positive that legally he couldn't ask me that. Just like he couldn't question if I was pregnant or if I had children or was planning on having any.

But at the end of the day, what was he going to do? Fire me for telling him nunya? It wasn't like he could get me for anything else. I was never late, never called in, never left early. When the new assistant manager asked me if I could stay, I usually did. The only time I said no was when *he* made the request. There was proof to all of it.

And I wasn't going to use Zac, not for anything, but especially not for this person.

Not when he was so busy with his new opportunity. His new chance. His future.

Since the weekend of Lola's quince, I had only seen him twice. He'd come over to my apartment the day after his first practice with the White Oaks and eaten leftovers on the couch beside me, telling me all about what the team did differently than what he'd done in Oklahoma. He'd been calm, centered, and pretty matter of fact. He'd kissed me on the head when he'd left that night and called me right after I'd closed the door to ask, "Did you lock the door?" And I'd laughed and told him, "*Yes.*"

Then I'd seen him again the day after his first game with the team—he hadn't played—and he'd invited me over. Trevor had been there, and so had CJ, and we'd hung out. Zac had made his "world famous" spaghetti and had made me play them the two versions of the videos we'd made together for my Lazy Baker channel.

Well, he and CJ had both made me replay their videos three times each to boost the views. It had been pretty cute how excited they'd been with how they'd come out. The uploads were doing *amazing*, like I knew they would. People ate up having these big guys standing in my kitchen with bright aprons on that barely fit.

Since then, Zac had texted me almost every day, usually at night to check in or tell me he'd watched one of my videos. Sometimes I messaged him during the day but not that often since I knew how much he had going on. He was busy either at practice or getting a massage or squeezing in film or napping or physical therapy or doing one of the other million things that he needed to. I understood, and I was so happy for him. I wanted him to kill this opportunity he'd been given.

So I could keep my head up high for that, for him and for his life and privacy. I would. No matter what.

So I didn't look away as Gunner's gaze narrowed, and I'd swear even his ears moved a little. Yeah, he was pissed. That was obvious as hell.

His little pouty faces weren't going to sway me either.

There were plenty of people I would throw under the bus, but Zac wasn't and would never be one of them.

And I hoped my face said that.

Gunner seemed to think about something, and I watched him wrinkle his nose. We kept on staring at each other for another moment or two before he said, "It doesn't have anything to do with your job."

I looked at him.

He looked at me.

And if he thought he was going to win this standoff glaring at me, well he had another thing coming.

His lips twisted, and I clear as day heard him, even Deepa had to hear him, say, "I'll be posting the October schedule pretty soon. I'm not sure anymore if I'll be able to get that request of yours in after all, by the way. Considering we're short staffed."

I had never, ever wanted to hurt someone more than I did him right then.

Not my cheating ex.

Not Zac's old girlfriend.

Nobody.

He was threatening my vacation. Why? Because I wouldn't let him use my friendship?

It was nothing less than a miracle that his cell started ringing from his pocket or wherever the hell he kept it. Between his butt cheeks, tucked under his balls, wherever. But he still focused on me with those hateful eyes as he put the cell up to his face and took the call with a "Gunner speaking."

My second thing to be grateful for was that he was a paranoid asshole because he walked away too, heading back toward the side door so that we couldn't hear him.

The second that door slammed shut, I fisted my fucking hands at that same moment Deepa said, "Oh hell, Bianca."

Because she knew exactly what he had threatened me with, what he was taking away. My fucking Disney World vacation that I had been looking forward to.

This *fucking fuck asshole.*

———

I kept planning the rest of my shift and the entire drive home.

I didn't regret what I'd done, *but* I couldn't help but be pretty pissed off at Gunner for being such a jerk. He couldn't fire me over that. I was pretty sure. He was just going to do whatever he could to piss me off. Maybe he didn't actually think he'd be able to push me away—that I'd be so desperate I would eat all the shit he tried to feed me—or maybe that was exactly what he wanted. Me to quit.

But he didn't know me. I wasn't going to do anything unless it was on my terms, especially when it concerned him. He wasn't going to get to bully me.

Now I was going to stick around on principle, or at least until Deepa got out of there, like my original plan.

But what his little threat made me do was think about what was to come after. My lease was about to end, and I hadn't renewed it yet. I wasn't sure what I wanted to do or where I wanted to go. The more I thought about it, the more uncertain I got.

I had gotten an email that afternoon from the photographer and food stylist I was hiring to shoot my cookbook. She had an opening in November and wanted to know if I wanted to move up my booking.

I had *a lot* more work left to do, and I wasn't sure how I could make it happen but knew it was a good idea to let her move me up in the queue. I had a gut feeling about what I'd have to do to get everything done in time... but I wasn't ready yet to make that decision and break my own heart. Even if it kind of seemed like fate.

Oh well, I thought as I headed up to my apartment hours later.

It wasn't like Zac had showed up to Maio House with the intention to see me and get me into this predicament. But I wondered again how the hell Gunner could have found out in the first place. Part of me had expected someone to post a picture or a video of Zac at Lola's quince, but I hadn't seen a thing pop up, fortunately, and if it had, I hadn't been tagged in it, and neither had he. Gunner didn't have social media accounts anyway, so I doubted he'd seen Zac on my channel.

I sighed and scratched at the tip of my nose as I stopped at the top of the landing to my apartment that evening.

Because right next to it, leaning against my door, was a man.

A tall, lean man.

His head lolled over from where he had been holding it, facing the blank opposite wall.

I recognized his slow, slight smile before I noticed the familiar clothing of jeans, broken in boots, and very white T-shirt.

"Hey, Peewee," Zac drawled with about as much enthusiasm as I had for cleaning out my shower drain when it clogged.

Something was wrong. He'd had practice that morning and afternoon. He'd told me the night before via text.

"Hey, Snack Pack," I said carefully, taking a step forward now that I knew he wasn't some serial killer creeper. I stopped right in front of him, taking in the bunched muscles of his biceps from how he'd been standing there with his arms crossed before slowly letting them drop to his sides.

There was something definitely wrong. His smile was half pulled up, but it was all off. Plus his eyes didn't look all that right either. They were dim, and his skin looked tightly stretched across all those sharp, pretty bones of his face.

"What happened?" I asked him, letting the strap of my purse slide off my shoulder and land in my opened palm. I set my opposite hand on his forearm. *Please God, tell me they didn't release him.* "Want to talk about it or no?"

His Adam's apple bobbed, and it tore me up some more.

"Do you want me to trip someone? Need a hug? Want a back scratch on the house?" I offered some more, rubbing my thumb over his tight, muscular forearm.

Those broad shoulders seemed to sag right in front of my eyes, and I wondered what the hell had happened. Things had been fine. They'd been great. He'd seemed normal just last night. Everything about him the last couple of weeks had screamed cautious optimism. He seemed to like his coach and teammates. I'd even asked him if he was fine with not starting, and he'd just slid me that lopsided smile of his and said, "Somebody reminded me I should be thankin' my lucky stars even if I'm number two, and that's what I'm doin', darlin'."

So yeah, I was goddamn worried now.

"Zac, what happened?" I whispered, instantly reaching up and sliding my arms around his neck. I hugged him. Uninvited, yes, but something wasn't right.

And he'd tell me to back up if he didn't want me there.

I stroked my palm up and down along his spine as I looked up into his Disney prince face.

But he didn't respond, at least not with words. What he did do was exhale. His body loosened and then curled into me, some part of his head coming to rest against the top of mine. One forearm went around the lowest spot on my back, anchoring me in place, right there. Against him.

I held him, and he held me, and I stood there and listened to his deep breaths. If he didn't want to tell me what was up, that was okay. I didn't need to know.

It wasn't like I didn't keep things from him that my gut believed he had no business hearing. Or more like, he didn't need to be bothered by comments that had no purpose. Not anymore.

More than anything though, if he really wanted to tell me, he would. He'd told me about signing with Houston before he'd told anybody else. I'd been in the car with him when he'd called his mom and grandpa on the way back to Houston after the night of the party. Part of me still couldn't believe even that.

We kept on standing there. With his chest inhaling and exhaling in front of mine. With his arm around the back of my neck and what might have been his cheek or his forehead resting against the top of my head. With the tips of our shoes touching. My purse resting on the top of them.

And I kept on moving my palm up and down his back, trying my best to soothe whatever the hell was bothering him.

What could have been half an hour later, he finally lifted his head off mine, and I took that moment to take a small step back, arching my neck upward to take in his features again.

He was already focused down on me, those baby blues stark against his face, his mouth still formed into a shape that wasn't anywhere near the happy one I was used to.

I didn't like it.

I reached up and set the tip of my finger on the end of his nose in the longest boop of all time. We didn't need to talk about it. That was all right with me. "I'm having a crappy day and was going to order some delivery. Want to eat with me?"

Those blue eyes stayed on my face, and I was glad I'd gotten a little more sleep than usual the night before and that I hadn't been stingy with makeup. Just because I realized we had no chance in hell for that to matter, I still cared. Whatever. I could take pride in my appearance.

He gave me another one of those half smiles that said everything and nothing at the same time.

I tapped my finger on his nose again. "I'll let you pick what we eat if it'll cheer you up."

He didn't laugh... but he did smile. A small but genuine one. A genuine one with something in its depths that made my little heart ache a bit at whatever was bothering him.

"I could use a chalupa," he told me. "It's been that kinda day."

Chalupa? That was what he wanted?

I was probably going to regret it, but I still said, "Okay. The nearest one is too far for delivery, but I'll drive."

He made some kind of noise that almost sounded like a sniff. "It'll taste better warm."

I bet it would. "I'm gonna get the shits, so I hope it'll be worth it."

He blinked, and at the exact same time, we both burst out freaking laughing.

Zac covered his eyes with his palm as he muttered, "Jesus H. Christ, kiddo."

He didn't see me smiling as I poked him in the ribs, but I caught his own mouth beginning to form into one. All right, maybe everything wasn't totally right in the world, but it was getting there.

Zac's hand dropped from his face to settle briefly on my shoulder, giving it a light squeeze. "Need to do somethin' inside first?"

"Nah, we can go."

I led the way down the stairs, asking, "Want me to drive after all or do you want to take your fancy-ass car?"

"Whatever you want."

We could take mine. He seemed too distracted to be a good driver.

Zac didn't say a word when I steered us toward my car and still said nothing when we got into it and I pulled out of the complex and onto the road. That was when the idea struck me. We glanced at each other when I stopped at a red light, and I wasn't even a little sneaky when I slipped my phone out of my purse and tapped a few times at the screen. Just as the light turned green, I found what I was looking for and hit the little triangle at the bottom of the screen.

I waited a second.

Two seconds.

The speakers in my car finally picked up, and I still waited.

And my beloved Zac didn't let me down.

It took two beats of the song to ring through my car before he snorted and the back of his hand nudged at my upper arm.

I grinned at him just as I hit the gas. Lifting my finger, I pointed at him and sang the last two words of the first bar, "... go girls." The shoulder closest to him moved in time to the beat of the song I'd been forced to listen to like half a million times around him when I'd been younger. Zac snorted again.

Out of the corner of my eye, I could see his fingers tapping along to the beat on his thigh, and I kept on singing, knowing I was pretty much yelling out the lyrics totally out of tune and not giving a single shit, especially not when he started laughing right before the chorus.

And then, *then,* this fool joined in.

At the top of his lungs, with that accent that felt like a hug, he sang all about forgetting he was a lady.

And together, almost at the top of our lungs, we sang about feeling wild, about short skirts, and mostly... about feeling like a woman.

We were both dying laughing at the end.

There were tears in my eyes, and he was leaning against the seat, both hands on top of his head as that lean torso puffed in and out with ragged breaths as he kept on cracking up.

"Oh, I needed that," he wheezed, dragging those big palms down his face to wipe at his eyes and cheeks.

"Then get ready for the rest of my playlist, bubba," I warned him right as the next song started.

And then, we were at it again. I did it for his sake. To get that smile back on his face. The light behind his eyes.

It worked.

We sang about just breathing, about someone named Jolene, and right as I was pulling the car into the parking lot, we thought we were performing on The Voice while we sang about having friends in low places.

I turned off the car then and turned to Zac, wanting to ask him if he was better but not wanting to ruin it when I could see it in his eyes that he was. Because he was smiling that big, old Zac smile that made his entire face resemble Christmas lights. And I couldn't help but return the expression.

He took my hand from where I'd set it on my lap and brought it up to his face, kissing the back of it with those firm, warm lips.

I'd be lying if I didn't admit my little heart stuttered a second.

But I didn't think twice about leaning over and planting a quick kiss on his cheek. "There's my Big Texas." I tapped him on the cheek with my free hand and said, "I'm always here for you if you need me." He knew that. Then I booped him on the nose once more. "Come on. Let's get this over with so we can gas each other out on the way back."

He barked out a laugh. "I'll be fine. It's you I'm worried about now."

I pulled my hand out from his and snorted as I sat back and went for the door handle. "You should be. I haven't eaten this in years. If you'd let me choose, we'd be eating roast beef and melted cheese sandwiches."

I was pretty sure he snickered as I got out, and he met me by the trunk, sliding sunglasses on to cover his face. Maybe we should have ordered through the drive-through and eaten in the car, but he'd say something if he had too much trouble being in public. I figured. We'd gone grocery shopping. Gone to a quinceañera together. Plus, it was his idea, saying it would taste better warm. We weren't in a rush.

He eyed my car for a second and then looked at me.

I was parked pretty crooked. Fine. I could admit it. "Leave me alone," I muttered.

Zac smiled tightly but he nodded.

No one paid us any attention inside as we each ordered a meal and we both pulled out cash at the same time.

"Let's split it," I tried to offer.

"I got it," he said at the same time.

We stared at each other.

"How many times have you made me dinner now?" he asked, arching one of those annoying blond eyebrows. "I gotta start buying you groceries."

We stared at each other some more.

The cashier cleared his throat, and we both must have realized we were being annoying holding up the line.

"I'm sorry," I apologized to him, still looking at Zac. "Might as well get me some of those cinnamon things while we're at it if you're paying."

"The cinnamon things too, please. Thank you."

The employee rolled his eyes and took his cash, huffing something under his breath, probably calling us assholes. Yikes. Zac and I made a face at each other after he took his change, and we moved off to the side. "You got any plans tomorrow, kiddo?"

"Work in the morning but nothing in the evening. You?" I wanted to know how practice had gone—and if his mood had anything to do with it—but I didn't want to *ask*.

Honestly, I just wanted him to tell me on his own, but I knew better than to hope. Expectations and all that. *We're just friends*, I'd reminded myself no less than once a day since I'd woken up in his hotel bed holding his hand.

Through his sunglasses, I could see his eyeballs focused on me as he lowered his voice and said, "Nothin' much. One of my teammates asked if I could drop by this haunted house he invested in that's openin' tomorrow. Wanna go?"

"Go with you?"

He made a little bit of a face. "With who else?"

I made a face back at him.

He squeezed my shoulder. "So yeah?"

He really wanted me to go with him? "You don't want to ask one of your other friends?"

That had him tipping his head to the side. "Other friends?"

"Yeah, your other friends here."

Those eyebrows of his just knit together, and even that bottom lip of his got fuller with the movement. "You're my only friend here, honey," he explained, his voice careful. "If you don't wanna go, that's all right."

Shit balls. At the second part. Not at the first. The first was obviously... well, I guess I understood it. I knew a lot of people, but I was also aware they weren't all my friends. There was a difference. "I'd go with you to an opera if you really wanted me to, I just thought...."

He raised his eyebrows.

Okay, there wasn't any getting out of this. "I know you don't have a lot of time, and I know we hang out when you do have a chance. I didn't want you to...."

"Feel obligated?" he asked slowly.

"Yeah, maybe." I pressed my lips together. "Don't make that face at me. You had all those people over at your house that day I first went over and—"

"Those are my friends, but they aren't my *friends*, darlin'. Not like you." He stared down at me with those baby blues. "And I'd rather hang out with you. If you're gettin' tired of me...."

I made another face at him. "Oh, get a life, loser. You know I'm not."

He coughed. "Loser? Me? I'm writin' this down and tellin' Mama about it."

I snorted. "What are you going to tell her? *Mama, Bianca was bein' mean to me.*"

His upper body jerked, and I heard him choke, "Is that what you think I sound like?"

I was 95 percent sure that the cashier at the register who had been looking blankly forward, whispered under his breath, "It is what you sound like."

I raised my eyebrows at Zac like *see?*

"Well, now you've done fucked up, and you're sharin' those cinnamon things with me."

That got me to laugh.

And it got him to grin at me, not taking me or himself seriously. "I'm still tellin' Mama," he threatened with a little side smile and a nudge.

"Your food's ready," the cashier finally called out, shoving a tray on the counter forward, his expression watchful all of a sudden.

I smiled at him.

He didn't smile back.

I grabbed some sauces and let Zac carry the tray over toward the drink station. We each filled up our cups and took the table in the corner, farthest away from the front counter. I was going to be hurting soon. I'd make it worth it in the meantime, though. My stomach was grumbling.

I took a bite of my crunchy tacos and then said, "I'll go with you if you want me to. I've only been to a haunted house once, and I closed my eyes the whole time, but it'll be fun, right?"

Zac, who had his mouth full of chalupa, nodded. "Very fun."

Liar. I had no problem with scary movies, but I did close my eyes from time to time—most of the time.

Speaking of doing things together. "Hey, have you watched the video I uploaded of us lately?"

He shook his head.

"It already hit four million views."

Zac set his chalupa down. "You serious?"

I nodded at him and grinned. "Yeah. They went up like crazy over the last week. It's been years since the last time I got that many views so fast. Everyone loved it." Especially me. It made me smile the times I watched it. All right, I'd smiled the entire time I'd edited the video, but that was a different story. I just loved watching Zac talk and do everything in general.

Oh God, I was screwed and needed to stop thinking that way.

"Thank you again for doing it for me," I added, giving him a smile I hoped was as appreciative as possible.

His own smile in response was big. "Mama and Paw-Paw watched it and loved it. Mama said I should do more with you."

"Hey, whenever you want."

"Whenever you want," he insisted.

I couldn't help but beam at him. "Deal. My subscriptions went up about ten thousand after the one I did with CJ and Amari." That one had done really well too. "It went up another twenty after yours."

"'Course they did, darlin'."

"Your fans seemed to be super excited about it. Did you read any of the comments? One guy wrote that he'd never been a fan of yours before, but he was now," I told him.

He grinned.

So I told him another one. "Another lady said you're cuter in an apron than in your uniform."

His smile widened. "What else you got?"

I thought about it for a second, thought specifically about

a handful of comments that implied more or less the same thing. They loved our video.

SOMEBODY PLS TELL ME THEY'RE TOGETHER

Number one fan???! #dead #deceased

Get married already!!!!

I think I just died of cuteness overload. Zac Travis + The Lazy Baker = magic

ThE sExUaL tEnSiOn!!! AnOtHeR ePiSoDe PlEaSe!

I love you, Bianca, but please change the channel to THE LAZY BAKER AND ZAC TRAVIS SHOW. I need more!

Came for the baking, left needing to masturbate.

"Go read them yourself," I said instead and decided to change the subject. "Everything going okay with the team? Sucks y'all lost the last game, but they could've put you in, so it's kind of their fault."

He gave me a long, long look as he chewed.

Oh God. They'd released him. Those pieces of—

"I'm gonna be startin', Bibi."

I dropped the packet of hot sauce I'd just torn open. "Excuse me?"

He didn't look happy, which didn't help convince me I'd heard him correctly. "I'm gonna be startin'. Fisher tore his ACL this mornin' durin' practice."

Yup. I gasped and only barely managed to keep my voice down as I asked, "Are you serious?"

He nodded.

"Why don't you look excited then, Snack Pack? I thought you'd be overjoyed. *I'm* overjoyed," I whispered.

His pink mouth twisted to the side just a little, and I knew in that instant whatever had driven him to come over and get a huge hug was back in business. "I should be, you'd figure."

Yeah, he should be.

Zac's hand went up, and he fiddled with the short hair by his ear. "I'm just...."

"Nervous?"

His mouth twisted a little more. "Somethin' like that," he admitted. "Haven't felt like this in a while, but so many things seem to be on the line now. Things that didn't seem to be on the line before and...." Zac blew out a breath toward his food, and he seemed to eyeball his chalupa for a minute before he continued. "I'm lettin' dumb shit I heard get under my skin. I should be excited, but I'm worried I'm gonna fuck this up too."

"You're not going to fuck anything up," I told him as calmly as I possibly could.

"My last coach said I could fuck up a done deal if somebody left it alone with me long enough," he said with a deceptively casual shrug. "I don't wanna screw any of this up. I wanna do well. I always have, but it's just different now. Now it feels like this could be it. Most of my life, Peewee, I've felt like I was missin' somethin'—just this little somethin' I can't shake off no matter what.... Maybe it's just me needin' to really live up to what other people used to think of me, what they expected. I don't wanna be a disappointment, to me or to anybody else."

"You're not a disappointment, Zac. You're amazing. You're tremendous. Some people are just assholes, and you shouldn't listen to them. You know that. You've got this."

"But what if I don't?" he asked softly, still looking down at his food and breaking my heart. "What if I've lost it? What if I'm broken, like they said?"

I didn't know who the hell *they* were, but I was going to light them on fire if I ever found out. It took every single thing in me to keep my voice calm, my face neutral. "You're not, but if we have to, Snack Pack, we'll go buy a lot of super glue then. Just to reinforce everything. Make sure you're better than ever."

His eyelashes lifted, and he settled those milky light blue irises on me. Zac didn't say anything or even sigh, which I'd consider to be a good thing. He just... looked at me. Calmly. Totally. His eyes roamed my face for so long and so intensely, I couldn't do anything but smile at him.

It was like... he was looking at me for the first time and something had caught him off guard.

After a moment, with his gaze still locked on me and with his eyebrows knitted together, he just said, "All right, kiddo. That's a plan then."

And it was my turn to wink at him.

We finished eating our food pretty quickly with Zac changing the subject and telling me about a conversation he'd just had the night before with Paw-Paw in a tone slightly more restrained than usual. He gathered our trash and went to dump it while I washed my hands. We had just made it to the door to leave when the fucking cashier called out, "The White Oaks suck," just as Zac started to push open the door.

He paused for a second, and I saw something ripple across his face.

And I didn't like it.

I didn't like it at all, especially not after the conversation we had just had.

And this fierce protectiveness I felt for Zac, one I had always felt for him, surged up inside of me, and I turned around to frown at the guy standing there with a surly expression on his dumb face.

"Your face sucks. Have a nice day," I called out to him right back, even giving him a sarcastic wave as I gestured super over the top for Zac to keep moving.

He blinked, and it took maybe three seconds, but his

smile went wide before he walked out and I followed after him.

"What a dick. I'm sorry, Snack Pack."

My friend stopped right on the edge of the curb and turned to me with an expression that wasn't anywhere near being devastated like it had been before. He looked... amused. But more than that. And he was still looking at me differently. "You tell him his face sucks?"

"I should've said his attitude sucks too, but it was all I came up with in the moment. Next time."

That big palm of his went to the top of my head and squeezed it. Those blue eyes glittering. Those white teeth out and flashing at me in a smile so sweet, I sucked it up like it was made of gold.

I winked at him again. "You have to be nice, but that doesn't mean I need to."

"You're the best, kiddo."

I shrugged a shoulder at him. "I'm all right."

"You're better than all right," he said, still watching me closely. "It ain't even a competition."

And my heart... my heart did some shit it had no business doing. It thumped. Again. With recognition. With a love so deep I knew it would crush me if I let it.

And that scared the shit out of me.

I was falling in love with him.

Fortunately, my stomach did a roll right then too—a different kind of roll—right at that moment, and I knew what was happening. I was giving myself a chance. Reminding myself of what we had. And that was friendship. A friendship that would span decades.

And I was going to hold on to it with both hands.

Or at least with one at the moment.

Reaching behind me, I smiled and swiped at the air... and then I made it so I was throwing an imaginary ball at him.

It wasn't all that imaginary.

I threw my fart at Zac.

I threw it at him and said, "Attack."

In the time it took him to blink in surprise, he farted too, but not a quiet one, a loud one that must have rumbled his butt cheeks...

Then he was cupping and throwing one right back at me, laughing.

I loved him, and I knew it. I really did. And I had no fucking business doing so.

CHAPTER FIFTEEN

Zac had been staring at the heels of my boots on and off from the moment he'd pulled up to find me outside, waiting for him.

And he was staring at them again now as we walked from the enormous parking lot settled across a few acres surrounding the haunted house.

There weren't too many cars in the lot yet. Then again, we were there fifteen minutes before the doors even opened in the first place. Zac had said that his teammate had wanted them to be the first "visitors" through on opening day. To avoid the crowds, I guessed, and to have pictures taken of them to put up on social media.

Them being Zac, CJ, and Amari, who had been in his car when he'd pulled up to get me. We'd talked about CJ "practicing" cooking the entire ride over. Zac had been trying to teach him.

"You sure about those?" Zac finally asked, pointing toward my feet with his chin.

I lifted my toes. "Yeah, why?"

"You don't think tennis shoes would've been better to go through?"

"They're only wedges, and they aren't even three inches. I can run in taller than these," I scoffed. "I got this."

His face implied he didn't believe me.

"Promise. Connie trained me to run in heels."

That got me an eyebrow lift. "Trained you?"

"We were bored one night."

He blinked, but he shook his head with a smile after that.

In jeans, his usual boots, and a light gray T-shirt I'd seen him wear once or twice by that point, he looked happy and great—not at all like the man who had shown up to my apartment looking so sad the day before. More like the man who had thrown his fart at me... after I'd thrown one at him. And even more like the man who had sang about walking a line, crying in the rain, and then cried laughing with me after yelling at the top of our lungs about carving our names into pickup trucks.

And today, he seemed back to normal when he'd rolled down the window and hollered, "*Let's roll, Bibi. Ticktock.*"

Based on the expression he was giving my shoes *again,* he was definitely in a familiar mood.

"Don't worry about it, Snack Pack," I told him. "You're more likely to trip in your boots than I am. These are super comfortable."

Yeah, he looked skeptical as hell, and he wasn't trying to hide it. "You roll an ankle, and I'm leavin' you behind, kiddo."

I snickered. "Pssh. I go down, and I'm taking you with me."

Zac's hand landed on the back of my neck as he chuckled.

Behind us, Amari—I knew it was him because CJ's voice was really deep and this one wasn't on the same level; it was just a normal, nice voice—asked, "How do you two know each other again?"

Zac kept his warm palm on my neck as he answered with, "Bianca's grandma used to take care of me."

I looked up at Zac and found those soft blue eyes on me. I smiled. He smiled back.

Sure enough, there were maybe twenty people in line to get into the haunted house. There were a few handfuls of employees dressed as everything from zombies to these really ugly clowns with blood and fake guts stuck to their masks and clothes, creeping around the roped lines set and ready for the crowds that would no doubt start showing up. Maybe not today since it was only the beginning of October but closer to Halloween, for sure.

"Did one of y'all tell him we're here?" Zac asked over his shoulder.

It was Amari that replied. "I did. He said to hold up and he'd be here in a minute."

We stopped in a circle, right beside the entrance to the line. I could see around CJ's shoulder and noticed that the people already there were glancing over in our direction. At them. None of the guys were abnormally tall, but it was something about their postures that said "*Look at me*." So I sidestepped to the left so that CJ's ripped up body could hide me a little better.

If he noticed he was being watched, it didn't register on his face as he asked, "What's on the menu this week?"

"Vanilla mug cake and another attempt at those stupid brownies I screwed up."

"I can do another one whenever you want," Amari piped up. "It was fun."

"Yeah, whenever you want." I didn't want him to feel obligated. People always offered to do nice things, but only to be polite.

The extremely handsome man pulled his cell out of his pocket. "What's your number? I'll text you."

I didn't even think twice about it. I rattled the number off to him.

But I felt something weird and glanced up to find Zac staring at Amari. And I mean, *staring* at him. What the hell was that about?

A very deep voice, almost as nice as CJ's, called out some way that had us all turning to find a man the size of Zac and Amari combined making his way over with three normal-sized human beings trailing behind him, two of which were dressed in black clothing and held walkie-talkies and had different things clipped to their belts. The huge guy lifted a hand in greeting, and if the people in line hadn't been paying attention before, they were now.

I stood there as the big man slapped Zac, CJ, and Amari's back before Zac introduced me. "This is Bianca."

I held my hand out to him, and he shook it. "Hi, thank you for letting me come too."

The man made a face, squinted his eyes, and lifted up a finger to point at me afterward. "You're the baker girl, aren't you?"

Well, shit. I pressed my lips together and nodded.

"Yeah, yeah. Nice. Thanks for coming."

I was pretty sure my face went hot and pink. The baker girl. Well, well, well.

Zac's elbow nudged at mine, and I looked up to see him making a face. "*See? You're famous,*" he mouthed, and I rolled my eyes and elbowed him back. But seriously, I was pretty sure my heart started beating faster.

"I'll get you in line to go through first, take a few pictures, and you can walk through in no time," the man explained while I daydreamed about him knowing who I was.

I elbowed Zac a little more as we were led toward the line, and the guys stopped to sign autographs for the people who had figured out who they were. I stood there and took a few pictures for them and pretended like I didn't notice the curious glances being shot my way. But they were mostly all teenagers. No one minded when the biggest man maneuvered our small group to the front of the line, and I could hear the clicking of more phone cameras going off behind us.

Then the person holding the "real" camera started gesturing the guys together, and I tried to take a step back to hide behind Zac, but the big man said, "Baker girl! You too! Say, are you coming to my party?"

Party? What party?

I didn't get a chance to ask before Zac reached behind and took my wrist. "Come on, kiddo. Front and center."

That had me snorting and settling in beside him, my left side totally lined up to his, Zac's arm sliding over my shoulders, his hand draped in front of my chest. On my right, CJ stood an inch or two away, close but not touching me. The flash started going, and it was right then that I realized what they were going to use these pictures for.

For the internet. For social media.

At least the good part was, I wasn't *trying* to hide my friendship with Snack Pack. I'd already been busted by the one person I had wanted to keep it a secret from.

I just... you know....

Whatever. I smiled and tried not to look constipated.

The sound of a chainsaw going off inside the building had me meeting Amari's gaze, and he shot me a funny expression.

"You scared?"

He tilted his head to the side. "Why? If I say yes, will you hold my hand?"

Well, I hadn't been asking to flirt. I'd just been joking. But....

"No," I replied. "I'm going to be too busy holding Zac's hand. I don't want him having nightmares tonight."

He chuckled just as I felt a hand land on the back of my neck again, molding itself around it.

Tilting my head back, I found those familiar baby blues on me. I whispered, "But for real, I don't think I'll get scared, but if I do, I'm using you as a human shield. You've lived a much fuller life than I have. Technically, Amari's bigger but—"

My old friend scoffed. "We're the same size. You know people still call me 'Big Texas,' don't you?"

"Yeah, I know, but I started calling you that back when you *were* the biggest guy I knew. You're not even that big."

"Excuse me?"

It was too much fun to pick on him. "You're big, but you're not *that* big."

Zac's head reared back. "Aren't you five feet tall?"

"Five foot two."

Zac blinked.

I blinked.

He narrowed his eyes. "Swear to God, I'm tellin' Mama on you."

"If you're ready," the big man, whose name I had no idea what it was, called out with a wave of his hand in the direction of the gaping black hole of a door that led into the haunted house. The sound of a chainsaw going again made my little heart speed up a bit. The outside of the place really did look pretty creepy.

Yikes.

It was fake. They were all actors. It was going to be *fine*.

Somehow, someway, Zac got shoved to the front—I'd bet it was for pictures because, hello, he was the *quarterback* of the White Oaks now—and he'd reached back, dragging me up to stand directly behind him instead of further toward the end of our five-person line. The fifth person was the owner. CJ was directly behind me.

"Bianca," he whispered as we trudged forward.

"Yes, CJ?"

"I think you should try less peanut butter on the brownies next time."

I was glad he was at peace and could think about food. "I was thinking the same thing," I replied over my shoulder.

"I can do another video too if you want," he offered.

"It would be my honor." The chainsaw started roaring even louder.

I faced forward again and saw that Zac had stopped right at the entrance. I jogged over to him and pushed at his hip. I didn't think twice about slipping a finger through one of the belt loops of his jeans as he entered the building. Strobe lights flashed as computerized voices screamed and cried from up ahead. What felt like spiderwebs grazed my face and head, even though I was hunching forward directly behind Zac, clinging to his jeans for dear life.

"You okay?" he asked... with laughter in his voice.

"Yes!"

A face popped out of the fucking wall to my left, out of nowhere, and I screamed, stumbling to my right, because *where the hell had that come from?* Behind me, I heard CJ hiss something that sounded an awful lot like "Motherfucker."

And in front of me, Zac must have felt my pull at his jeans because he'd stopped, and in the brief flash of the strobe light, I caught glimpses of his amused face.

Yeah, I grabbed his fucking jeans again with both hands that time and pushed at the middle of his back with my forehead.

To our right there was a nook with a couple of caskets under pale yellow light, and I knew, *I knew* something bad was going to happen. Why the hell had I agreed to this? Jesus. I'd been to a haunted house before; it wasn't like I'd enjoyed it all that much.

I was too old for this shit. My heart was too old for this shit. I had so much left to live for.

Zac and I had gotten to almost the edge of the coffin display when this motherfucker came flying out from a trap door that the coffins had distracted us from, and I heard someone behind me yell, "Damn it!"

It was a split second later that something hit me in the back.

While I was taking a step.

I stumbled.

And I felt my ankle just go... sideways.

Yup.

Sideways.

"Whoa-ho-ho," I screeched, lifting my leg up and wrapping my hands around it, bumping into Zac's back.

CJ called out from behind, "Sorry! Amari pushed me!"

Something grabbed my shoulder, and just as I was about to push it off, Zac yelled, "What the hell happened?"

"I'm fine," I told him, not sure if he could even hear me but knowing what he was going to say if he did.

He crouched in front of me, the lights flashing against his face and features. "Did you roll your ankle?"

I nodded.

His mouth went flat under the lighting.

"It's fine. I'm fine."

He looked at the foot I was still holding for a moment, then stood up and turned around.

Zac dropped into a squat position and said over his shoulder, "Come on. Hop up."

I tried to set my weight down and *nope*.

"You all right?" CJ asked from behind.

I waved my hand at him. What was I going to do? Take a piggyback ride from him instead?

Nope.

I set my hands on Zac's shoulders and tried to hop up as far as I could. Those big palms grabbed onto the backs of my thighs, hefting me up higher until I was pretty much straddling him from behind. Over his shoulder, he said, "Remember this, Peewee."

"Yeah, yeah, thank you," I said into his ear just as someone jumped out of fucking nowhere again, and I was pretty sure Amari screamed. Someone laughed, and I was glad one of us was having fun, even though I was pretty sure it was the owner having the time of his life laughing at his teammates.

"Hey?" Zac yelled so I could hear him.

"What?"

"Remember that time you said you'd be fine goin' through a haunted house in heels and rolled your ankle two minutes in?"

I made a face he couldn't see because mine was right next to his. The short hairs on his face tickled me. "Mind your business."

I felt him laugh more than heard it as we approached a long length of hallway that was pitch-black. *Great.* Really, just *great.*

I tightened my arms around Zac's shoulders, just in case he took off jogging. I doubted it; he hadn't screamed so far, unlike my new friends who I hoped were still behind us and hadn't been murdered. I didn't want to risk looking behind me to see someone following us, trying to scare me. There was only one thing I could remember ever scaring Zac, and it sure as hell hadn't been scary movies.

The last time I'd brought it up—a decade ago—he'd still insisted he hadn't actually been scared and that he just hadn't eaten breakfast and *that's why I passed out.*

Yeah, right.

"You scared?" he hollered as we started down the hall.

"Scared you're gonna drop me," I said, even as my heartbeat sped up. I mean, my heart and most of my brain recognized that this was fake and that all these people were actors who wouldn't even touch us... but the rest of me picked up on the scary music and the chainsaw still going from somewhere coming up ahead....

Well, whatever.

"I'm not gonna drop you, kiddo."

"Okay," I croaked into his ear when someone started banging on the other side of the walls we were walking by. "This is so stupid. I should have just stayed home."

A chin appeared in my vision as Zac tried to glance at me over his shoulder. "We got this."

"Eh."

One of the hands on the back of my thighs patted it. "We got this."

"I'll poke them in the eyes, and you run."

Beneath me, I could feel him laugh. "Throw some fart bombs at 'em."

Pressing my forehead against his shoulder, I laughed. "You liked that, huh?"

"Kiddo, I like everything—*goddamn it! Don't do that!*"

I didn't get a chance to get scared because the actor who popped out of nowhere had appeared on the side of Zac where my face wasn't. But when he shouted, I lifted my head and looked over to see someone in a creepy clown mask walking beside us, his nose literally inches from Zac's face. Yeah, fuck this. I closed my eyes and put my face back where it had been, right by his throat that smelled like his nice cologne.

"Fuck it, just run. Amari and CJ are on their own. They're big guys. They can save themselves."

"All right, he's gone," Zac advised me a moment later. "Let's wait a sec. I want to see if they scream too."

I kept my eyes closed but my ears open.

"Oh hell no, this is the devil's work," I was pretty sure CJ hollered.

We snorted. Then I felt Zac start moving again.

"Are your eyes closed?"

I nodded against his neck. "They're really dry."

He was cracking up again. I could feel it. "I'm sure they are, darlin'."

The sound of the chainsaw got louder with every step Zac took, and a couple times I heard him suck in a breath. I wrapped my arms around him even tighter, but he didn't complain. Twice I felt his hands flex beneath my thighs.

"I believe in you," I whispered. "Save us."

At the sound of the chainsaw right up ahead, he started walking faster, and I peeked an eye open to see a figure standing at the mouth of what was an open door with fog swirling around. And sure enough, he was holding what sounded like a chainsaw but didn't look like one.

"If we don't make it out alive, I want you to know I love you," I said into his ear and felt him laugh again.

"See you at the gates?"

"Of hell? Yeah, I'll see you there."

I knew he shook his head because I felt his chin graze my forearm.

Then he walked, going forward, my instincts warning the chainsaw guy was right there.

Something flashed beyond my eyelids, and I knew someone had taken a picture.

Well, at least they'd think it was scary and come check it out.

I opened my eyes just as Amari, CJ, and the other big guy came walking out. And by walking, I meant, CJ was making a face, Amari was directly behind him looking pretty damn disgruntled, and the owner was grinning wide.

"You can drop me. I can limp back to your car," I told Zac, tapping at his upper arm.

I saw a flash of his chin. "So you can roll the other one on the walk back to the car?"

"Ha, ha, ha."

―――――

"How's your ankle, kiddo?"

The icepack I'd slapped on it the second we'd gotten up to my apartment left my toes bared and covered the lower hem of my jeans. He'd carried me up the stairs, and I knew it was going to be a long time before he let me live this down. I wiggled my toes at Zac, who was sitting on the opposite end of the couch from me. He was sipping on one of the cans of grape soda he'd pulled out of my fridge when I'd gone for the icepack to help the swelling. It wasn't hurting too bad, but it was stiff, and since I was going to have to work tomorrow, I wanted to prevent it from being worse than it needed to be.

"It's all right. I just tweaked it." I kept my face even. "It could have been worse."

The corners of his mouth twisted up around the rim of the can. "Could it? Could it have been worse?"

I reached for the remote to turn the television on. "Yeah. It could have. I could have actually sprained it, and then my boss would have been mad at me."

"Your boss would be mad at you for sprainin' an ankle?"

I blew out a breath. "He'd get mad at me for letting my polo shirt get wrinkled." He'd get mad at me for breathing too, I'd bet, if I did it loud enough.

He frowned. "This the same boss you hate?"

"The one and only."

"Things haven't gotten any better?"

Plucking the icepack off, I tossed it onto the side table to my left. "Nah, they've gotten worse," I admitted before realizing what I'd said.

Of course he picked up on it. "Why?"

I didn't want to tell him, but... I didn't want to not tell him either.

"What happened?" he demanded quietly.

I scratched at the tip of my nose and stretched my leg out a little to end up on the cushion between us. "He's just been more of an asshole because I keep telling him no when he asks me to work longer shifts. Now he found out we're friends and tried to ask me about it, but I shut it down."

Those dark blond eyelashes dropped, and the pleasant expression on his face fell off. He even set the can of grape soda on the floor by his feet. "What?"

"I think he might have wanted me to ask you to come to the gym or something annoying."

A frown took over his perfect face.

"It's fine," I told him, even throwing in a shrug so he'd really believe me that it wasn't a big deal.

"If you say so, but you tell me if there's somethin' I can do to help. I don't see why you haven't quit yet—yeah, I know because of your friend—but you don't need to be puttin' up with that kind of nonsense, Bibi."

"I know," I muttered. "I'll be out of there soon, come hell or high water. Which speaking of, I didn't tell you but the photographer that's going to be doing my book asked if we could move the booking to November, so I'm trying to figure that out."

He was still frowning as he stretched his legs out in front of him and kept going. He shot me a little side-look that was mostly a frown. "If there's somethin' I can do to help, I'm serious, let me know."

I knew he was serious, so I nodded at him.

"We goin' to that Halloween party?" he asked.

I'd forgotten all about it, even though the owner-guy had brought it up again—pointing a finger at me as he said it like there was another Baker Girl around—after everyone had made it through the haunted house. But I'd been too distracted bickering with Zac about my wedge boots to do more than smile and nod. But now I wasn't distracted.

"I thought he was just being nice inviting me."

He slanted me a look. "He told you twice and texted me as we were leavin'," he explained. "You'll come then?"

"When is it? I don't have a costume, and I'm trying to save my money right now to pay off the photographer." It was the truth. Regardless of how far I took my willingness to quit, I had to save everything I possibly could until then. "I shouldn't be spending on things like that."

He gave me the same exact expression he had a moment ago. "You need money? Why didn't you tell me?"

"I don't need money. I just don't need to be spending it right now." I smiled at him. "But thank you for worrying. I'm sure you can get—"

"Bianca, I swear if you try and pawn me off on some make-believe other friend again—"

"*I'm gonna tell Mama,*" I mocked him before bursting out laughing.

He pressed his lips together.

I laughed harder, so hard there were tears in my eyes by the time he decided to ignore what I was doing and saying. He hadn't forgotten what we were talking about.

"I'll let you borrow whatever money you need to pay for your photographer," he stated, that frown back on his face.

I would never take his money... unless I absolutely had to, but I wasn't there yet. I didn't feel like arguing with him, so I said nothing instead and let him keep yammering on.

"And if you go with me to pick out a costume, I'll get yours too."

I sighed. "You can go by yourself, you know."

"If I wanted to go by myself, I would."

I bet he would.

I'd bet if he wanted a date with some pretty woman, he could get it in about a split second too. That's what I'd been on the verge of reminding him. But instead, he wanted to go with me. I wasn't sure why. I really didn't understand it. As far as I knew, he hadn't been out with anyone, anywhere, not since the day of his party. All his posts had been football related.

Every time I wondered why he liked to spend time with me, the only question in my head that came up was that it might be because he could be himself around me. But that didn't add up because he didn't act differently around other people. Maybe he was slightly more ridiculous in my presence, but the true essence of him, he shared with everyone. It was part of what made him so likable and charismatic. Also, it was those damn eyes.

And the rest of him, honestly.

It had touched me that he'd gone to the haunted house to support his teammate. It said a lot about him. At least I thought so.

Well, whatever. I wasn't going to bring it up, so I was never going to know; therefore, I had to take the information available to me—that if he wanted to go with someone else, he easily could—and make a decision.

"Okay. It can be my Christmas present," I agreed.

He huffed but nodded. So I leaned forward and poked at him and got poked back in return. We smiled at each other.

"My friends are plannin' on comin' to visit to watch a game," he said. "Not sure when yet. They've got three kids. I really want you to meet 'em."

He did? I nodded. "Okay. Tell me when."

His attention moved forward again, and a moment later,

his phone started ringing from its spot on the middle cushion between us, right next to my foot. I took a peek at the screen and saw the name flash across it before he hit the ignore button.

ALICIA BLONDEATTY HOU

I swallowed.

Zac was silent for a second, but he wasn't looking at his phone—he'd barely glanced at it. He was focused on the television.

He wasn't even looking at me either when he dropped his hand over my ankle and held it there, giving it a light squeeze. It was warm and dry.

He left it there for a while.

I couldn't help but wonder some more who the Alicia person was. Someone he'd met in Houston apparently. It shouldn't be a surprise.

Maybe it was even the same blonde from the party. More than likely though, it was a different one. He hadn't remembered her when I'd brought her up a while back. Cool. Fine. Okay.

My phone beeped right then, and I peeked at the screen to see I'd been tagged in something.

Tagged by **HTWONHAUNTEDFACTORY**.

I unlocked the screen and hit the icon to open it.

I nudged at Zac's shoulders, getting those baby blues swinging in my direction. I showed him the screen.

On it was Zac, mostly, mouth open as he laughed, and behind his shoulder—like the other twenty pictures that my grandma had had in her house of us—was me. A forearm wrapped around his neck, face scrunched up, eyes closed. Behind us was the man holding the fake chainsaw, acting like he was chasing us out, which he probably had been, but I'd been too busy having my eyes closed to know for sure.

The owner man tagged me in the post. And Zac.

Me. The Lazy Baker.

Zac. Zac "Big Texas" Travis.

Well, if our friendship had been a secret before, it wasn't any longer.

The hand on my ankle gave it a light squeeze, and I looked up to find Zac's light blue eyes on my face.

"It's a good picture, huh?" I asked him.

His thumb rubbed along the sole of my foot. "Yeah, kiddo. It's a real good one," he agreed, looking me dead in the eye.

CHAPTER SIXTEEN

I would have paid money to have a picture of Trevor's face when he saw us walking up to the front doors of the club where the Halloween party was being hosted weeks later.

Honestly, from the handful of interactions we'd had, I wasn't sure he was physically capable of doing more than rolling his eyes, scowling, or making his features go completely emotionless. So that was something. I mean, Zac had needed to lift his hand to get him to shake mine the second time we'd met.

First, he blinked.

Then I'd swear that he rubbed his eyes with a fisted hand and looked at us again, like maybe his eyes had tricked him.

They hadn't.

While I didn't enjoy his disbelieving face anywhere near as much as Zac did, I still got a kick out of it. And I knew without a doubt that Zac got a huge kick out of it because he started elbowing me and giggling. All "hehehe" under his breath while we made our way through the parking lot with CJ and Amari trailing behind us, more than likely tugging at their own costumes. I'd helped them come up with a quick costume the day before when I'd gone over to the house to pick up Zac so we could go grocery shopping.

Salt and pepper.

It had almost brought a tear to my eye.

But nothing had made me laugh quite like what Zac and I had managed to find at the costume store.

But Trevor wasn't laughing as he gazed at us with a sigh and muttered, "Really?"

Zac's plaid-covered elbow hit my bodysuit-covered one.

I mean, it had been freaking fate—like we'd planned it when we hadn't. Yet it had worked out perfectly. Beyond perfect honestly. Even CJ shook his head when he'd met us outside of the house while we waited for the ride Zac ordered. "You both would" was all he'd said before snapping a picture of us. Zac had an elbow on my shoulder, because why not when it was level and I could basically be used as a crutch?

I'd asked CJ to take one for me too on my phone, and then Zac had taken my cell and sent it to himself.

"Whatcha think, Trev?" Zac asked as we stopped in front of his longtime manager.

Trevor scrubbed at his face again, finally making me take in the "costume" he had on.

It wasn't much of one. Honestly, he looked like he usually did. I was pretty sure I'd seen him wearing the same suit like a week ago when I had gone to pick up Zac before going to the movies. He'd been stressed as hell that day—I was able to tell by his face—but it had been because of the game the White Oaks had been set to play the next day. Going to the movies had been my idea to try and take his mind off things. Unfortunately, the team had lost the first game that Zac had started, but they'd won the second one and scraped by with another win during the third.

Boogie had come down to Houston, and we'd watched

that home game together—the first one since Zac had taken over—low in the stands, while we'd screamed our asses off. Afterward, Zac had come over to my apartment, and he'd barbecued on my patio to celebrate. It had been a lot of fun.

It had been a good few weeks—weeks in which I hadn't seen Trevor again, even though I saw Zac just about every other day when he didn't stay late to watch film or do whatever it was he did at the White Oaks facilities. On the days I didn't see him, we still texted. Sometimes he called. Being around him so much had started to be second nature.

And then there had been us going to the Halloween store on one of his half days.

Trevor, on the other hand, hadn't gone to a costume store. He was in a sleek, slim-cut, black suit with a crisp white shirt and a black tie. The only difference was that the hair he usually had combed and gelled backward was parted down the middle and might have had a little bit of oil in it. It was a lot longer than it looked when he had it styled normally; it just about hit his chin.

Was he...?

"I think I shouldn't be surprised," he said dryly in response to Zac's question about what he thought about our costumes.

Zac looked down at the same time I glanced up, and we both grinned, elbows meeting again, like this pleased us. Because it did. There were so many times you had to act like an adult, but if I had the opportunity not to... well, I was going to take it. *"You're only as old as you tell yourself,"* Mamá Lupe used to say. And I was so lucky Zac felt the same way.

Even though I felt like his costume wasn't much of a stretch, but that's what made it even better.

In his most "country" boots, which his mom had mailed to him overnight, with spurs on them and everything; skintight blue jeans that hugged every inch of those long, muscular legs; a big, old, vintage belt buckle that he'd told me belonged to Paw-Paw, which his mom had also sent; and a yellow plaid, long-sleeved, button-down shirt... he could have passed for a cowboy. But it was the cow print vest, red bandana, the big fake star clipped to the vest, and his tilted cowboy hat that really sealed the deal.

I'd sat outside the dressing room door laughing my ass off for at least two minutes when he'd come out with what the costume store had provided.

And it was while I'd been laughing that he'd been the one to ask the employee if they had the costume that I was currently wearing.

They did, and he'd brought it to me as an offering.

I hadn't thought twice about it. I'd agreed. And even though it was meant for someone taller and bigger than me— a small man—I was glad that it wasn't totally skintight. It was just regular tight. The white spandex had a few green lines around the stomach and the forearms. I had a thick black belt on, and over my chest was a foam chest piece with red buttons, shoulder pads, and more green accents. The hood of the spandex suit was purple and hid almost all of my hair. I had silver ballet flats that I'd put green fabric over the toes with double-sided tape that I had a feeling would fall off in the first thirty minutes. The only thing I was missing was a laser and retractable wings.

But whatever. It wasn't sexy, but it made me and Zac laugh, so I was happy with it. I was so stressed and confused about other things going on, I needed it.

I'd asked him how I looked, and he'd crossed his arms over his chest, shook his head, and said, "*Absolutely beautiful, darlin'.*"

A lie, but I'd take it.

I focused back on Trevor. "Hey, Trev."

Beside me, Zac choked. He'd already explained how much

he hated being called Trev, but since he wasn't particularly nice to me—more like he suffered through my presence when I was around—I figured we were good.

"Trevor," he corrected.

Yeah, yeah. "Are you supposed to be John—"

"Wick. Yes. Let's go inside. I want to be out of here in an hour. I came straight from the airport. I've got things to do."

A hand landed on the padded shoulder of my Buzz costume, giving it a squeeze for a moment before those fingers curled around the nape of my neck and stayed there as we followed after Trevor. There was a line, of course, but he headed straight toward the bouncers, holding out what looked like laminated, holographic passes that the men checked with flashlights and then some kind of blue light before they waved our small group in. I couldn't hear Amari or CJ over the music coming through the doors and walls as we went through them. It wasn't anywhere near as loud as a club usually got, but it was still noisy enough that I figured I'd have to stare at mouths the rest of the night to understand what anyone said —if anyone even talked to me in the first place.

There were *a lot* of people already inside.

And like he could read my mind, Zac leaned in real close, the light wisp of his breath tickling my ear as he reconfirmed, "Hang with me, all right?"

I had already been contemplating this since I'd heard about this thing. "That's okay. You don't need to babysit me or anything. I know you might have to do your thing. I'll be okay for a while. If I want to leave, I know how to get home." I smiled at him.

His eyebrows went flat under the low brim of his cowboy hat. "Get home? By yourself?" he asked like I'd just said I was going to compete in the Olympics for gymnastics.

I glanced up at his handsome face and nodded. He really

was the perfect Woody. But, what? Did he think I was going to go home with someone? He knew I had to work the next morning; I'd mentioned it a minimum of six times. I wasn't going to stay here all night. He hadn't planned on it either from what he'd said.

Zac moved closer, dipping his head so I could get a real good look at his lips. "How about this: we'll stay for an hour, and then we'll get outta here like Trev is plannin'. We can do whatever you want after that. Deal?"

The "yes" was there, but so was the knowledge he knew people here. "Zac, you know my feelings won't be hurt if you would rather hang out with—"

He pressed his index finger against my lips.

I blinked at him and said with his finger still over my mouth, "I will lick your finger, and you know I will."

Zac laughed, booping me on the nose. "I would rather hang out with you than here. You got me? Or do I gotta say it again for the... what? The fiftieth time?"

I didn't need to watch his face to know he was telling me the truth. So I nodded and asked, "Whatever I want?"

He nodded pretty seriously.

"Okay."

"What are you thinking?"

"Drive-through Taco Bell."

Zac blinked. "Drive-through?"

"What, you're too good for drive-through now?"

"I created a monster."

"Travis!" someone hollered out of nowhere.

It was some big, burly guy who came walking over. Big. Real big. As Zac turned us toward him, his arm didn't move an inch.

"'Sup, man?" the man asked. "Are you... Woody?"

"Woody, and I got my sidekick, Buzz, here."

They hugged each other, and the other man glanced from me to Zac and then back to me again.

Zac slipped his arm over my shoulders before leaning his head against mine. "Bianca, this is Milton. Milton, Bianca," Zac told him.

I stretched my hand out toward him, and he took it in his huge one, the arm on me not going anywhere. "Nice to meet you."

"Nice to meet you." The other man jerked. "You're *the* Bianca?"

The Bianca?

"Yeah," Zac was the one who answered. "The one I was tellin' you about."

He was talking about me?

"No shit." He suddenly seemed so much more interested. "The Baker?"

"Lazy Baker," Zac corrected him for me. "She's got more than two million followers on WatchTube. Get it right."

Here I went keeping my life a secret from just about everyone, and here he was telling everybody.

"Yeah, yeah, yeah," the guy snapped his fingers. "With the recipes. Zac showed me your page."

He *had*?

His smile was so sweet, I had to blink. I stayed there as they talked about something, but I was too hung up on him telling his teammates about me that I stayed pretty quiet, absorbing it all.

Marveling at it.

He really was the best guy.

And not for the first time, my heart gave a little twist at the fact.

But the second the other man walked away, I snuck out from under his arm and asked, "You told people about my channel?"

He gave me a funny little smile. "Yeah, why?" He ticked his head to the side. "Did you not want me to say anything?"

I had told myself at least twice a day for the last month that I *wasn't* back to being in love with Zac. That I wasn't. No way. No how. It wasn't happening.

Sometimes I managed to believe myself; other times, I knew I was full of shit.

And he was making it really hard to go with option A. Really hard. "No, I mean, you can do whatever you want. But it's no big deal—"

"Why are you always tryin' to downplay it, huh, darlin'? It is a big deal, and I'm so damn proud of you, even though it isn't like I had somethin' to do with it." He moved his head to the side. "Well, you did used to make me things, so I was kinda your early guinea pig, huh?"

I.... Well....

"And you never downplay me," he argued.

"Because there's nothing to downplay."

"I'm only in the organization now because the White Oaks lost both their quarterbacks, kiddo."

He was about to get jabbed in the side. "And? You're amazing. You're awesome."

"You think I'm amazing?" this dummy asked.

I kept my face even; I wasn't about to egg him on. "I know you are. You're the one that seems to forget that."

He watched me closely with those eyes. Just as he opened his mouth, someone to the side stumbled backward into me.

But just as I was shoved by the stranger's weight, Zac's hand struck out, pushing the person back to where they'd come from before he, or she, could fall on me. I looked up at him and didn't miss the frown on Zac's face as the man turned around to look at who'd pushed him.

From the face he made, he recognized him. "Sorry, sorry," the guy apologized quickly.

Zac didn't say a word as he grabbed onto my shoulders and moved me closer to the wall beside us, putting his body between me and the crowd.

"You okay?" he asked when the guy turned back around and moved away.

"Yeah, I'm all right. He just stomped on me a little." I glanced up at him as I kneeled to rub the top of my foot. "Thank you for protecting me."

One side of his mouth tilted up. "Peewee, I'd never let a thing happen to you."

There went my heart again, and I tried to hide it with a grin. "Like you know I'd never let anything happen to you?"

He nodded once. "Just like that."

He held out his hand and helped me to my feet.

And that was when I saw them.

I knew immediately who they were under their costumes of Morticia and Gomez Addams. The skintight, clinging black dress and black lipstick didn't hide who she was. The black suit and what I knew was a fake black mustache didn't hide his identity either.

I squeaked, and Zac gave me an interested look. "What is it?"

I grabbed his forearm. "Oh my God, Zac, that's Jasmine and Ivan Lukov!" I whisper-hissed.

His head turned in the direction I was staring, and I wasn't even sure he was looking at the same couple I was, because he asked, "Who?"

Who? Was he kidding me? "They only won a fucking gold medal! Oh my God, I'm going to faint. They're only the greatest figure skating pair of all time!" I wasn't kidding. I might faint. I had watched every single figure skating competition they were going to participate in, just to see them skate. I'd watched a WatchTube video of them once that happened to come up two years ago, and they had sucked me in completely since.

"How do you know that?" Zac asked, almost with a laugh, as his hand wrapped around my wrist.

I glanced up to meet his gaze and tugged on the forearm I was still holding. "How do you *not* know that? Introduce me! Please!"

He looked at me and shrugged, his fingers giving mine a gentle squeeze. "All right, all right. I don't know 'em either, kiddo, but we can make somethin' up. Come on."

I had just come out of the bathroom stall following the longest pee of my life—after struggling for five solid minutes to take off the foam padding of the top half of my Buzz Lightyear costume and then peeling off the spandex suit until it was pooled at my knees—when I spotted the next person who had me stopping in place. I seriously had no idea why people wore rompers. I would die. Or pee all over myself. It had been enough of a close call.

I'd been holding it for at least an hour. An hour in which twenty minutes had been spent talking to the gold-medal-winning figure skating pair that I was even more in love with after meeting. They were self-deprecating and funny, and Jasmine had been even prettier in person than on TV. And I wanted to have a smug face as good as hers. Ivan Lukov was also just about the prettiest man I'd ever seen—his beauty was only surpassed by Zac's, but in a different way. Zac had taken a picture of me with them, which made my year.

Another twenty minutes had been spent with us on the dance floor, and then the rest of the time with me standing at Zac's side while he talked to a couple people he knew.

And when that hour of us being at the Halloween party

had hit, his phone had started vibrating with an alarm I hadn't even known he'd set, and I'd decided to make my way to the bathroom before we left.

And it was for that reason that I happened to be in there at that exact moment.

To find her at the sink, washing her hands, wearing a Little Red Riding Hood costume with a wolf mask sitting on the counter.

In the goddamn bathroom, of all places.

Ten years had passed, but I recognized that fucking face.

The face that had belonged to a Disney princess—a Disney princess I had thought originally belonged to a Disney prince.

As an adult now, maybe she still deserved a Disney prince... in a different fucking movie.

She was a bitch Cinderella... and I was Mulan. And Zac... Zac was... well, Zac looked like the prince in Sleeping Beauty, but inside, he was an Olaf.

And Olaf was my favorite.

He didn't deserve this asshole. He never had. Part of me understood he had been thinking with his dick and not his head back when they'd dated for a few months, but it still blew my mind he'd let someone so shitty into his life. Had he not seen it? Had he not known? I wasn't sure.

What I did know was that *now* she was here. In front of me. In the fucking bathroom.

I had never looked her up once in all the years since she'd crushed my pride and self-esteem into smithereens. I'd *thought* about it once or twice but had stopped myself in time.

But that didn't mean I hadn't made a promise to myself— a promise I had made the day I'd decided I was going to be more than a little kid someone hung out with out of pity. The day I decided I was going to be proud of myself first.

If I ever see that bitch again, I'm gonna tell her. I'm gonna tell her "thank you for that time you were an asshole to me and you hurt my feelings for years. Eat a dick."

Most of the time, I thought I was mature, or at least mostly mature. But in that second, with her standing there at the sink, as pretty as ever—part of me wished she'd grown a bunch of facial hair over the years—whatever maturity I had in me, disappeared. Like *that.*

She looked up, her gaze catching mine through the reflection.

And maybe, *maybe*, if she had smiled or done anything other than look me up and down, maybe I might have let it go. But the words still rang fresh in my soul.

She didn't do anything friendly. She seemed to size me up with her still-heartless gaze, found me lacking, then finished rinsing off in the sink. Unimportant and forgotten.

I stood there as she shook her hands off, water flying everywhere, and leaned forward to get closer to the mirror mounted on the wall.

And I knew what I was going to do.

What I had to do. For younger me. For anyone else she might have ever been ugly to that hadn't stood up for themselves either.

Especially when Zac was standing somewhere close by outside that door, ready to hang out with me after he'd already spent hours in my company. Because he cared about me and I cared about him.

Because we had been meant to be friends. To be in each other's lives. Over the last few weeks, he'd become my best friend too.

Because it had been both my fault and Zac's that we had grown apart over the years, but Boogie had been right: you had to work on friendships and relationships, and there was only so much that could happen since I'd basically given up and retreated. Because of her. And maybe if I'd even remotely kept trying after I'd initially given up, he would have reached back out toward me with both hands.

Either way, she had been an asshole, and I wanted her to know that I hadn't forgotten her words and deeds.

That was when a sliver of a thought of Zac seeing her hit me right in the chest. Of seeing her and remembering that they had dated for a little bit. Of the chances of him still finding her attractive and rekindling something.

But... oh well. If he wanted to start up a relationship with someone like her again all because she was beautiful, then... whatever. It would be on him.

But this, *this* was about me.

Pushing my shoulders down—I'd slipped my costume back on—I stood exactly where I was and said her name. "Jessica?"

The woman instantly looked at me in the reflection of the mirror, her eyebrows knitting together in confusion. She paused, like she was thinking about it, like she wasn't sure if we knew each other and she'd forgotten, but answered after a second, "Yes?" She turned around, that confused expression growing on her still-pretty features.

Zac doesn't have time for you anymore, sweetie. He has things to do, and he's too nice to tell you that. Maybe if you tamp down how needy you are with him....

"My name is Bianca," I told her, not expecting her to remember and not surprised when she didn't react at all. "We knew each other a long time ago. You dated my friend Zac." And just in case she had dated more than one Zac, I went into details. "Zac Travis."

I had never in my life seen in person someone literally go white. I was pale and got even more pale during the winter, but I had nothing on her then. Not even close.

Then something else slid over her face. Fear. Panic.

Did she remember what she'd said?

Well, I wasn't going to risk that she didn't know what I had carried around word for word for the last ten years. "I don't know if you remember, but you told me—"

She took a step back, bumping into the washbasin in a way that seemed like she didn't even feel that she had. "Oh shit," she whispered under her breath so low I barely heard it. "I'm sorry."

She was already apologizing before I could even remind her of what she'd done? I'd been waiting for this shit for *years*. "Do you *remember* what you said to me?" I asked her as her hands went to the edge of the counter, like she was trying to hold herself up.

"I—I—shit. *Shit,*" the woman stuttered. "I'm sorry, I forgot. I... I forgot. I meant to only do it for a little while.... For a couple months, but I for-forgot until now.... Shit. Shit, shit, shit," she echoed, staring at me with wide, fearful eyes that made zero sense.

What the *fuck* was she talking about?

"You only meant to do what for a little bit?" Did she have me confused with someone else? Had she been ugly to another person in Zac's life? One of his cousins, maybe?

But she didn't respond, because she was too busy chanting, "*Oh shit, oh shit, oh shit,*" under her breath as she lifted her hands to her face... and then dropped them suddenly.

Drama queen much? I'd had this planned for years. I'd lain in bed and worked out my speech a long time ago, ready for just this opportunity, and now she was trying to turn it around and make it about her? Nuh-uh.

"You *said* things to me. Do you remember? You told me I was—"

The pretty woman shook her head, face still paler than pale, and took a step forward. "Look, I'm sorry. I'm so sorry for what I did. I shouldn't have come—"

My mouth ran off before I could stop it. "Yeah, you should be. You were *mean.* I had just been a kid and you—"

She put up a hand, like to try and keep me away from getting too close to her. "He loved you so much, and I was just jealous, and I'm so sorry—"

"I don't want your apology. You *hurt* me. I let one of my favorite people in the world go for ten years because of what you said."

If I'd thought she looked scared before, her features went straight terrified after my last comment.

"Oh God," she muttered before turning around, nearly stumbling as she headed straight for the door, saying over her shoulder, "I'm sorry. I'm so sorry."

She was out of there, leaving her mask behind.

And goddamn it, my hands were dirty—maybe I could touch her face with my dirty hands as payback—but I went after her, stopping to squirt some hand sanitizer because I wasn't a total monster.... but confused by the fact she looked so sick and scared. Because something told me that wasn't the reaction of someone who felt bad for how she'd behaved in her twenties. It was deeper than that. Somewhere in my heart, I knew it.

And that was why I went after her through the door.

And that was why I pretty much instantly stopped on the other side.

Because she'd bumped into Zac, and her whole body was shaking and her mouth was running off a long line of words without a break, without a breath, without the blink of an eye.

"I'msosorryIforgotIonlymeanttodoitforalittlewhilebut-thenyoubrokeupwithmeaweeklaterandIwasmadanddidn'tcare-andIfiguredyouwouldnoticeandthenyou'dfixitandI'msorry."

I wasn't even sure if Zac recognized her from the what-the-fuck expression on his face as she blew through her apology.

But the man I didn't recognize who had moved to stand beside Zac must have understood enough because he set a hand on her shoulder and said, "Baby, what are you talking about?"

Baby? Her boyfriend? Husband?

Actually... he did look a little familiar.

She swooned. She gulped. She looked like she wanted to fucking run but physically couldn't because she was shaking so bad.

"Jessica, what did you do? What did you think he would fix?" the tall, super strapping man asked the woman who had kicked me as a teenager with her words.

Zac's baby blue gaze met mine in confusion, and I knew I had to tell him. What she'd said, what she'd done, and what I had done.

Grown apart. Stopped messaging him. Totally retreated.

I had given up on him in a way.

Just as I opened my mouth to tell him, Jessica looked at me, then to Zac's confused face, and back to me. And she exhaled three words that made no sense. "I was jealous."

It was the man who gently asked, as his own expression went about as confused as Zac's, "About what?"

I wasn't sure what it said about me that I felt zero sympathy for her. None.

It was then that Zac blinked and then asked, "Wait a minute. You look familiar. Did we—" He stopped and glanced at the man he had to have known, looking sheepish all of a sudden. "—go out? A long time ago?"

I was going to slap him. On the ass so I wouldn't ruin his photogenic face. *He didn't remember her.*

I wasn't sure if that made it better or worse.

Maybe he needed more information. **JESSICA**

BRUNETTESTUDENT DAL. At least she'd been a student back when they'd dated.

I wanted to kick him right in the asshole.

The woman, Jessica, made a noise in her throat as she lifted her eyes slowly to make contact with Zac, a surprised expression sweeping over her features. I was 99 percent sure there was anger in her eyeballs as she looked at him.

Then, *at that exact moment*, I might have felt for her a little bit. But just a teeny bit. Because *yikes*.

Only for a second. Until she opened her mouth again, the anger morphing into incredulousness in the blink of an eye. "For three months, Zachary Travis," she told him coldly.

She'd busted out his last name. Yeah, she was definitely pissed and insulted.

The other man blinked in surprise, but whether it was at her tone or the fact he didn't know they had "dated," I had no clue. I was so mad that I couldn't finish what I had wanted to do, damn it.

"Still dumber than a box of rocks, huh?" she told him in a mean voice that had the other man stilling. Zac, on the other hand, narrowed his eyes like he was trying to remember... and failing. I could tell by the expression on his face; one eye got more squinty than the other.

But I hadn't forgotten.

And she wasn't about to say shit like that to him.

"Don't talk to him like that," I snapped, annoyed.

She rolled her eyes, the fear and the body shakes magically gone. "You. Still defending him. Still following him around like a little puppy, huh?"

Where the hell had the scared bitch gone? I wondered, offended and mad all over again. I was nobody's puppy. I was a German Shepherd, maybe a Belgian Malinois; not the smallest or the biggest but strong, proud and loyal.

Fuck her. Asshole.

"So?" I asked her because it was the first thing that popped into my head. I almost said *at least he remembers me*, but it didn't come to me fast enough.

"Jessica," the man stated, distracting us. "What are you talking about? What did you do?" He paused. "And don't lie. Don't even think about."

And there she was, back to being scared. Or maybe it wasn't so much scared as... caught. Resigned, and terrified about it, that's what it was.

And I must have not been the only person to pick up on it because even Zac said, "I remember you now." And in the blink of an eye, his head lifted, his expression changed into one so serious it was scary, and he asked, "What are you talkin' about?"

The man said her name all slow and tense.

She gulped again, and a deep feeling of dread filled my stomach. A warning. A premonition.

Tears filled her eyes. Tears I didn't really believe from how fast they appeared and how effortlessly she batted her eyelashes. "I'm sorry, okay?" she whispered in a tiny voice that made me want to smack her too. Not in the asshole.

And since I didn't trust these guys to not boo-hoo-woo-woo over her pretty little blue eyes getting teary, I jumped in. "What are you sorry for? What you said to me?"

Nope. Not that. "For what I did," she answered, still using that tiny voice I wanted to stomp on. "For the phone numbers...."

The phone numbers?

I thought it was Zac who actually said those same words out loud in a question.

Jessica nodded all timidly and at the floor again.

What phone numbers?

It was the man who asked with a bewildered face, "What phone numbers? What did you do? Tell the truth."

The fact he kept asking what she had done wouldn't settle in my brain for hours. What kind of person were you? I would wonder later, that someone would assume you had *done something*. But I wouldn't worry about that for hours. Until later. Until after all this had come to the surface.

She started to cry, just a tear, then two, and she sniffed. *"The phone numbers."*

What the hell was she talking about?

"I... I'm sorry. I was j-j-jealous, Enzo. Do you understand? I was jealous, and I... I was a lot younger, and I'm sorry, okay? I'm sorry I did it." She broke off, sniffling and sniffling and sniffling.

Fake, fake, *fake*. Did people really fall for this act? I glanced at my old friend to check his reaction and froze at his expression.

"What did you do?" Zac asked in the calmest, flattest voice I'd ever heard from him. His shoulders were down, and that sparkle in his eye, which was about as steady as the sun, was gone. Even all the lines on his face were smooth. Two stripes of pink flagged his cheeks, and I knew it wasn't a blush. It was anger.

Zac was angry.

She moved her gaze toward him, tearing up, and murmured, "About swapping your numbers...."

What?

Zac looked at me. "Darlin', do you know what she's talkin' about?"

I had no idea and I said so.

The woman started weeping, and I could see a couple faces turn at the sound. The tears sounded so goddamn fake, I couldn't believe it. My niece had been better at fake crying than that by the time she was one. I'd seen Connie make herself cry a hundred times, and she could have won an Academy Award for her acting job.

Jessica had experience, I could tell, but she didn't have the same talent as my sister or my niece at doing it. Plus, I didn't like her, so I didn't get a kick out of it.

My stomach tensed.

"What numbers did you swap?" the Enzo guy asked, carefully, slowly too.

She sniffed again, and I barely heard her answer. "Theirs...."

What the hell was she talking about?

One of them must have asked because she answered. "I'm sorry, okay? *I'm sorry.* I just forgot, and I thought that they would eventually notice and it wouldn't be a big deal, and I didn't know, okay? I didn't mean to—"

"Jessica." The man named Enzo took a step back before he asked, "What did you do exactly? Don't. Lie."

She put her hands to her face as her shoulders hunched, and I was pretty sure we all barely heard her.

But we heard her all right. At least most of it.

"I swapped your phone numbers out in each of your phones." She wept. Fake, fake, fucking *fake.* "I... I... you left your phones around, and I took them, okay? I took them and swapped out your numbers for my granny's, and I'm sorry. I'm *sorry.*"

I sucked in a breath that only I heard, mostly because I was pretty sure Zac had made the same sound. And the Enzo man stilled.

She....

She....

"You...," Zac started to say in a voice so hard and brittle, I figured he'd learned it from Trevor. It was mean. Relentless. Unpliable. "You sayin' you took my phone and changed Bianca's phone number in it?"

No.

He kept going, all frost and ice and absolutely unlike the man I knew and loved. "Is that what you're tryin' to say?"

"You've complained to me about your grandma having a cell she refused to use...." Enzo trailed off, sounding stunned.

She cried even harder.

And it made me feel so fucking cold.

Sick.

Mad.

Because I was pretty sure I understood what she'd done.

She had been jealous.

She had taken our cells from wherever they had been lying around close to her during one of the few times I'd met her.

She had changed the numbers under our contacts to her grandmother's phone?

Was that what she was saying? A phone that might have never been answered or checked? My parents had given Mamá Lupe a prepaid phone that had lived in her glove compartment. She had only used her home phone.

And then Zac broke up with her sometime soon after that and she never fixed it? Never said anything?

"Why would you do that?" I asked her before I could stop myself, arms tingling and nearly numb.

She had changed our numbers.

She had changed our numbers.

This Jessica Asshole hiccupped. "I'm sorry!"

I didn't think I'd ever wanted to punch someone so much in my fucking life. And I hoped I never would. My hands were freezing, and my stomach cramped.

I could hear Zac saying something to her. Could hear the other guy speaking too. All three of them seemed to be talking at the same time, but my heart was beating so fast it made my ears buzz, and all I wanted right then was one thing.

To beat her ass, but since I couldn't do that—wouldn't do

that, she wasn't worth going to jail—there was only one option left, considering I wanted to kill her.

To get the hell out of there and away from this fucking monster.

I didn't even really process taking my phone out and requesting a car.

I knew Trevor said something to me as I walked by him on my way out, staring at my phone and at the blinking dot that said my driver was close. Maybe even CJ said something when I passed by him, and maybe I said something to him back, but I wasn't sure.

All I knew was that I wanted to fucking... I wasn't sure what I wanted to fucking do. Scream. Cry. Kick someone's ass.

I wanted to kick my own ass most of all.

But what I did know was that I wanted to get the hell out of there at least.

I wanted to go home.

And that was what I did as I got into the car that was already parked and waiting in the lot by the time I pushed through the crowd. Maybe it was the same ride someone had taken there. It wasn't like it mattered.

It might have only been five minutes later, maybe less— just long enough for the driver and me to introduce each other—when my phone vibrated. The screen showed **ZAC THE SNACK PACK** on it. For one millisecond, I thought about not answering it.

But that wasn't me, and this wasn't the right moment. He hadn't done anything.

Maybe he'd been right.

Maybe he really had tried to call me. Or text me.

Maybe he hadn't gotten some of my messages or calls either.

I couldn't think of a single person I hated as much as I

hated Jessica in that moment. Not the ex who had cheated on me. Not the girl he had cheated on me with who had known he had a girlfriend. Not anyone. Not even Gunner. Not even the meanest people to ever leave comments on my uploads.

Who did that kind of shit? Who went into someone's phone and *did that*? Because she was *jealous*? I'd been seventeen and basically a family member. It wasn't like he'd been in love with me or had treated me in any way that was different than a beloved, pesky little sister. I'd been at the age where I was barely building my sense of self-worth, and she had stolen almost all of it with her terrible comments. She had made me second-guess one of the most important relationships in my life after I'd lost Mamá Lupe, when I had literally been at my lowest.

And now, apparently, that hadn't been the only thing she'd stolen.

She's taken something so much more precious: time.

So I answered. Because I wasn't going to lose what I'd just gotten back, especially not because of Jessica again.

"Hey," I answered, rubbing over my brow bone with my index finger. "I'm—"

He cut me off. "Where you at?" His voice was off, all tight and rough.

"I'm sorry, Zac. I left. I had to get out of there."

He said something under his breath I couldn't understand.

God, I felt like an asshole. I should have at least warned him on the way out instead of just... leaving. "I'm sorry. I just got so mad. I wasn't thinking straight. I was upset—I *am* upset...."

There was a pause, then a sigh over the receiver. "You goin' home?"

"Yeah," I whispered.

"Okay. I'll meet you there."

Oh hell no. "No. No. It's okay. Stay there. I'm fine. I'm

just… sad and mad and want to think about stuff." Maybe he wanted to go home and think about things too. "I'll call you tomorrow. I'll go by the house. Deal?"

There was a beat of silence. Then I might have even heard him swallow hard. "Bibi—" he started to say before I interrupted.

"Promise."

I managed to hear him breathe over the line.

"I just can't believe what happened. I think I'm in shock a little, but I promise I'll go by the house tomorrow. I'm fine. I'll be home in like twenty minutes."

He made another sound before, "Text or call when you get there?"

She had stolen this from me.

I had *let* her steal this from me.

I couldn't believe it.

"Yes."

"All right."

"Are you okay?" I asked.

"Not really, darlin'."

I feel you, I wanted to say but didn't. "Tell me all the gossip tomorrow, okay? And I'm sorry you spent all this money on this costume and I barely got to wear it. I'm sorry for leaving. I'm sorry…" *For being an idiot.*

He hummed just as Trevor's familiar voice said something in the background that I couldn't understand—my cue to get off the phone.

"I'll let you go. I'll text you when I get home. Be safe, okay?"

His "yeah" was a little too simple, but I let it go.

"Bye."

"Have your key ready when you get out of the car, 'kay?"

That brought a smile back onto my face.

This was the man who had loved me for half my life.

"Yeah, I will. Be safe too. Love you."

His "Love you too, kiddo" was instant.

And I carried his words with me on the silent trip home and up the stairs and into my apartment. My hands felt like ice cubes, and my heart seemed to have grown to the size of a boulder inside of me. Something deep within my nasal cavity burned too.

I couldn't fucking believe it.

I sucked in a breath through my nose as my eyes tickled and my chest hurt. I started peeling my costume off, the shoulder pads going first.

I had cried real tears because of how some insignificant asshole had made me feel.

The hoodie part of the catsuit went next.

I had lost ten years of friendship with someone I loved because of one person's words and deeds.

One or two hot tears slipped out of my eyes, but I held the rest of them back.

I wasn't going to cry over this. *I wasn't.* I refused to.

I collected the pieces of the costume that Zac was going to need to return—or that I would probably offer to return since he had paid for the rental—and folded it neatly on the floor beside the door, wiping at my face once with the back of my hand. Back in my bedroom, I took a rinse in the shower while my eyes tried to tear up some more, and I had just managed to slip on a cropped tank top and pull some old leggings on when my doorbell rang.

Then a fist pounded at the door. "Bibi, it's me."

I froze.

That was when my cell phone started ringing from where I'd left it on the kitchen counter.

"Bianca?"

Shit!

"I can hear your phone. I'm worried about you."

I wanted to tell him that I was fine and to go home, but I already knew how that was going to end. He'd wonder why I wouldn't open the door, expect the worst, and threaten to come in.

"I'm not dressed for company," I called out weakly.

"Like I care."

I was worried he'd say that.

Neither one of us said anything until he knocked again, weaker that time.

"Please?" Zac pleaded quietly.

I sighed as I made my way over to the door, unlocking and then cracking it open to find him in his Woody costume, standing there, leaning a shoulder against the wall with an expression on his face that just screamed... exhaustion. And for once, he didn't exactly smile as I stood there in my old pajamas, showing off my not-a-six-pack. I wasn't going to assume he didn't notice that my eyes were more than likely red from trying my absolute hardest not to cry since I'd gotten home.

"Hey."

"I was worried about you," he said steadily, that soft gaze moving over my face slowly.

"I was worried about you too," I told him, squeezing into the opened doorway just enough so that it didn't swing wide and show him the inside of my apartment. "I'm sorry I left you there. I just... I'm sorry. I shouldn't have left you. I know you wouldn't have left me. That was a shitty thing I did."

His handsome head tilted to the side, but there was no smirk there. He was off. I could see the steadiness of his breathing from the way his shirt and vest rose and fell, the little star pinned to his breast doing the same.

"I'm sorry, Zac." I felt the tears pop up in my eyes all over again as my throat started to close up. I tried to hold my breath so that I wouldn't cry. And failed.

As my gaze went fuzzy, I reached up and used part of my shirt to dab them. Zac's shoulders dropped down, and I barely heard him say, "Oh, kiddo."

I sucked in a breath through my nose and lifted my shoulders, dabbing at my eyes even more. "I should have told you," I whispered, looking down at my bare feet balancing on the doorway before I stepped onto the concrete outside.

But the tips of his boots came into my view, lining up right along my toes a moment before those warm, strong arms came around me, pulling me gently into his chest, into a hug that had my cheek going to the yellow button-down shirt. "You ain't got nothin' to cry over."

"But I do."

"No, you don't." His warm hand curled over my bare hip.

I shook my head, his star badge digging into my cheek. "Yeah, I do. I never told you."

The hand he had on my shoulder slid across and down my spine, his fingers warm when they landed on the naked small of my back. "Tell me whatever you want, inside, yeah? We need to talk."

Oh fucking, fucking hell.

I went tense.

And maybe if I hadn't gotten tense in his arms, he wouldn't have noticed. But I was in them, all nice and safe and warm, and he felt it. His chin went down close to my ear, the bristles scratchy. "What was that?"

"Nothing," I lied, trying to think of any excuse possible why we couldn't go in and failing.

That was when I heard the door creak open and he shuffled me back a step before I could stop us. It was enough for him to see my bare bones living room.

"What are all those boxes?" he asked slowly.

Shit. "Some of my stuff."

It was his turn to tense, like he could sense something was

off and there was a reason why I had boxes sitting in my living room. "Your stuff? You donatin' it?" he asked, the pads of his fingers skimming my back just enough to make me tense up even more.

"No?"

"No or no?"

"No?"

"Bianca?" He pressed his palm flat against my skin, warming it instantly.

I had to fight back a shiver at his touch. "Yeah?"

His chin dipped in, brushing my temple. "Why didn't you want me to come in?"

I turned so that my forehead went to the middle of his chest, and the only reason why I didn't try and pull away was because I didn't want to look at his face. And apparently, I didn't want to talk to him either because I shrugged, like a weak shit.

What was he going to do? Tell me I couldn't pack my things? Or that I couldn't move?

His chin went back to my temple. "Why?" he asked so sweetly, I almost wanted to tell him.

"Because."

"Because why?" Those clever fingers tickled again. "You movin'?" His chest rose. "You movin' in with somebody?"

"I don't know yet," I answered honestly, still speaking into his shirt. "I had free time the other night and figured I might as well start packing a few things."

His whole body tensed; I even felt his stomach muscles harden against mine. "Who are you movin' in with?"

Did he sound mad, or was I imagining it? "I don't know. My lease is about to end in a couple of weeks. My coworker said I could move in with her until I decide what I want to do, but I've been thinking I could go to Connie's or stay with Boogie's parents or...."

He went very still.

I lifted a hand and picked at one of the pearl buttons of his shirt with my fingernail, still keeping my attention down.

I had planned on telling him, talking to him about it. I just hadn't gotten that far yet. I kept yo-yoing back and forth between staying in Houston, going to Austin, or possibly even heading to Killeen to be with my sister. I'd also been looking for a nice apartment I could rent on a month-to-month basis in the meantime until I made a decision.

Gunner *had* ended up not scheduling my vacation, and even though it pissed me off beyond words, in a way, it ended up being for the best. I ended up rescheduling the photographer to come in, and I still had a lot of work to do before then. And, of course, this was all happening right when my lease was coming to an end. I had my eye on a couple of houses I could rent in Austin and Houston where we could do the photoshoot for my book at since I wasn't going to have my place for much longer.

I just hadn't wanted to bother Zac with the details, especially not since he'd been essentially promoted and had the weight of a team back on his shoulders.

I didn't want to stress him out after what he'd admitted to me that day at Taco Bell.

He had enough shit to worry about without adding me and my problems to his plate.

Zac's hands went to my shoulders, drawing me away so that those light blue eyes were there, hovering inches from my own as he frowned in concern. "Tell me the truth right now, Peewee. On Mama Lupe's soul, what the hell is goin' on?"

Aw, shit. "You had to go there?"

He nodded, not even looking a little bad he'd resorted to it. He looked... well, he didn't look all that tired anymore either. He seemed... concerned.

"Nothing *bad.* My lease is fixing to end in a month, and they won't let me renew it for month-to-month, and I don't want to sign another agreement. I don't know if I should stay here, or if I should go be closer to Boog and Con. I'm getting ready for whatever I decide. And I know I mentioned my shoot with that photographer for my cookbook being changed, and that's in a few weeks, so I have to figure everything out...."

The tendons along his neck popped. "You're not movin' in with somebody then?"

"Not some random stranger, if that's what you're asking...." I trailed off, taking in his strange expression.

His mouth twisted, and it took him so long to say something, I had no idea what was about to come out of his mouth. His hand went to palm his head as he blinked slowly, his words a trickle. "Why didn't you say somethin'?"

I went up to the balls of my feet, squirming. "I was going to.... Don't you look at me like that. You have enough going on; I'm not going to put my shit on you. You have to focus. I don't need to distract you. You have to worry about your own career and finances."

His mouth was parted, and he was staring at me and staring at me... and....

"Do you think I'm tight on money?"

"I'd hope you're fine. You said you were...."

The palm on his forehead turned into two big fingers pressing into the delicate skin at the corners of his eyes. "Darlin'." He blew out the deepest breath and might have followed that up with a tiny prayer to Jesus before he continued. "I own twenty rental houses, seven Six Guys Burgers, five Pedro's Pizzas, and I invested early into a shoe app that's killin' it. My friend doesn't do anything else but mess around with stocks during the day." His gaze pinned me. "I'm fine on money, and I can focus on my career and worry about you at the same time."

"You *what?*"

He blinked.

I blinked. "Why didn't I know that?"

"'Cause you never asked."

Why would I? "Does Boogie know?"

"He knows about some of it." Before I could ponder over that, based on the expression he made, something dawned on him, and he reeled. "Isn't your trip to Disney supposed to be comin' up? You haven't said a word about it in a while."

Just the reminder of my sacrifice made me flinch. And *that* reminder almost made me cry. I shrugged. "I postponed it. I got most of my money back. I have to get everything together for the shoot for my book. I can't take a whole week off and be ready for it. I knew what I was doing letting her move the date up, but... I'm still a little disappointed." More like a lot disappointed, but I couldn't cry too much over it. It was my choice.

"Aww, Bianca." He exhaled, dropping his head back at the same time as his hand settled over his heart. I'd swear those soft blue eyes glittered and his voice was pained as he said, "You're killin' me, kiddo."

"I don't want to kill you, and you don't have to worry about me—"

"Too bad."

Sometimes I wondered how it was possible for me not to fall in love with the same person once but *twice*. This was how, by him being so great.

It made me smile even though it was mostly bittersweet. "You're a good friend, Snack Pack, but seriously, you don't have to worry about me. I'm lucky that I have places to go, people I can stay with in the meantime. I just hadn't told you because you have enough stuff to think about, and it isn't like if I move somewhere else we'll lose touch again."

And that reminded me about fucking Jessica.

If that reminded Zac too, it didn't show on his face at that point. If anything, he got this gleam in his eye that made me worry. "Yeah, you're right, you got places to go. And none of 'em are that far," he stated. "You're comin' with me."

"What's that?"

He was already nodding to himself, because it sure as hell wasn't to me. He had his thoughtful face on. "Don't worry about it. I'll get it sorted. All you gotta do is be ready to go."

Did he say I was going with *him?* "Zac. No."

His focus was back. "Bianca. Yes."

"No. I'm not your responsibility. If anyone, Connie's my big sister and has to worry about me—"

"Didn't you hear what I said? Worryin' about you is like... lovin' the goddamn sun on my face, kiddo. Like breathin'. It's never not gonna happen." He stared at me with those tight shoulders and tight face, going up to that impressive height that had me straining my neck to look at his handsome face. "Lemme figure it out. Stay with me as long as you need. As long as you want. I guess as long as I'm here and the White Oaks don't get rid of me."

There he went, killing me too a little. "Oh, Zac, they'd be stupid to let you go. You and the team are doing amazing."

Yup, he was still staring down at me.

I cursed. "You're a sneaky, manipulative little bastard, you know that?"

"Yeah. Pretty sure Mama's called me the same thing a time or two."

How the hell had today gone to shit so fast? "I don't need you to feel like you have to take care of me."

His shoulders dropped just a little. "Tell me you wouldn't do the same for me."

Damn it. He had me there, and he knew it.

His fingers wrapped around my wrist, warm and solid. "And even if you wouldn't, I'd still do anything for you." His voice was serious. "Maybe I fucked up and had my head up my ass there for a minute, but I'm *always* gonna worry about you. For the rest of my life. I'm never gonna be too busy to be there for you. You hear me?"

His words sliced me down the center. Flaying me wide. Leaving everything important and everything not important open and vulnerable.

So all I could do was press my lips together, look up at that face with its immaculate bone structure and straight into those soft blue eyes... and nod.

And all Zac did in that next second was lift his free hand and bury those long, valuable fingers into my hair, cradling the back of my head... and focus down on me.

I smiled, and he... kinda smiled.

Sort of.

It was mostly in his eyes somehow. Something moved in them that I didn't know what to do with or how to begin to recognize. Something... big.

Before I could think about it too much, those fingertips scratched as my scalp lightly, and he exhaled, his breath touching my mouth.

Oh *man*.

"Darlin'?"

"Yeah?"

His fingernails scratched a little more. "Now that we got that sorted, you wanna tell me now what happened?"

I was in a daze. His lips were right there... and that meant nothing to him, but it meant too much to me. "With what?"

Those fingers of his did their little scratch thing that I now realized I could feel across the backs of my knees too. "With Jessica."

Like I'd thought I was really going to get away with not talking about this anymore. Damn it.

Shoulders dropping down and back, I grabbed all of my inner strength and told him—ignoring the scratches that were making my knees weak as much as possible. "You want to know what happened in the bathroom or before?"

He thought about it for a second. "Before." His exhale touched my mouth again, and I had to remind myself all about my expectations. "I put together enough of it outside the bathroom. I saw Trevor talkin' to you and thought he'd stick with you, but by the time I went lookin' for you, he said you'd left. Should've gone with you, darlin', but I needed to understand what the hell she'd been talkin' about. I had no idea...."

He shut his mouth, and the muscles in his cheeks rippled.

I sucked in a breath that made my eyes water at the reminder of what she'd done.

I still couldn't believe it. I didn't know if I ever would.

"She told me," Zac continued on after a second, in something very, very close to a croak that had me staring straight into those light blue eyes. "Enzo is a good guy. Used to be a quarterback here but he retired two seasons ago. He was tellin' me all about his new wife and how they were in town visitin' his family before y'all came out, and how she hadn't wanted to go to the party but he'd begged her... He made her explain. I couldn't believe she did that, but the more I thought about it, the more sense it made. You said I never wrote you back or answered, and I told you there was no way I would've let that happen. I know I tried gettin' in touch with you too, kiddo. There's no way I wouldn't have. And I know that's no excuse for all of the last ten years, but I really did start to believe there that you just didn't want me to be part of your life anymore."

Something terrible and bitter pinched my tongue at the

memory of the joy on his face when he'd realized it was me that first day, of how happy he'd seemed to be.

And he'd thought I didn't want him around?

"Zac, why were you so nice to me that first day if you thought I had felt that way?"

He closed his mouth and looked at me. "'Cause I was happy to see you. I missed you. I wasn't lyin'. I never forgot you. I asked about you less and less, but I still wondered... when I wasn't busy havin' my own head up my ass."

Tears stung my eyes again at the infinite kindness in him. When I'd seen him, I'd been so hurt, and all I'd wanted was to keep my distance so that I wouldn't give him the opportunity to hurt me again. And he'd—he'd tried and kept on trying, even thinking I hadn't wanted him around either.

Of course I was still in love with him. Of course I'd fallen in love with him again. I had no choice.

His fingers slipped from my hair, and he stared at me even harder. "She changed your number in my goddamn phone. Changed my number in yours because she was fuckin' jealous. *Fuckin' jealous.*"

He took a step back then as he shook his head, leaving me reeling again as he walked toward the living room wall and then pivoted on his heel, stopping instantly. His hands scrubbed at his denim-covered thighs, and he made this terrible noise in his throat that made me want to go to him.

"There's more to the story, isn't there?" he asked me softly, forcing me back to the present.

"Yes."

Here it was.

"I'm sorry, okay? I want you to know now that I'm sorry for... being dumb and young and for letting it happen, okay?"

I loved him more than ever when he nodded without hesitation.

"When I was seventeen," I started, "you were in your

second season in Dallas... Boogie and I went to go visit you. We went to see a game. We went out to eat with two of your teammates, and you had brought Jessica along. I'd already met her before. I sat next to you, I guess. I don't know, maybe I had been talking to you too much instead of letting you talk with everyone else... and Jessica came up to me in the bathroom and said... she said... stuff. About me being an inconvenience. About you not having time for me. And she said some other things. I had to go sit in Boogie's car afterward. You guys thought I was upset about Mamá Lupe."

I'm telling you this to make you feel better. You're young, but it's not going anywhere. He doesn't like you like that, okay? You're a baby.

Fortunately, I didn't tell him more than that. I didn't have to, and I didn't really want to.

Mostly because, with each word out of my mouth, that normally placid and easygoing face melted into one so serious, one so... so... thunderous... there were thunderstorms brewing behind his eyes and thunder bubbling beneath his cheekbones... and I forced myself to rush ahead.

"I believed her, Zac. Maybe not at that moment, but then you stopped answering my texts like two weeks later. You went to my graduation and everything was fine; then you came home again and she was with you, and then it seemed real. That's when I stopped getting your messages, and it broke my heart... and I just... I tried after that, you know, texting you. I tried to tell myself that it wasn't a big deal and that I'd give you time to not bother you, but I still never heard back from you, and it broke my heart even more. Then I got embarrassed and started telling Boogie I was busy when he'd invite me to go see you... I moved... and the next thing I knew, it had been years. But I never stopped following your career or anything; I always kept up with everything. I was still... maybe not your number one fan but at least in the top five. I'm sorry, Snack Pack. I'm sorry I believed her, and I'm sorry I didn't say anything, but I was ashamed—"

He was there.

His "kiddo" was sighed into my hair the moment his arms wrapped around my shoulders, his cheek settling against my head.

Zac hugged me tightly, so fucking tightly I wouldn't be able to take a deep breath, but I didn't care. I didn't care, I didn't care, I didn't care. And my own cheek was against his chest as regret and pain and disappointment in myself and in Jessica, and even a little bit in Zac, filled my lungs.

Disappointment for all the things I could have had for years but hadn't. But what else was there to do or say? Nothing. Because it was in the past, and all I could do now was be here and present like I could have and should have been all those years ago.

"I'm sorry," I told him again. "My feelings were hurt, and I didn't want to bother you any more, even though I *knew* you cared about me, but it was just easier to not try than to have it get thrown into my face."

His arms tightened even more, pulling me in so close there was no escaping his presence or the light mix of cologne and that natural Zac smell that filled my nostrils at being so close to him. "You ain't got nothin' to be sorry about, you hear me? Nothin', Peewee. *I'm* sorry." I was pretty sure his nose pressed against my head, because his voice got even quieter, like his mouth was muffled in my hair. "I'm sorry I spent time with somebody capable of that in the first place. I'm sorry I didn't try harder or bother Boog more. I'm sorry I got so busy I guess I thought you didn't want me around either and I let the years go by. I haven't been a good friend, and I'm so damn sorry about that too. But none of that was any of your fault, you understand? It's mine."

His arms loosened as his head pulled backward, and he

aimed those pastel blue eyes at me. Anguish showed in the lines of his forehead and mouth. "I do wish you would've told me she said somethin', but I must've not been a good enough friend then either if you didn't feel comfortable enough to tell me."

His words punched me right in the chest. "No. *No.* You were always such a good friend, even when you had a lot going on. You had barely been in the NFO for like two seasons, and you were busy and getting busier and..." *I'd been in love with you and hadn't known what to do with myself.* That was the truth. But I wouldn't say it. It wasn't like I was ashamed. If he put the pieces together, he'd figure it out on his own. There just wasn't a point in me bringing it up.

One of those big quarterback hands cupped the nape of my neck under my hair, and his gaze turned even more intent. "I'll never believe that," he told me. "And nothin' is gonna make me feel better. You don't need to make excuses for what I did and for what I didn't do. This was Jessica's fault for sure, and I hope she gets what's comin' to her eventually—I think she will, if the face Enzo was makin' at her meant anything— but at the end of the day, this is my fault."

"Zac—"

"I'm sorry, kiddo. I'm so damn sorry for all of it."

"No, it's my fault too. I was just so sad after Mamá Lupe died and—" I gulped, and my shoulders bobbed under his forearms. "—I'm sorry I didn't believe in you more. I'm just.... I was just used to people getting busy and forgetting about me. And I guess I convinced myself that you had only been nice to me because of the snake thing that I don't even remember."

Zac's mouth went flat, and I saw his Adam's apple bob. "I didn't like you so much because you saved my life, kiddo. Bein' around you has always made me happy. Even when you were a baby, you were always makin' me laugh." His head tilted forward, and I barely heard him, but I did. "You still do. That's why I... that's why I'm always botherin' you. You make everything fun. Everything good. You've always been my favorite girl, kiddo. Hands down."

I wasn't sure if he smiled first or if I did, but what I did know was that I loved him with my whole heart, even though I knew better.

At least he loved me too. In his own way.

CHAPTER SEVENTEEN

Me: I'm going to be late getting home. Get dinner without me. Sorry to bail, but I'll make you some almond cake to make it up to you. XOXO

I sent the message with my right hand, leaned back against the seat I was in, and sighed.

I couldn't fucking believe it.

Part of me wanted to glance at the man in the seat beside mine, but I couldn't talk myself into it. I knew that this was my reality. Otherwise, I wouldn't be sitting where I was, with him beside me.

Having one of the worst days of my life.

The only positive side to all this was that he was pretending I wasn't next to him too.

Thankfully, he was still doing that when my phone rang maybe a minute and a half after I'd sent my text message.

I LOVE ZAC CALLING flashed across the screen—I wasn't sure when the hell he'd snuck onto my phone and changed his contact information, but it had made me smile when I'd first seen it—and I answered.

"Hey," I said.

"Hey. You stayin' late at work? Want me to bring you somethin' to eat before you get hangry?" my friend asked in one quick breath, in almost a whisper that had me wondering what the hell he was in the middle of doing exactly. He'd told me he had a meeting at White Oaks headquarters with the coaching staff. We had only made plans to squeeze in dinner because... well, I think we were both shook up after what had happened with Jessica and the switching of our numbers, and we both probably felt bad about it. Maybe. At least I did. I'd had a lot to think about lately, and that was at the top of my list.

I rubbed at my brow bone with my right hand and glanced at the man beside me to make sure he was still hung up on his phone. "No, I'm not working late." Unfortunately.

But Zac beat me to speaking before I had the chance to explain. "You goin' out tonight or... got, uh, a date or somethin' you're standin' me up for?"

I straight-up snorted into the phone and glanced to my right once more to make sure he wasn't paying attention. "Pssh. I'd never stand you up for some guy. I'm at urgent care—"

"Where?" he asked.

"Urgent care—"

There was a sound in the background a split second before his voice went soft but sharp. "*You're at the hospital?*"

"I'm okay," I tried to rush out, glancing at my phone to make sure the person snarling at me over the line was really Zac. It was. "I fell at work and cut my elbow—"

There were some noises in the background, and I was pretty sure I heard someone say his name before he basically demanded in one long breath, "You all right? Did it just happen?"

"About an hour ago? We just got here. I'm in the waiting room. I'm not going to bleed out or anything but it hurts."

There were more sounds in the background, a few whispers before Zac asked, "Which one?"

"I just need a few stitches maybe."

He blew out a breath that filled the line, and his voice was steadier during his next question. "Bianca. Where you at?" I'd swear I could hear him moving. Walking. Something.

"You really don't need to—"

He didn't let me finish. "I really do. What urgent care are you at?" Before I could get another word out, he added, "I'm comin'. You better not even start with your nonsense again either."

I sighed, holding my throbbing elbow a little tighter to my stomach. I rattled off the name of the urgent care clinic that Gunner had driven me to, and that was when my boss finally turned to look at me instead of his phone for the first time since we'd gotten here. He'd had the nerve to roll his eyes when I busted my ass in front of him, and Deepa had screamed for someone to call an ambulance.

There was no ambulance. He'd driven me himself. After he'd reminded everyone that he'd had much worse happen when he used to fight. Asshole.

"Be there in no time," Zac told me. "Let me know if they take you to the back so I know where you're at, all right?"

He was coming. God, he really was the best. "Okay, I will, but if you can't come, I promise I'll be fine. I just didn't want you to wait around to eat with me."

"I'll be there as soon as I can," my friend said before ending the call without a goodbye.

I sighed and set my phone down on my thigh, staring at the black screen.

"Boyfriend?" came Gunner's question out of nowhere.

I slid up a little straighter in the barely cushioned chair of the waiting room of the urgent care facility he'd driven us to.

"No, my friend. He's on his way if you'd like to leave. He should be here in a little bit."

And actually, I really would prefer for him to leave. I had asked if Deepa could just drive me instead of him, but he'd said someone had to stay and work the juice bar since we were going to have to leave the front desk empty, so *no*, Deepa *couldn't* drive me. This man needed Jesus. And maybe an exorcism.

And apparently, he was going to ignore my request again. "I'll wait," Gunner said, sounding like he would rather be just about anywhere else.

He was doing this to spite me.

"It's all right though. I know it was an accident. I can give you the bill when I get it. I'm sure they won't give it to me tonight," I told the man who I did actually hold responsible for all this shit.

All because he hadn't listened.

And he knew damn well it was his fault too.

"No, I'll wait," Gunner repeated himself, sounding annoyed. Like I wanted to be here. Like I'd wanted to slice my elbow open.

Like I'd wanted any of the shit that had happened today to happen.

I just wanted to crawl back into bed and start the whole day over again.

It had started with a phone call from Deepa while I'd been getting dressed to go into work for a few hours. Her mom *was* sick, she had stage three breast cancer, and she was going to go back home to help her out. She'd apologized over and over again for deciding to leave, and for moving out of the house she was splitting with two roommates—a house she'd offered to let me come live in while I figured out what I was doing. She had offered to let me take over the bedroom she rented, but I didn't want to live with people I barely knew. My assistant, my friend, was leaving, and I had no idea what the hell I was going to do or who was going to help me from now on. I was going to miss her a lot, but at the end of the day, what really mattered was that Deepa was there for her mom, and that the other woman fought as hard as she could for her health.

So there was that.

And then there was the second thing. The email that started it all. Another stupid, *stupid* thing I'd done.

I'd only been holding it together because I was at work when the emails had started coming through from my viewers. I'd read their messages and checked my WatchTube channel on my own to confirm what they'd been trying to tell me during my brief breaks in between members and Gunner's loops of terror around the building.

My viewers hadn't been lying. The profile on my channel had been changed to some bogus person.

And maybe I'd been pretty distracted over *that* when I'd busted my ass and landed myself at urgent care, waiting to see a doctor so I could get stitched up or glued back together or whatever it was they were going to need to do. I was pretty sure I'd stopped bleeding finally, but my elbow was just throbbing like crazy to the same beat as my pulse.

Squeezing my eyes closed, I tried to tell myself it—everything today—wasn't the end of the world. That I hadn't actually lost anything. That I could get it all back. Most of it. Not Deepa. I needed to make some phone calls, fill out a form or two, and then everything would go back to normal, which had been my plan the instant I'd realized what had happened.

I had just been formulating a plan to start pretend-gagging to try and leave work early when this shit had happened.

How the hell did I let this happen? I asked myself as I shifted around in the uncomfortable chair and made eye contact with a woman across the room who was leaning her head against the wall and genuinely looking like shit.

But... I knew. I knew how it had happened. I had just prayed it hadn't. But I'd had to leave for work, and I'd been distracted by Deepa's call and had just told myself what I'd done was enough.

And now....

I squeezed my eyes closed so that I wouldn't cry. I wasn't helpless. Everything would work out. I had everything that WatchTube would possibly need or want to confirm my identity.

But this tiny little thread of fear still pulsed through my body at the *what-if*.

What if they wouldn't give me my channel back?

Breathing in deeply through my nose, I told Gunner, "You really don't have to stay. I'll be fine."

"I'll wait," he repeated himself. Unfortunately.

The old owner of the gym I worked at, Mr. DeMaio, once told me that there was no one more stubborn than a professional athlete. *"It doesn't matter if they're retired or in the middle of their prime, Bianca, they're stubborn asses. Just look at my granddaughter."* And I remembered then how he'd said that right as she had been walking by because she'd pointed at him on her way to the manager's office and replied with *"Shiiiit. Look in the mirror, Grandpa."* And all three of us had laughed, and man, did I freaking miss them.

One of them would have come with me if this had happened while they'd still owned Maio House.

The difference was that I wouldn't have complained if one of them had been around, taking Gunner's place. I wouldn't have minded at all. They weren't assholes.

I guess that stubbornness explained why Zac was coming even though I told him not to.

I sighed and tried to dig deep in my heart and be more

patient. Be a better person and not be aggravated by Gunner just for the sake of being aggravated because it was him here.

I had bigger shit to worry about.

Sure, he was annoying. And a micromanager. And a dick. And not charismatic or likable enough to get away with the passive-aggressive stuff that spewed out of his mouth.

"I'm getting something to drink," my current boss said suddenly, standing up. He paused for a second, and I was pretty sure it wasn't my imagination that it hurt him to offer, "You want something?"

"No, thank you." See? I was trying. Because I finally knew I wasn't going to be at Maio House much longer. That was the one and only bright side to today, even though it was a double-edged joy. Losing my friend but gaining my freedom.

Gunner shrugged though and headed off toward a corner as I sat there, cradling my elbow against my side and breathing in and out through my nose.

If I had just walked the other way toward the bathrooms....

I pulled my phone out again and started to send my sister a message before deciding I should wait until I was all stitched up. I didn't want her freaking out, because she would, or blowing up my phone, because she would do that too. I'd send her a picture when I was done and out of here. That would be perfect.

Leaning back against the chair, I closed my eyes and tried to think about what I could work on in my next video. It would have to be something easy because of the stitches, that was for sure. At least it was my left arm.

Hmm. It had been a while since I'd made something cold. It was still warm enough, in Houston at least, to where that would be a hit.

More frozen yogurt?

Something touching my knee had me jerking my leg back and opening my eyes with a flinch.

But the second I focused, I found a familiar set of light blue eyes inches away from me.

He really had come.

Zac's face was careful as his gaze slid from my head down to the elbow I was holding on my lap, wrapped in a towel. The hand he had touched me with flexed on my knee, and he tipped his head to the side before asking softly, "You all right, darlin'?"

"Yeah," I answered. "It just hurts."

He frowned, and one of those great big hands landed on my inner forearm, his callused thumb making a small circle there. He was in sweats and a T-shirt, a cap pulled down low and covering his hair and most of his face. And he'd never looked better to me as he gazed down at my arm with his forehead furrowed. "I bet. What happened?"

"Someone had broken a glass earlier and they didn't sweep it all up. I tripped and fell right on it like an idiot. Just busted my ass. We asked the manager for a vacuum to get all the pieces, but he never brought it," I explained as he stared at me. "Why are you looking at me like that?"

"Why didn't you call me?" he answered, lifting his head. His eyebrows were knitted together, and the corners of his mouth were tight.

"Because it's just a little cut, and you have more important things to do."

That got me a blink. "Yeah? Like what?"

I pressed my lips together. "I don't know. Doing your thing with your coaching staff. Football stuff. I don't want you to get in trouble because of me."

"Bianca." He was still watching me carefully. "Why you always sayin' stuff like that?"

I partially smiled as the thumb on my forearm did a little

circle that felt pretty freaking nice on the sensitive skin there.

And I felt that thumb, and his entire palm, slide to my upper arm and squeeze it gently, gaze still intense. "Didn't I tell you already I'll never be too busy for you? Are we clear on that now? Once and for all?"

I gulped, and he just raised his eyebrows. I might have swooned if I wasn't already sitting down. *And you better not take his words like that because he doesn't mean them that way,* I reminded myself. Futilely.

"You say things like that, and it hurts my feelings, darlin', but we'll talk about that later when you aren't bleedin' to death. I'll think about forgivin' you once I know you're gonna live."

"Aww, Zac—"

"Don't '*aww, Zac*' me. Your feelings would be hurt too if I got hurt and didn't tell you because I thought you'd be too busy."

I hated it when he had a point. But it *was* different. I groaned, and he shook his head just a little as he squatted there in front of me.

"No. Don't you dare say some dumb shit. I can see it in your eye you wanna say somethin' pointless. Knowin' you, something like '*oh, but I'm not you,*' am I right?"

Okay, that might have been almost word for word what I would have said.

The thumb on my arm did another little circle, and all I could get myself to do was nod.

He wasn't amused by the fact he'd guessed correctly. "I'm not more important than you. You're more important than me—"

I snorted, and that earned me a raise of one of those tawny eyebrows.

"Now, my darlin', tell me what I can do. Want me to go

talk to 'em and see if I can get 'em to squeeze you in quicker? Give you a painkiller?" He rubbed up and down my arms a little more, strong and warm. "I'm sure it hurts like hell, huh?" he asked gently with a small smile of pity that I ate up with an imaginary spoon.

I nodded. "I'd show you, but you probably don't want to see it." In fact, I was positive he wouldn't want to see it. That was part of the reason why I hadn't wanted to tell him where I was.

"Bianca?"

I eyed Zac and wished all of a sudden that he was wearing some sunglasses or something else that hid his features more than just hiding his hair. I turned my head at the same time that the hand Zac had on me jerked just a little and met Gunner's eyes as he stood just off to the side. There was a frown on his face. "My friend is here now. I think he'll stay with me so that you can go."

I could feel Zac's gaze on my face, hard and hot.

I turned to him. "You'll stay with me, right?"

He tilted his head to the side. "All night if I need to, darlin'."

I smiled at him before glancing back up at Gunner. "He's staying," I confirmed.

The frown on my boss's face got a little deeper. "I told you I'd stay. I need to see about your bill."

Zac squeezed my upper arm before he stood up. He turned that long body toward the last man I would have wanted him to interact with and said, "I've got her bill. You don't need to worry about it."

Was this the right time to tell him that I didn't have insurance and wouldn't mind milking Gunner for it?

"It's my responsibility. I'm her boss."

"I know who you are," Zac said in a deceptively slow drawl that tickled at the base of my neck. I wished I could see his face, but he was turned away too much. What I could see was the way his shoulders went down and his chin tipped upward. "You've done enough, buddy. I've got it from here."

"Bianca Brannen?"

I shot up to my feet and sent my boss a blank face. "Thank you for driving me, but I really will be all right." I'd figure out the bill later.

Zac still wasn't looking at me as he said in a low voice, "I've got her."

Gunner glanced down at me, his harsh face emotionless. "Take three weeks off then, paid sick leave. Come back then." After another glance at Zac, he turned and walked away.

"Bianca Brannen?" the nurse called out again, and that time, Zac lifted his hand in a wave at her.

I poked his side. "Want to wait out here?" I wondered if he knew that I remembered his not-a-phobia. I didn't want to put him under pressure.

That gaze slid to me, and his nostrils flared. His Adam's apple bobbed hard once before he surprised the shit out of me and shook his head. "I'll come with you."

He *what?*

I mean... "You can wait out here."

His response was to brush the tip of his finger against the corner of my mouth.

And I responded to that by holding my breath.

He was touching my beauty mark.

"Are you sure?"

His Adam's apple bobbed.

Right. "You can just... look at me the whole time if you want to come in. Not at the doctor or anything in the room," I whispered the suggestion to him.

He was looking in the direction of my mouth when the corners of his went up and he ducked his chin in agreement.

He was being serious. He wanted to go in with me.

I couldn't believe it. He had to love me. I knew it then.

But I didn't say another word because I didn't know what to say. Or think.

A tired-looking nurse started to say, "He needs—oh." She blinked, and her eyes widened. "*Oh.* Umm, never mind. Follow me."

Over my shoulder, I smiled at Zac, wincing only a little when I bumped my elbow by accident.

The nurse took my vitals, being really freaking polite the entire time as Zac stood by the chair I was sitting in, a hand on top of my head. I could feel him fingering my curls, tugging on one and then another. He could've put me to sleep if he would've done it any longer, and I stayed quiet, just enjoying his touch.

The second she walked out though, I turned to Zac, ready to distract him. "So, you ready for tomorrow?"

"Move your hands."

I moved them to the side and watched as he turned and settled himself across my lap, not dropping all of his weight down on me, but most of it. I lowered my arms, thought about it for a moment, and set them around him, resting one hand on his thigh and holding my elbow with the other. "Look, you fit."

His smile wasn't totally bright, but it was mostly warm as he set his hands on top of my free one. "It's been a long time since I sat on someone's lap."

"Lucky me." His thighs were like a rock. "You're lucky I don't have boney legs; otherwise, it'd be pretty uncomfortable."

He flexed the long muscles of his quadriceps as he set an arm around my shoulders. "You got a lot of experience sittin' on people's laps?" he asked quietly.

"Only some people's."

"Whose?"

I smiled at him, fucking around. "People's," I answered. "So, you ready for tomorrow?" So far, the White Oaks had played three games at home, and I'd gotten to go to all of them. Boogie had come down, and we'd enjoyed it. I'd even sucked it up when Lauren had tagged along one time and tried my best to be nice to her and ask questions about the wedding. They had decided to have a small one and weren't having best men or bridesmaids or anything. Worked for me.

Zac was still frowning and looking like he really wanted to say something else that wasn't football related, but he finally said, "Yeah. About as ready as I can be. You're comin', aren't you?"

I pressed my cheek against his biceps and smiled up at him. "You rushed over here when you were probably in a meeting, and you're sitting on my lap when we both know I'm probably going to need to get stitches. Yes, I'm coming, Snack Pack." And then I remembered what happened with my channel and the ache in me grew fierce. "I need to tell you what happened earlier."

His fingers skimmed the back of my hand lightly. "What happened?"

And it was right then that the doctor knocked and peeked her head inside the door.

———

An hour and five stitches later, Zac was heading out of the urgent care room by my side, holding a small paper bag with gauze that the doctor had shoved at me. By the lack of surprise on the doctor's face when she'd walked in, either the nurse had already warned her who was inside the room or she had no idea who Zac was. She hadn't batted an eyelash.

Especially not when she'd seen Zac sitting on me.

The doctor was really polite as she took a peek at my

elbow and claimed I would need stitches just like I'd thought. And when Zac took a seat on a stool that the doctor slid over, he slipped his fingers through mine—looking sweaty and uncomfortable—especially as she injected me with some numbing stuff. He kept on holding it too as she stitched me up, whispering, a retelling of his last conversation with Paw-Paw as I'd squeezed the shit out of his hand, imagining that I felt that damn needle puncturing my skin, and instead forcing me to press my lips together to keep from laughing.

"How bad is it?" I had asked him while we'd waited to get discharged. He was staring intently on our hands, making it a point not to look elsewhere.

"You want the truth?"

"Yes."

"You're scarred for life, darlin'."

There hadn't been an initial bill, and I wasn't going to bring it up either. I could pay for it, even though I felt like Gunner should. But with the three weeks he claimed to be giving me off, I figured it balanced out. It was his fault for not just opening the closet and getting us the damn vacuum like we'd asked. And Deepa was going to be leaving anytime now and her poor mom was sick, so....

I managed to make it all the way until we were about to get into his car before I started crying.

Finally.

I was pretty sure he froze in his spot next to me, about to open the passenger door, when he stopped. "What's wrong? Does your arm really hurt?" he asked in just about the softest, most tender voice in the world before palming my cheek. Tears splashed against the skin of his million-dollar hands.

But I managed to tell him, with big gulps in between every other word, "Zac, I lost control of my Lazy Baker channel. Someone hacked me this morning."

Before any other words came out of his mouth, he was

there, right in front of me, his other hand going to my waist. "Say that again, honey. I'm not sure I heard you correctly."

So I tried to tell him again. From the beginning. "Someone hacked my account this morning. My Lazy Baker WatchTube account. I got an email from a company asking to advertise on my channel this morning. It looked legitimate. When I clicked on the link for the product they wanted to push, an installer buried itself into my computer.

"I knew what was happening, and I forced my computer to restart and changed all my passwords, but I guess I was too late. The hacker bypassed my two-factor authentication and got into my account and pulled my WatchTube information from my email. It happened while I was at work and... and...."

Zac stepped in close, and I felt his chin brush my temple. "Take a deep one. All right. Someone hacked your account then, darlin'?"

"It's all my hard work," I whispered.

Something warm and damp pressed against my temple. His lips. It had to be his lips. "I know. Okay, take another breath. What can we do? How do we get it back?"

"I need to call—"

"Hey, shh. You can cry, but don't do that sobbin' thing. I don't like you hiccupin'. Okay, so we need to call. Can you call on the drive? What if I call too, will that help?"

I shrugged under his face and felt the press of his mouth against my temple again. "Probably. Yes. I'm sure it will, but you—"

"If you tell me I don't have to, I'm gonna wring your neck, kiddo. 'Course I'll do whatever I can. I'll tell Trev to call too if it'll help. I'd ask if you could go through some other way of gettin' back into your account and changin' the password to get them out, but you know better than I do what can be done. Hey, no, no. No more cryin'." He leaned back, and I saw his hand go toward his stomach before he pulled his T-shirt up and used the bottom of it to mop my cheeks and under my eyes with it. He even swiped under my nose with it, and that made me cry more.

"Bibi, darlin', this has happened before, right? Other people have gotten hacked too? We'll get it back, I promise. You're not losin' all your hard work. You're not losin' a thing."

I sniffled under his gaze as he dropped his shirt back into place, but lifted his hand to frame my cheek. "But what if they delete all my videos? Or delete my channel?"

"Is that why they hack into 'em? To delete 'em?"

"Well, no. They sell them...."

He started to nod that perfect face. "Okay, so then they'll sell it. For how much? I'll buy it back for you."

I reached and grabbed his hand, giving it a squeeze. "I really do love you, and I don't know why you're so nice to me after what I did."

"You didn't do a single goddamn thing, do you understand me? We're not talkin' about that and what happened with that girl anymore. She's nothin'. You're my friend, and I'd do anything for you. All you gotta do is tell me."

All I had to do was tell him.

He didn't understand. I loved him, but not like that. Not when he was doing all this nice shit to me like coming to a hospital even though he had to be sweating it and sitting beside me while I got stitches and offering to pay for my bills and pay to get my channel back and—

His hand slipped out of mine, and then both of them were on my face, cupping my cheeks. "Hey, shh. We're gettin' it back, all right? You'll still get to quit your job. We'll make these hackers regret ever even hearin' your name by the time we're done with them, yeah? You don't need to worry. I've got you, kiddo. I'm not goin' anywhere." His head ducked, and that warm mouth brushed across my forehead. "We'll go to Trev's, you call WatchTube, I'll make you some soup, and I'll call too. And if they won't do anything, we'll unleash our secret weapon: Trev."

He was killing me.

I had learned to trust my instincts over time, and they all got fried in his presence. Tilting my head back, I looked at him through blurry eyes. "Zac, you know you've paid me back about a million times over for the snake thing, right?"

I thought the corners of his mouth tilted up, but I couldn't be sure when my eyes were trying their best to turn into water fountains. I felt his thumb rasp over my chin. "We're not even close to bein' even. Come here, gimme another hug, and then let's get in the car and do what we need to do."

I didn't nod or anything. I went straight into his arms and wrapped my good one around his waist instead of his neck, one of his going around the middle of my back and another around the back of my neck. Zac curled around me and into me, his presence warm and steady. Eternal.

"You scared the hell outta me earlier, kiddo. Tellin' me you're at urgent care." His fingers nudged a spot right behind my ear that made my knees weak. "Don't you dare ever do that to me again, okay? Next time just don't get hurt, is that a deal?"

I snickered, watery and light, but nodded against him.

"What else you need?" he asked, nuzzling my head while his fingers did that thing by my ear again. "What else will make you feel better, huh?"

I only had to think about it for a second. "Can I smack one?"

His arms jerked, and I felt his chest do a little puff. "Are you askin' for what I think you're askin'?"

"Yes." Pressing my nose into the bone between his pecs, I said, "It'll make me feel better; I know it will."

He was trying his hardest not to laugh, but I could feel

him doing it. "If it'll make you feel better," he said, and I could hear the amusement in his voice.

He took his time pulling away. He gave me a long look too before turning around with a smirk on his face.

Zac glanced at me over his shoulder, then popped a hip to the side... which also popped his butt cheek out. His smile pulled his mouth into the best grin of all time, all teasing and loving and amazing. Just like Zac.

Then I did it.

I smacked the underside of his butt.

And I was right. It did make me feel better.

CHAPTER EIGHTEEN

Two days later, I was driving home and **OLD FART ZAC** flashed across the screen of my cell as an incoming call.

I didn't think anything of it. I had seen him the night before after his game—the second loss under him—and he'd seemed all right. He'd even done a shoulder shimmy out of nowhere while sitting on Trevor's couch, and I'd scratched his back. He'd *oohed* and *aahed* the whole time. I figured he was good and not totally down on himself. So I answered his call with "Hey, old man."

"Peewee, you heard back about your channel?"

I smiled even though it wasn't necessarily a totally happy one. "Not today. Apparently, they're very busy. But they said they're working on it."

"I'm sorry," he said sincerely. "What are you up to then?"

"On my way home from the grocery store. You?"

He'd groaned at the reminder I was driving around with one hand, like I hadn't been driving with one hand for the last ten years. He'd gotten on my case about it after he'd driven me back to Maio House following my meltdown in the parking lot of the urgent care and after going to his house for soup—that he'd made at home just for me, with meatballs, spinach, rice, and beans—and several phone calls to Watch-Tube headquarters from me, him, and even CJ.

One of my viewers had emailed me yesterday to tell me that they saw my channel for sale on a website that sold hacked WatchTube channels, and all my videos had been taken down. Which then resulted in me blowing up and calling WatchTube again. And, truthfully, crying again.

After everything I'd gone through, the fear of losing it, of having to stay at Maio House after all, terrified me.

Forty-eight hours later, I still hadn't gotten my channel back. They knew what was going on and claimed to be doing something. Personally, I didn't get what the hell there was to "do" other than take it away and give it back to me, but...

I was trying to be optimistic. I had every hope I'd get it back, and if I cried a little between now and then, well, that was part of it. I was worried.

And my elbow hurting didn't help any either. It didn't help any at all.

Anyway.

Over the phone, Zac said, "Nothin'," in a way that sounded... suspicious.

So I asked, "Did you want to come over? Was there something you wanted me to do for you?"

Then his "Mmm. Somethin' like that. I'll see you at your place, kiddo. Drive safe," set alarms going off in my head.

I was already wary when I parked my car and spotted a small crowd hanging around the stairwell myself and three other neighbors shared. The thing was, Santiago rarely had company, and my other two neighbors were only home on the weekend. And today wasn't a weekend.

I looked around. There wasn't an ambulance or a firetruck. What the hell were they...?

I sped up, holding my purse and single bag tight in my

right hand, watching the group of eight or nine moving like they were trying to get a better look at whatever was on the second floor. A few of them were holding their phones up, either trying to take pictures or record something. I slid through the group of people to get to the staircase.

Sure enough, I was still only halfway up when I heard Zac's "You're welcome, sugar."

But what I wasn't expecting was the "No problem" that I had spent enough time with now to recognize as CJ's.

And there was a third voice that sounded familiar.

It was Amari, I confirmed a second later. Because all three of them were on the landing with my neighbor Santiago and three other people I didn't recognize at all. Two men and one woman.

The woman was holding Zac's forearm between her two hands, gazing up at him like he was a ten-carat diamond.

He was holding a small plastic bag in the same hand.

But the second I cleared the top step, Zac's head swung toward me and he nailed me with a big smile and a "Took you long enough, darlin'."

I smiled at him, eyeing the woman still clinging to him for a moment, and then grinned at CJ and Amari; it was Amari who turned and gave me a hug first, careful not to hit my left arm. CJ and I bumped elbows—well, he bumped my upper arm and I bumped his hip with my good one, but close enough. I slid Zac a look, pretty sure I caught a glimpse of a small frown that he quickly wiped away before he asked, "What? Nothin' for me?"

I tried not to look at the woman who jerked her hands away from him. Was she a neighbor? I wasn't sure. It wasn't like it mattered.

Stepping toward him, I reached up and wrapped an arm around his back, feeling a heavy palm cup the back of my neck, his cheek pressing to the top of my head as his other hand landed on my left upper arm and gave it a rub with his warm, dry palm while his bag swayed against me.

"Hi, Bianca."

Lowering my arm to let go of Zac, I turned my head to see my neighbor. "Hey, Santiago."

The hand on the back of my neck twitched.

I reached up and set my fingers on his forearm, digging my fingertips in, and mouthed, "*Muscle spasm?*"

That Disney prince nose wrinkled for a moment before he lifted his gaze, held up a hand over my head, and said, "Sure was nice meetin', y'all. Thank you so much for all the support. We hope to see y'all at a game in the future. Have a nice day."

And if that wasn't my sign to open the door and get inside the apartment, I had no idea what could be.

So that was exactly what I did, catching another glimpse of the people standing around, looking disappointed that Zac had cut their visit short.

A visit I was going to want an explanation for sooner than later.

And it came the instant I unlocked the door and led the three professional football players in.

Zac went right into it as he headed into the kitchen and opened a cabinet while I locked the door. "Y'all want some water? Bianca, we're here to get your stuff. How long will it take you to finish packin'?"

Just as I was wondering what he was talking about, Amari said, "Yes," and CJ said, "I'm good."

He was already filling up the third glass of water, the bag hanging from his wrist, by the time I managed to ask, "What stuff are you talking about?"

Zac was handing Amari his glass when he answered. "Your stuff. What you don't already have boxed." He held one out toward me too, and I took it, watching him carefully, still confused. "Clothes. Kitchen things. We got boxes in my trunk. Between the four of us, we can get everything ready in an hour or two max, I bet."

I held my breath. "And where are we moving my stuff?"

He had his back to me as he picked up his own glass of water to take a sip. "It's goin' to Trev's, darlin'."

Were my ears ringing? "And why would they be going to Trevor's?"

"Because that's where we can get you moved in right now 'til I figure out a better option."

I repeated the words out loud like I hadn't heard them correctly.

But apparently they were right before he nodded at me like *yeah*. Like *no big deal*. Like he'd thought about it and it made perfect sense to him.

"Zac...." I trailed off, trying to think of what in the hell to say.

But that was when CJ piped up from his spot by my windows. He was peering at the paper covering them. "Trevor doesn't care."

I highly doubted that, and that must have been apparent on my face because Zac said, "I asked. He shrugged as he walked out and said he'd be back in two weeks."

What in the hell was happening?

Zac kept going. "In the meantime, Bibi, while I figure it out."

"Zac...." I smiled at CJ who had glanced at me for a second before returning his attention to the diffusion-paper-covered windows. I focused on my friend again. "Can we talk in my room?"

He shook his head.

"Zac," I kept going, scratching at my cheek. "My friend... my favorite friend who I know is just trying to help me and who I love very, very much... can we please talk in my room? Please?"

His smile went lopsided, and still, he shook his head. "Let us do this. You need to be out soon. This'll give you time to clean up the place so you can get your deposit back, and if you wanna film more videos, I've seen you checkin' out Trev's kitchen. You can do your shoot there. Plenty of space."

I blinked.

And he kept going. "Trev won't be back for a while, and we're good roommates. Aren't we, Ceej?"

CJ nodded.

Amari... Amari was just leaning against the counter, watching and sipping water.

Zac tipped his head to the side and walked over to me, standing right there, watching me with those light blue eyes. His free hand searched for mine, the tips of his fingers tickling mine. "Darlin', come on. We're not home most of the time, so you can do whatever you want. Trev's got most of the same stuff you do at his house. You can film and do your shoot there, rent free. And this is the only time we're gonna be free for at least two weeks. With your poor little arm, you're not gonna be able to carry things on your own, and you know it. Might as well take advantage of us." His nostrils flared for a moment, and it was only because I knew him so well that I heard the hitch in his voice. "Unless you decided already you're movin' to be closer to Connie." His fingertips traced up, grazing my palm. "Or you can live close to your best friend in the whole world. You're already over there all the time anyway."

I had thought about it since the last time we'd discussed it. But I still wasn't sure what I wanted to do or where I wanted to go. And... a small part of me was holding onto Houston because of Zac. Not because I thought I needed him, but mostly because he still sought me out so much instead of the million other people he had to know. I didn't totally get why.

But on the other hand, I was a pretty good friend, and I knew he had to miss home to an extent, so maybe it wasn't that much of a mystery.

I was his old sweatpants.

And maybe... maybe it wouldn't be so terrible to stay a little longer, at least until I made a real decision that wasn't weighed down by a million other things going on. And Trev *did* have a nice kitchen, and the guys weren't home....

Once the season was over, maybe his feet would get settled again, and he'd be off, going on his trips and living his life like he'd been before. Expectations. I knew what they were.

He tipped his head to the side like he knew what I was pondering. "Bibi?"

I knew what I was going to say before the words found their way into much more than my heart.

"I can get more people to do videos for you at Trevor's," Zac kept going. "But even if you don't wanna stay, I was still gonna offer." He slayed me with another smile as he lifted his shopping bag. "Got you a housewarmin' present though. Whatcha think about that?"

And there, right there, lay the biggest problem I had with Zac.

That he was terrific.

He was a good grandson, son, best friend, and regular friend.

He was a great person.

And my poor little defenseless heart had carved out this niche that was just his size over the years.

I loved this fool. So, so much.

And in that moment, I decided it wouldn't hurt to stick

around a little longer. Zac had thought this option through for me, and he was here.

It took everything in me not to clear my throat as I stared at where he stood, his two teammates in the background, and asked, "What's in there?"

"Check it out."

I took the bag and opened it. It looked like a shirt or something folded.

"Take it out," he coaxed.

I peeked at him and pulled out the gift, knowing almost instantly it was an apron. I shook it out and couldn't help but grin and shake my head. It was yellow, had images of spices on it, and said, "DROPPIN' A NEW RECIPE ON YOUR ASS." I looked at Zac and said, "Thank you. I love it. Blue Q aprons are my favorite."

He winked at me.

This terrific, amazing man. Well, there was only one answer I could give him. So I did. "Okay. You're right. As long as Trevor is fine with it."

"He is."

"Then okay." I smiled at Zac and mouthed *"Thank you"* again.

He replied out loud, that lopsided-forever grin still on his face. "You're welcome, darlin'."

———

It took four hours to pack up my things.

Four hours of the guys asking about a dozen questions over just my cast iron cookware—*is it supposed to be this heavy?*—and then another thirty minutes with me making them something to eat so I could "clean out" my fridge. It was basically just omelets, cheese, and some leftover veggies I had in the bin, but no one complained. I caught CJ licking his fingertips.

Zac filled my suitcases in a way that was so organized it kind of surprised the shit out of me at how efficient he was. Then again, he'd used a suitcase more than I ever had or more than likely would, so he had the experience. With only one good arm, I was pretty thankful all three of them had helped. The only thing I had really done was pack my night-stand, underwear and bra drawer, tearing up just a little at the fact I was moving out of my apartment. I wasn't *that* heart-broken over it, but it was still sad to know I wasn't going to be staying here any longer. This place had been a haven for me after everything that happened with my ex. But I had the future to look forward to.

Now I just had to get my channel back. I hadn't been about to cry over that in front of them.

"Everything fit except for your TV," Zac said as he shut the back of CJ's Jeep the moment we were done unloading the last of my things at Trevor's.

"I'll ask CJ if he wants to get up early and pick it up before practice," he offered, setting his hands on my shoulders and lightly kneading them as we stood in the driveway of Trevor's house.

"You don't have to do that. I'm sure if I ask my neighbors, they'll help me carry it down and put it into my car. Then maybe one of you can help me put it in the garage or some-where." I had decided I was going to call around first thing tomorrow to donate my couch and bed. The mattress was the same one I'd had from when I'd lived at Mamá Lupe's, and I could treat myself to a new couch finally when the time came. I wasn't going to be staying at Trevor's that long. Just a few weeks, max. Long enough to finish my book and have some time to really think about my future. And regardless of whatever I decided, I'd definitely see Zac play a couple more times. I'd drive. Now if they made it into the playoffs....

In the meantime, I could get out of the house as much as possible, stay in the room when I was home, keep the house clean, maybe cook, and basically not be an inconvenience. I'd be a good houseguest.

And an even better friend.

The hands on my shoulders gave them another squeeze, those light blue eyes solid and steady. "Or CJ and I can get it if you gimme a key."

"I don't want to bother you guys any more than I already have."

He made that face again.

"Don't you roll your eyes at me, old fart. It's true. You've all already done enough. Way more than you needed to."

Those big hands went to cup my face, the palms squishing my cheeks together as I stared at him, blinking slowly. "What. Did. I. Already. Say? You're. Not. A. Bother. You're never gonna be a bother."

It was my turn to groan.

He squished my cheeks some more. "Let me, yeah? If he doesn't wanna help, you can wake up extra early and we'll ask your neighbor that likes you if he'll help."

I squinted at him. "What neighbor?"

He stopped squishing my cheeks, that light blue gaze holding mine. "The one across the hall."

"You think? Santiago?" I asked. "Huh."

Zac's thumbs slipped under the collar of my shirt as he massaged my muscles there. "CJ will help," he said, changing the subject away from Santiago liking me.

I flashed him a smile and ducked out from beneath his hands when I just about moaned at what he was doing to me. "Okay, but if you can't, I can handle it. Promise. I have people I can ask."

"Yeah. Me."

There went my poor little heart again, all defenseless and raw. So I poked him in the stomach. "Thank you again for doing this."

"You're welcome."

I smiled up at him, and he smiled down at me.

He took my hand. "Come on. I've got film to watch, and you've got computer stuff to do."

I snorted. "Computer stuff. How old are you?"

"Too old by the way you talk to me."

I poked him again, and he tapped the tip of my nose before steering me into the house through the front door. The front door of the home where I was going to be living for a little bit.

Suddenly, out of nowhere, I thought about the pretty blonde who had been at his party the first day we'd seen each other, the one who had known where his room was.

Was he going to be bringing other girls there? To the room two doors down from the one I was going to be staying in?

If I could have started sweating on command, there would have been a drop sliding down my spine.

Why hadn't I thought of that before? *How* hadn't I thought of that before?

I kept my gaze forward as I said, "Hey, if you or CJ want me to leave at any point, you know, because you're having company or something"—holy shit did my stomach hurt—"all you have to do is tell me. Okay?"

He stopped suddenly, and it took me about two steps into the space between the dining room table and the office to realize it.

"What?" I asked him.

I could see his tongue poking at the inside of his cheek as his gaze settled on me. His chest rose and fell as he looked down, and I was pretty sure I caught a nerve pulsing along his jaw. But after a second, he nodded once and all he said was "All right" before he started walking again.

Just *all right*.

Not "*No, that isn't going to happen.*" Not "*Don't worry about it.*" Just, nothing.

And I had to hold my breath and remind myself that this wasn't a mistake. I wouldn't let it be.

It'd be fine.

And I was a goddamn liar.

I was a goddamn liar because I suddenly felt nauseous and sick and jealous. So jealous that I scratched the back of my neck even though it didn't itch. I had built this fantasy in my head that, when he wasn't hanging out with me, he was busy with the White Oaks or doing something at home. Not... out partying like he used to.

I knew better.

But I owed it to him to be a good friend after everything he'd done for me. I could do it for him. I *would* do it for him.

We made it to the living room and found The Sports Network on. There was no one watching the television, but that didn't change what the evening correspondents happened to be discussing. I guess CJ had turned it on.

Because the rerun from the morning had the headline in bold letters.

DO THE WHITE OAKS HAVE A CHANCE?

It was the Michael B anchor who was in the middle of talking, and of course he'd be talking about Zac. His voice loud and electric. "*Sure he's been showings signs of brilliance, but that doesn't mean it's going to last! I need to see more! Zac Travis is past the prime of his career, and I can't help but not be convinced this isn't some kind of fluke. He doesn't have the consistent record to stoke any kind of belief.*"

I felt Zac stop directly behind me, and I didn't need to turn around to know he was watching and listening.

So I did the only thing I could. I dove for the damn remote sitting on the couch and changed the channel.

But I wasn't fast enough. Because when I did finally turn, I saw it. The hidden hurt and insecurity in his eyes. And I knew him too well to not recognize it.

I hated it. Absolutely hated it. And knew I needed to change it.

So I did what I did best when I felt awkward: I smiled. And I told him, "Want to go get a chalupa? I got a new playlist, and I've been waiting for a reason to remind you that all your exes don't live in Texas, no matter what the song says."

It took a second, but just a second.

But his expression slid off.

And the next thing I knew, those long, strong arms were wrapped around me, and he was pulling me into his warm, solid body. Those dry, firm lips pressed against my forehead, my temple, and my cheek as he said quietly, holding me there, "I don't know what I'd do without you, kiddo."

The truth was, I didn't know what I'd do without him either.

CHAPTER NINETEEN

There weren't a whole lot of things more awkward than waking up in a place that wasn't yours.

I'd mentally prepared myself for it the night before as I'd settled into a spare bedroom at Trevor's house, one door down from CJ and two from Zac. The house was beautiful, and everything was clean—thanks to the service that came by twice a week—and the room I was staying in even had its own bathroom. When I'd been living with Connie, and even with my roommate, I'd had to share a bathroom.

Even though CJ and Zac had both assured me that Trevor was "okay" with me staying at his house for a little while, it was still weird.

It wasn't the first time I'd stayed with people out of pity. That was how I'd ended up at my aunt and uncle's house after Mamá Lupe had passed away and my parents had decided that they had to go back to the Dominican Republic as soon as possible, so that I could finish my senior year in high school. No one had wanted me to live by myself, and no one could pay her mortgage so they'd put the house up for sale. If my relationship with Connie had been any different, I would have thought it had been a pity invite when they'd told me to come up, but I knew her and Richard, her husband, too well to confuse what they'd offered.

Anyway.

The house was empty when I headed downstairs. I made sure to clean up after myself following breakfast and kept busy showering and then sitting at the kitchen island, working on my computer for a few hours. It wasn't until after I'd made lunch and was sitting there eating it that my phone rang.

I glanced down at the screen and cursed. "Hello?" I answered, knowing I was going to regret this conversation.

"Blanca, it's Gunner."

No shit. He was calling me from work, which was listed on my phone now under **MAIOHOUSESUCKS**. *And did he call me fucking Blanca again?* My stomach turned in annoyance and I propped my fork against the plate. "Yes?" I replied tightly.

He went right into it. "I was thinking, while you're on paid vacation—"

Vacation? Is that what he was calling it?

"—Could you get your friend Zac to come by and post a picture or two of him working out here?"

This asshole. I winced, shaking my head in disbelief. Did he really expect me to say yes? "No, he doesn't have time," I told him, straight up. What was the worst he would do? Fire me?

There was a sharp sound. "No?"

"No." I should have known there was going to be a catch with his offer. If anything, it should be surprising it had taken him this long to call with his plan. He had more than likely come up with it from the moment he'd made the offer in the first place. "Is that all you needed?"

"No?" he repeated, sounding stunned.

I hoped he was.

"No," I confirmed. "He can't. Like I told you last time you asked. I have to go now, bye." Before he had a chance to say anything else, I hung up. I was snorting at the nerve of him as the front door opened and heard a familiar "Kiddo?"

"I'm here," I called out as I set my phone down and saved the footage I'd been in the middle of editing and turned on the barstool to find Zac coming in, holding a small duffel bag in one hand and a glass bottle of water in the other.

The only thing off about him was the weird smile on his face.

"What's wrong with you?" I asked him instantly.

He froze for a second as he dropped his bag against the wall and then headed over to where I was sitting. Zac wrapped his forearm around my neck from behind and pecked me twice on the cheekbone, right by my eye. He smelled like he'd just gotten out of the shower, and I liked it. A lot.

Too much.

"Darlin', how can you always tell when somethin's wrong?" he asked, his cheek coming to a pause over the top of my head. I liked that too much too.

Well, if he wanted to be affectionate... I tucked my chin and pressed my lips to his forearm briefly. "Because I know you too well. You've made just about every face possible in front of me at one point or another. And you look extra pale. Are you sick?"

He didn't move from his position, cheek still on my head, and I could feel his chest right behind me, rising and falling.

"Zac?" I cupped his forearm and tried to tilt my head upward to look at him. "If you don't want to talk about it...."

"I think I might have a fever."

His arm felt nice and cool under my hand... and he hadn't

looked flushed coming in the house. My Zac senses were going off. "Want me to check it?" I asked him suspiciously.

He paused, then nodded.

"Bend over then," I told him and felt his arm flex.

"*What?*"

"I'll check it rectally." I laughed. "It's the most accurate, you liar. What's really wrong?"

He pulled back a little. That handsome face was still looking totally off even as he narrowed his eyes at me and said, "I'm tryin' to tell myself I don't feel good," he admitted carefully, sounding sheepish. Which was rare because I didn't think he had a sheepish bone in his incredible body. I mean, *body.* "I gotta get PRP done on my knee in an hour."

"What's PRP?"

Zac took out the stool beside me, pulled my bowl of pasta toward him, and started eating it as he explained to me the treatment that required his blood platelets being reinjected into his body to reduce inflammation he was having that was making his knee achy. The thing was... he looked sick the whole time he told me about it, and I wasn't surprised once I understood why.

They had to take blood from him, which was bad enough. Then reinject him, several times in several places. To most people, that wouldn't be a big deal, and part of me was surprised it was still a big deal for him considering the fact he was fixing to be thirty-five and had more than likely gone through who knew how many cortisone injections over his life.

But apparently, Zac was still scared of needles.

Or *not* scared as I was pretty sure he would insist if it came down to it.

He didn't need to say the actual words, but I understood.

It was his dirty secret.

I got up, scooped the remainder of the pasta I'd set aside into the same bowl he was still demolishing, and grabbed another fork. I stabbed a couple more pieces of pasta and chicken and watched his face as he then tried to switch the subject to a phone call he'd had with Paw-Paw on the way home.

But he wasn't fooling me.

"Zac?" I asked him after I swallowed a piece of chicken.

"Hmm?" he answered as he ate more pasta.

"Not that you need me to go or anything... but would you like me to go with you to get your treatment done? So I can drive you home if you... aren't feeling well after?"

Wasn't feeling well after. Pssh.

I remembered the stories of him passing out when he'd had to get allergy shots every month there for a little while when he'd been younger.

His blue eyes peeked at me as he speared a piece of cauliflower and chewed it slowly. "You got the time?" he asked carefully. "I was gonna take a car there and another on the way back."

I couldn't laugh or smile. I didn't want to hurt his feelings. Because God knew if the day came that there was a flying roach, I was going to scream at the top of my lungs for him to come kill it.

"If you want to take a car, go for it. But I'll drive you if you want."

He eyed the bowl between us and pushed it toward me for the last bite. "Yeah." He cleared his throat and dragged the knuckle of his index finger across his eyebrow. "All right. Yeah."

———

"Mr. Travis, I'm ready for you, if you'll follow me," the nice-looking woman in khaki pants and a tucked-in blouse called out an hour later.

Zac and I had taken a seat in the tiny waiting area of the small facility where his trainer had scheduled his appointment. He'd admitted to me on the way over that he knew people who had gotten this kind of treatment before, but it was his first time. I'd driven his car over one-handed and had tried my best not to look surprised when he'd made the suggestion.

Two light blue eyeballs glanced at me.

And I had to pinch my lips together to keep from smiling at what I was pretty sure was him asking me to follow.

I was touched.

And I wasn't going to ruin it.

"Can I come too?" I asked the nurse practitioner, knowing I probably looked and sounded like a clingy girlfriend, but I didn't give a shit. I was only asking to follow because I had the feeling he wanted me to go.

She glanced at Zac, smiled a little, and nodded.

I was pretty positive that Zac was breathing a lot harder than normal as he led the way after the woman, and I had to bite my lip, then bite my tongue to keep from cracking up at the fact he was so nervous and trying desperately to hide it.

I set my hand on his waist, feeling how trim it was, and gave him a squeeze of support.

He set one hand on top of mine and kept it there as I followed after him, inches away as we headed into the tiny exam room. We introduced ourselves as Zac took a seat on the exam table, and I could see the big gulps of breath he was trying not to take but failing and taking them anyway.

He was already pale, or at least paler than he'd been when he'd gotten to the house.

And I knew the woman could tell too because her gaze moved from his slightly trembling hands to his face and back.

I met her eyes, and we smiled at each other.

She knew. "Okay, Zac, this won't take me very long. I'll draw the blood from your right arm, and then we'll work on your knee. If you're fine with it, I've got this handy spray that will help you not feel a thing, is that okay?"

His "Yes, ma'am" nearly killed me.

Well, I was here for a reason, even if he was in denial.

"Hey, Zac?" I asked before taking a seat right beside the table and then scooting it closer to him.

Those blue eyes moved to me, and his Adam's apple bobbed savagely. "Yeah, Bibi?" he asked in a weak voice.

I slipped my hand between his and his thigh, sliding my fingers through his, linking them together. They were ice cold. He'd changed into some shorts, and I could feel his leg hair under my fingers. "I called WatchTube again. They won't tell me what's going on yet. Can you believe that?"

"They won't tell you what's goin' on?" he asked, gaze moving in the direction of the woman who was busy pulling needles and who the hell else knew what out.

"Nope," I told him with a sigh that sounded shaky to me. "All they're saying is that they're 'investigating it.' Mother-fuckers. And to 'give them time.'" His gaze was still on the woman who had turned to face him as she fiddled with the packaging for a needle. "Can you believe that?" I asked, trying to get him to look at me. "I cried again."

That had him turning to me, a frown on his drawn face. "Don't cry. We'll get it back. I promised you. I'll get Trevor to see if he can find someone's number and give 'em a call to get it sorted."

Good, he was still looking at me. "He doesn't need to do that, but if you want him to…." I smiled. Out of the corner of my eye, I saw Zac's right arm get pulled out, and I knew she was about to withdraw his blood, so I squeezed his opposite hand. "I'm sure I'll get it back, but they took down all my videos, and what if they can't restore them?"

"Then we'll get 'em to restore 'em," he said, moving his fingers around mine in a massaging gesture. "You almost ready for the photographer? When is she comin'?"

"Getting there. And next week." I rattled off the dates she would be over at Trevor's house. "You have a home game, and I'll try to get her out of the house by the time you're there so you can relax."

His mouth went flat. "Why you gotta rush her out? I wanna see everything too. Anything you need, all you gotta do is ask." His fingers massaged mine a little more. "I'm so damn proud of you, Bibi."

"I'm so proud of you too, old man."

He was looking at me as his phone rang. Letting go of my hand, he pulled it out of the front pocket of his jeans, made a face, and set it on top of his thigh before leaning over just enough to take my hand again. He hadn't looked at the woman, who had since withdrawn his blood and put it into some spinning, centrifugal machine thing that was busy going, and I knew I had to keep his attention until after he got the rest of his treatment finished. But my mind wandered for a second.

Had it been a girl calling?

Some pretty redhead in Houston now?

Or maybe a blonde in Dallas?

A brunette in Oklahoma?

"What's that face for?" he asked quietly.

I met his gaze and shook my head, ignoring that little—okay, not so little—spike of jealousy in my stomach. And my chest. And head.

"Whatcha thinkin'?"

I shook my head again, knowing I needed to keep talking to him and not be some jealous friend who had no business feeling any kind of way.

"Tell me," he insisted.

Well. I looked him dead in the eye and shrugged again. "You really have that many girls in your phone that you have to put in what they look like and what they do so you remember them all?" I asked, hoping like fucking hell I kept my face blank.

The fingers around mine twitched, and he got this funny expression on his face that made me feel like he was thinking about what I'd just asked. Zac even glanced down at his phone like he was considering it. "I...." He closed his mouth but met my gaze again. His eyebrows were knit together, and for the first time since he'd walked into the house, there was some color on his cheeks. Pink specifically.

"It's all right; I was just being nosey," I lied, offering him up a little smile that I also hoped like crazy was neutral. "You don't need to tell me anything, Zac."

"I don't even know 'em," he said quietly after a second. "I never answer or text 'em back. Not anymore."

Why the hell had I even brought this up? I should have just kept my mouth shut and minded my own business.

I felt nauseous all of a sudden.

"Not in a long time," he added in a soft voice that had me glancing down at the floor. I saw him give his phone a little flick that made it move across his thigh an inch. "Delete 'em for me."

I pretended to look at my fingernails, draped between my thighs.

"All of 'em like that." He kept going in that sweet voice that didn't do anything for me.

I shook my head and hunched forward, placing my forehead on top of his thigh, my gaze glued to the tiles on the floor. "I'm too expensive. You don't want to pay me hourly for that," I mumbled. "And I'm starting to get a headache," I told him as I straightened my fingers and tried to slip them out from his.

He didn't let me.

Those million-dollar fingers tightened around mine in a super hold. "You wanna know what I have you under in my contacts?"

I wanted to shrug, but that felt way too personal. "Peewee?"

"No." His fingers moved out from around mine, but before I had the chance to ball up my fist and take it away, his were back, stroking my thumb before doing the same to my other four fingers. "Try again."

That time I did shrug. "Bianca?"

"Nope." He linked our fingers together again, and I noticed then that they weren't as cold or clammy anymore.

"I don't know, Zac," I told him.

The thigh under my forehead bounced a little. "Guess."

It took everything in me not to sigh.

He loved me. Of course he liked women and had sex with them. Of course there were a ton of women who wanted to have sex with him and probably jumped at the opportunity to have his number.

I would have been one of them.

You know, if there was a chance. But there wasn't.

And that wasn't his fault.

If it wasn't for our friendship, or the fact that we had grown up together, or the fact that we got along so great, I wouldn't have any kind of friendship with him. I wouldn't have him in my life period. It was a one in a billion chance that we'd even met in the first place. That circumstances had connected us.

I didn't want to punish him for not returning my feelings. Because they were dumb, pointless feelings that did nothing but twist me up into knots and hurt me.

So I tried my best to lighten my voice as I offered, "Okay. Bianca the Baker?"

His leg moved under my forehead again. "No. You don't need a thing after your name," he said calmly.

I had to dig in deep to pull a joke out of my heart. "My New Daddy?"

He laughed lightly. "Nope. My Little Texas."

I snorted weakly and felt him start playing with my fingers again.

"Bibi—" he started to say before the nurse practitioner cut in.

"Zac, I'm going to numb your knee a little and start the treatment, okay? You might feel some pressure."

I sat up then, moving my grip to sneak through his fingers again. This was why I had come, to be here for him. And I knew I'd done the right thing then when I found him already pale and staring at the needle she was holding at his side like she was about to murder him.

"Remember to breathe," she reminded him.

He wasn't breathing. He was staring at the needle.

"Hey." I squeezed his fingers.

The woman held up a placating hand. "It's okay, Zac."

Oh dear God.

I squeezed his hand tighter. "Hey you. Bubba. Look at me. Let her do her job. You sat through me getting stitches like a champ."

Yeah.

He made it about three minutes before he fainted.

———

"How are you feeling?" I asked Zac a few hours later.

He was sitting on the couch, head resting against the back of it. His gaze just slid over to me without the rest of his head moving. "I'm good," he replied, actually sounding okay.

He hadn't been sounding okay an hour ago. He hadn't looked that okay either.

It had taken everything inside of me not to laugh my ass off when he'd opened his eyes after passing out and asked, "What happened?" I'd had to hold it in until I'd run over to the pharmacy next door and bought him an orange juice, which he'd downed after a bottle of water that the nurse practitioner had provided. She'd told me immediately after his eyes had rolled to the back of his head that men passing out while giving blood or getting injections was pretty common.

I'd told him that on the drive back home, but he'd just given me a dirty look and said, "If you're gonna laugh darlin', go ahead and do it."

It was only because I loved him very much that I held it back, tried to keep a straight face, and said, "I'm not going to laugh. I already knew you were freaked out by needles. I'd probably pass out if I saw a spider."

"A spider I could handle."

But not an itty-bitty needle. I didn't say that, but I thought it. Once he was conscious and his blood pressure was fine, we left the facility and headed home. I'd made him lay down on the couch with a cold towel over his head while he napped and I worked on my computer, trying not to think about the looming possibility of permanently losing my channel.

Plopping down on the chaise right beside his knees, I cupped one. "You want some water? Need anything?"

He sniffed. "A back rub would be nice."

A back rub?

He sniffed again.

Ah, shit. "All right. Come on, you spoiled ass. Did your grandma turn you into this monster? Because I don't see your mom doing it."

He chuckled as he scooted over a little on the chaise and patted the spot between him and the armrest, and I scooted back, wiggling in there. My hands went straight to his shoulders, taking in the heat of his skin through his shirt, and worked the muscles there.

He made it seem like he'd had surgery instead of just fainting a little. I was going to have to tell Boogie so he could laugh. He'd be the only one to understand.

"Is that all right?" I asked him after a couple minutes.

"Oh, that's so good," Zac moaned, slumping forward so that his T-shirt stretched tight across his muscular back.

I snorted as I dug my thumbs into his shoulders, kneading the muscles as hard as I could. "You sound like you haven't gotten a massage this century, you perv."

His reply was a groan, and it made me snort again. "It feels so good when you do it."

"Don't they pay people on the team to do this for you? They're way better at it than I am."

Zac shook his head as it dangled forward. "Yeah, but none of 'em do it with love like you do." The moan he made went straight to my nipples. "Oh, that's the spot right there."

Oh God, this was a bad idea. Too late now. I dug in to the spot right at the base of his neck and moved one hand up to massage along the column of his spine, and I felt him turn into goo.

None of them do it with love like you do.

He had no idea.

But I did, and it was a tiny reminder that I'd only been here a couple of days and needed to figure out what I was doing so I could get out of here. I wasn't Zac's responsibility, and it would be a terrible idea to stay here too long.

To risk the chance of seeing something I absolutely, positively didn't want to see.

Did I want to leave Houston? Did I really want to move to Killeen? Or even Austin?

I had no fucking idea, and that was the biggest problem.

Under me—well, my hands—I was pretty sure Zac purred as he curled his back even more. "I'd pay you to do this every day," he murmured.

My hands were starting to tire out, and I let go of him before sliding my fingertips down the sides of his back and fluttering them against his ribs. His arms slammed down on top of my fingers, trapping them against his skin.

"You're a bully."

I laughed as I caught sight of CJ coming down the stairs and into the living room right as I tried to curl my fingers back into his side to tickle him. "Am I? Am I a bully?"

I must have gotten enough pressure in there because he sucked in a breath and said, "YES!"

"You picking on Zac again?" CJ asked as he walked by us, a small smile on his face.

"She sure is." Zac leaned back, maybe hoping to push me out of the way so I'd let go as he said, "Do you see how she treats me? You see how she manhandles me, Ceej?"

The back of his head came to rest on my shoulder, pushing me just enough away so my fingers couldn't reach his ribs anymore, but I set them on his shoulders and pecked him on the side of the head as I laughed again.

"Are you putting this down on your list of things to tell Mama about?" I teased him.

He turned his head to look at me, those eyes of his striking despite how pastel they were. "Yeah," he claimed, but I could see part of his mouth going up into a smile.

"Tattletale."

He snorted as he smiled, still staying in place as he leaned his weight against me. "What are you doin' the rest of the evenin'?" he asked.

"I don't know. Reply to some emails maybe. I did everything I wanted to do today. This working-from-home thing is pretty nice. You?"

I regretted asking the question the second it came out of my mouth.

But he shook his head. "Nothin'. Don't feel up to much with my blood sugar levels bein' all weird." He slid me a look like he was waiting for me to contradict that's what had made him faint.

I just pinched my lips together.

"Wanna watch a movie?"

"What are you going to watch?" CJ asked from the kitchen. From the sounds of it, he was pulling something out of the fridge and was going to heat it up.

"I don't know what's on. I haven't checked, but there's gotta be somethin'," Zac answered before leaning back again to look at my face. "Unless you got a date or somethin'."

"I'll watch a movie," I told him. "I could use a break."

"I bet, Miss Popular."

"I will crawl across the floor when you're sleeping, take off your socks, and tickle your feet, don't try me."

He grinned. Then he tried to stick his finger into my ear.

Somehow he grabbed the remote without looking and started changing the channel. I didn't think much of it until he sat up and scooted all the way back onto the chaise, his hip directly against mine, his leg lined up with my own. One arm went over the back of my neck, and he hauled me into his side.

Then he tossed the blanket over us.

He's just being affectionate, I told myself as he faced forward again and started going through the movie channels.

He liked... to snuggle.

And I was lucky I was the girl around for him to do it with. The safe one. The one he felt so comfortable with.

Lucky me.

CHAPTER TWENTY

I was downstairs washing my dishes about two weeks later, listening to Zac talking on the phone with his agent—CJ had left to run errands—when the doorbell rang.

He glanced at me, and I shrugged. It wasn't like I'd invite someone over.

Well, no one other than the photographer who had been by. I still couldn't believe it had happened, much less grasp just how amazing the pictures she'd taken were. It had taken five days to get all the shots done.

Five days of Zac oohing and aahing with me as he spent his bye week—a sort of week vacation every team got during the season—on the couch and around the kitchen, watching the woman in action. He'd helped me cook and clean and been my moral support the entire time.

Part of me had expected him to say *bye* and go off on vacation like CJ—who had gone to the Virgin Islands with Amari and another player whose name I couldn't remember. But he hadn't gone anywhere, not even to visit his beloved Mama or Paw-Paw. He'd hung out with me. We'd gone grocery shopping, to the movies, to the beach even though it was crazy windy, and we'd gone for a couple of long walks.

And if it hadn't been for the fact that I *still* hadn't gotten my channel back, it would have been a great week we'd gotten to spend together. But the loss had loomed over my head and in my heart even though I tried my best not to think about it since there wasn't all that much I could do but call and email repeatedly.

Anyway.

By the time I'd rinsed the soap off my hands and dried them, the doorbell rang again. Zac put his hand over the receiver. "Gimme a sec, darlin', and I'll get it."

I mouthed "*I got it.*"

He needed to focus on his conversation about next season. I'd been eavesdropping the whole time he was on the phone and knew exactly what kind of plan they were formulating.

Sign another year with the White Oaks if they'd take him, or he would go just about anywhere else if they didn't.

But it all hinged on one major thing: the remaining games of the season.

If he managed to get the team to the playoffs—which I was hoping more than anything happened—then there was a shot. The White Oaks were the dark horse of the season. Mostly because of Zac and the way he'd played and led the team. I'd been on the edge of my seat days ago when he'd been in Arizona and they pulled an upset out of nowhere in the last quarter. I was glad Trevor hadn't been at his house, because I'd been screaming at the top of my lungs and jumping up and down when Zac threw a pass that CJ connected with and won them their game.

I'd stayed up that night to make them donuts that they could eat when they got home the next morning as a treat. Even Deepa had texted me with firework emojis at the end.

I'd said bye to her a couple of days ago when I'd gone over to her place and helped her pack before she drove home to be with her mom. I was going to miss her a lot, but I knew she had to go. We would keep in touch, I'd make sure of it.

I still had no idea what I was going to do without her or in general. Zac had helped me the last time I'd filmed, but I knew I couldn't rely on him always being there. I was still recording videos, getting ready for the day I'd get my channel back. Zac was trying to keep me optimistic.

Anyway.

Sure, the current season wasn't over-over yet, but they had to win the next couple of games to make it into the playoffs. If they made it into the playoffs, that was one thing. If they didn't... well, that was going to be a totally different story for Zac.

The pressure he was under kept me up at night.

Well, that and the fact WatchTube still hadn't taken access of my channel away from the motherfucking hacker assholes who had taken it from me. I'd raised hell this last week and had some of my viewers call and email too. I'd even had a couple of other blogger friends post about it.

And they still wouldn't give me an update or just straight-up give it back to me.

But the more time it took, the more convinced I made myself that I was going to get it back and shoot straight for the damn moon with it. I wasn't going to lose it, especially to some assholes. If I had to sue WatchTube, I would.

I'd just sell a kidney to get a lawyer.

Or ask one of the two people who loved me who would give me the money without a blink, if I stopped being stubborn.

If I wasn't feeling so stressed from Zac's future being on the line, me not knowing what the hell I was going to do and where I was going to live, and all the drama with having my channel hacked, I would have been overjoyed that some things were progressing.

Things were going to get better though; I could feel it. I just had to stay strong and keep my eye on the prize.

And quit my job.

I was doing that shit the second I got my channel back, I'd decided. My three weeks off from work were coming to an end, and I was ready to cut ties now that I didn't feel any obligation to stay at Maio House. My two weeks' notice was already typed and saved as a draft.

Now, I just needed my channel back.

I made my way toward the door after gesturing to him again that I would answer it, instantly spotting a woman standing in front of the glass door, holding a baby on one hip and her cell in the other.

She was pretty. Beautiful really. Way taller than me. And the baby in her arms, squirming to get down from the looks of it, couldn't be three years old. A toddler.

A neighbor?

A... friend of Zac's?

The woman had dark blonde hair tipped at the ends in a dark green. The baby had dark hair and rich brown skin. I waved through the glass, and it took the woman a second to see me before she lifted her hand almost hesitantly in return.

Oh God. *Please God don't let this be some woman Zac hangs out with*. I didn't want to have to leave right that second. But I would. I would, I would.

I had planned for this, thought about it during the empty spaces in my day since I'd moved in. I'd mentally prepared, or at least I liked to think I had. But I accepted in that moment that I wasn't prepared for shit.

And that terrified me.

Unlocking the door, I tried to smile as I stood in the

doorway, keeping the door about as close as possible to my side as I said, "Hi."

The woman looked a little older than me and had a wary expression on her face. "Hi," she responded in an equally careful voice I wasn't sure what to do with.

"Can I help you?"

Yeah, her smile went straight-up tight. "Is Zac here?"

This was what I'd been ready to dread. I pressed my lips together, not sure whether to agree or not because... what if she was a fan? What if she didn't actually know him and had just gotten lucky she'd found his address somehow?

"Zac?" I asked slowly, still holding out hope that this wasn't what I thought it was.

"Yeah. Zac," she answered warily, her gaze going from me to the little girl and back. She seemed uncomfortable. "I've been trying to call him, but he won't answer."

None of that meant anything to me. She could be making it up.

"I'm Vanessa," she said, extending her hand out toward me. "You are...?"

Vanessa.

Why did that name sound familiar?

Oh. The Vanessa I'd seen that didn't need a description in his phone. I'd seen her texts a handful of times coming through. And I'd seen Zac grin when he responded to them. He'd mentioned once how much she'd been there for him years ago, but that was about all I knew.

My stomach dropped a little as I took her hand and shook it. "Hi. Bianca."

The smile that rose up out of her caught me completely off guard. "*The Peewee?*"

I wasn't sure if her knowing about me was a good thing or not.

Had she dated Zac too? Was she here to do it some more?

It wasn't like I'd be surprised he'd date a mom. I wouldn't be surprised if he'd done it plenty of times before.

And oh my God, did I hate that fucking thought.

I needed to get used to it, and I knew it.

But it still took the breath from my lungs.

"Yes," I told her and tried not to feel bad that it sounded like I was getting an anal probe without lube.

She was still beaming a bright smile at me, and I was still trying to picture her pretty face right in front of Zac's, loved and appreciated and *just Vanessa.*

And I was wallowing in that thought when a deep male voice called out, "Is he here?"

A massive figure came walking up the path, coming from what I realized was an SUV I didn't recognize parked in the driveway. But it wasn't his huge, hulking body that caught my attention. It was the two little boys each holding a hand that interested me the most. Both of them were wearing jerseys. One was in an Oklahoma Thunderbirds jersey. The other in a San Diego jersey.

And even though their faces looked like they were supposed to be little boys, they were huge.

The closer the man got, the more familiar he started to get. Was he an old teammate of Zac's? All dark-haired with a short beard, massive and muscular, and attractive in a way that wasn't Zac's Disney prince quality but more medieval warrior. He was bigger than Zac, CJ, and Amari.

"I don't know...." The woman trailed off, casting me a quick glance because... well, she didn't know. I hadn't said yes or no.

"Is he still not answering his phone?" the big man asked as he lifted each of the boys by their arms, earning happy-boy shouts—and the man smiled down at them.

I knew I knew him from somewhere. I just wasn't positive

it was from his days with the Three Hundreds or the Thunderbirds.

"No—"

"Bibi, nobody's tryin' to kidnap you, right?" Zac's familiar voice called out from the hallway.

All I managed to say was "uh" before the big man I was pretty sure was an ex-teammate of Zac's called out, "You got time to answer your phone now?"

I heard Zac's footsteps falter behind me.

Then he said, "*Aiden?*"

The oldest of the two little boys let go of the big man's hand and went charging forward, screaming, "Uncle Zac!" at the top of his lungs.

Uncle Zac?

"Sammy?" I heard Zac say. The other boy kept clinging to his dad's hand, but the little girl tried peering into the hallway too, her eyes bright and interested as she asked, "Uncle Zac?"

"Yeah, your Uncle Zac, Fi. You remember him?" the woman, *just Vanessa*, confirmed.

The little girl nodded.

A moment later, Zac touched my hip, balancing a little boy on his shoulders. He winked at me before going straight for the woman with the toddler, blatantly ignoring the big man who rolled his eyes in exasperation. "How's my sugar and how's my mini sugar?" he asked before hugging the woman—Vanessa—and the holding his arms out to the little girl. "Do you remember me, Fiona? I'm your uncle Zac."

The little girl hesitated for a second before nodding and reaching out her own little arms so he could take her too.

And in less than a minute, Zac had two children on him—one on his shoulders, the other in his arms, giving him a kiss on the cheek. If that wasn't cute enough, he was grinning wide.

God needed to have mercy on my soul.

I needed to get away from him. Recharge. Get my mind back on track and remember my expectations.

Remember that I didn't want to be hurt in the future if I let my heart go too wild.

"I don't think I'm ever going to understand what you did to become the child whisperer," the woman named Vanessa muttered in slight surprise but mostly exaggeration as Zac gave her another hug. "But we're all good. We'd be better if you *answered your phone for once, Zac*."

He laughed as he tickled the little girl. "I was just about to call you back, honey. I was on the phone with my agent, and Bibi hadn't come back, and I was worried somebody was tryin' to steal her from me."

Like someone would kidnap me.

Zac straightened, turned in my direction, and said, "One second, darlin'. Forgive my manners. I got one more very important person to say hi to, and then I'll introduce you all." He winked at me a second before he dropped down to a knee, still balancing both children in his arms and shoulders, and grinned at the other boy. "How you doin', bud? You got a hug or a high five for me?"

The littlest boy, who had to be... I had no idea since he was so big he could have been three or fifteen, shrugged then held out his hand. Zac smacked it. Then he stood up and tilted his chin just a little higher to look at the man maybe an inch or two taller than him. They stared into each other's eyes, and then Zac snickered and leaned in to pat him on the back. "How's it goin', Big Guy?"

The big guy indeed gave him a single hard smack to the spine that I was pretty sure would've broken my back.

Then, finally then, did my friend turn back. "Where was I now? Bianca, this is Vanny, and this is Aiden. And these little angels are Fiona, Grayson, and Sammy." He bounced the girl. "My niece and nephews."

The big man rolled his eyes again, but the pretty woman —Vanessa—grinned.

"They're some of my best friends, even though they only come visit about once a year."

"You know, I'm pretty sure you only come to visit once or twice a year too...." The woman trailed off, inching her way toward the big guy, who took her into his side, reached over, and put his hand on the hip farthest away from him.

They were pretty cute together.

"I thought y'all weren't gettin' here 'til tomorrow?" Zac asked before whispering who knew what to the little girl.

Vanessa shrugged. "We were in Austin visiting Diana. My brother is here on business, so we came down to see him too. We were calling to see if you wanted to go eat with us, but you weren't answering, so we decided to come over and make sure you were still alive."

Aiden slid the woman—she had a huge colorful rock on her ring finger, so I had to bet she was his wife—a look. "And?"

She slid him a look back before sighing. "And I wanted to see Trevor's house," Vanessa admitted. "Part of me still can't believe he doesn't just have a coffin in a castle somewhere."

Zac laughed, and so did the massive man, the sound of his kind of rusty, not likes Zac's which was clear and happy and well used.

"I don't go into his room, so you never know what he's sleepin' in in there." Zac bumped my elbow with his free one, blue eyes catching mine. "You seen it?"

"No, not yet," I said, not sure what to say.

Zac's hand landed on the back of my neck, giving it a squeeze before it slid down and rubbed between my shoulder blades. "Come on in then. I'll let you snoop around. Where y'all goin' to eat?"

The woman rattled off a place that wasn't a restaurant

but more of a family-fun center with tokens and games that I'd taken Guillermo and Luisa to before about half an hour away.

Her answer also happened to be my cue to go do something. "Well, I have some things to do, but it was nice meeting—"

"Come with us," Zac interrupted.

Had he missed the part where he'd been the one invited and not both of us? I tried to tell him with my eyeballs what I was thinking, but when his smile didn't falter or do anything, I whispered, "Ehm, they came to see you."

Zac didn't whisper back. "Vanny, tell her she can come."

"Of course you're invited. I didn't know you were *the* Peewee."

She'd just thought I was **BIANCA BLACK-HAIRGYM HOU**.

Zac winked, which didn't help any either.

"Aiden's treat," he said.

The Aiden guy just stared at him, but Zac was oblivious.

"You comin'?" He busted out the big guns as he beamed that Zac smile at me. "Please?"

I wanted to tell him that I really should get to work, but... how could I say no to that 'please'?

I was pretty sure he knew the answer to that was that I couldn't say no to him and his pleases.

That was how, an hour later, after all three kids peed, I found myself realizing that I had to be the only person who didn't know who the Aiden guy was. He had played in Dallas, like I'd wondered. And while I had no doubt he'd played some defensive position based on his size, he must have been really well loved and admired since Houston fans weren't exactly Three Hundreds fans. Because the second we entered the family entertainment center—which I knew from memory had pizza, burgers, and chicken nuggets—it seemed like every eye turned toward the big man and the Disney prince quarterback who threw farts at me.

If someone were to ask me, the Aiden guy sure wasn't hard on the eyes, but Zac... well, Zac was Zac. If I was going to look at anyone, it was going to be him. And not just because of the way his bones and skin had been put together, but also because of the rest of him. The stuff you couldn't see on the outside so easily.

All I had to think about was the way he'd picked on the kids and showered them with attention from the moment he'd seen them.

It shouldn't have been surprising; he'd always liked kids even when he'd been nothing but one himself. I was living proof of that. God forbid there was a baby-baby somewhere; he was going to try and kiss it, then steal it. I kind of wished there had been a baby, honestly. But he was so cute with the toddler and the boy I'd learned who was now almost seven and the quiet one who I thought might have been thirteen with a fake birth certificate that said five.

"Can I help you with something?" I asked Vanessa after we'd arrived at the huge facility with an indoor playground, bowling alley, and hundreds of games. The Aiden man had bought us wristbands and the kids digital "tokens" to use. To give Zac credit, I had seen him saddle up next to him at the register, they'd bickered, fought with credit cards, and then Zac had rolled his eyes and shoved his back into his wallet.

"Can you watch Fi for a second?" the other woman answered as the younger of the two little boys whispered a question to her.

Standing off to the side, Zac was talking to Aiden with the oldest boy standing there, his head tipped all the way back, listening to them. From the bits and pieces I caught onto, they were talking football.

"Sure," I said before taking a seat in the empty chair beside her.

The three-year-old blinked at me with these crazy-long, black eyelashes that I was way more jealous of than a grown woman should ever feel.

I smiled at her. "I like your hair bows."

Those big, dark eyes blinked up at me. "Mommy did it."

"Wow. My mommy never gave me hair bows that pretty," I told her and winced.

Lord, that struck a little too close to home.

To be fair, my mom had done some things to my hair, but only in the month or so a year she was in the States. My God, that really did sting a little when I thought about it. She had emailed me two weeks ago to check in. She'd even sent me a picture of her and my dad with some villagers.

"How old are you?" I asked her, pushing my parents aside. They were close to retirement, but I knew things were never going to change. I was fine with it.

She held up two fingers right as Vanessa finished telling her husband—Zac had confirmed it on the way to the complex, explaining all about how all three of them had lived together for a few months years ago during the end of his time in Dallas—that the other boy needed to pee. "Fi, one more finger," she corrected the little girl as she turned toward us.

Fiona flashed me three fingers, and I ooh and aahed over them. Out of the corner of my eye, I watched Zac walk off with Aiden and the two boys to where I could only imagine was the bathroom.

"Your kids are so cute," I told her. "The boys are huge."

Vanessa snickered. "They take after their dad. I told Aiden they're going to have beards by the time they're thirteen, and women are going to think they're full-grown men."

I laughed. "I told Zac in the car that I thought the oldest

one—Sammy?—could have been seven or fifteen, and I wasn't sure."

That made her laugh too. "They were both ten-pound babies."

I didn't mean to make a face, but I did, and fortunately it only made her crack up more.

"Everyone makes that face. Don't feel bad."

It was my turn to laugh, all awkward. "I'm sorry. How big was she?" I asked.

"She was a preemie. She was only about four pounds." Her hand went to tweak the little girl's bow.

Zac had explained in the car that they had originally meant to be Fiona's foster parents, but they'd only made it a few months before deciding to adopt her.

The other woman glanced over her shoulder before turning back to me. "Bianca, before they come back, I wanted to ask... how's Zac doing? I've been really worried about him. I've been so busy, and he doesn't tell Aiden the same things he tells me, so I don't really know if he's doing okay mentally."

Did I want to talk to this woman who I barely knew about Zac?

One look at her face, and thinking back on her brief mentions, and I knew he cared about her a lot.

So yeah, apparently, I did.

"He is now. He's stressed, you know. During the off-season, I was worried about him too just from some things he was saying." She frowned like she didn't know about that. "But he's really been focusing, and he hasn't been going out at all that I know of except to do things with me. He's under a lot of pressure, but he's still being himself."

She was already nodding before she finished talking. "I didn't know about the off-season. Last year, I knew he was really struggling and making some dumbass choices I wanted to kill him over, but I wanted to make sure he wasn't blowing steam up my ass when he'd tell me he was doing better now." One corner of her mouth went up a little. "He told me you'd kick his ass if he didn't keep his shit together."

I snorted. "Nah, he doesn't need me. He knows what he needs to do."

She squinted at me a little, kind of smiled, and then shrugged a shoulder. "He's got a heart of gold, that one, but I still—"

"What are you two gossipin' over?"

It was Zac who set his hands on top of my head, fingers slipping through my hair.

"You," I told him.

He groaned, his fingers still kneading at my scalp. I wanted to moan it felt so good. And of course that was when his phone started ringing. I heard him sigh and knew he pulled it out after he took his hands off my head. He tapped me on the shoulder. "It's Amari. I'll be right back."

I tipped my head back to meet his gaze and nodded.

He smiled at me before he turned around and walked off a little bit. When I turned back toward the table, five faces were looking at me. Three small ones and two big ones. Vanessa was the only one smiling. I hadn't even heard the other three come around.

They stared at me. They stared at me expectantly. I didn't think a child had ever made me want to squirm more. Because I knew what they were doing. What they were asking themselves.

"I'd never do anything to hurt him or take advantage of him. He's been my best friend since I was Fiona's age, give or take," I explained, so hopefully they wouldn't keep looking at me like I was the bad guy.

The older boy narrowed his eyes at me with his little-kid/teenage face. "What's his favorite color?"

"Sammy!" Vanessa hissed at him. "Don't use that tone of voice with her, and you aren't giving an interview."

He was interviewing me? I almost burst out laughing. He really was worried I was going to... what? Hurt Zac? Not be his friend?

"Mom, you said that we need *good friends*. Not a lot of them, just *good* ones. And I just want to see if she's a good one or a bad one," the little boy replied, super seriously.

Well.

I met Vanessa's eyes right as she was going to scold him and tried to tell her it was fine. She must have got what I was implying because she said, "Three questions before he gets back and that's it, only because it's okay with her. We don't assume we know what other people think or feel, do we?"

"No, Mom."

I was pretty sure even the Aiden man was trying to bite back a laugh when I glanced at him. He was staring at his wife really hard, telling her who the hell knows what with his eyes.

Then the little boy focused back on me and asked, "What's his favorite color?"

I folded my hands on top of the table and told him, "Green."

It was the right answer because he asked another question, ready to fucking go. "What's his favorite food?"

"Spaghetti."

He narrowed those little boy eyes at me a little more. "Do you love him?"

Wasn't that the fucking question. But I told him the truth. "Very, very much."

The seat beside mine got pulled out, and the next thing I knew, Zac was slipping into it, asking, "What are y'all talkin' about now?"

I nudged him. "Still you."

That hand of his landed right between my shoulder blades as he smiled. "What about me?"

"Wouldn't you like to know?" I joked right before the older boy, Sammy, asked about food.

It wasn't until a couple minutes later that my phone vibrated. I took a peek at it.

ZAC IS MY FAVORITE 2 new message.

When the hell had he changed his contact information again?

I opened the text.

ZAC IS MY FAVORITE 2: Want to run around with me after this?

To do what? I wondered. I really did want to go home and get a video edited. I'd only come here because he'd asked.

I texted him back.

Me: I'd rather go back to Trevor's if that's all right. I really need to get some things done.

It wasn't until half an hour later, while we were busy tearing up a pizza—while I noticed that the Aiden man ate three salads—that he messaged me back.

ZAC IS MY FAVORITE 2: Whatever you want darlin

———

I woke up in the middle of the night to get a glass of water and peeked out the front door.

I paused.

There were only two cars in the driveway: mine and CJ's. A certain BMW was missing.

Back in my room, I texted Zac.

Me: Are you okay?

I waited an hour to get a response that never came.

CHAPTER TWENTY-ONE

It was my cell phone ringing that woke me up the next morning.

Cranky and tired, I glared as an unknown New York number flashed across the screen as I held it up to my face with one eye closed.

Was it WatchTube?

"Hello?" I hoped I didn't sound as tired as I felt. I'd forced myself to go back to sleep after an hour of waiting for Zac to text me back, and I'd tossed and turned all night, totally restless. The times I woke up enough, I'd checked my phone to see if I'd had new messages in my inbox.

But there hadn't been shit. Just a couple emails and some social media notifications.

I'd been expecting a stranger, but that wasn't what I heard. "Bianca, it's Trevor. Where the hell is Zac?"

Both my eyes shot open even as that slightly disgusting feeling from the night before—at the reminder that his car hadn't been out there last night—ballooned up all over again. Gross and thick and reckless.

And totally useless because who was I to get jealous over

him? He was my friend, and that was the beginning and the end of it. I had never expected any different.

"I don't know, Trev," I answered him honestly.

Because I didn't want to rat him out. I didn't need details, but Trevor wouldn't be calling me at... nine in the morning for no reason.

He must have believed me because he dove right into another question while I was still struggling with the fact he was calling me in the first place. To ask where Zac was. *And how had he gotten my number?* "When was the last time you heard from him?"

What was this? *Who Wants to be a Billionaire?*

"Last night. We spent some time with his friends, and then he came back, dropped me off, and said he was going to run some errands." I'd checked a few news sites while I'd been up to make sure nothing had been posted about Zac being in an accident or something.

He huffed.

"Why? Did something happen?"

"I texted him last night, and he hasn't responded."

Welcome to the club. I rubbed my eyes with my wrist as more of that gross feeling welled inside of me. Jealousy, okay, it was fucking jealousy. I highly doubted he'd been in an accident. "Maybe he was just having too much fun?" That made me want to throw up, but I kept it to myself.

He snickered in a way that had me blinking up at the ceiling. At *his* ceiling. "We're under crunch time, Bianca. If I text him, he needs to answer. He needs to be on his A game, not partying, getting his picture taken with random women at clubs—"

He'd gone to a club?

He stopped talking, and I was pretty sure it wasn't because I gasped or anything. At least I hoped more than anything that I hadn't made a sound. My lips were pressed tight for a reason. And what pictures was he talking about? How did he know there were women?

I'd figure it out later. Maybe.

No. No, I wouldn't. Because it wasn't my business.

Oh God, I really was nauseous. I just needed to keep it together a little longer. "Trevor? You there?"

There was a pause. Then I heard him sigh. "Bianca, look, kid, I like you, all right? I got a feeling about you, so I'm saying this because I don't want you to lose that shine in your eye...."

I didn't mean to say it, but I did it. "You're scaring me." Did he say... did he say he liked me? Just last night, Vanessa had told me all about how mean Trevor had been to her. How much neither one of them could stand each other and about how glad she was that he didn't manage Aiden anymore.

I felt like there was more to this story, but I hadn't gotten a chance to ask Zac about it.

So for him—who had never so much as even smiled at me, but he'd eaten my food—to say he liked me and didn't want me to lose the shine in my eye?

I wasn't going to like what he was about to say, and I knew it.

"Zac's the closest thing I have to a son. I know everything about him, all the good and the bad—like you do—and it's been my responsibility to keep him on track as much as possible because I want the best for him."

Yeah, I didn't like where this was headed.

He kept going. "But he's had one nice, sweet, perfect girl after another in his life since we've known each other, and I'm sure you know that. I know he cares about you. Anybody with eyes can see that, but I don't want you to have any expectations that will end up—"

Why did it feel like I got punched in the chest as hard as possible?

Why did I want to cry?

And of all the words in the world did he have to use 'expectations'?

It wasn't like I'd genuinely thought that I'd ever had a chance. I knew that some of my dreams were just that—dreams. Some dreams you have a say in. Some dreams you can make happen...

And there are some dreams you had zero shot at.

You couldn't make someone love you.

Most importantly, you couldn't make someone who already loved you, love you any differently.

"No, Trev, it's all right. I don't... I don't have any expecta tions. I know... I know not to expect anything. I learned that a long time ago," I told him, trying to keep my voice light and failing. Or maybe not failing. Maybe he wouldn't notice.

He didn't believe me, and I knew it instantly. "I don't want you getting disappointed. Zac is just Zac. He doesn't ever mean to hurt anybody, and I can tell you're at the top of the list for him. But sometimes we hurt people without meaning to."

Sometimes we did. He was right. "I know he doesn't like to hurt anyone. I just opened the door for him yesterday when he found a lizard in the house. He didn't want it to die inside." Trying to be an adult, I held my breath a little, trying to cling to the fact that Trevor had said he cared about me—not that it was a surprise. I knew he did. But *one nice girl after another?* I could have done without that, not that I wasn't already fully aware of it. "But thanks, Trev. I appreciate it."

There was another pause. Another sigh. "Maybe I'm saying this as a selfish asshole because I don't want you to get hurt and leave him hanging. You're good with him. To him. Just... hear me out."

I pressed my lips flat for a moment and tried my best to keep my voice level. "I will."

At last he changed the subject. "And don't listen to everything that Vanessa says."

That Vanessa? I didn't say anything. How the hell had he known she would say something?

And that must have made him laugh because he knew exactly what I was doing. "You hear from him or see him, tell him to call me. Bye, Bianca."

"Bye, Trev."

He didn't even correct me that time, and it made me feel a little worse.

Dropping my phone on top of my chest, I exhaled and stared at the tall ceiling.

Before I could convince myself that it was a bad idea, or that I had no business, or that friends didn't do that kind of stalker shit, I grabbed my phone again and opened up the old trusty Picturegram app and went to the search option.

I wasn't proud of myself, but I typed in what I typed in.

It didn't take long to find it. Just a few rows down, I found what Trevor had to have been talking about. A picture someone had posted hours ago.

It was of Zac sitting with a woman on his lap.

He was in what looked like a wide booth, with that smile of his that annoyed me, and she was there, perched, with her boobies all up in his face.

My fingertips went numb. The rest of my hands tingled too, if I was going to be honest. I might have even felt nauseous.

I tried to look for any sign that I was wrong, that the picture hadn't been taken yesterday, but I couldn't remember what the hell he'd been wearing. And the girl was covering most of his clothes with her body anyway. Did his hair look longer or was I imagining it?

And what? If it hadn't been taken last night, then it would

suddenly be better if it had been a week ago? Two weeks ago? Three weeks ago? I tried to reason with myself.

Mostly, I was so proud of myself for calmly exiting the app and slowly rolling up into a sitting position.

This was nothing new. I had seen this before even though it had been months. He had invited me, and I had said no. Maybe it would have happened even if I had gone along.

It was fine.

I sniffed.

Okay, it wasn't fine, and I was a fucking idiot for thinking I could do this shit. That I could see it and deal with it. That my lack of expectations would keep me grounded.

He didn't need me. I was just his old friend who made him feel... safe. He hated silence. He missed home.

I was a fool. A fool in so many ways I couldn't even begin to count them.

But I wasn't going to be for much longer, and I knew what I needed to do.

I dragged myself out of bed and headed for the shower.

That was when my phone rang again. It was a one-eight-hundred number.

Chances were, it was nothing to be excited about, but....

I answered it. "Hello?"

"Hello. Can I please speak with Ms. Brannen?"

"That's me," I answered.

"Great. I'm so glad to get you on the phone, Ms. Brannen. I was calling you in regards to the claim you filed...."

―――――

The next thing to wake me up was the knocking at the hotel room hours and hours later.

The super light knocking.

One peek at my phone showed that it was eleven thirty at night. There were a couple of missed texts from Connie... and from Zac too, apparently. I'd answer them in a minute, I figured, getting to my feet with a yawn. I peeked into the room with the kids. The two little boys were sharing a roll-out, twin-sized bed, and the little girl, Fiona, was passed out in her crib.

We'd had a lot of fun earlier.

I wasn't sure who had been more surprised by it: me or them, the Graves family. Because when the doorbell at the house had rang that afternoon, when I'd known Zac had to be at practice, I'd been surprised to see the family standing on the other side of the glass door.

Zac had told them I was there. Zac who had texted me shortly after Trevor called to tell me he was fine and *was I okay?* Like he hadn't gone missing.

Then somehow, one thing led to another, and the next thing I knew, I'd taken them to the Children's Museum and to do a bunch of other fun shit.

The Aiden guy still didn't talk much, but he smiled a lot around his kids and his wife. He'd even given me a tiny smile when I'd let his kids chase me around and acted super over the top as I fell to the floor when they'd gotten me. I'd learned that huge man was now retired from the NFO, and according to Vanessa, Aiden was very happy as a stay-at-home dad. I had to admit it was pretty adorable to imagine him that way. So it hadn't been any kind of hardship to offer to watch the kids if they wanted to go out.

And surprisingly, they had agreed, promising to be back around midnight.

Which was a few minutes away.

Why would they be knocking on the hotel door anyway? They wouldn't risk waking their kids up, and I'd given them my phone number.

With a yawn, I went up to the balls of my feet and glanced through the peephole.

I'd be lying if I said my heart didn't twist a moment before it started beating faster. Racing. Okay, it was racing... like a horse that wanted to get away.

But I wasn't that kind of person, and like I'd told myself already multiple times over the course of the morning and afternoon, Zac hadn't done anything. None of his actions had anything to do with me. Now if he talked shit about me, that was one thing; if he failed me or lied to me or wasn't there when he'd promised to be, that was something else too.

But all he'd done was go out, like he had every right to, and hang out with women, like he also had every right to. It wasn't like I hadn't known he had a life. Yet none of that knowledge did a single thing for my heart.

It didn't change the decision I'd made earlier either. If anything, I was more determined than ever to do what I had come up with.

So I opened the door and forced a small smile on my face before closing it mostly behind me, standing there in the gap to hopefully block our voices.

And Zac was there, in his oldest jeans and an old burnt orange college T-shirt, looking tired and worried. He had a big game this week, after all. His future depended on it. It was also past his bedtime.

"Hi," I whispered, noticing how those light blue eyes moved over me. What? Making sure I was fine?

"I tried textin' and callin' you when you didn't get home, Bibi. I was worried about you," he said carefully, still looking me over.

I kept that stupid smile on my face. "Sorry, I had my phone on silent." Lies, it was on vibrate. I just hadn't seen a point in replying while I'd been awake.

Or even looking at the messages in the first place.

And that made me feel like a jerk now that I thought about it.

He must have thought I was full of shit because the lines across his forehead creased. "What are you doin' here? I called Vanny, but she didn't answer." Why would she do that? "I called Boog and your sister, and they both laughed and hung up on me when I said I was worried you weren't home."

Part of my mouth moved up at that. Of course I was fine. They knew I could take care of myself. And I'd been texting Boogie earlier about Baby Boog stuff.

"I am fine," I told him, keeping that stupid smile on my face even as I lifted a shoulder. "Just here babysitting the kids. Your friends will probably be here soon, but I'll stay even if they aren't."

Those blue-blue eyes roamed my face, and those creases on his forehead didn't go anywhere either. "I was worried about you," he repeated.

And still, I gave him the same face.

"What's wrong?" he asked.

"Nothing."

"You sure?"

I nodded.

"Want me to wait with you 'til they get back?"

"It's fine. They're sleeping. I'm sure you need to get your rest," I told him calmly, maybe even coolly, staring him right into his eyes at the subtle, petty reminder that he hadn't come home last night because he'd gone out. And stayed out. Which was none of my stupid business.

"I can hang out with you 'til they get back."

"It's all right. Probably shouldn't be talking in there and wake them up. I'm a big girl; I'll be all right." That stupid expression still didn't go anywhere. "Thank you for offering though."

He hesitated, and something moved across his face. "You sure, kiddo?" he asked softly.

"Positive. Get some sleep. You need it."

And maybe that was the wrong thing to say, because he definitely frowned then even as he took a step back.

A step back right before I closed the door in his face.

CHAPTER TWENTY-TWO

"What's wrong with you?"

Snapping out of the daydream I'd been right in the middle of while standing in front of the refrigerator at Trevor's house, I glanced over my shoulder to see Zac's manager sitting at the kitchen island with his computer opened in front of him. He wasn't looking at me. He was focused on the screen, but it wasn't like there was someone else he'd been talking to.

I hadn't even known he was back until he'd come out of his bedroom earlier, talking away on his cell, and set his laptop down on the counter. From the bits and pieces of his conversation that I'd caught onto, he'd made it back at the crack of dawn and had taken a nap. Maybe Zac had known he was coming, but he hadn't passed the message along to me.

I wanted to think that it was because I'd barely talked to him, but I knew that was only because I'd made it that way.

Just yesterday Boogie had come down to watch Zac's game with me. We'd gone out to eat afterward, and I'd gone mostly because I didn't want to alarm either one of them if I tried to bail with some stupid excuse. And also because I knew those two could talk each other's ears off for hours, so I wouldn't even really need to pipe in more than I wanted to, and that hadn't been much. They'd noticed but had accepted me having a lot going on.

I had my mind on a lot of things, including but not limited to the call that had come in the same day as Trevor's call, confirming that I had my channel back. It was the one, bright shining light in my life at the moment.

Andddd that was negative and pathetic and not true.

I had a lot of bright, shining lights in my life. Just because I got my feelings hurt was my own damn fault, and Zac was still one of the bright, shining lights in it. I wasn't going to hold it against him that he didn't feel for me the way I wanted him to. It wasn't his fault. I wanted to think it wasn't mine either. You try not to fall in love with Zac.

Anyway.

I was the only one at the house, or so I'd thought. CJ and Zac were both at practice until late, and I'd be lying if I said it wasn't a little bit of a relief that he was gone.

You know, my friend who I was in love with.

But Zac, fortunately, had nothing to do with what had me zoned out in the middle of the gleaming white kitchen that I had finished filming in right before Trevor had busted into the living area, back from New York or Los Angeles or wherever the hell he'd gone.

Turning around to face him and his shiny laptop, I folded my hands on the counter and told him the truth. "I'm supposed to start working tomorrow, and I'm debating whether I should quit my job immediately or if I should put in my two weeks' notice. I can't decide." I'd asked Connie for her opinion, and that hadn't been any help.

Trevor muttered, "Hmph," so I wasn't totally sure he was paying attention.

But he was more of a neutral party than anyone else I

knew, so since he'd asked and he was here.... "Can you tell me what you think? My worry with trying to put in a two weeks' notice is that my boss is going to be an extra asshole and make me even more miserable than usual, but I feel guilty quitting all of a sudden so...."

That had his eyes flicking over to me from the top of his computer for a moment before he went back to typing. "You're putting your notice in, Bianca. He doesn't need to be nice to you." His fingers stilled over his keyboard for a moment, gaze flicking back before he added, "Wait. How are you quitting? Did you get your channel back or did you suddenly get a book deal?"

How the hell had he known about me wanting to release a book in the first place? I'd wonder about it later.

"I got my channel back. They called the day before yesterday and told me. I'm so happy." Because I *was*.

The most ridiculous, unexpected thing happened then.

Trevor smiled at me. Maybe I couldn't see all of it at once, but I saw most of it from over the top of his computer. And it was a smile. A real, live smile.

And he wasn't even being sarcastic when he said, "That's great."

"Thank you. I'd jump up and click my heels together, but I'll probably land wrong and sprain an ankle, so you can imagine it."

Even though my chest burned, I had texted Zac about it that afternoon after I'd found out, and he'd sent a reply with a bunch of smiley faces.

I'd replied with a single smiley face that made me feel bad all over again for not being as nice to him as he deserved.

And just like that, the smile fell off Trevor's face like it hadn't existed in the first place. Maybe it hadn't. Maybe I'd imagined it.

I nodded. "What do you think? Two weeks' notice or nah?

I'm thinking a notice. It won't hurt to be professional." My sister had said that I shouldn't bother saying anything period. In the background, Richard, her husband, had shaken his head at me, telling me not to listen to her either, like my gut said. What if I lost my channel again and didn't get it back? It had taken way too long. Or what if my viewers didn't come back? What if I had to apply for another job in the future and they called for references? I wasn't sure it would be smart to leave on bad terms.

And I'd already made enough dumb decisions.

"I think so too," he admitted, thoughtfully. "The sooner the better."

Oh, he had a point there. "Tomorrow?"

"Or today."

I'd admit that kind of made my stomach hurt. "And go back to work when I'm not on my shift?"

He rolled his eyes again before focusing back on his computer. "Do it today. Let your boss sleep on it since you're so worried about him being mean or whatever that means, and he'll be over it tomorrow."

I was pretty sure that wasn't how Gunner worked, but I wished. I also got Trev's point though. But....

I was still thinking it over a few minutes later when he said on nearly a huff, "I'll go with you if you'd like. Zac's told me about your boss, and I'm curious."

There was only one answer to that. "Yeah, sure. Maybe he'll be less of an ass with an audience. He tried to get me to have Zac come by and post a picture of himself online, and I said no. I'm sure he's still going to be upset about it. I'll be quick. I've had my letter written for a while now."

He nodded and waited until I was in the living room to ask over his shoulder, "What's the name of this boss again?"

———

Forty-five minutes later, with a fifty-five-year-old man at my side who probably looked like more of a sugar daddy than a real dad—because why he would be keeping me company while I did this would make no sense to anyone, but luckily I didn't care what other people might presume—I walked straight in, clutching my two weeks' notice in my hand.

And lo-and-behold, my arch nemesis was standing at the counter where I worked, an arm propped where it always was... as he bitched at a new hire I'd only seen a time or two. I didn't need to hear the words to tell what was going on. I'd made the same face that the new guy had just about every day since Gunner had started working at the gym. It was a *"fuck my life"* face.

Poor guy.

But thank you, Mary, Jesus, and Joseph, I was going to be out of this bitch *pronto*. Thank you, Deepa, WatchTube, and my photographer.

And I had backup with me. Maybe I could report Gunner to OSHA or something if he overheard him being ugly to me. I hadn't thought about that until now.

Sure enough, Gunner turned toward the door almost instantly. Trevor moved to follow just behind me. He had his sunglasses on and already had his cell phone out, tapping away at the screen.

My boss blinked, so I blinked back.

"Hi, Gunner. Can I speak with you in your office?"

He stood up straight, eyes flicking toward Trevor, probably taking in the casual jeans and polo shirt he had on, and dismissed him. "I don't have time, and I'm not giving you any more leave if that's what you're trying to ask for."

What a wonderful human being. "No, I'm not here to ask for more time off," I assured him. *And thank you for asking, my elbow is healing just fine.* Dick. "I wanted to give you this." I handed him the sheet of paper.

He didn't take it.

"It's my two weeks' notice," I explained, holding it out closer to him.

I'd swear he scoffed. He might have even snickered too as he raised an eyebrow as well. "Your notice?"

Did it seem like that ridiculous of a thing to do? I nodded.

I held it out to him just a little closer. "I'll work through two weeks from now until then—"

"I'm already short staffed thanks to your little buddy Deepa leaving out of the blue. You can wait until—"

Was he for real? That was a dumb question; of course he was. "I'm not going to wait."

He definitely scoffed then. "I don't give a shit what you—"

I hated him. I hated him so bad I could taste it. I had been so relieved the last three weeks being away from him and his toxic behavior that I'd forgotten how crappy he made me feel. And you know what? I hated myself too for not just using the edge of the paper to papercut his ass across the neck, but c'est la vie. Hopefully, he got one between the webbing of his fingers on his own. He was *such* an asshole.

"Take her notice," came Trevor's voice from behind me.

Shit. I poked at Gunner's stomach with my notice, set and ready to take advantage of my ally. "Yeah, take it."

He didn't.

What he did do was look at Trevor with a frown.

"Take the notice. Let her work her two weeks," Trevor said in that calm, cold voice.

I nodded and poked him again with the edge of it.

But he didn't listen. "No."

"That's not how this works," Trevor said calmly before sliding a glance toward me. He already looked exasperated two minutes in. "Just do it and tell him."

I paused, then mouthed, "*Tell him what?*"

He tipped his head to his side like he genuinely thought I knew what the hell he was talking about.

Trevor though rolled his eyes again. "What would the other kid tell you to do?"

The other kid? Zac?

Oh. Oh.

He'd say he was proud of me and what I'd built.

He'd tell me not to let this ass push me around.

Then he'd probably say, "*What would Shania do, kiddo?*" Just to make me laugh.

And Shania... Shania would probably tell me I didn't deserve this shit.

And I'd had it.

Tipping my chin up, I thought about the man who would elbow bump me. My friend, who if I would have told him what I was doing, would have come with me. But I hadn't. Because of my own damn fault and my own dumb feelings.

Instead, I had his manager in his place.

Which reminded me again of what I needed to do later today or tomorrow at the latest.

But right then wasn't the moment to focus on that too much.

This was about now. Right here. My future.

The one I had made mostly all on my own but with a bit of help and support from people who cared about me.

I was doing this in honor of all the employees this man had driven away. And I was going to do it with a whole lot of pride. I'd tried to be the responsible one, even though I didn't want to. So.

Maybe Jessica the Asshole had forgotten me. Maybe so had Zac for a little while, and if this fucker only remembered me for a little while, I was going to give him a reason to.

"Actually, I'm going to go ahead and quit now," I said.

It was his turn to scoff. "Don't expect me to give you a reference."

"I don't need one, Gunner. I have a successful business that pays me *a lot* more than you do. I was going to quit before Mr. DeMaio even sold the gym, but... I'm done now. One day if you're bored, look up The Lazy Baker online. Maybe she'll look familiar." I shot him a bright smile, while he dead-eyed stared, and turned around before lifting my hand and wiggling two fingers at him. "Good luck with employee retention!"

Trevor wasn't smiling when we made eye contact, but it was pretty damn close. "Good job."

He didn't even complain on the drive back to his house while I went over all the details again like he hadn't been there to witness them in person. He even nodded and kept the eye rolling to a zero. And when we got to the house and I saw Zac's car in the driveway that couldn't dampen my good mood either while we got out of Trevor's car, and I practically skipped up to the front door, relieved and honestly feeling about fifty pounds lighter. I was free! *Free!*

"Thank you so much, Trev," I told him again as he walked behind me into the main living area of the house. "That was one of the best moments of my life."

He didn't snicker or chuff or anything, but I could tell there was pleasure in his voice as he said, "No need to thank me. If you tell anybody I like seeing birds spread their wings, I'll deny it until I die."

I started laughing just as I spotted Zac standing beside the kitchen island. He was watching us.

That took a little bit of the wind out of my sails, but I still managed to say, "Hi."

"Hi." He frowned for about a split second. "Did you eat already?" he asked, his voice slightly funny. "I was just textin' you to find out." He looked at Trevor again as the older man went around to grab his computer from where he'd left it on the island. "Hi, Trev."

"Zac. I'll be in the office. I have a call I need to make." Then he was heading down the hall, leaving us alone.

And those blue eyes that were mixed with milk moved back to me.

Right. "I ate earlier," I admitted. "Thank you though, but I'm not hungry." That was a lie; I was always hungry, but I'd blurted out the words before reminding myself that this wasn't how I wanted to be with him.

It wasn't what he deserved.

And he knew I'd screwed up, or regretted it, from the frown that carefully formed over his features again.

Shit.

"Bibi," Zac said slowly, maybe even carefully, his gaze roaming my face while he kept on leaning against the island. He looked tired. "What's goin' on?"

He deserved better than this. Better than me, I told myself. So I had to try for him. "Nothing. Why?"

"Because you sure have been actin' weird, darlin'," he replied, still speaking slowly.

I shrugged both my shoulders, but it didn't work.

He kept going, his frown getting deeper and deeper by the second. "You barely talked yesterday. Then you ran up to your room the second we got back after dinner."

He'd noticed that?

"You didn't text me this mornin' either," he told me. "If I did somethin', tell me."

Was I supposed to tell him that I had fallen back in love with him like a moron? No. That wasn't what he wanted. And that was fine. Great.

"You didn't do anything," I told him, exhaling, telling myself I might as well do this now before I lost my confidence. "I didn't mean to give you that impression, Zac."

He took a step closer, his jaw tight, looking intent and worried and focused. He knew I was full of it. "I can't fix it if I don't know what happened."

"Nothing. You didn't do anything. All you've done is be a good friend, and I appreciate everything you've done for me."

He was the one wrinkling his nose then. Those eyebrows knitting together even more.

So I barreled on. "Please don't think I'm not grateful for everything."

"What are you doin'?" he asked, standing up straight.

"I've been thinking a lot about it, and I think since you're not going to be here for Thanksgiving, I'm going to leave early to head to see my sister and the kids. I'm going to take a look around at some apartments in Killeen, some in Austin—"

His "What?" sounded breathless, and there were so many lines crossing his forehead, it would have taken me too long to count them.

"I don't want to impose on you and Trev anymore, and it makes sense. I might as well take advantage of going up there." It didn't make sense. At least not total sense. I didn't love Killeen. I really didn't. And Boogie was about to get married and have his first baby, and I wanted to be there for him, but how much could I really intrude on his brand-new family? I guess if I was going to be anywhere, it might as well be closer to my sister. "I don't know when I'll be back, but I'm going to stay with Connie."

"Stay with me. If you don't wanna be alone for Thanksgiving, fly up to New York. I'll get your ticket. We can get room service."

That felt like a punch straight to the heart that I hadn't even been a little prepared for. "No, you've done more than enough, Zac. CJ told me how the team does its thing for Thanksgiving when you play away games."

"Stay with me after that. That's what I meant too."

Oh man. "I can't stay here forever. You know that. I was only supposed to stay a little while."

Those soft blue eyes, all baby blue and more pastel than vibrant, were totally and completely levelled on me. His shoulders were down, his mouth was tight... and it was breaking my heart telling him all of this.

But I knew I had to. I didn't have a choice.

"What are you doin'? You said yourself you didn't even like Killeen that much not too long ago. I'm not kickin' you out. Neither is Trev. If you don't wanna live here a little longer... I can have Trev find us an apartment."

Us?

And then what? He'd go on his off-season vacation and party it up, and I'd sit around and work and see his pictures online? See him bring girls back? Wait around for him to come back? He wanted us to be... roommates?

A little part of me died inside at just imagining it. I couldn't see it in person. No way. I knew I had already gotten lucky that I hadn't witnessed it happen, but I'd blamed it on him being tired and stressed after every practice and not wanting to go out again. *Again.*

There was only so much my spirit could handle. "No. You don't need to do any of that. I've got it. I'm not your responsibility."

He took a step forward and lifted his arm to palm the back of his neck. "You kinda are," he told me softly.

Why did he have to do this? Why did he have to be such a good friend? "No, I'm not, but I love you for thinking that." I tried to give him a smile. "You've done enough. I don't want to take advantage of you."

"Advantage?" He was standing so still. "Of me?"

I nodded, not trusting my words.

"Bianca," he said, frowning and brooding in the blink of

an eye. "What the hell are you talkin' about? I thought you liked bein' around me. Little Texas and Big Texas reunited."

That was the problem. "I do, Zac. I love being around you. I love *you*. So much. Forever. But I can't stay here for the rest of my life. I can't... live with you. You have a life. You have things you like to do that you probably can't do with me around."

His head jerked back. "Like what?"

"I don't know." That sounded weak even to my ears. "Going out. I don't know, stuff that doesn't include... me. I don't want to be an inconvenience. I don't want to step on your toes. I don't want to take advantage of your great, big heart."

"Bianca, what do you do to inconvenience me?" he demanded, dropping his hand so that it dangled at his side. "When have I ever given you the impression I don't want you around? I invite you to go do everything with me."

The reminder of the picture gave *me* a papercut right along the seams of my fingers, shallow but painful. And it took everything in me to keep my voice almost level, to keep from probably crying, honestly. "Never. You never have, and I love and appreciate it so much. You're one of my favorite people in the whole world, but you don't owe me anything. You never have. You don't have to feel guilty about how we lost touch or feel like you owe me shit because of that dumb snake thing when we were kids and try to make it up to me now by being so great."

Those blue eyes bore into mine, and I'd swear he almost went pale. "You think that's what I'm tryin' to do?"

"Isn't it?"

"No, it's not."

Oh man, I wanted to scrub my face off. "Zac, I'll come back, okay? We aren't going to lose touch. We aren't going to go our separate ways and not see each other again for ten more years. I cross my heart, old man. I'm just going up there for Thanksgiving, and I'm going to stay a while after that to look at places and stuff."

He wasn't listening, or if he was, he wasn't paying attention because he said, "Why are you tryin' to leave so fast?"

"I'm not."

"Tell me what I did then. Tell me why you wanna go. You said you'd stay, and you never go back on your word, so I wanna know why you're tryin' to do it now."

Go back on my word?

"Tell me on Mama Lupe's soul," he demanded.

That time, I couldn't hold my hands back from rubbing my face. I wanted to cry. "Because there's no point in me staying here. There's no difference between me leaving now or in a few weeks."

"Why do you have to leave in a few weeks? Why can't you stay here?"

"I already told you why I moved to Houston in the first place. There's no reason for me to still be here."

His throat bobbed again. "I want you here, kiddo. Is that a good enough reason? I like havin' you here. You think your sister or Boog like havin' you around more than me? 'Cause they don't. I'm sure they don't."

I held my breath as my nose burned. There was no getting out of this. I knew there wasn't. *I had done this. It was my fault.* "Oh, Zac, please don't make me do this. I told you I'll come back. We'll always be friends. I'll see you as much as I can, as much as you have time for, even if we live in different places."

"I wanna know why you won't stay," he said, like the stubborn ass he was, and I knew I wasn't going to get out of this.

He wanted it. The truth. And he wasn't going to fucking let it go.

"I don't want to," I told him honestly, clenching my fist closed afterward when I felt that it was shaking a little. I had to lift my hand and brush the knuckle under my eye when it started to tickle, and I was more surprised to see it come back wet.

His frown got even bigger. "If it's makin' you tear up, I wanna know even more, darlin'."

"I don't want to lose you."

"Lose me?" He looked stunned. "Now you're assumin' you're gonna lose me? What the hell is goin' on? We go from me askin' you to lunch to you bein' all closed off and then sayin' you wanna move somewhere else even though I'm standin' here tellin' you to stay with me, and now you're implyin' you're gonna lose me? What the hell happened? What am I missin'?"

How the hell had this gotten so out of control? I wanted to cry. I wanted to bury my head in the sand and pretend like none of this was happening, but that wasn't going to be reality. "Look, I'm feeling overwhelmed, and I don't mean to take it out on you. I just think it would be for the best, and I'm not going to change my mind."

"Why?" he asked, his voice rough then. "You said you liked Houston. You said you like bein' around me."

"Oh my God, can you please just drop this? Can you please just say, '*I totally understand, Peewee. I want you to do whatever will make you happy….*'"

"I want you to be happy, kiddo," he said with a tremendous frown that was eating me up by the second. "But I don't get why that can't be here."

He was going to kill me. "Because you don't need me here."

"Who the hell said that?"

I was seconds away from crying. "No, you don't."

"Yes. I do," he insisted. "You were snugglin' on the couch with me the other day, and now you don't even want to be in the same city."

Lifting my hand, I rubbed my forehead, taking in his perplexed face. His confused eyes. And I had no idea what to do with them. "If you want someone to snuggle with, you've got a thousand girls in your contact list who would love to do it, Zac. If you want a best friend, you don't need me here. You've done that with Boogie for the last fifteen years. If I live somewhere else, we're not losing each other. I love you, and I know you love me too."

His shoulders dropped, and something enormous moved over his face at the mention of Boogie. Something like exasperation or defeat. Or something I couldn't understand. His gaze went to the ceiling, and he squeezed his eyes closed as he said, in a rough voice, "Of course I love you, kiddo."

I was going to have to tell him. There was no way around it. Fear rose up in my chest, swift and steady, but he was never going to understand otherwise. And I was going to have to believe that we could get through just about anything together.

Including me and my dumbass feelings.

"That's the problem, Zac. I know you do. I know that. But, I... I love you differently than that. In a way that isn't... friendly. In a way that I have no business, okay? And I know that," I told him softly. "Please don't make me talk about this anymore. I lost you for ten years, and I don't want to lose you for another ten again because I made things weird. You were Boogie's first... and I get it. You and I were just meant to be friends. Best friends."

All I could hear was his soft breathing in the moments after that.

He was watching me with this devastated expression that cracked me in half.

"Bianca," he started to say softly with the heaviest blue eyes. "I love you, darlin'...."

I tipped my head back with a sigh.

"Can't tell you how many times I've wished you weren't Boogie's cousin."

He was flaying me alive now.

I wish you weren't my best friend's cousin, he'd said.

Maybe in another lifetime... those words felt like.

And in the story of our lives, in our friendship, his phone rang.

But he didn't even look down at it. The "cousin" was perched on his lips. The *I love you* that sounded so right and natural, he had never needed to say the words out loud because I had known them so well. It was our silent song to each other. The one only each of us understood.

He wasn't telling me something I didn't know. Because I did.

It just wasn't his fault that he loved me, but not... not like that.

It wasn't either of our faults that we both loved Boogie so much either.

I understood everything.

"Get your phone, Zac. We'll talk later," I told him... lying. Knowing I was lying.

He said nothing.

"It might be important," I warned him.

His chest expanded, and his expression was pained. "I need to go back soon for a meetin'."

It was my turn to nod. "You need to focus. I know. I want you to."

But those words weren't enough because this man I loved just kept on staring at me, mouth slightly gaped with something in his eyes that looked like... something I couldn't recognize. But finally he exhaled when his phone stopped ringing and then started up again, and his question was low and nearly hoarse, "We'll talk later?"

I nodded, lying again. He'd forgive me, I knew. Eventually.

But more than likely, it wouldn't take that long because he wasn't that kind of person.

But I was going to find out.

Because I was leaving.

It would be better that way. For both of us. I just knew it.

CHAPTER TWENTY-THREE

"Peewee, are you going to tell us what's going on or are we going to have to annoy it out of you?" my sister asked from across the kitchen as I pulled a tray of chocolate chip cookies out of the oven and set them on top of her range.

I'd made them per my nephew's request. He'd asked all sneaky and extra sweet, by coming to lay on the bed with me that morning and pointing out a gray hair he'd found about three minutes into his visit. Then he'd made it up to me—in a way—by offering to pluck my eyebrows... then telling me I could trust him with tweezers because his mom was always asking him to pluck her upper lip. And sometimes her chin.

And here this heifer had been lying to me for years—bragging—about how she was "naturally" hairless.

Making Guillermo cookies was a no-brainer after that. That was going to be ammo I could use against her for the rest of my life. The lying cow.

Needless to say, that little tidbit of knowledge had been the highlight of my last two weeks. Under normal circumstances, I would have been full of glee at being able to pick on my sister. But apparently, I wasn't being very good at hiding that something was bothering me, even though I'd tried my best to play it off.

Because no matter how hard I'd tried, Connie was calling me on my shit. One quick glance at Boogie told me he was in on it too, even though he'd only gotten to her house that morning. It was Richard's birthday, and we were celebrating it over the week-end. It was mostly going to be a day and a half of doing two of the things he loved the most: going bowling today, and tomorrow we were driving to Houston to watch the White Oaks' game against the Three Hundreds. Zac's old team. I was still bitter toward them even so many years later for letting him go.

Thinking about Zac....

My chest ached a little. More than a little. An awful lot.

"There isn't really much to tell," I said, trying to keep my voice as nonchalant as possible, smiling and making it seem like everything was fine. Which was what I'd been trying to do since I'd gotten to Connie's house.

After I'd snuck out of Trev's house while Zac had been gone, I'd driven up to Killeen and knocked on my sister's door at eleven o'clock at night. I'd even made sure not to cry so she wouldn't get suspicious. I'd waited to let go—just a little—until I was in Guillermo's room to really do it, and I'd covered my face with my jacket so that I wouldn't make a sound.

Zac had started texting me about three hours into my drive, when I'd figured he'd gotten home and found me... not there.

ZAC THE OLD MAN: Where you at?
ZAC THE OLD MAN: Peewee?

I texted him back at the first red light I got to with my heart in my throat. I didn't want him to worry.

Me: On my way to Killeen. I'm sorry, Zac. I under-stand if you're mad, but I really want to see my sister

and check out a few places. Get out of your hair for a while too so you can focus. I promise I'm fine. I'll text you when I get there if you want me to.

His replies came in almost instantly, but I waited until I got to another red light, right before getting to her house, to read them.

ZAC THE OLD MAN: Bianca

ZAC THE OLD MAN: Please tell me when you get there

ZAC THE OLD MAN: Or come back. You said we were gonna talk

Me: I will. And we can talk whenever. [smiley face emoji]

I waited until I was parked to send him another message and then put my phone on silent so I wouldn't do anything in front of Connie that would give her a clue that things weren't great. Then it wasn't until I was in my nephew's room that I read his next response.

ZAC THE OLD MAN: Glad you made it safe. Not glad you left in the first place. Come back

ZAC THE OLD MAN: Can we talk tomorrow?

ZAC THE OLD MAN: Eating that chocolate zucchini bread you left. You should put it in your next book.

That had been what made me cry in my nephew's room.

Because how much did I *wish* that he would really want me back?

Finally, when I was able to, I texted him back once more, wiping at my eyes with the backs of my hand once I'd gotten it together.

Me: You're busy tomorrow, remember? I'll text you. Also: yes, if there is a next book, I'll put it in there. Maybe with more walnuts.

He texted me back immediately, even though it was hours past his bedtime.

ZAC THE OLD MAN: There's gonna be another book.

ZAC THE OLD MAN: Miss you already kiddo. Come back. We can talk and get things sorted.

I didn't text him back after that. I didn't know what to say. I wasn't going to go back until I had a real plan. I'd left most of my things in the bedroom at Trevor's after all.

But that didn't stop Zac. He sent more messages the next day. And the one after that. And had every day since.

Messages that said what he was doing (practicing, eating), things Trevor said or did, but mostly though, he asked me to drive back and said he missed me.

I texted him back every single time, even though my heart hurt.

Every message nearly made me cry, but I smiled instead because Connie didn't need to be all up in my business more than usual.

And I'd thought I'd done a pretty decent job at keeping things to myself, but apparently that wasn't the case.

Especially not when Boogie, who was sitting at Connie's table, piped up too. "I thought I was imagining it."

"You're both imagining shit," I said, focusing on the cookies that were making my mouth water.

My brother-in-law, who was sitting at the table too, popped open a can of orange soda before he said, "Me three, Bianca. 'Cause I swear I heard you crying in bed a couple nights ago, but sometimes your sister cries for no reason when she's on her period, so I wasn't sure if that's what was happening to you or not."

I turned on my heel slowly to stare at the man taking a sip out of his soda without a care in the world.

I wasn't the only one staring at him either because my

sister was doing the same but with her mouth open a little while she did it.

"What?" her husband asked, like he was confused by the silence. "Tell me I'm lying. You don't even try to hide it."

"What happened?" Boogie asked, snapping out of it. "You got problems with WatchTube again?"

I wanted to lie, I really did. I wanted to blame it on my channel being stolen, because that would have been a real good excuse. But I wouldn't.

"Nope. Everything is good with them now."

"Is Kenny trying to talk to you again?"

Kenny. Ugh. My ex could eat shit. "Nope. I haven't heard from him since he took all my money."

"Then what's wrong?"

Out of the corner of my eye, I saw my brother-in-law shift a little, bringing his can back to his mouth for a little sip. "Is it Zac? Did he cheat on you? Because if he did, I'll tell everybody he's on steroids. Try me."

Silence.

Total and complete silence filled the kitchen and breakfast nook area.

Our faces were all different though.

I'm pretty sure mine was in horror.

Connie looked like she didn't know who the hell was sitting beside her.

Boogie looked like someone had just told him his mom was an alien.

And my brother-in-law, all average height and skinny and adorable, was looking at us like he had no idea why we were all staring at him.

"What? You want me to kill him or something? Because one time I went hunting with my dad, and no lie, I fainted when he—"

Dear God.

"B, is there something I should know about you and... and...?" Boogie stuttered, looking somewhere between his mind being blown and the start of being mad.

"Honey," my sister started to say, her voice almost... a whisper? And why did she look horny? And why did I know what her horny face looked like? "What would make you think there's something going on with B and Zac?"

"There's something going on with you and Zac?" Boogie echoed.

What the hell was happening?

My brother-in-law shrugged casually, still sipping his soda without a care in the world... like he hadn't just dropped a hydrogen bomb on our asses.

On all of us. Seriously.

On Boogie in the form of there possibly being something in the world between his best friend and me.

On Connie who was looking at this man she'd been with for nearly two decades like she didn't know him... but the little freak liked what she saw.

And on me, for not being as secretive as I'd thought.

Or maybe, actually, he was just a hell of a lot more perceptive than any of us had ever given him credit for.

Then he kept going, lifting an index finger. "Well, Peewee didn't want to talk about him for years. Now they're friends again and seems to me like they spend all their time together, and then she moved in with him. Hello, and ya know, I always figured he was a player, but he's not going to hang out with a girl he doesn't like."

"They've known each other since we were kids," my cousin muttered, still looking and sounding out of whack.

Shit.

My brother-in-law snorted. "So? He didn't see Bianca for ten years. What? You think he's going to think of her as being a little sister? You're smarter than that, Boogie. And Yermo told me all about them at Lola's quince, m'kay? There's 'I love you like a sister' and there's 'I love you as a person.' I know I couldn't have been the only one to feel the chemistry in that video they did together either... but okay, maybe I was. Man, you two need to pay more attention."

None of us could say a single freaking thing.

And apparently my brother-in-law took that as a sign to keep going, so he did.

"But, B, did he cheat on you? Lie? Because he seemed like a nice guy, but I've never been a White Oaks fan, so I'll do it. Next time I get a B-12 shot, I'll save the needle and use it as proof," Richard claimed, everything about his narrow face totally serious.

"What else do you know that you haven't told me?" my sister whispered.

"I don't know anything for sure; I just have my guesses."

His guesses. This man was wasting his life in the army when he could probably make a fortune being a goddamn psychic—or at least fool people into thinking he was a psychic.

I was stunned.

"What's going on? Is there something going on with you and Zac?" Boogie asked again, aiming his nearly black eyes at me.

Shit balls.

Scratching the tip of my nose, I held my breath for a second and decided I'd walked right into this—asked for it really, because why had I thought they wouldn't notice something was wrong with me? They knew me better than anyone. Including Richard.

But one thing at a time, starting with my cousin. "No, there's nothing going on with me and Zac," I told him.

He sagged, but it was Connie who sat up straighter before pointing at me. "You're lying."

"Don't use your mom voice on me, heifer. I'm not lying. Nothing has gone on with us other than hugs and some kisses on the cheeks, which I give everybody in the first place."

My cousin still looked relaxed, wary but relaxed. He knew I wouldn't lie to him, and that made me feel better. He just wasn't going to like what I was going to tell him next. That was for sure.

But there was no way around it now.

"*But* I was dumb and I started to really... like him, as more than a friend. It's not like I meant for it to happen, but it did. Again. I told myself not to let it happen, but again, it did. And I knew I had no shot in hell of him being interested in me like that, but...." I shrugged, resigned to being in the same damn position all over again—the idiot who fell in love with her cousin's best friend. And not just any normal, mere man. But Zac Travis. The butt cheeks of Texas. "I've just been upset a little because I let my guard down and he did something innocent that reminded me of why I knew better."

The looks on their faces were questioning, so I sighed.

"Some girl posted a picture of them together, okay, nosey? She was sitting on his lap. It hurt my feelings, but we aren't together. At all. He doesn't even like me like that. I told him, and he started to say something about how he wished I wasn't your cousin, Boog. So there. He didn't do anything wrong. I don't want to stop being friends with him. If anything, I just need to remember what kind of friends we are, and that's platonic, and I'll be fine in no time. I'm not planning on spending the rest of my life spray painting 'Bianca loves Zac' onto any railroad cars or overpasses. I'll find someone else to date, maybe we'll get married, and maybe I'll have a couple kids, but maybe I'll have a couple dogs or cats and be a cougar someday. I don't know. I'm pretty open. So anyway, I'm fine, nothing happened. I'm not traumatized for life or anything, so can we please never talk about this again?"

Boogie didn't exactly look stunned, but he looked... surprised? Thoughtful? Maybe even... uncomfortable? "Nothing ever happened between you two then?" he asked slowly.

I shot him a look. "He's your best friend, Boog. No. We're both affectionate and comfortable around each other. I've never seen his wiener, even though I might have tried."

He jerked back, and his eyes almost bugged out. "Bianca!"

"What? That's what you were asking, I could see it."

Connie nodded, one eye still on her husband. "That is what you were asking, and I would have asked if you hadn't beat me to it."

She totally would have.

"He's my best friend too, Boog. You're my best friend. All three—four of you—are my best friends."

And fortunately, my cousin had to know that to his bones because he didn't wait to nod even though his uncomfortable expression went nowhere. "But you like him as more than that?"

I lifted a shoulder. "I didn't mean for it to happen, but yeah. I love him, but I can learn to love him as just a friend. That's where more than half of it goes to anyway. So we're good, or does someone else have any more dumb questions?"

"I have one question, and it isn't a dumb one," my sister piped up, lifting up a hand like she was still in school. "Is that why you're here looking at apartments?"

"Only like 10 percent," I told her, a little bit lying but not totally. In reality, it was more like 60 percent... 70 percent.

It would still be nice to see her and the kids and my way too perceptive brother-in-law all the time though.

"I have another question, still not a dumb one either," she said, and unsurprisingly, she raised her hand again.

"Yes, Connie."

"Has he checked on you to make sure you're fine since you left?"

I nodded at her.

And my sneaky sister nodded back slowly.

I turned to Boogie, who was the person I worried about the most. "Are you fine, or are you still about to have a shit attack even though nothing happened and getting my feelings hurt was my own fault? And you can't get mad at him, because he never ever tried to put the moves on me or anything, even though I kind of wished he would have."

"I don't have shit attacks" was what he said first.

Even Richard looked at Boogie.

He ignored us though. "I'm fine. Really. Not really. You could've told me, Peewee," he said, turning his dark eyes to me with the start of what seemed like a hurt expression. Maybe because I *hadn't* told him before. I usually told him everything.

Then again, he hadn't told me he was even thinking about asking his girlfriend to marry him, so he wasn't one to talk anytime soon.

I was still a little salty over it, even though I'd say we were both even at this point. But we didn't need to get into that. What we needed to do was smooth this over, because the last thing I ever wanted to do was mess up my friendship with him, or Zac's friendship with him.

"What was I going to tell you, Boog? '*Hey, I've been hanging out with Zac a lot, and I think I'm in love with him? Again?*'" I gave him a look. "I'm sorry I didn't say anything and just sprung this on you, but I know it was dumb. I knew it was dumb back when I was a teenager. I know it's dumb and pointless now. It's like that kind of love is the only thing my heart knows, but I'm going to get it under control. That sounds lame as shit, but it's true. He's your best friend, and the last thing I want is to make things weird between you two, when he hasn't done anything."

"It's not dumb," my cousin muttered thoughtfully after a few moments, after a deep sigh that had him rubbing his forehead as he looked down at his lap.

"I'm sorry. I only kept it a secret because I'm embarrassed and know better," I told him. "I love you, and you mean the world to me. I don't want to mess anything up."

Out of the corner of my eye, I could see Connie's gaze bouncing back and forth between Boogie and me. Richard was doing the same thing, still sipping that orange soda. None of us said a word for the longest time.

Until Boogie broke the silence with another sigh before lifting his head and looking at me with a small, wary smile on his face that told me everything was going to be okay. "You can't help who you love sometimes, even if you know that maybe you shouldn't or that maybe it's going to hurt."

Well, shit. I guess in a way I'd never thought about it like that with him. I still didn't like his future wife, but....

"He is my best friend, but so are you, B. It's a little fucking weird—it's a lot fucking weird—but...." He sighed one more time. "You're really fine?"

"I only hurt myself, promise."

Because that was exactly what had happened. I'd hurt myself. I could admit it.

But I was going to fix it. I was going to be okay.

———

"I can't believe you didn't tell me," my sister said a couple hours later right before striking out at me like a viper, going straight for my nipple like she was going to give it a twist.

It was more experience than instincts that had me karate

chopping her hand out of the way and covering both my boobs with my hands.

She tried to go for me again, so I reached forward and pretended like I was going to do it back to her.

But I wouldn't, because the one time I had done it, she had made sure to get me back twice as hard to teach me a lesson. Nothing was worth getting a titty twister, not even giving one.

"I was wondering what took you so long to ask," I told her. I was still covering my nipples, and if anyone noticed, I didn't really care. I'd been too busy reading a text Deepa had just sent me that I hadn't been paying attention to Connie creeping over.

The message read:

DEEPA IS COOL: Did you hear they kicked Gunner out of the gym? Rumor is somebody bought him out.

I was going to have to celebrate that one later. It was too late to benefit me, but that jerk had it coming. It was about time the other owners noticed they couldn't keep employees because of him.

Looking up, Connie leaned up against the counter of the bar at the bowling alley, because that was where we were celebrating my brother-in-law's birthday. It had been his favorite thing to do for as long as I could remember. I used to go to his tournaments back in Fayetteville. I was just taking a break after our last game, and apparently so was my sister.

"I was *waiting* because I promised Richard I'd leave you alone."

Aww, Richard. He'd told me he was sorry for blurting out my business on the drive over. Then he'd offered again to spread the rumor about Zac and steroids if I wanted.

"And I guess I was hoping *my sister* loved me enough to come give me all the details in person."

I snorted and picked up my Sprite. "You really thought I was going to make it that easy?"

She sent me a flat look that had me smiling.

"And there's nothing to tell, Con, so there's nothing to share."

"'There's nothing to tell'," she mocked me using quotation fingers and everything. "Bullshit."

"Not really, because nothing is going to come of it, so...."

"Punkin!" Richard shouted as he approached us from the lane he'd been bowling in while we took a break. "I thought you were going to wait to harass Peewee."

"She just started talking on her own."

My brother-in-law and I shot each other a look too, and we let it go.

"You're *really* thinking about moving up here?"

I nodded.

Richard stopped beside my sister, draping an arm across her shoulders as he stole her beer. "You can stay with us however long you need."

"I'm hopin' to get her to come back to Houston," a different but very familiar voice said.

My brain froze. My whole *body* froze. I wouldn't be surprised if even my red blood cells did too.

And my heart went straight into my throat.

Straight there. Nonstop. Flying express.

I *knew* that voice.

Setting my Sprite on the counter, I took the beer from Richard, took a sip, handed it back, and then finally turned my chair around enough to see the man who hadn't moved from where he'd been standing behind my chair while he'd spoken.

Because sure enough, there he was. Zac. Brown cowboy hat on, his usual jeans, and a T-shirt that stretched across his

lean, muscular chest. Those big hands were on his hips
and he…

Well, he was focused on me.

He looked tired.

"Snack Pack?" I asked like I didn't know his face inside
and out.

His smile was small but sweet. "Hi, darlin'."

"What the hell are you doing here?" was the best I could
come up with as I took in his exhausted features some more.
"You have a game tomorrow," I stated like he didn't
know that.

What was he *doing?*

He did this nonchalant little shrug like his game the next
day, another game that represented his potential future, was
no big thing. "I changed my cell phone number a little while
ago. Wanted to come tell you face-to-face and give you the
new one," he explained slowly, looking me dead in the eye.

"What are you talking about?" I asked him before I could
think twice about it. "Why did you change your number? You
need to be home resting, you old fart, not… being here."
Because *what the fuck* was he doing here in the first place?
And why did he change his number?

And why couldn't he just text me and tell me he'd gotten a
new one?

My comment had his smile cracking even bigger, into a
full-grown, big, natural Zac smile that was basically my kryp-
tonite. "Some things are more important than restin', kiddo."
His eyes scanned my face slowly, his expression staying right
where it was. That big palm of his came right up to the center
of his chest, and he rubbed a circle right there as he said on
an exhale, "I sure did miss you."

Out of the corner of my eye, I saw my sister smack
Richard with the back of her hand on the upper arm.

And maybe I would've reacted if my heart didn't feel like it had just gotten zapped with a defibrillator.

"I've missed you too," I told him, struck by the way he was looking at me, like he really had missed me. A lot.

So much that all I wanted was a hug in that moment.

I hesitated for maybe a second before I slid off the stool and approached him, throwing my arms around his neck before he realized what I was doing. I hugged him tight. And in the time it took me to take a breath, to fill my lungs with the sweet, subtle scent of his cologne, his arms were around me, squeezing me tight and close, his cheek or his mouth pressing against the top of my head.

I'd swear on my life I heard him mutter, "Oh," softly as his palm slid down the length of my spine, stopping only once it covered the small of my back.

I took in his heat and the long length of his torso pressed to mine so solidly for a moment. Then I released him from one breath to the next, taking a step back so quickly it forced him to drop his arms. I watched him take a breath, watched a determined little notch appear between his eyebrows, and then saw him watching me like...

Like he'd made some kind of decision and he was preparing himself for the consequences.

Those powerful, fit lungs of his filled before he spoke up. "I came to talk to Boogie too," he said tightly, his hand going back to lay right smack in the middle of his chest.

I took another small step back. "What do you need to talk to him about that you couldn't just do on the phone or tomorrow?" I asked, way too confused by the fact he was here, by him changing his number, and mostly by the way he was looking at me right then. "Are you okay? Did something happen?"

What was going on? He'd finally lost it. He'd gotten

sacked really hard last week, and I'd stood up in front of the television—

That regal chin lifted. "I'm good."

He was good, but none of this made sense.

"I should've talked to him months ago, but I can't put it off anymore," he said carefully, still watching me closely.

I wanted to think it was my sister who kicked me in the calf, but I wouldn't be surprised if it had been my brother-in-law.

I went up to the balls of my feet, swallowing up the face I hadn't seen in weeks like a starving person who knew she should take it easy. "Not that I'm not happy to see you, but are you trying to piss off Trevor and your agent?"

A partial smile lifted the corner of his mouth. "I'm not worried about Trev or anybody else, and you said you'd talk to me on the phone, but it's been weeks and you still haven't called."

Well, he had me there, damn it. I swallowed hard. "Zac...."

His eyes roamed my face long enough that I raised my eyebrows, and it was then that he sighed and flicked his gaze to the side. "I'm bein' rude. Connie, Richard, hope y'all are doin' well. Can I have Bianca now?"

"Yes, if you get us tickets to another game in the future, please," Richard answered.

I stared at both of these vultures who were supposed to love me... but who were giving me up for possible football tickets.

And had Zac worded that weird or was it my imagination?

He nodded at them. "You got it." Then he glanced back toward me, and my heart gave two hard whacks. "You got time to talk to me now?"

I still couldn't believe he was here in the first place. "Zac, I'd talk to you on the phone if I knew you were coming.

What the hell, man? And why did you change your number? You got a stalker now?"

"Come with me to talk to Boogie real quick, and then I'll tell you whatever you wanna hear," he said, watching me with those blue eyes I loved.

I was pretty sure my sister smacked her husband again.

"You're scaring me," I told him, going through about a dozen different scenarios in my head. They were all terrible.

The corners of his mouth went up again in that smile that made me feel funny. His eyebrows too. "You trust me?"

I sighed and made a face. "Yes. But I already told him... what I told you." *That I was in love with you.* "He knows you didn't do anything, that nothing happened. Boog knows you love him too much to ruin your friendship."

His mouth went flat and white at the edges, and his nostrils flared for a moment before those light blue eyes moved over my face again, and he said in a steady voice, "Don't worry about that. Just trust me, would ya?"

He held a hand out toward me.

And I took it, pretty sure that yet again, my sister whacked Richard.

Just trust him, he asked.

Well... it wasn't like I had another choice. So I took it.

"I'll be back," I told them, meeting my sister's beady, smug gaze over my shoulder.

She snorted. "Yeah, sure you will."

Zac squeezed my fingers, and I forgot about her cryptic comment before following after him, asking, "Zac, seriously, what are you doing here?" as we headed toward the lane where Boogie was standing, watching a friend of Richard's go up for his turn.

I tried to slip my fingers out from his, but all he did was knit his longer ones through mine instead.

He smiled down at me too. "I told you, darlin'. I came to talk to you and your cousin."

But about *what?* "I know Trevor is going to be on your ass for leaving. You should be home."

He tugged on my hand playfully. "I can't stay all night, kiddo. Just a little while." He gave me another one of those sugar-sweet smiles. "And he knows where I am."

I eyed him.

He kept on smiling. "Come on. The faster we do this, the faster we can talk."

"I could've talked to you on the phone. I don't want you to mess anything up, not when you have a game tomorrow."

"I'm not messin' a thing up. You can ask Trev. He gave me his blessin' to come so I could put him out of his misery."

Trevor's blessing? "Were you being a pain in the ass?"

He shot me a little side look that made me snort.

"You're always being a pain in the ass, my apologies."

He chuckled at the same time that my cousin happened to turn around, in the middle of smiling when he caught sight of Zac first. Then me holding his hand.

And he didn't stop smiling, but his face got a little weird. A little tight. Maybe even a little uncomfortable, just like earlier. Basically, it was all three.

I didn't know what to think of it.

I had told him the truth, and I knew he'd believed me about there not being anything going on between us.

What I was though, was glad that I'd told Boogie how I'd felt. I hated keeping secrets from him, but I knew he understood why I'd done it.

I glanced at Zac to see if he was tense or awkward, but he only looked determined. I'd seen him make the same facial expressions before on game days.

Boogie said something to the friend beside him before coming over, his mouth forming a flat line. He stopped directly in front of us, expression calm but careful and totally like my cousin.

Only then did Zac let go of my hand and go straight into giving him a hug that my cousin returned. A normal one. Easy. Slapped him on the back and everything. It relieved me.

But as he pulled away, my old friend set both hands on my cousin's shoulders. "You know I love you," Zac said steadily.

And my cousin nodded seriously, his face grave. "I know. You know I love you too."

Only these two could tell each other they loved each other like it was the most natural thing in the world. I'd always loved it. And I understood why Zac wouldn't put anything between them. I really did. Who was I to mess this up?

I really was doing the right thing. I just needed time to get over it—time and maybe a distraction. Maybe I could reschedule my trip to Orlando and make an extended vacation out of it.

"You're the brother I never had and never wanted," Zac kept going, bringing my focus back to him and the way he was looking down at my cousin.

That had Boogie grinning.

And it was me who felt a little uneasy. Was this sounding like a breakup, or was I imagining it? I had to be imagining it. I'd seen marriages less supportive than these two's friendship.

"I love you, all right?" Zac repeated.

My cousin sighed.

What the hell was he sighing for?

Oh God, I had a bad feeling in my stomach. "Why are you two acting like you're splitting up? Nothing happened, Boogie, I swear."

"Who says we're splittin' up, darlin'?" Zac asked, dropping a hand from my cousin's shoulder to reach over and take my forearm gently, his rough thumb grazing along the inside of it.

"We're not breaking up," my cousin confirmed before focusing back on his best friend with a deep breath and then a long, drawn-out sigh that came straight out of his soul. I was pretty positive even his shoulders slumped for a second, but he set them back into place, and it just made me feel again like they were breaking up. "Say what you have to say so I can move on with my life," Boogie told him, tipping his chin up and everything. "Is this why you've been calling me every day to talk about nothing?"

He was calling him every day?

Zac didn't hesitate. "Yeah. I should've told you when I realized it. I didn't expect it to happen, but it did," he told him steadily. "I fought it, I swear, but I didn't have a goddamn chance, Boog. It was like fightin' the inevitable. Tryin' to fight a brick wall. I swear on Paw-Paw's life, I had zero chance. She came up behind me when I wasn't expectin' it and gave me the beatin' of a lifetime."

"Somebody beat you up?" I asked in confusion, looking him over but finding no bruises on any of his exposed skin.

Boogie said nothing.

I literally had no clue what the fuck they were talking about and wanted some more context clues so I could figure it out.

Zac, though, didn't let anything stop him. He licked his lips and set his own shoulders firmly down, preparing for... something. "I don't wanna keep tryin' to fight it anymore. I can't. I know you'd want the best for me, and this is it, and I think you know that." He took a breath and said very carefully a sentence that sent my heart into overdrive. "My whole life, I've felt like I was missin' somethin', tryin' to find somethin'. I don't know how to explain it, and now, it feels like I found it, Boog. It was right in front of my damn face all along."

My cousin stared at him, and his thinking face was on. It

took him a moment, his breathing long and deep, before tilting his head toward the ceiling and eventually saying, "I want to say you could've told me all this over the phone, but I'd be lying. I could tell for a while now there was something you wanted to tell me, but I was caught up with Lauren and the baby and let it go." He lowered his gaze and sighed again. "And I know you never had a chance. You never did. But we need ground rules."

"Okay."

Boogie's face went serious. "There's only one. You never talk about shit I don't want to hear. That's all I want; everything else I might worry about, I know I don't need to. We wouldn't be having this conversation unless you were totally sure you knew what you were doing."

Zac nodded solemnly.

My cousin looked at me, and then he smiled.

I frowned. "I don't know what you two dorks are talking about. At first, I thought it was me, and now I have no idea."

His smile just got that much bigger.

"No, I'm serious. What are you talking about?"

Boogie laughed then, erasing every trace of the pressure that had been on his cheekbones a second ago. "We're clearing things up."

Clearing what up? I elbowed Zac, who was still holding my forearm. "I'm not trying to mess anything up. I promise. I love you two, and each of you knows that, and I don't want this bromance to need therapy because I was being dumb."

My tall friend gave me a lopsided smile. "How were you bein' dumb?"

I eyed Zac since he'd asked the question. Then I looked at my cousin because he knew since I'd just explained it to him. Did I want to remind him how I felt about him? Absolutely not. But it didn't seem like I had a choice anymore, damn it. "For having feelings and making things weird, but I promise I already talked to Boogie, and I was going to tell you that there's nothing to worry about because I'll get over it in no time."

"Get over it?"

Why was Zac sounding choked?

My cousin smirked, then snorted and turned, saying over his shoulder, "Bianca was saying earlier that she's going to get some dogs or cats and be a cougar someday. You're on your own with that. Thanks for dropping by for a whole minute to see me. You're a real friend."

That had Zac snorting all over again. "I'll see you tomorrow."

"Whatever you say." My cousin laughed once more, going straight for the lane again, shaking his head.

"What was that about?" I muttered to the one still holding my forearm, confused. "Who beat the shit out of you?" Had he... started dating someone? Had he started seeing someone in the last *two weeks*?

It was Zac's turn to laugh as he tugged on my arm, taking a step back. The dark circles under his eyes were more apparent as he tipped his head down to look at me, another big smile on his face. "I was talkin' about you, kiddo."

For a moment, it felt like I fell through time and space before I croaked, "Me?"

He nodded, tugging on my arm to follow, and I did... mostly because I could barely feel my legs and I was beginning to question whether this was real or not. "Yeah, you. Who else?"

He was leading me toward the exit, which I guessed wasn't weird or unheard of. He just wanted some privacy? To talk to me about...

Hold on.

I repeated some of the word choices they'd used during their conversation and thought about them some more as Zac pushed through the doors, holding one open for me before letting it shut behind us. I'd been so worried about them being upset with each other that I'd been mostly focused on each word they used rather than the whole message.

But now....

"Zac?" I asked as he led me toward his car.

"Yeah?"

He beeped the locks and opened the passenger side door too. I stopped beside the car, tipping my head up to meet those blue-blue eyes that seemed to sparkle even under the streetlights. He was smiling down, slowly and lazily. He didn't look nervous or even that tired anymore. Zac looked... well, he looked alive and bright and... determined and relieved.

"What was the inevitable you were talking about?" was the first thing I managed to ask.

His expression—that one that made me feel like there was nothing in the world that could ever be that bad if he was near—went nowhere as his hand took mine once more. Possessive and protective and steady, he took the whole thing. He tilted his head to the side, that very Zac smile making me rise up to the balls of my feet in anticipation. "You, kiddo, what else?"

I almost fainted.

And he noticed my almost faint because he laughed all rich and perfect. "Come on. Get in the car. We gotta have a chat."

I got in the car, mostly because I wasn't sure my knees would hold me up much longer. Also because I wasn't sure I wouldn't swoon, smack my head on the side mirror, and forget everything that had just happened. At least the parts I could comprehend.

And this fool was still smiling as he shut the door after I got in, and he was smiling as he climbed behind the wheel and turned on the car. All while I reeled. Stricken. Stuck.

Amazed. Terrified. Confused too.

Mostly confused.

He... he....

I took a breath in through my nose and put my thoughts in order as he turned on his car and turned toward me.

"Zac?"

He looked so earnest. "Yes, darlin'?"

I couldn't look at his face while I asked this, so I focused on the screen of his console as I asked in a steady voice, "Do you... do you...?" I could barely think the words, much less say them out loud. "Were you...?" I couldn't fucking stop stuttering. Because I couldn't comprehend what he'd been trying to imply.

He made a soft sound in through his nose. "Did you steal my damn heart, run off with it, and say I'll see ya later? 'Cause the answer to that is yes."

I really was on the verge of passing out, and it took everything in me to whisper, "No, for real."

"I'm bein' for real," he replied easily, one corner of his mouth curled up into a lazy smile. "I've thought about it. I'm thinkin' it happened sometime between you givin' me that awful pep talk about old Zac kickin' this Zac's ass and you throwin' bombs at me, I'd say."

He was saying....

He was trying to tell me....

I forced my eyelids not to blink, thought about it a little more, and asked again. "Zac?"

He leaned back into the door and crossed his arms over his chest, looking smug and good and still relieved. "Yes, sweetheart?" he asked with so much love and patience, I didn't know what to do with it even more.

"Why are you really here?"

"'Cause I love you," Zac answered.

I glanced away again. I wasn't going to look at him. I

couldn't. But I would tell him the truth. "You literally said to me that you didn't think you would ever fall in love because you'd never be able to trust someone enough to do that," I admitted, willing my heart to be reasonable. To be smart. To not jump the fucking gun and start imagining all kinds of shit when it damn well knew better.

He made an amused sound that only made my heart drop. "True enough."

I blinked and turned toward him again.

"But...." He trailed off.

I shoved my fingers under my thighs.

"You're not just 'somebody,' are you, kiddo?"

The fuck did he just imply?

He kept talking. Because he couldn't read my mind. His arms uncrossed, and he sat up straight in the small interior of his fancy car, his head millimeters from grazing the roof as he aimed that gaze straight at me with the strength of a thousand lighthouses. "And there was no fallin' for you, Bianca. I just did. Just do, you know? Love you, I mean. It was like I told Boog, you snuck up behind me when I wasn't lookin' and beat the livin' shit out of me 'til I didn't have a choice but to see you. See who you've become. See who you'll be. You amaze me, kiddo. You're gonna take over the world one day, and I wanna be there to see it. I wanna be there to help you any way I can. Lovin' you is the easiest thing I've ever done, and it's the easiest thing I'm ever gonna do. I just know it." He paused, and his eyebrows went up at the same time his shoulders did. "I've never said that like that to anybody before, and I was a little scared, but I figured nothin' could be worse than not sayin' it and you leavin', and wow... that actually felt right. Real right."

I held my breath, and I'd swear I could hear my heartbeat. Maybe even his too. And right then, I felt like he could read my mind because he smiled at me, and it was tender and different and something I would remember for the rest of my life.

"I've missed the hell out of you," he said, staring right at me.

Yep. I was going to pass out.

"Zac?" I whispered.

"Yes, darlin'?"

If I didn't throw up, I was going to faint. Maybe throw up and then faint. Maybe shit myself too. Who knew?

But I was nobody's coward. And I had to know. I had to. "Are you sure you... really feel that way about me?" I asked, swallowing. "Enough to say that? To Boogie? Because there's friend-love and there's—"

His hand settled on my thigh. Tilting my chin up, we made eye contact. "More sure than I am of anything." He gave my leg a squeeze. "More sure than I am of myself. That's what I wanted to tell you that day you left, but I didn't know how. I'd never wanna make you pick, and I guess I was worried you'd pick Boogie. By the time I got home though, ready to tell you to gimme some time to sort things out, you were gone."

I flicked myself on the chin just to make sure I wasn't imagining it. I wasn't. It stung.

And Zac saw it because he chuckled, his smile warm and eternal as his fingers moved to slide through mine. "I didn't wanna risk ruinin' what I got with Boogie, Bibi, but these last two weeks without you... I've been miserable. I wanted you back. I missed every single thing about you. And I had to think about what I had to offer you when you've got so much already goin' on. Today I finally did the last thing I needed to before I could talk to you about it all. Before I felt like I could deserve to try."

I pressed my lips together for about a split second, my nose tingling. My eyes burning. My soul screaming.

"Bibi?"

"Yes, Snack Pack?"

"Are you gonna ask if I'm sure I'm crazy about you?"

This idiot.

That finally had me digging in deep to figure out how I felt. And there was only one answer I could give him. "No, I wasn't planning on it. Why wouldn't you be?" I joked.

And I meant it.

All the little signs... the ones I'd ignored or taken to be something else—friendship, it had been a deep-rooted, immovable friendship—had been there along the way.

Like my cousin had said, he wouldn't say something and he wouldn't be here if he wasn't completely serious. I knew Zac as a jokester as much as I knew him as the man who usually had incredible self-discipline and dreams bigger than anything. He was a man who earned people's friendship and devotion.

He knew what he wanted out of life more often than he didn't. But sometimes we all just needed a little push. Whether it was a gentle one or a hard shove was the question though.

And his smile in that moment was as wide as Texas. "And here I was thinkin' I'd have to make you a list of reasons why I am," he said with amusement, with so much affection it threatened to break my heart in half.

But only threatened, because I didn't spook easily. I was used to being given these tiny microscopic chances and running with them. All I ever needed in anything was an opportunity and my greedy ass would take it all.

Because he cared for me.

He was here on this night, before his game, because he'd missed me.

Because he said he loved me.

Because I mattered.

They were all things I had known but in a different way. A very different way. And I had wanted this so badly, I had just never seriously hoped of thinking it was a possibility.

But of course it was. It should have always been. He could do a hell of a lot worse than me.

"Nah," I told him, reaching across the console and booping him on the nose with my free hand even though it shook. "I believe you."

And just as quickly as that subtle joy had risen inside of me, it went away.

Because I remembered.

I remembered what the hell had driven me to come all the way here. To spend two weeks looking at apartments. To have spent my Thanksgiving missing him. To have my favorite people badgering me in my sister's kitchen.

My mood dropped just. Like. That.

I drew my hand back like he'd burned me, and his happy expression instantly disappeared. "What is it?"

Tucking my hand back beneath my leg, I told myself to be an adult and just... say it. "You're being all nice and sweet to me and saying all this, and... and... it's bullshit."

"What's bullshit?"

"This. What you're saying."

That blue-eyed gaze narrowed. "No, it's not."

I nodded a little sarcastically, a little mean. "Well, *yeah,* it kind of is."

"Tell me why you think that."

"Because... two, three weeks ago, you let some girl sit on your lap and push her titties in front of your face. If that's how you think you're supposed to love someone, then you're doing something wrong. I know you said you're new to it, but you're not dumb."

He blinked once. "No, I didn't."

"Yes, you did. I saw the picture, Zac."

His forehead creased, and he was straight-up frowning as both of his hands held mine. That handsome Disney prince face was pulled into a deep frown, probably the deepest frown I'd ever seen on him. "No, I didn't."

He was denying it.

I eyed him, knowing in my bones that he wouldn't lie. Not to me. Not over something like this. I knew it.

So what the hell did that mean? I knew what I'd seen. I hadn't imagined that shit. I'd seen the date she posted it.

"I did no such thing, darlin'. I don't even know what you're talkin' about. I haven't had any girls anywhere near my lap in... I don't know how long. Forever." His frown got even more fierce. "Not since before you showed up. Longer than that."

I wanted to frown at him or think this was bullshit or at least claim that it was, but... I knew this person. I knew him well. Better than anyone.

I looked at his face, at his handsome, perfect face, looking confused and worried, and that sharp edge of jealousy and anger wavered big-time.

"What picture are you talkin' about?"

I held my breath a little. "This woman posted a picture of herself sitting on your lap."

"Who?"

"I don't know. Some girl on Picturegram."

He didn't even seem to think about it. "Show me."

I thought about it, pondered it and shook my head. "I didn't save it or anything, old man. I'm not a masochist. It came out the day after your friends showed up. Trevor saw it too."

He thought about it. "The day I went over to Amari's? After we hung out with Aiden and Vanny?"

Went over to Amari's? "Yes." Yes to the time we hung out with Aiden, Vanessa, and their kids. But Amari's?

Zac was still thinking about it even as he shook his head. "Bibi, we watched film at his place. I went to the store to buy some new underwear and went to his place right after. That's why he called while we were with Van and the kids, to invite us over. I asked you, remember? His mom made us food. I was tired and passed out on the couch. His mom was the only woman there, and she'd probably slap me if I asked her to sit in my lap."

I felt like an idiot.

"Whatever you saw, darlin', it had to be an old picture. Is that what Trev called me rantin' over? Tellin' me I needed to get my head outta my ass before I ruined my life?" He reached forward and took my hand, his fingers big and strong around mine. "I swear it had to be an old one. These girls take pictures and hoard 'em for a while and randomly share them. Sometimes they'll even ask for a picture, you'll say yes, and then they'll come and sit on your lap without askin'."

I stared at him. He pressed his mouth together as his gaze bounced from one of my eyes to the other.

"Cross my heart," he told me, his face serious. "You know I wouldn't lie to you, don't you?"

I stared at his face, at those blue-blue eyes for so long I was pretty sure he was squirming.

His fingers were warm around mine. "Bianca... I know I've done some things in the past I wish you didn't know about, but I'm not like that anymore."

Well, shit.

"Yeah, yeah. I know you wouldn't lie to me. The picture just looked recent; that's why I thought.... You're always surrounded by girls, Zac. You used to go out all the time. It just seemed to make sense."

"I used to, yeah, but I don't want that anymore. Only one thing I want. One thing that makes me happier than a million other people combined," he said. "I deleted all those numbers weeks ago. I changed my number so nobody would be callin' in the first place. I didn't wanna give you a reason to second-guess me. I want you to know I'm in this for real. None of that other shit has ever mattered. But you always have. Always will."

I took a deep breath.

"It had to be an old picture, I promise," he swore. "I know you believe me."

I did, and maybe in a way, I should be glad that I knew so much about him. There weren't secrets left between us. There wasn't a reason to doubt this scary thing that seemed like it was pulled straight out of my dreams and dumped into my lap. Him loving me wasn't new.

But this different kind of love *was*. Love 2.0. More like Love 5.0.

I had no reason to doubt it. Or him.

And I sure as hell wasn't going to run.

Zac loved me. *Me.*

And... I was going to milk this shit for the rest of my life, if I could. Maybe I hadn't been around the block like he had, but that didn't mean I wasn't going to terrorize him. Because I was. Because I could.

"I do," I agreed. I lifted my chin and curled my fingers around his, ready for this. I'd been ready for this forever. "Just to make sure though, if some guy posts a picture of me sitting on his lap in a year, it'll be an old one too, okay?"

His fingers jerked, and I just about laughed at the incredulous face he made. "What guy?"

"Some guy I don't remember. I've met a lot of them, so...." I glanced at him with a smirk.

He wasn't smiling.

But I was.

"You're not funny."

"I'm super funny."

It was his turn to side-eye me. "You believe me then?"

I groaned. "Boy, I said yes. If you want me to pretend like I don't and pitch a fit for a second, I will though."

Just like *that*, his smile was back, out and beautiful and everything in the world. "You'll stomp your feet for me?"

I nodded, feeling a smile creep over my face. "Just for you. But I swear to God, someone puts their titties in your face and you don't push them away immediately, I'll kill you, then bring you back to life and kill you again. I've already been cheated on, and I'm not doing that again."

"I'd never do that. Never." He smiled, and it grew and grew, and the next thing I knew, he was leaning forward and taking my hand, pulling it toward him. Pulling me toward him. "Come here."

"Why?" I asked him even though I wasn't putting up a fight.

"Because," he said as he kept on tugging me to him.

I had a hand on his thigh as I said, "For the record, you told me you were crazy about me before you even kissed me. What if I don't like the way you kiss?"

He laughed with his face inches away from mine. "Is that what you're worried about?"

"I mean..." I shrugged, teasing the hell out of him. It was like the best of both worlds. "What if?"

He shook his head, still grinning. "You're a real sweet pain, kiddo." His breath brushed my lips. "Let's see. If you don't like it, I'll try again until I get it right. I ain't scared of practicin'."

I was laughing when he leaned over, closing the distance between us.

And I was still laughing when his lips brushed mine.

Finally.

But in that following moment, they were kissing me. They were mine, and I knew that he was mine. Because he always had been. We'd just lost each other for a while, but we wouldn't again.

His mouth was warm as it touched my own. Softly. Lightly.

I'd been waiting for this shit forever. My teeth caught his bottom lip, tugging on it gently, making him suck in a breath.

Reaching for him as I kneeled on my seat and hovered over the center console, I slid a hand through his hair, cupping the back of his head in my palm, and opened my mouth, kissing him slowly back, like there was nowhere else I would rather be. No one else I would rather kiss.

Because there wasn't.

He pulled back just a little. "Who taught you to kiss like that?" he asked, his voice gruff.

"People," I joked, brushing my lips across his.

He grunted. And Zac... he responded. Big-time.

His hand went for my cheek, the other one went to palm my nape over my hair, and he opened his mouth, his tongue instantly brushing against mine, lightly the first time, then deeper the second. He was warm and sweet, and I loved everything about the way he tasted. Loved the soft way he moved his tongue against mine, the way he held me there.

He took his time. Savoring. Lingering.

His lips took my bottom one between his, sucking it gently before brushing his tongue against mine again.

I really, really loved the way he kissed my top lip before doing it all over again.

Zac kissed and kissed like he had all day. Like there was nothing else he would rather do either, and he gave my tongue a little suck as he held my face in those tremendous, outstanding palms. Warm, firm lips teased the corners of my mouth and chin before taking mine once more.

He loved me, and if he hadn't already basically said the words, I would have been able to tell.

Because no one had ever kissed me like this before, and I had a feeling no one else ever would.

No, it wasn't a feeling. It was knowledge. He was my past, but he was going to be my future too.

Zac hummed deep in his throat, the sound soothing and so pleased. His lips grazed the edge of my chin as he murmured, almost drowsy, "Mmm, darlin'. You're gonna be the damn end of me; I can already tell."

I pulled back a little and smiled up at him, licking my lips because, *yeah,* I could kiss him all day. He was good at it. Great at it.

But I wasn't going to tell him that.

"Yeah, I think we need a little more practice first," I told him instead.

His chuckle made me smile against his warm, wonderful mouth. "Yeah? You think so?"

I nodded, leaning forward to kiss his chin, loving the feel of the bristles of his facial hair on my lips and the way his thigh felt under my hand. "Practice makes extra perfect."

He booped me on the nose. "Extra perfect sounds like fun."

I took him in then as his face hovered so close, his hand stroking my shoulder all the way down to my arm.

"Are we good for now?" he asked.

"For now?"

"Yeah, we still gotta talk about a couple other things."

We did?

"And I wanna show you somethin'."

I made my eyes go wide. "I want to see it, but okay, perv."

Zac burst out laughing. "I wasn't talkin' about that... but that too."

I snorted, and he laughed.

"You're comin' to the game, right?"

"*Yes.*"

"And you'll let me show you somethin' after?"

I held my breath and nodded before leaning toward him and brushing my lips over his one more time. Because I could. Because he wanted me to. And if I had doubted it, the low moan in his throat and the hand he used to cup the back of my head would have confirmed it for me.

So I told him, "Yes."

His lips took mine once more, and then he whispered, "Good."

CHAPTER TWENTY-FOUR

"What in God's name is on your face?"

I fully turned around and smiled up at Trev in the stands behind us, seated at the end of the row that Ms. Travis and Paw-Paw were in.

I'd already given Paw-Paw and Ms. Travis a hug. Boogie had texted me when he'd been on his way with them, and I'd headed up to wait for their arrival, before leading the way back down the steps in front to try and break Paw-Paw's fall if he happened to lose his balance.

The older man had laughed nice and deep when he'd realized it was me standing there to greet them.

Raising both hands, I twirled the fake blue mustache that Connie had glued to my upper lip right before we'd left her house. "I don't know, but I like it," I told Trevor.

The man sighed and took in my sister when she turned around. Her whole face was covered with blue paint—instead of red like mine—and she had a killer white mustache that curled at the ends halfway across her cheeks. I'd called it an old prospector mustache. Her husband, Richard, on the other hand, had a white face with a red mustache. We were triplets.

It was only Boogie, who was sitting in our row, who didn't have anything on his face. He was wearing a TRAVIS jersey though, tucked into his perfectly pressed jeans. Connie and I had giggled at him, and he'd given us the middle finger.

Trevor shook his head and might have even rolled his eyes, but it just made me grin. I could tell by then that it wasn't an ugly eye-rolling. It was his *"I guess I can put up with you"* eye roll.

Basically, he really, really liked it.

Connie whacked me in the arm then, and I turned to glance toward Boogie, who I hadn't really gotten a chance to talk to since the night before when we'd last seen each other. We'd only managed a hug when I'd met up with him by the concession stands because I'd gotten too busy talking to Paw-Paw. He was staring forward, and I nudged him with my elbow. "Boog?"

Was he thinking about Zac and me?

My cousin nudged me right back with his elbow. "I'm good," he answered, still facing forward, like he knew exactly what I was wondering.

"Are you sure?" I whispered so that my sister, hopefully, couldn't hear. I wasn't sure what I would do if he said he wasn't fine, but... I could only hope that he hadn't been lying last night.

I'd gone over the pieces of the conversation that he and Zac had had, at least the parts that managed to sink in, and it had kept me up for a few hours once we'd gotten back to Connie's. Boogie had seemed fine after I'd gone back into the bowling alley once Zac left, but I hadn't wanted to push his buttons more than we potentially might have already. My mouth had tingled for a while after he'd kissed me goodbye. Zac and I had sat in his car for at least half an hour while he told me about CJ—he had made a halfway decent cake while I'd been away—and some other gossip about a couple other players I'd met the night of the Halloween party. He admitted that *Trevor* was the one who bought Gunner out of the gym after I brought up Deepa's news. Apparently the gym was a good investment.

He even said the Enzo guy—the man who had been at the Halloween party with Jessica—had reached out to him and apologized for her actions. They were married, but apparently not for much longer. There had to be more to that story, but Zac hadn't asked. I didn't blame him.

If anything, sitting in his car and talking to him had just cemented the fact that not only was he my best friend, but that I loved him with my entire heart.

And if he loved me too—which it absolutely seemed like he did—then I needed to hold on to that with both hands and never let it go. Maybe it was all new and fresh and wonderful, and maybe I should have been in total shock—I was only half in it—but the truth was, I saw it. I could feel it. So what was I going to do? Not accept it?

Hell nah.

But, more than anything, I loved Boogie, and Boogie loved me. I didn't want to pick, and I hoped he would never ask it of me, especially not when he loved the same person I did.

My cousin looked at me over his shoulder, giving me a smile that *was* a little reluctant but only a tiny bit. "I mentally prepared for the possibility of this when you were seventeen," he admitted. "Then you two stopped talking, and I forgot, and I've been so busy, I forgot about it. I didn't pay attention."

I blinked. "You did?"

"Yes." He nudged me again. "He's always loved you and worried about you, B. Same as you." He shrugged and rolled his eyes before sliding me another look and another nudge. "I wasn't sure it would happen, you know, but even Laurie brought it up. Mamá Lupe said something right before she passed away too. I don't remember what you two were doing, you were painting your room or something, and he was in there, and we could hear you laughing, I think, and she told me not to be jealous—I wasn't jealous, B. I was never jealous of the both of you. Never. And she said some things are just meant to be or something like that.

"I thought about it back then. I'd watch you two, and yeah, you got along so well. I thought, if something happened, it would be a long time from then, and that maybe nothing would ever happen anyway. He didn't look at you like that back then, but I knew how you felt. And I guess I've thought about it a little since yesterday when you told me how you felt and... I guess Mamá Lupe was right. Some things are meant to be. What were the chances that he happened to be in Houston? He had almost gone to Dallas instead to train. That had been the plan up until the day before he left, and then he changed his mind."

Boogie's dark gaze moved toward me, and he gave a little laugh. "You never wanted me to talk about it, but he asked about you all the time, Peewee. Even when he thought you didn't want to be his friend anymore, he asked how you were doing. He never forgot about you. I remember, for a while, his feelings were hurt when you lost touch, but then both of you went off and did your own thing and it seemed to be fine." His shoulders went up. "Maybe he didn't come into my life for me. I'm starting to think maybe it was for you."

I was going to need to lie down, pronto. But there wasn't anywhere clean, so I was going to have to keep it together even as my world rocked a bit right then.

"Or maybe he was supposed to be in both of our lives."

Boogie smiled.

"But are you okay with it?" I asked him quietly. "Because if you're not...." What the hell would I do? Beg? Plead?

"Stop." Boogie gave me another long look like he thought I was being a pest. "I know what he's done. I know who he is. And I know you too. And I guess, if I could've picked someone for you, it wouldn't be Zac."

"Who would it be?"

"Jesus."

I leaned against him as I snorted.

He nudged me again with his elbow, but the part of his mouth I could see was curled up into a smile. "But I guess he'd be my second choice. I know he loves you. I saw it with my own eyes the last few times we hung out. I didn't want to see it, but I did. I do. Then he wore that shirt earlier, and if I'd had any doubts, they would've gone away then."

He saw it?

But wait... "What shirt was he wearing?"

My cousin blew out a breath as he pulled his phone out of his pocket. A moment later, he had the TSN app open and an ad was playing. "Give it a sec," he warned me when I glanced at him. It was a short pregame video, and a second later, the footage moved to players entering the stadium.

The second one they showed was the only one who mattered.

And when I saw what Boog was talking about, my knees went weak.

He had on a T-shirt I had never seen before—a heather blue one with huge white font on it that said, "THE LAZY BAKER."

Me. He was wearing me.

"You see?" he asked before hip bumping me. "But for real, I was serious about that ground rule, so you two need to figure it out."

"Thank you for being okay with it," I managed to murmur while I kept watching his cell phone screen until they focused on another player arriving.

Had he made the shirt? Had he ordered it? It wasn't like it mattered, but I couldn't help but feel this incredible, overwhelming shot of straight-up love filling my veins at what he'd done.

And he hadn't said anything.

"What am I going to do? Tell you both not to be happy? Loving you, B, is the easiest thing in the world. He never had a chance," Boogie said, getting me to lift my face up to look at him and that face I really did love so much. I set aside Zac and his shirt for a minute. "Some things do good by themselves, but some things do better together, like cheese and burgers."

I nodded at him, keeping my eyes wide so that I wouldn't tear up still. "Cheeseburgers are pretty amazing."

My cousin grinned. I shoved his shoulder a little, and he shoved mine right back.

"I told Liz that night after you dropped him off at the hospital that it was only gonna be a matter of time."

Boogie and I both turned around to the row above us to find Paw-Paw with a smile on his face. It was him that had made the comment. Liz was Zac's mom's first name.

"Paw-Paw," Ms. Travis groaned from her spot beside him. She had a temporary tattoo on her cheek with Zac's number 4 on it, and his jersey on under her jacket.

The older man put his hands palm down on his chest, covering the White Oaks logo of the thick jacket he had on. "I did say it. I'm not lyin'. The last time Zac came by and he told us *all* about Bianca, didn't I say it again?"

She blew out a breath and glanced at me with a faint smile. "You did."

Oh man. I hadn't even thought about being quiet or telling Paw-Paw or Ms. Travis about... us—not when it was just yesterday that he'd said anything.

Maybe Zac had wanted to tell them? Maybe... he didn't want them to know?

Nah.

Well, too late now anyway.

Folding my hands together, I looked up at both of them with hope in my heart. "Are you both okay with me and Zac seeing each other?"

"You're going to be doing more than seeing each other," my fucking sister scoffed under her breath as she pretended to look toward the field, but I didn't take my eyes away from the two Travis family members. I kicked her in the leg instead.

"Yes," Ms. Travis confirmed, that faint smile turning into a fierce one. "I need help keepin' that boy in line. I hope you're up for it."

I was up for it, and I told her so with a laugh.

A second later, my phone vibrated from inside of my pocket, and I took it out, wondering who would be texting me. Deepa?

The name on the screen had me freezing.

ZAC THE SNACK PACK: You make it?

I smiled down at my screen.

Me: Yes. Paw-Paw and your mom are behind us.

Me: Connie glued a mustache to my face, by the way.

I got a response almost immediately.

ZAC THE SNACK PACK: A mustache??

Me: A blue one. I think Trevor might have done the sign of the cross when he saw it.

It showed he was typing up a reply before I'd even hit Send on my second text.

ZAC THE SNACK PACK: I've always had a thing for mustaches

I laughed.

Me: You're in for a treat then. It's a good one.

Me: Also, you're going to do great today. I'm so proud of you and so is everyone else.

I almost expected not to get a reply from him, but my phone vibrated after about a minute with a new text.

ZAC THE SNACK PACK: In that case, I'm gonna try even harder not to let you all down.

My heart squeezed.

Me: You could never let us down. And even if you don't win and the team doesn't go to the playoffs, you're still invited to go to Disney World with me once I reschedule my trip.

ZAC THE SNACK PACK: You're only supposed to go there if you win it all.

Me: You're winning just by being where you are right now.

The typing icon stayed on the screen for almost a minute before I got another text.

ZAC THE SNACK PACK: You right.

ZAC THE SNACK PACK: Follow Trev after the game, okay?

ZAC THE SNACK PACK: Love you kiddo

"Love you, kiddo," he said like he'd said it a hundred times before.

Which he had.

But I read it in his text then. The difference. I wasn't sure how I could ever explain the nuance, but it was there, as different as day and night.

He loved me. *Me.* And he meant it.

I thought about that until he was running out onto the field with his teammates—some of whom were my friends now too—to play another big, important game that most commentators had going in favor of the Three Hundreds because they'd had a slightly better season.

Zac was too nice to ever rub anybody's face into anything —well, most of the time—but I hoped they cried silent tears when the White Oaks won.

I stood there in the stands with my cousin on one side, and my sister and Richard on the other, and Zac's Paw-Paw, mom, and manager directly behind me, cheering just as hard as everyone in the stadium as the game prepared to start. And we stood like that for a long time.

For the entire game.

Because it was stressful as hell. The Three Hundreds were out to prove a point. Unfortunately for them, so were the White Oaks.

For three quarters, the teams were tied nearly neck and neck. The Three Hundreds would score and then the White Oaks would do the same. Every fan in the stadium screamed at the field over tackles and fumbles and interceptions.

And then, with less than fifty-five seconds left on the clock, Zac and Amari did it.

They scored.

They had won.

THEY WON.

And just about everyone went apeshit.

Boogie and I hugged, and I know for sure that Connie and I held each other as we jumped up and down. Richard and I grabbed each other by the shoulders and yelled in each other's faces so loud the earplugs I'd slipped on at the start of the game didn't do much. I hugged Paw-Paw and Ms. Travis too. He had tears in his eyes, and she was crying, so I hugged them again.

It was then that Trevor grabbed me by the wrist and made a face to tell me to follow him. I pointed at the Travis family, but Paw-Paw waved me off to go alone. Trev led me through a maze of people, around a barricade, down some stairs, and through a checkpoint as White Oaks fans were going insane at their win.

It was one step closer to the *playoffs*.

"Bianca!" a voice yelled from around the security guard.

It was Zac, holding his helmet in one hand as one player after another walked by him, slapping him on the shoulder, hooting and yelling as they went down the dark tunnel that we had approached. His face was pink, and his hair was matted to his head, but he looked happy and alive and amazing.

What I would remember for the rest of my life was meeting him halfway and how he held me with his arms banded right under my butt after he pulled me into them, grinning so wide as I hugged him and kissed his cheeks and his mouth and his cheeks some more.

"I knew you were going to do it! I fucking knew you were going to do it!" I told him, pressing my mouth against his damp ear so that I wouldn't have to yell in his face from the deafening noise of the fans still going crazy.

He pulled back a little and smiled at me, the biggest smile to date, probably ever in existence. His hand moved, and he palmed my cheek as his gaze traveled over my painted face, that perfect grin still there. All for me.

"How do I look?"

He drew the pad of his finger over my fake mustache. "Like the best thing I've ever seen."

And then he kissed me again.

———

Hours later, after he'd had to let me go—after kissing my face a bunch more times even though I warned him about my face paint bleeding—and after one interview after another, Zac celebrated with his team in the locker room while the rest of us headed over to Trevor's. The Travis family, Connie and Richard, and Boogie waited for him there. We ate food that Trev had ordered and scarfed down celebratory cake. CJ went out with some of the other players on the team, but Zac didn't.

It wasn't until after Connie headed back to her hotel and Boogie had decided to drive back to Austin so he wouldn't leave Lauren alone for longer than necessary, that Zac grabbed my hand and asked if I wanted to go look at something with him. His mom and grandpa just smiled and waved us along.

I held up my promise and said yes.

Nothing could have prepared me for the three-and-a-half-hour drive that led us awfully close to Liberty Hill. I hadn't even realized how long we'd been in the car because we'd been too busy talking about the game and how incredible it had gone and all the other little things that had been said in the locker room before and afterward.

"Are you planning on driving me out to the middle of nowhere and dumping my body?" I asked as he took a sharp right turn onto a dirt road that I hadn't seen until the last minute.

"Not today. Maybe in sixty years," he said with a smile I barely caught the edge of thanks to the light from his dash.

My heart thumped like a little kid who just got told she was going to Disney—not that I knew from experience, but I could imagine. "Oh? Sixty years?"

His smile got even wider as he navigated us down the pitch-black street. "You play your cards right and maybe it'll be seventy."

I was too busy taking in the magnitude of his words to respond.

He glanced at me. "Too much?"

Too much? I squeezed my hands into fists and put them

under my thighs for the second time in two days, but this time, it was because... I didn't know what to do with them, not because I wanted to smack him. "No. It's just... I'm not used to it. It doesn't feel real, I guess."

"What doesn't feel real?"

"You. This. Everything." I laughed, feeling nervous all of a sudden. "I mean, I'm fine. I'm not complaining, but it's just... a lot to take in."

Zac reached across the console, and I took his hand, sliding my palm across his warm one.

"Just yesterday I thought I was going to need to go far away for a while to get over you, because there was no way I could keep going with you a few feet away and now—"

"And now we're pulling up to what I wanted to show you," he cut me off with a squeeze of his hand as he turned the car into a fenced-in property with a gate with horses on it.

I squinted through the side window, but it was too dark to see anything other than a white fence along the sides of the car. "Where are we?"

Up ahead, the headlights caught onto a two-story home circled by a handful of big trees.

I eyed Zac and caught him looking at me with a small smile on his face.

"Why do you look nervous?" I questioned.

"I'm not nervous."

"That's your nervous face, Snack Pack."

"It's not my nervous face," he tried to claim.

But it was his nervous face. What the hell did he have to be nervous about?

He slowly pulled the car to a stop along the gravel driveway and put it into park.

"Whose place is this?"

He snickered as he turned the car off. "So many questions. Come on. Come with me."

I shot him another look but opened the door and got out. He was already circling around the front and, again, putting his hand out toward me. I grinned at him, feeling nervous myself, and took it. "If we get arrested for trespassing, I'm blaming you, okay?"

He tugged me closer and pressed his mouth against my temple before leading me forward. Unable to see much as we headed toward the front door, I tripped on something and just barely kept from busting my ass when Zac pulled my arm up with a laugh too.

"You got those heels on again?"

"No! Maybe...." I laughed as I got my feet under me.

He pulled his phone out and flashed the screen toward the ground. Then he slowly looked back up at me. If I had any hopes he wouldn't recognize my shoes, they would've gone to hell with the look he sent me.

They were the same boots I'd worn the day we'd gone to the haunted house.

His mouth twitched.

I just blinked at him.

He blinked back.

"Are we going in or...?"

He shook his head, and he didn't need to say anything as we kept going to the front door and stopped there. Using his phone, he illuminated the doorknob, and I saw that there was a keypad above the knob. He pressed in a couple buttons, and it unlocked.

Zac shot me another glance as he opened the door and reached just inside, flicking the lights on. "Come on," he said.

So I went on. Zac led me through a doorway off the white-walled foyer and into an open area with a spacious living room on the left with a wall full of windows, and on the right was a big, big kitchen. The first thing I noticed was the double fridge, then the double ovens, an island with a beautiful white countertop, and a six-range oven with red knobs. And then there were the two-tone cabinets; the ones against the wall were white and the bottoms ones were navy.

"Oh wow," I said. "This place is awesome."

The fingers holding mine twitched. "You think?"

"Yeah. I mean, Trev's place is amazing, don't get me wrong, but this one...." I looked up at him with a smile. "Is this a vacation rental? I feel like we're not that far from Paw-Paw's house, but I would know if they remodeled their place."

"No, this isn't Paw-Paw's," he confirmed. Zac leaned his hip against the island, crossed his arms over his chest, and fucking said it. "I don't want you to move to Killeen."

I blinked. "Okay...."

Then he nodded. "You move, I'm goin' with you."

Andddd I froze. The weight of his words kicked me in the stomach. "What the hell are you talking about, Zac?"

"If you move to Killeen, to Morocco, to Orlando... I'm comin' with you."

My stomach cramped suddenly.

"I know you said this is all new and it doesn't feel real and it's too fast, but... Bibi, I've always known what I wanted. Maybe sometimes I don't think straight and I might fart around, but once I get my head on and decide on somethin', I'm gonna do it. And if I've learned anything the last couple weeks, it's that I don't wanna be without you. I'm so damn in love with you, kiddo, and I wanna be where you are."

He stood up straight suddenly and blazed those light blue eyes at me, his hands going to my wrists, where he swallowed them up, making them feel small. He took a deep breath, and his shoulders fell. "I know you've got your own life, and I know you've got these dreams and plans that you don't need me for, but I'll buy you the nicest kitchen I can afford if you don't leave." One hand let go of my wrist, but all he did was stretch my fingers out, and then he rubbed them. "If you stick with me. If you gimme a chance."

My heart was going to hammer out of my chest at this rate. In about three seconds. Maybe two.

"Zac—" I started to say.

"I don't know where the hell I'm gonna end up a month from now, or two weeks from now, and I'm sorry—"

"Zac," I tried to cut him off again.

He wouldn't let me. "But I bought this place. I closed on it two days ago. There's twenty-seven acres, plenty of room for us to build you a studio or somethin' like you said you wanted. I can't promise I won't have to move around in the near future, but I wanna have some place to come home to. Some place that won't go anywhere." He bit his bottom lip. "If you don't like somethin'—"

"Zachary James Travis," I whispered.

He stopped talking and raised his eyebrows. "Bianca Maria Brannen."

"You told me you loved me yesterday, and today you're telling me you bought a house? You bought me a house?"

His smile popped up out of nowhere. "I'm hopin' you'll let me live in it with you. We can save space and share a room."

Setting my hands on his shoulders, I went up to my tippy toes, letting the thrill of his words seep into my bones, overwhelming me, taking me over. This maniac. This... this amazing psycho. "You're never going to make things easy, are you?" I breathed.

"Nope." He smiled.

His palms cupped my cheeks a split second before that mouth—that *mouth*—settled on mine. Not with a peck like I'd been more than halfway expecting but like he was in this for the long run.

Because that's what felt like happened almost immediately after he took hold of me and brushed his tongue against mine.

I brushed mine against his right back, kneading his shoulders and upper arms as I held him close.

I couldn't believe it. Any of it.

His hands moved slowly as his mouth did the same after time. That warm mouth brushed softly against one corner of mine, then moved to my jaw, making a sweet, perfect line on it before trailing downward toward my neck. I tipped it to the side to give him better access, loving the way he just barely grazed the skin, so light and damp, it made goose bumps pop up on my arms and even the backs of my knees. And he must have sensed how much I loved what he was doing that he started softly sucking on that thin skin that seemed to have a line straight to my nipples.

I moaned and was grateful as hell there was no one else in the house.

That I could have him now all to myself on such an amazing day.

How could I not love him? Not want him? I'd wanted him for what seemed like chapters in my life. And now he was here, and his hands were on my hips as he sucked one spot after another along the column of my throat, convincing my nipples to go hard against his chest when I pressed myself closer to him.

That was when I felt it. The long, hard length that was trapped within his jeans, tucked up against his thigh while I flattened our bodies together.

Zac was hard. For me.

And I didn't need to use my hand to know that he wasn't just long, but he was thick too.

Shit.

He was hiding a monster in there, hidden along the strong but lean body of his.

I was going to climb him like a fucking tree.

Zac's head moved as he nipped and sucked at another spot on the other side of my neck, and I dug my fingers into his hips, pushing us even closer together, earning a groan from the man. He retreated, eyes dark and almost glazed over, and I knew I wasn't imagining the deep breathing his lungs were going through in the second before I lifted my chin up again and he kissed my lips more.

And then it was just hands.

My hands back on his upper arms, keeping him there, in front of me, close, then my hands back on his hips, holding them against my stomach as he ground his cock there. Then more hands, on my ass, then upper thighs, and he was hoisting me up. I wrapped my legs around his hips, so high up on him that the seam of my stretchy jeans was pressed against the hardest part of his lower abs as we kissed.

And made out.

And sucked and nipped at each of our mouths like the world would end if we didn't.

I ground my hips against his stomach, arms wrapped around his neck as he kissed me and kissed me some more.

And I wouldn't regret pulling back, breathing hard, to ask, "Is there a bed in this house?"

"The sellers left one, the headboard was too heavy to move it." He breathed hard against my jaw before pressing that soft, wet mouth right below my ear as he answered, "I don't wanna rush you into anything."

He wasn't rushing me into shit, and that's what I tried to tell him before angling my mouth back onto his, holding his head steady so he could keep kissing me.

He must have gotten my message because he started walking, holding me in his arms, a muscular arm banded around the middle of my back and the other underneath my ass, holding me in place as I rocked my hips, sure my underwear and jeans had to be wet by then, wanting friction and him and everything.

"I love you, Zac," I whispered against his ear when I had to pull back to catch my breath, and he hugged me even tighter to him, his face tucked against my throat as I realized he'd walked us into a small bedroom with a queen-sized bed.

He hummed into my shirt, squeezing me hard as he said in a quiet, calm voice, "You don't even know...."

"Do you want to get naked? Because I don't want to rush you either."

He burst out laughing. "You're gonna rush me?"

"Well, only if you want to. I'm sure you've gotta be tired."

Zac lowered me to the ground so fast, we both cracked up. He smiled before fisting the bottom of his shirt and pulling it over his head. I was still laughing as I did the same to mine, throwing it across the room like the further away it was, the fewer chances there were I'd have to put it back on any time soon.

"Seriously though," I told him, pausing while undoing my pants when reason really hit me. "I know you didn't get enough sleep, and we don't need to do anything."

Zac turned to me before taking a seat on the edge of the bed and scooting backward on it, shirtless and tan and so perfectly built, I didn't understand why no one had ever put him on an underwear ad. "We can do whatever you want, darlin'. Why don't you come here for a sec though while we think about it?"

Think about it?

I smirked and nodded.

And maybe I was jumping the gun a little by taking my pants off, but I did it anyway. It got me a little murmur from Zac that had me side eyeing him as I stood up straight. "What? I don't wear jeans when I go to bed."

He was sprawled on the mattress, his upper body propped

on the headboard—this thick engraved thing with horses and cowboys on it that was pretty epic—his smile lazy but different as his eyes moved over me standing there in my underwear. "Come here. Come sit with me."

He didn't have to tell me twice. I crawled up on the bed, totally conscious of the fact that I didn't look like a super-model or even a wannabe model in any way, but I didn't care. It had taken me half an hour to get the face paint off, and I was pretty sure there were streaks around the edges, close to my hairline. I had a cute bra on and underwear that didn't exactly match but were close enough.

But most importantly, I could see the tent in his jeans as one of his hands went down to the button and flicked it open. "What? I can't sleep with them buttoned up," he drawled with a wink.

I laughed as I made it between his outstretched and slightly spread legs when he reached for me, leading me in and onto him so my hip settled beside his, my legs between his own and my upper body mostly draped on top of his, our heads sharing the pillow he had cushioned between the head-board. His hand didn't waste time going to my hip and sliding up my ribs as he smiled at me, warmly and with so much love, he didn't need to use the word again or any time soon for me to understand.

His fingers tickled the sensitive skin of my ribs as he palmed them. "This is real nice," he said as his opposite hand went to my thigh, his thumb making a line.

I set my hand on his chest between his pectorals, feeling the light hair under my fingers. "This *is* nice," I agreed, lifting my head to give his throat a peck. His skin was warm and soft.

He turned and kissed me, pecks and slow, slow kisses that had his tongue dipping into my mouth, then open mouth kisses and more pecks. I wasn't even sure when it happened, but at some point, my hand was on his cheek as I held him there. And I definitely had no idea when his hand slid beneath my underwear, his palm cupping my bare ass cheek.

But the second I knew, the second I realized it, I arched against him, wanting him to touch me more as we kissed.

"Did I tell you already how nice this is?" he asked as he dragged his lips to my throat and gave me another slight suck there as his hand cupped the meatiest part of my butt. "How good you feel? How much I love lookin' at you?"

"No. You can always tell me again," I murmured, trailing my hand down between his pecs until it reached the center of his flat, hard abs before making a line back up.

Then he kissed me more, and I wasn't even sure when his hand lifted my right leg up even higher so that it was hitched over his opposite hip, my left leg still resting between his thighs. And the next thing I knew, I was leaning over him, kissing him, my leg restless as it rubbed against him and part of his jeans. His fingers moved, sliding lower and lower until the pads of them brushed over my lower lips, soft and almost feather-like from the back going to the front.

I moaned as they went back in the direction they'd come. I arched my hips, trying to get more of his touch as he brushed my seam, back to front and back to front, as I kept trying to follow him. Them. His fingers.

"You good with a little more?" he asked after tearing his mouth away, his lips millimeters from mine.

All I could do was nod, my words gone.

He nodded too, eyes hot, as one of his fingers finally grazed my seam, sliding between my lips and just slightly brushing my clit as he did so. It had to be his middle finger because his index and ring finger still grazed the sides of me before the tip of it dipped inside. Just the tip. He moved over my seam again, sliding and brushing, petting me. Then he slipped a little more of his finger in, groaning at what I was positive had to be me soaked.

Every pass, he dipped a little deeper until his whole finger was buried inside of me, and I was wiggling my hips, grinding against him as he pushed in and out, groaning. "Jesus Christ, Bibi," he whispered, pumping away.

I bit his neck, and his chest went rock hard.

He pulled out of me all of a sudden and squirmed down on the bed, meeting my eyes the entire time as he rasped, "Come here, darlin'."

I sat up and instantly straddled his stomach, thinking that was what he wanted. Because I knew what I wanted. I wanted to pull him out of his underwear, and I wanted to sit on him.

And that was exactly what I told him.

His groan was long and husky, and I had a feeling I was going to remember the way it sounded for the rest of my life. "You can sit on whatever you want," he whispered, "however long you want, darlin', but take a seat up here for a minute, would you?"

He patted his chest, mouth damp from our kisses, his face and neck and chest flushed.

And I knew what he meant.

He didn't have to tell me twice. I was aching and hot and wet, and I'd do anything he wanted for a minute. So I climbed up over him, nervous and excited as I threw my leg over his head, and he didn't wait. He tugged my underwear to the side. When I dropped my hips, he must have met me in the middle because his mouth was there. Tongue *there*. Everywhere.

I moaned from within my soul as he gently sucked one of my lips into his mouth and then the other before his tongue dipped into me like his finger had.

"Zac!" I hissed as his fingers curled over the tops of my thighs, holding me in place as he suddenly sucked on my clit.

Lifting my hips, I met his eyes as he looked up at me and asked, "Can I...?"

Those hands I loved went to my hips, lifted me up, and guided me down his chest and along his abs. I went for the zipper on his jeans as I leaned forward and kissed him. My hand snuck into his underwear, palming the hot, hard base that had his dick tucked along his thigh, and pulled him out. He let me slink down as I gripped him with both hands, taking in the deep pink penis that was the size I'd imagined.

My God. He was fucking big.

And all he let me do was wrap my mouth around the head once, give it a single suck, before he groaned, "Oh, darlin' baby, that's all I can take."

I pulled him out and trailed my lips along the length of him, inch after inch, as he lifted his hips and smiled down at me with a crazy look on his face.

"Don't embarrass me like that our first time, Bibi."

I laughed and licked right under the crown of his head once, earning me a lift of his hips. "What? You'd rather embarrass yourself inside of me?" I teased him.

He howled as his hands went to my upper thighs and he nudged me forward, closer to him. And I went.

"I don't have a condom, but if you wanna grind up and down my cock...."

I gripped him, laying him flat against that tanned stomach, and straddled his dick, sliding my seam along his hot organ. I didn't want to wait anymore. I didn't need to. "I don't think you need one, but if you want...."

He tipped his head back, the tendons in his throat flexing as I rubbed myself against him. "Swear on my life I got tested when I joined the team, and I haven't even looked at anybody since way before that, and I've never not used—"

I leaned over him, biting high up on his jaw before whispering, "Me neither, and I'm on birth control. You sure that's okay?"

His hands kneaded my thighs as I dragged my seam along his cock some more, leaving the thick base shiny and damp. "More than okay, honey, please...."

I slipped my hand between his dick and his stomach, raised him straight into the air, and took his tip inside of me. Just an inch, an inch that had both of us groaning before he sat up all the way and took my mouth. I lifted my hips before dropping back down and taking a little more, thankful I'd sucked him a little, even more glad that I'd rubbed my wetness onto him. Slowly but surely, I worked myself all the way down on him, teasing. Zac's hands were on my ass as I worked up and down his length until finally I was down on his thighs and he was stuffing me full in every direction. I gasped, and he groaned.

Then it was furious, me working my hips, Zac lifting his with those strong hip and ab muscles. My clit rubbed against his pubic bone. He lifted me up and brought my legs around his hips, and then those arms were working, lifting me up and dropping me down on him, halfway down and then back up. Most of the way down and then back up so only his head was inside. Over and over and over again.

I moaned into his ear, and he groaned and grunted, his palm cupping my nape as he held me there against him. Totally against him. Sweat dripped between his pecs, wetting my chest as I moved up and down.

I could feel it. I held my breath and ground my pelvis against him, right, right, there....

"Oh," I whispered, pressing my mouth against his neck as I cried out, my orgasm rolling through me, making me pulse around him.

"Shit," he hissed too, thrusting up faster and pushing me down harder and quicker.

"Zac," I cried, squeezing his shoulders tight, desperately.

He held me tight too, one arm banding around the middle of my back as I rode his lap. "Fuck! Fuck!" he choked, growled, and held me down on him as his hips slowed, his thrusts long, and I could feel him throbbing, pulsing warm and wet. The muscles in his thighs were clenching on and off, like they were spasming, and I was pretty sure I could feel his biceps popping too.

"Oh my God," he whispered into my hair, my face still fully shoved into his damp neck. "I think you might've killed me," he croaked. "My toes are crampin'."

I snorted, rubbing my hand up and down his spine as his cock twitched once more.

Zac slid his hand down my back, and if he hadn't been so sweaty, I would've been self-conscious about how sweaty I had to be too.

"I don't think I have any cum left in me," he whispered, still out of breath.

I pulled back just enough so I could look at his face, raising a hand to bury it in the back of his head, tangling my fingers through his hair. "Let me check."

He tossed his head back with a laugh. "No!"

He was grinning as his hands stroked my back, ribs, hips, and back up to my hair. He kissed me softly and sweetly as his gaze moved over my face before he hugged me again, chest to chest, his head tucking against the top of my head.

"Snack Pack?"

"Hmm?"

"I don't need fancy houses or sweet kitchens, okay? Or these grand gestures like you driving up the day before one of the biggest games of your life. I just want you. That's all I've ever wanted. I don't have these crazy expectations. You have so much pressure on you, and the last thing I want is to be one more thing you've got to work too hard at. Especially now, after today."

His body tensed under mine, but I felt his hand stroke my back slowly, taking his time. His breathing was a little uneven, but it was there, puffing against my hair. "Kiddo, look at me."

I sat up a little, just a little, so I could look at his face, and I smiled at him.

His hand stroked my ribs; his face was intent. "I'll tell you as many times as I need to because I know you haven't heard it enough and you deserve to, and because I like to say it too, all right? You're important. You matter to me more than any game. Any practice. Anything. Where you go, I go. You are never gonna be something I have to schedule in. You are never not gonna be a priority to me." He leaned forward and stroked my face then. "You've popped up into my life when I've needed you the most so far, and I'm gonna need you to stick around for the rest of it." He paused. "We're in this together, understand me?"

I understood. I understood big-time.

And somehow, I managed to pull one thought out of my head as I sat there looking at this man who I adored. That I would do anything for. Go anywhere for. "Does that mean... you'll go to Disney with me when I reschedule my trip?"

His smile softened, and he pressed his forehead against mine, those warm fingertips tickling my back. "You better believe it, kiddo."

CHAPTER TWENTY-FIVE

About two months later, he kept his word.

We went to Disney World.

Zac waved at people as he held up a trophy as big as my niece, and I got to ride in the float he was on beside the driver, sucking it all up.

The papers, analysts, and commentators called it the *"greatest upset in NFO history."* I called it Zac being cheap and knowing if he won the biggest game of his life, he could take me for free. Regardless of what anyone wanted to call it though, there was one thing I knew for sure.

Sometimes dreams really did come true.

One of mine just happened to be six foot three, two hundred and ten pounds, and had the cutest little peach butt in the world.

He had a name, and it was Zac.

And I knew this was just our beginning.

EPILOGUE

I tried to be as quiet as possible as I tiptoed into the bedroom, holding a glass of water in one hand and my dead cell in the other.

I didn't want to wake up Zac.

He'd tried to stay up with me, but the second time I found him with his head drooped to the side, eyes closed while he sat on the couch in my office, I'd told him to go lay down. And from the side lamp that was still on and the tablet lying facedown on his chest, I knew he'd *still* tried to wait up for me. Just when I didn't think I could love him any more than I already did, he did stuff like this, staying up when I knew he was exhausted.

Setting my glass down and plugging in my phone, I sat on the edge of the bed and peeked over at his sleeping, perfect face.

I'd won the damn lottery with this guy.

He looked so sweet and innocent with his eyes closed. As tan as ever, he was still lined with those long, lean muscles that stretched and flexed with every one of his movements when he was awake. His breathing was nice and soft. His lashes lay long against his cheekbones.

I was such a creeper, but I could stare at his face all day.

And with him sleeping... well, I could. At least without him noticing and then winking at me and tugging me over. Part of me kind of hoped he woke up now that I thought about it. But I knew he needed his sleep.

I'd never tell him to his face, but it was taking him a little longer and longer every year to recover after a game. He'd just gotten home that morning from a win in fucking Oklahoma. I'd gotten way too much pleasure at the White Oaks kicking the Thunderbirds ass the night before.

As I had every time they did over the last five years. It was a deep, personal satisfaction that I thought all of us who loved Zac felt when the other team lost. Even Boogie's daughter had run around the living room giving out high fives when everyone watched the game at our house the night before. I could still hear Paw-Paw hooting up a storm.

Part of me couldn't believe we were still in Houston. Or that Zac was still starting, not after everything that had happened to him during the first half of his career.

Then again, the other part of me—the majority of me —*could* believe it. Easily.

Zac had found his feet, his place, and he'd flourished. Even the TSN commentator, Michael B, who had done nothing but criticize him for the longest, sang his praises now.

And Zac had two enormous rings to prove he was worth all his accolades.

Then again, he'd always been worth every positive word ever said about him—at least I thought so. I was biased though.

"But neither one of 'em is my most important ring," he'd told me

with a wink a few months ago, when he'd locked them into the safe at our house near Austin.

"You starin' at me again, kiddo?" Zac yawned, peeking an eye open before slowly smiling. His shoulders hunched up around his chin as he stretched a little. "You okay?"

"Yeah, just counting all the gray hairs in your beard," I whispered, taking the tablet off his chest and setting it on the nightstand.

He chuckled as he wiggled deeper under the sheets before turning onto his side and lifting them up for me to sneak under. I caught a peek of his black boxer briefs and all the beautiful, endless lines of his body as I slid in, tugging my pillow closer to his. Zac smiled at me before yawning again and scooting over too until we were face-to-face in our bedroom. "How many did you count this time?"

"I lost count after fifty, old man," I lied.

He laughed as he settled in. "You got your website fixed?" he asked, referring to what I'd been doing in my office when he'd passed out.

"Yeah, it just took a lot longer than I had expected," I answered him, stroking a finger down the line of his nose.

That big, warm hand of his curled around my hip for maybe the one-hundred-thousandth time over the last few years. "Good. Did you finally get back to Trevor and tell him you're gonna do the show?"

The show. Trevor.

That was another thing I couldn't believe, the fact that Trevor was now somehow my manager too. My agent and manager in one. He'd come to me with the proposition about a month after Zac had won his first ring, weeks after we'd headed to Austin after our first Disney trip. *"You've got the potential, and I've got the connections. What do you think?"* he'd offered. And I'd taken the leap, trusting in him, and I could honestly say I hadn't regretted it much... only when he nagged me. And even then, it wasn't really regret I felt, more like temporary annoyance.

But I definitely hadn't regretted him when he came to me with an offer to have me judge a kids' baking show for the Food Channel.

That opportunity, I still couldn't believe.

"Yeah. The dates work out perfectly with your off-season," I told him, scooting in closer to his toasty body. He wrapped his arm even more around me, bringing me in so close my knees brushed his thighs.

"I'm so excited for you," he said softly as his fingertips grazed my back. "Next thing you know, they're going to be offerin' you your own show."

I could only dream. My WatchTube channel had grown over the last five years, slowly and steadily. I'd managed to squeeze in so many more "guest" appearances since, with CJ alone hitting ten videos with me, Zac clearly in the forties now because he was a viewer favorite—and my favorite—and I'd even had more of his teammates and two coaches join in. Even Vanessa, Zac's close friend and now my very good friend too, had done one with me.

But it was my books that had really taken off.

Some days, I didn't know what the hell I'd done to deserve any of what I had, starting with the man looking at me on our bed with the goofiest, most tired expression on his face. He could barely keep his eyes open. And that made my stomach feel goofy.

Well, goofier than it had been feeling lately.

I'd been waiting to tell him in person what I'd found out the day before, not wanting to give him the news over the phone.

I was pretty sure he had an idea, but... knowing Zac, there was a chance he was totally oblivious to it too. But I knew I had to tell him, and I had to tell him ASAP. I just hadn't found the right time during the day because Paw-Paw and Zac's mom had been over, then my site had crashed, and I'd wanted a quiet, calm moment to let him know.

"Snack Pack?" I whispered as I set my palm between his pecs, touching the curly hairs there.

He blinked at me sleepily before leaning forward and giving me a kiss and a "Hmm?" Those light fingers brushed my back a little more. He really was too handsome for his own good.

"Did you decide if you're doing the next Anatomy issue?" I asked, going for that question first.

Part of his mouth curled up. "Not yet, darlin', but if you're fixin' for my Texas peaches, you know they're all yours."

I snorted. "I was just wondering. But it would be nice to update the framed picture I have on my desk with a more recent one."

His tired laugh was a puff against my mouth that made me smile.

He was fading fast, and I knew I could wait until tomorrow, but... I didn't want to.

"Zac?"

His eyes were already drifting closed again as he asked, "Yeah, sweetheart?"

"What would you think about... a Tiny Texas?"

Zac's light blue eyes went wide in a fucking instant. He shot up to an elbow and stared at me, giving me a full view of that incredible chest. "A Tiny Texas?" He blinked. "You serious?"

I pointed at him. "Big Texas." Pointed at my chest. "Little Texas." Then I pointed toward my stomach, totally exposed by the cropped top I had on. "Tiny Texas."

Before I knew what the hell was happening, his hands pulled me over and across, so I was straddling his hips. His eyes were brighter than ever, his face shocked but not white.

Even his mouth was a little parted as he basically gasped, fully awake, "You serious, Bibi?"

I licked my lips and nodded. We'd talked about kids right before we'd gotten married that summer after his first season with the White Oaks, but it had been one of those things that we'd both shrugged off, thinking *someday. Whenever. What's the rush?*

But it wasn't like I hadn't known he loved children. I did too. One night about a year ago, we'd casually talked about what we'd name our kids one day, if we had them. "Lupita," he'd suggested, if we had a girl, and my heart had nearly exploded at the tribute to my grandma. Or "William James," after Boogie and Paw-Paw.

I touched his cheek. "I haven't gone to the doctor yet, but I took the test yesterday, and... it was positive," I told him, watching his face and his eyes as he did the same right back. "So... is it feeling like a 'yay' or are you scared? Because, true story, I'm a little scared. But also, this is technically your fault. I told you I forgot to take a few of my pills, and then you started tickling me, so then I started tickling you, and then we both got all...."

If someone had told me a decade ago that one day I would be sitting on Zac's lap one night, with him in his underwear, in our house, on our bed, I would have thought they were repeating something straight out of dreams.

And if someone would have told me that I'd be doing that, telling him I was pregnant with his *baby*, a baby Zac, and that he'd sit up and wrap his arms around me, kissing my cheeks and my mouth and my neck and chest... well, I would have thought they were just being cruel.

But that was what happened.

Zac kissed me and kissed me as he whispered things into my skin that sounded like "I love you so much," and "I can't believe it," and "Are you serious?" and "We need to go to the doctor tomorrow mornin'," and "What the hell do you have to be scared of? We got this," and "You're the love of my life, kiddo."

And he was right.

Together, we had this, me and the love of my life. Hands down.

ACKNOWLEDGMENTS

Thank you so much for reading HANDS DOWN! First and foremost, thank you so much to all of my incredible readers for all of your support and love.

Eva, thank you so much for your diligence, memory and suggestions. I don't know what I'd do without you. (Well, Zac would have brown hair, I'd have the kids mixed up, and there would be a Mark/Marcus in every book, among a thousand other mistakes, haha.) Thank you for everything, dude. You're the best.

Sita and Isa, thank you for your help with the blurb! Judy, I can't thank you enough for always answering all of my audio questions and for just being wonderful. Letitia at RBA Designs, Virginia at Hot Tree Editing and Ellie with My Brother's Editor, thank you for being amazing. Kilian, I'm so grateful for all your help.

Thanks also to Jane, Kemi and Lauren of Dystel, Goderich & Bourret for all of their work with getting my books into different markets.

To my friends who I know I'm forgetting: thank you for everything.

To my Zapata, Navarro, and Letchford family, you're the greatest families a girl could ever ask for. A very special thank you to my mom for being a great travel partner, always agreeing to be my assistant even before I tell you where we're going, and for being more organized than I am.

To Chris, Kai, and my forever editor and angel in the sky, Dorian: I love you guys so much.

ABOUT THE AUTHOR

Mariana Zapata lives in a small town in Colorado with her husband and two oversized children—her beloved Great Danes, Dorian and Kaiser. When she's not writing, she's reading, spending time outside, forcing kisses on her boys, or pretending to write.

MarianaZapata.com
Book Store
Merchandise Store

Join my Mailing List

ALSO AVAILABLE

Printed in Great Britain
by Amazon